**Reviewers love *New York Times* bestselling author
SUSAN ANDERSEN!**

"This start of Andersen's new series has fun and interesting characters, solid action and a hot and sexy romance....The introduction of the heroines of the future stories whets the appetite for more."
—*Romantic Times BOOKreviews* on *Cutting Loose*

"Snappy and sexy... Upbeat and fun, with a touch of danger and passion, this is a great summer read."
—*Romantic Times BOOKreviews* on *Coming Undone*

"Deft characters, smart dialogue, laugh-out-loud moments and sizzling sexual tension (you might want to read Chapter 15 twice) make this hard to put down.... Lovers of romance, passion and laughs should go all in for this one."
—*Publishers Weekly* on *Just for Kicks*

"Andersen again injects magic into a story that would be clichéd in another's hands, delivering warm, vulnerable characters in a touching yet suspenseful read."
—*Publishers Weekly*, starred review, on *Skintight*

"A classic plot line receives a fresh, fun treatment...well-developed secondary characters add depth to this zesty novel, placing it a level beyond most of its competition."
—*Publishers Weekly* on *Hot & Bothered*

"Sassy, snappy and sizzling hot!"
—*New York Times* bestselling author Janet Evanovich on *Baby, I'm Yours*

"Lively and fun!"
—*New York Times* bestselling author Susan Elizabeth Phillips on *Be My Baby*

"Sizzling, snappy, sexy fun."
—*New York Times* bestselling author Jennifer Crusie on *Baby, Don't Go*

8-09

Dear Reader,

I love Opposites Attract stories. And if they punch your buttons as well, have I got a hero and heroine for you!

Poppy Calloway was raised by hippie parents in a home full of love, artistic expression and the belief that one gives back to the community whenever possible. Far from a material girl, she's perfectly happy scraping a living out of designing menu boards and making greeting cards. She feeds her soul by bringing art to at-risk kids.

Jase de Sanges comes from a long line of career criminals. He was on the verge of joining the family tradition himself when a cop named Murphy intervened to show him there was more than one direction in which to steer his life. Now he, too, is on the job—a detective who's made *by the book* his personal mantra.

So when Jase and Poppy are charged with guiding three teenagers caught defacing property through the cleanup process, you can bet they approach the task from different angles. The free-spirited artist who sees the best in people and the bend-no-rules cop who expects the worst have nothing in common.

Well, except for that pesky attraction that's sunk its hooks deep and refuses to turn loose. And it turns out *that's* just for starters.

As always, I hope you enjoy!

Happy reading.

Susan

Susan Andersen

Bending the Rules

HQN™

Recycling programs
for this product may
not exist in your area.

ISBN-13: 978-0-373-77393-0

BENDING THE RULES

This edition published by arrangement with Harlequin Books S.A.

® and TM are trademarks of the publisher. Trademarks indicated with ® are registered in the United States Patent and Trademark Office, the Canadian Trade Marks Office and in other countries.

www.HQNBooks.com

Printed in U.S.A.

PROLOGUE

Dear Diary,
I will never understand why people paint their walls white. If it were up to me I'd color the world.

June 13, 1992

"SO WHAT DO YOU THINK?"

Anchoring herself against the ladder she stood on to paint the Wolcott mansion's morning room wall, thirteen-year-old Poppy Calloway looked at her friend Jane, who had asked the question. All but swallowed up by a man's paint smock, her slippery brown hair falling out of the banana clip she was using to hold it off her face, Jane gazed back at her from the west wall where she had painstakingly painted the woodwork around the bank of mullioned windows. Through the panes behind her, rain clouds blew across the sky over the Sound. The Space Needle, however, had a halo of pure azure above it.

"It looks wonderful, Janie," she said, admiring the velvety cream-colored wood against the deep melon wall. "Doing trim is the hardest." Blowing a blond curl out of her eyes, she flashed Jane a grin. "Which is why I gave the job to you."

A wry smile lightened Jane's solemn expression. "So I'm the chump of the Sisterhood?"

"Nah. I just knew you'd do it right." Then she turned to their redheaded friend, who was eating a Milky Way and dancing to Nirvana's "Smells Like Teen Spirit" over by the boom box they'd brought with them to Miss Agnes's mansion. "*You* planning on actually giving us a hand sometime today?"

Generous hips swiveling, arms moving in rhythmic counterpart, Ava met Poppy's gaze across the room. "In a minute. I'm communing with Kurt Cobain."

"You've *been* communing with him since you bought the *Nevermind* tape—what?—six months ago? Do it with a roller in your hand."

"Aw, Pop. You know I'm not good at the physical stuff."

"Hello!" She eyed the fluid movement of Ava's body. "Aren't you the one who dances good enough to star on an MTV video?"

Dimples punched deep in Ava's cheeks as she smiled in delight. But almost immediately she made a scoffing sound. "Yeah, right. Like they'd ever put my fat ass on one of those vids. Those are for skinny girls like you and Jane."

"Well, lose the candy bar and pick up a paintbrush—maybe you'll burn a few calories."

"Poppy," Jane remonstrated.

She merely shrugged and turned back to her own painting, feeling both guilty and impatient. She knew that was mean, but sometimes it was just hard to dredge up the proper sympathy. Ava's weight was a constant source of unhappiness for her friend. Yet she never *did* anything about it.

Still, she felt bad and watched from the corner of her eye as Ava trudged over to an empty paint tray and squatted to pour paint into it.

"Dancing burns calories," Ava muttered as she brought the tray over to start rolling color onto the lower part of the wall where Poppy's roller hadn't reached.

"That's true. It just doesn't help paint the walls." Still, Ava had a point and she offered the first olive branch that popped to mind. "That Courtney Love is all wrong for Cobain."

"I know!" Ava rubbed her cheek against a plump shoulder, dislodging the bright strand of hair that had swung forward to stick to the corner of her mouth. Dimples peeped again in her round cheek when she flashed a look up at Poppy. "I think he's just killing time with her until I'm old enough to marry him instead." She nodded sagely. "Men need sex, you know?"

"I'm sure that's the reason."

"Without a doubt," Jane agreed.

"But you can have Cobain," Poppy added. "I'm holding out for the Sheik."

Ava and Jane howled, because that was the fantasy man they'd invented last year during a backyard camp-out. Secretly, Poppy had to suppress a shiver. Because the dark, larger-than-life, lean-fingered man of their combined imaginations was her private ideal.

A regular real-life boyfriend wouldn't be too shabby, though.

"Are you girls ready for a break?"

At the distinctive sound of Agnes Bell Wolcott's deep voice, all three of them turned toward the door where she stood, decked out in designer couture from her snow-white, exquisitely coiffed hair to her expensively shod feet. They'd met Miss A. at an event at Ava's house two years ago and shortly afterward, she'd invited them for tea at the infamously ugly Wolcott mansion as a thank-you for spending time with an eccentric old woman known in certain circles for her adventurous travels, beautiful wardrobe and exquisite collections. She'd given them their first diaries at that tea and it was then that they'd started referring to themselves as the Sisterhood, after Miss Agnes said their connection to each other reminded her of such. They'd been coming for tea at least once a month ever since, and often dropped by—either as a group or individually—simply to talk to her in between times.

When Poppy had Miss Agnes to herself, conversation often turned to philanthropic endeavors. The older lady's enthusiasm for "giving back" left an impression on Poppy. There was just something about Miss A. that made you think about things in ways you'd never done before, and Poppy wouldn't be surprised if she was sporting the same fatuous, pleased-to-see-her smile now that she saw on Jane's and Ava's faces. To make up for it—conscious as she was about her dignity these days— she said sternly, "If you're going to be in here, you need to put on a smock." She nodded toward the pile that her parents had supplied. "I will not be responsible for ruining that outfit."

"And I will not ruin the beautiful lines of my Chanel with a paint-spattered lab coat," Miss A. said crisply, stepping outside the doorway so she was safe from wet paint but still in their line of vision.

Poppy grinned at the old lady's acerbic tone. One of the things she adored about Miss A. was that she never insulted their intelligence by pulling her punches. "There's a plate of homemade oatmeal-chocolate-chip-walnut-raisin cookies for you on the sideboard in the dining room," she said. "Mom said since I was no doubt my usual pain-in-the-patootie self trying to get you to agree to painting this room, the least she could do was supply a little sugar to sweeten the deal."

"How lovely of her. She obviously knows you well." The latter sentiment was offered in a dry tone, yet accompanied by a fond smile. "I'll tell Evelyn to add some to our dessert platter. Speaking of which, are you ready to break for lunch or would you prefer to finish your wall first?" She studied the completed one that was a deeper, more dramatic shade of the pale melon that Poppy and Ava were applying to the adjacent wall and nodded approvingly. "Divine color, by the way. It's going to look amazing with the draperies. You do have a wonderful eye for this sort of thing, don't you?"

"She's got the *best* eye," Ava agreed. "And if you don't mind, Miss A., we'll finish this wall first."

Slipping a foot from the ladder rung, Poppy gave her

friend an affectionate nudge with her toe. For she knew how much Ava loved Miss A.'s luncheons; knew, too, that she was sacrificing the immediate gratification of sitting down to one for her. She looked back at the older woman. "It shouldn't take more than ten or fifteen minutes, if that's okay."

"Darling, I'm getting free labor and beautiful new walls. You take all the time you want. I'll just go tell Evelyn."

She disappeared down the hallway and Poppy turned back to her painting with renewed energy. She knew the old lady was indulging her by letting them paint the room when she could afford to have it done professionally every month of the year if she wanted. That was the thing, though. Agnes didn't want the bother of it; she cared about the beauty of her collections, not the rooms they went in.

Even so, Poppy couldn't prevent the satisfied smile curling her lips. "I'm gonna talk her into letting me paint the parlor next."

"Good luck with that," Jane said from her position in front of the baseboard where it angled around the corner. She rose from painting the trim and stretched out her back. "That's where nine-tenths of Miss A.'s collections are kept. It would be a killer undertaking just to move everything."

"Still. I'm gonna do it. I'll wear her down—just wait and see. Dad says that's what I do best. And once I do?" She smiled dreamily. "We're going to paint it a lovely creamy yellow."

Jane and Ava exchanged glances. "We," Jane said. "Well, lucky us."

"Yeah," Ava agreed. "Sometimes there's a definite downside to this Sisterhood business."

But her two best friends picked up their painting tools and went back to work.

CHAPTER ONE

Of all the rooms in all the field houses in all the parks in Seattle, he had to walk into *this* one?

WHAT THE HELL IS he *doing here?*

Poppy did her best to continue her conversation with the manager of the Ace hardware store. But the man had a tendency to drone on at the best of times and with the new arrival striding through the milling crowd of business owners as if he owned the joint, it was difficult to focus her attention. Her gaze kept wanting to follow his progress. That *was* de Sanges, right?

She just barely swallowed the self-derisive snort that tickled the back of her throat. Because, please. This might be the last place she expected to see him, but of course it was.

Considering their one and only encounter, however, she didn't feel a burning need to beat herself up for allowing her mind to shy away from the admission.

Still, the truth was, it had taken no more than a glimpse to recognize the tall, lean, muscular body she'd seen only once before. She'd documented the prominent bony nose, those sharp cheekbones and that black-as-acrow's-feather hair. Was familiar with those long, white-nailed fingers and the dark olive skin that she had a feeling owed more to genetics than exposure to the sun.

And

Oh

My

God

Really remembered those dark, chilly eyes. Which she'd watched go hot for a few insane minutes last fall as they'd stood toe-to-toe in Miss A.'s parlor.

Whoa. She firmly corralled her wayward thoughts. *Don't even go there, girl.* Okay, so it was Detective Sheik, as Janie insisted on calling him. Big deal. But her face went hot and her mouth went dry, and she had to fight like hell not to squirm at the memory of Ava saying that for a minute there she'd feared Poppy and de Sanges—a man none of them had even met until that afternoon—might start going at it hot and heavy in the middle of the parlor.

Because her friend had been right. Poppy had never experienced anything quite so visceral as what she'd felt that day with the tall, dark cop.

"Everyone seems to be here," Garret Johnson, the president of the Merchants' Association, said over the babble of conversation in the Park Department's field house conference room. "Let's take our seats and get this meeting under way."

Eking out a breath of relief at having the plug yanked on that particular memory, she watched de Sanges from the corner of her eye until he pulled out a chair at the rectangular table. Then she took a seat at the opposite end.

It would have been even better if she could've nabbed one on the same side. That way she wouldn't be able to see him at all without making a concerted effort. But Penny, the owner of Slice of Heaven Pies, beat her to the last chair on de Sanges's side. Oh, well—too bad, so sad for her. Taking a seat across from the other woman, she exchanged idle chitchat for a few moments until the president rapped his knuckles on the wooden tabletop to call the meeting to order.

"Okay, as everyone knows," he said the instant the last holdout conversation fizzled into silence, "we're here today to decide what to do about the three boys who were caught tagging our businesses. But before we get into that, I'd like to introduce everyone to Detective Jason de Sanges from the Seattle Police Department. He's on the mayor's special task force to reduce burglaries and has kindly agreed to sit on our panel. Detective." He turned toward the cop and Poppy automatically turned in her seat to look at de Sanges as well. "Allow me to introduce you to our motley crew."

He went around the table performing introductions and, when he came to her, said, "This is Poppy Calloway. She's not actually a merchant, but she's on so many of our 'boards' that we consider her an honorary member of the association."

It was a standing joke, since she designed the menu and Today's Specials black or white boards for several of the business owners here today.

De Sanges nodded and looked at her for a suspended

instant with those dark, uncompromising eyes. "Ms. Calloway and I have met."

Everyone present turned to stare at her and she could almost taste the rampant curiosity and speculation. "Don't look at me as if I were a suspect in one of his cases," she said dryly. "You all heard about the theft we had at the Wolcott mansion a few months ago. Detective de Sanges came out to take a report when we were dissatisfied with the response we got from the first officer on the scene."

De Sanges had been dissatisfied as well—that Ava had used one of her many contacts to have him brought in. So he hadn't been there voluntarily, and he and Poppy had definitely gotten off on the wrong foot when she'd taken exception to what she'd perceived as his lack of concern over a break-in at the mansion that she, Jane and Ava had only recently inherited from Miss Agnes's estate. Well, could you blame her? He had all but said he'd been yanked off a real job in order to look for their silver spoons.

Which was nothing short of ironic when you considered that only Ava had been born to money. Poppy and Jane came from working-class neighborhoods. They'd all met in the fourth grade at Country Day school—Janie attending on a scholarship and her own tuition paid by Grandma Ingles, who was herself an alumni. Even today—despite inheriting an estate that was short on cash but long on priceless collectibles and valuable real estate—Ava was the only one of them who had any discretionary income. Jane was still inventorying Miss

A.'s collections and the mansion was a long way and a small fortune from being saleable, which was their ultimate goal.

Still, in the wake of Jane's run-in with the thief, they'd learned de Sanges hadn't just blown them off but had interviewed Jane's coworkers at the Metropolitan Museum—had in fact spent the most time talking to Gordon Ives. And since Gordon had eventually been arrested for the crime, Poppy thought she could probably cut the detective some slack and agree he had done his job after all.

"I'd like to open the meeting for discussion," Garret said. "I know everyone here was disturbed about how young our graffiti 'artists' were and you no doubt want to thrash out whether or not to press charges against them. Anyone whose business was tagged is, of course, free to do so at any time—this isn't a case of majority rules. But we're here to entertain all reasonable suggestions, both pro and con. So let's get some dialogue going, people."

No one said anything for a long, silent moment, then Jerry Harvey, whose H & A on the Ave on the corner had taken the biggest brunt of the vandalism, said, "I'd like to know who's going to clean up the side of my shop." He'd been the first to spot one of the kids tagging the café across from him when he'd gone to lock the front door of his funky home-decorations and art-framing shop for the night.

A few of the merchants grumbled agreement. The Ace Hardware manager pushed for pressing charges.

Poppy took a breath and quietly released it. "I have a suggestion," she said. "I know I don't have the same stake in the outcome of today's meeting as the rest of you. But I was at the Hardwire when Jerry caught the kids, and frankly I *was* disturbed by how young they are. The officer who came in response to your call, Jerry, said this is their first brush with the law. Rather than see them thrown into the system I'd like to offer an alternate solution that directly relates to your question."

All the merchants involved in Friday night's excitement gave her their undivided attention. De Sanges's eyes narrowed.

"I think it might benefit all of the businesses to give the kids something to keep them busy," she said. "To provide them with an artistic outlet that I believe we'd find more palatable than tagging—which I freely admit I don't get. At the same time we could teach them to take responsibility for their actions."

"How?" Garret asked.

"First by having them clean up the tagging with a fresh coat of paint that they either have to provide themselves or work off by sweeping or handling other odd jobs for the businesses they defaced."

"I like that so far," Penny said thoughtfully. "Except Marlene's place is brick, so how does that benefit her?"

"There are gels and pastes that dissolve paint from brick, and the same rules would apply—they'd supply whatever's needed."

Almost everyone nodded—including Jerry. But he

also pinned her with a suspicious look. "So where does the 'artistic outlet' part come in?"

Poppy knew this was where things could go south. But it wasn't for nothing she'd grown up with parents who got involved in causes on a near-daily basis. Not to mention the way her idea tied in to her own personal passion: bringing art to at-risk kids. Drawing a deep breath, she gave Jerry her best trust-me smile, then quietly exhaled. "I propose we keep them off the streets by letting them paint a mural on the south side of your building."

OH, FOR CRI'SAKE. Jase leaned back in his chair and examined the woman he had privately labeled the Babe. Which, okay, wasn't exactly a hardship since the whole package—that lithe body, exotic brown eyes and cloud of curly Nordic-pale hair—was very examinable.

He knew from experience, however, that she was a pain in the ass. And didn't it just figure? She was a damn bleeding-heart liberal to boot.

Earlier, when he'd walked in and seen her chatting up one of the guys in this group of small-business owners, you could have knocked him off his feet with a blade of grass. He hadn't understood why she was here, since as far as he knew she wasn't a merchant herself. Hey, as far as he could see, she didn't do *anything* useful. Of course, since he had firmly resisted the urge to run a check on her after their previous run-in, he could be wrong about that.

In any case, the president of the Merchants' Association had explained it when he'd said that Calloway was a board member.

Well, of course she was. He should have figured that out for himself after meeting her and her two rich-girl buddies last fall, when they'd used their connections with the mayor to have him yanked off a job where an old lady had been hospitalized by a mugger in order to look for their missing tea towels.

Okay, so it had turned out to be more than that—a lot more. But contrary to the Babe's accusation that he couldn't be bothered to do his job, he had been following the exact letter of the law when he'd told her there wasn't much he could do for them. But he'd nevertheless been digging into Gordon Ives's background when he got the call that a patrol officer had just arrested the man for another break-in at the Wolcott mansion—this one involving a threat against Jane Kaplinski's life.

All of which had squat to do with today's situation. He listened for a moment as Calloway outlined her hare-brained scheme. He kept waiting for someone to shoot it down, but when he instead saw several of the merchants nodding their heads, he couldn't take it any longer. "You're kidding me, right?"

Slowly, she turned her head to look at him. "Excuse me?"

"I figure this has to be a joke, because you can't possibly be serious. They broke the law. You want to reward them for that?"

Her eyes flashed fire, giving him an abrupt flash of his own—of déjà vu. Because he was no stranger to that phenomenon—her eyes had done the exact same thing when she'd leaned over him in the chair where he'd sat in the mansion parlor, taking their report last year. Serious chemistry had flared to life between them, but he was damned if he planned to fall prey to that again.

Maybe she was thinking along the same lines, because she didn't climb over the table to get in his face the way she had last time. Instead, she said coolly, "No, Detective, I am not kidding. I'm pretty darn serious, in fact. These aren't hardened criminals we're talking about—they're children, the oldest barely seventeen."

"Yeah, they start 'em young these days," he agreed.

"It's not as if they committed a violent crime—they didn't mug an old lady or attempt to rob someone at gunpoint at the ATM machine." Her eyes narrowed. "Or commit a burglary of *any* kind," she said with slow thoughtfulness, and he could almost smell the circuits burning as she followed that thought to its logical conclusion.

"They didn't commit a burglary," she repeated, gazing around the table at the other occupants. Then she looked him dead in the eye. "So why are you sitting on this panel, again?"

Excellent question. When Greer had offered to put his name in for the mayor's task force he'd given his lieutenant an immediate and firm "Thanks, but no thanks." Then, like an idiot, he'd let Murphy—the old cop who had stepped in years ago to take him in hand before the de Sanges genes could screw him up entirely—talk him into changing his mind. Murph had insisted that if Jase wanted to wear those lieutenant bars himself someday—which he did—he needed to start making his name known to the powers that be. And a good way to do that was to be part of these task forces—even if this particular one was more about election-year public relations than the war on crime.

So here he sat, proving once again that no good deed goes unpunished.

Not letting his thoughts show, however, he merely met her suspicious gaze with the cool straightforwardness of his own, evincing none of his reluctance to be part of this dog-and-pony show. "Because this is how we so often see it begin. Baby street punks grow up to be full-fledged street punks. Today it's tagging or stealing some other kid's lunch money at school—*if* they even bother to show up at school, that is."

"So perhaps we should make that a condition of my proposal. No school, no participation in the art project."

Slick, he thought with unwilling admiration, but said as if she hadn't spoken, "Tomorrow it's mugging some little old lady in the parking lot at Northgate." Pulling his gaze away from the Babe's, he included the entire table of merchants in his regard. "Or right here in your own community."

Okay, so maybe he was overstating the case a little, adding a dash of drama to get his point across. He was so tired, however, of watching punks bend the rules and not merely *not* be called on it but get special treatment for their efforts as well. That was just bogus. And it happened too often.

Still, he was surprised at the impact his words had. The business owners' voices started buzzing around

the table as they discussed the repercussions of allowing hardened criminals into their neighborhood business sector.

Wait a minute. His brows snapped together. Had he
given them that impression, that the boys in this case
were hardened criminals? *Jesus, de Sanges, the Babe is
right about that much at least. They're kids who committed their first offense.*

As if she could read his thoughts, she repeated to the
group around the table, "They're kids, you guys. Barely
past *puberty* kids without a single police record between them. Please keep that in mind."

"I'm keeping in mind that Detective de Sanges said
that's how all street punks start," the man who had been
introduced as the manager of Ace Hardware said.

"I didn't say *all,*" Jase disagreed. "But I do see enough
juvenile offenders to make it one factor to consider."

"Surely," Poppy insisted, "most of those that you see
are involved in an actual robbery or mugging."

"True. Most—but not all—are."

"Does anyone else have an argument, either pro or con,
that they'd like to throw out for discussion?" Garret asked.

"I'd just like to reiterate that these are kids who have
never been in trouble with the law," Poppy said quietly.
"I'm not saying let them skip out of their obligations.
Just, please, let's not be the ones to give them their first
police record."

"Anyone else?" Garret asked. Getting no response,
he said, "Does anyone plan on pressing charges?"

When no one said anything to that, either, he said,

"I'll take that as a provisional no." He turned to Poppy. "Can I hear an official proposal?"

She straightened her shoulders, which had temporarily slumped. Shook back hair so thick and curly the entire mass quivered. "I propose we teach the three boys who tagged your businesses a sense of accountability by making them cover or remove the vandalized areas with paint and/or paint dissolvers that they provide at their own expense. I further propose—"

"Let's do this one motion at a time," Garret interrupted. He looked around the table. "Would anyone like to second that?"

"You can't just turn kids that young loose with buckets of paint and a few brushes and hope for the best," Jerry said to Poppy. "Are you willing to supervise the project?"

Jase figured this was where her idealism would meet the reality of giving up her salon appointments or charity boards or however she spent her days in order to ride herd on three kids who—if his own experience was anything to go by—would be far from grateful.

He sat back, waiting to hear how she planned to get out of it.

But she merely gave Jerry a serene dip of her head. "Yes."

"I'll second the motion, then."

Garret looked at Jase. "Since we invited your and Poppy's opinions, we agreed to give you both a vote in this as well."

He was too astounded by the way Calloway had busted his expectations to respond.

Garret turned his attention back to his group. "All in favor?"

Poppy and seven of the eleven merchants raised their hands.

"Against?"

The remaining four raised their hands. Jase abstained.

"The ayes have it." Garret gave Poppy, whose smile was so bright Jase was tempted to whip out his shades, an avuncular smile. "I take it you have more to say?"

"Yes. I further propose we take this opportunity to teach these boys a more constructive way to decorate the buildings in their neighborhood. A way that, in the end, will benefit the entire community by giving us something we'll all enjoy looking at, and incidentally perhaps give them the self-esteem to redirect their creative urges in a more acceptable direction."

"Again, I have to ask," Jerry said. "You supervising?"

"Yes."

"I second the motion," Penny said.

"All in favor?"

Poppy and five merchants—one of them Jerry, the owner of the building she proposed the kids paint—raised their hands.

Garret looked around the table expressionlessly. "Against?"

The six remaining merchants raised their hands, and all eyes turned to Jase to break the tie.

He should abstain again and let them fight it out among themselves. What the hell did he care if they rewarded these kids?

Except…

He knew from personal experience what chaos could come from bending—never mind breaking—the rules. He fought the temptation to do so every day and saw no reason to pass that temptation down to another generation. Teach them young to stay on the straight and narrow—that was his motto.

Raising his hand, he threw in with the against group.

CHAPTER TWO

Well, *there's* a perfectly good fantasy blown to hell.

"I CANNOT *believe* I was attracted to that stiff for even a minute!" Poppy dumped her big tote onto the floor of Brouwer's Café, a pub that specialized in international beers. Pulling a chair away from the table Ava had scored near the long wood-topped bar, she dropped into it.

"What stiff?" Ava demanded over the raised voices of the crowd around them.

"Poppy!" Arriving at the table almost on her heels, Jane gave her an incredulous look. "You beat me here. How did that happen? You're *never* on time."

"She's mad at some stiff," Ava said. "It must have motivated her."

"Yeah, I gathered as much when you called." Jane hooked her bag over the chair rail and sat down, giving Poppy a concerned once-over. "That you're seriously hacked off, that is. What gives?"

At the thought of what—or rather who—"gave," her heart sped up and her hands wanted to clench. She flattened them against the wooden tabletop. "Guess who's on the committee with me?"

Ava leaned into the table. "What committee?"

"The one to do with those kids who were caught tagging the businesses she designs boards for," Jane reminded her.

"Oh, yeah. Sorry. You've got so many irons in the fire these days that I forgot about that for a sec. How did it go? Not great, I'm guessing."

"Not great." Her involuntary laugh tasted bitter and her fingers curled in toward her palms. "Oh, trust me, it was a tad worse than not great. It was a damn cluster f—"

The waitress, who'd had to weave her way through the throng of power-hour drinkers to reach their table, arrived just as she was about to cut loose with a truly grand-scale vent. "Get you ladies a drink?"

"I'd like the Leavenworth Blind Pig Dunkel-thing," Ava said.

"Weizen," the waitress supplied. "Dunkelweizen."

"Yes. Thank you. One of those."

"I'll take a Fuller's." Poppy drew a deep breath and blew it out, but she was still so irate she barely glanced up from her hands, which were once again firmly splayed against the tabletop, her fingertips white from her effort not to make a fist. "And a large pomme frites with the pesto aioli."

"Ooh. We're eating, too?" Ava wiggled with pleasure. "I'll have the Lembeck salad."

"I'll just have a Diet Coke with a lime, please," Jane said.

Ava's head whipped around to stare at her friend. "That's it?" she demanded as the waitress nodded and moved on to the next table. "Please tell me your skinny butt's not on a diet."

"My skinny butt is not on a diet," Jane obediently parroted. Then she grinned, her face radiant with newly-wed happiness. "In fact it's spuds-and-sausage night at Dev's folks and Mama K. hates it when I don't eat enough to burst. I'm just reserving all the stomach room I can."

That jerked Poppy out of her dilemma, and she grimaced at her own self-absorption. "You have dinner plans with your in-laws and you showed up for me?"

"Well…sure. We're the Sisterhood, aren't we?" Scooping her shiny brown hair behind her ears, she laughed. "Besides, this isn't exactly altruism at its finest. The Kavanaghs never eat until around seven anyway, and Devlin's riding over with his brother."

"Which one? Bren? How's he doing?" Jane's husband, Dev, had returned from the Continent last year to pitch in at Kavanagh Construction, the family business, when his oldest brother's cancer treatment called for chemotherapy. Jane and he had met when he'd headed the Wolcott mansion remodel, a project so huge it was still ongoing several months later. They'd had a rocky beginning and Poppy loved seeing her so flat-out happy.

"No, Finn, actually. But Bren is doing great. He's finally done with chemo, his oncologist is very optimistic they got all the cancer and his hair's even starting to grow back in."

"That's excellent news."

Ava flashed a smile. "I saw him the other day and he's got downy fuzz all over his head. If he wasn't such a big guy, he'd look like a newborn chick." Then she pushed back from the table. "I've gotta use the ladies'." She leveled a stern look on Poppy. "Don't you dare spill a single juicy detail until I get back."

"There are no juicy details," she muttered to her friend's departing back. Her thoughts turned inward to the day's earlier events, however, and she wasn't even aware of watching Ava cross the room. Only in the most absentminded way did she track the redhead's progress by all the male heads that swiveled to watch her go by.

"I never get tired of seeing that," Jane said.

"What?" she asked. Then realizing what she was staring at, she nodded. "Oh. That. Yeah, I know." They grinned at each other. Because fueled by eat-your-heart-out, revenge-inspired determination after being the butt of a humiliating bet when she was eighteen, Ava had changed a lifetime of bad eating habits. She'd refused to call it a diet, though, and she hadn't made the mistake so many full-figured women did of trying to whittle herself down to a toothpick-thinness unsuited to her bigger-boned frame. She'd stopped actively losing weight once she'd reached a size twelve—or what would be a fourteen, they liked to tease her, if she bought her clothing in the less pricey shops that the rest of them patronized.

But the actual size wasn't the point. Ava had curves, she wasn't afraid to accent them and men all but tripped over their tongues whenever she went by.

Apparently she didn't believe in wasting time when there was potential gossip in the offing, either. Back in under five minutes, she demanded even as she took her seat, "So let's hear it. Who's the stiff? And what on earth did he do to get you so bent out of shape? This is not like you."

"Yes, well, you can thank Jason de Sanges for my mood," Poppy said through her teeth. "That rat bastard wrecked—"

"Detective *Sheik?*" Jane snapped upright. "*That's* who's on your committee?"

"Oh, no. Not now." Her eyes slitted. "Thanks to him, the committee is no longer necessary. He torpedoed my wonderful plan." She explained how he'd slanted the information he'd given the committee to make the three teens sound like hardened criminals.

The waitress brought their drinks. After several sips of her British ale, Poppy felt the tension that had her neck muscles in knots start to loosen. She could thank Ava and Jane for that, because by allowing her, in the way of true friends, to unload on them they'd helped her shed a large portion of the stress she'd been carrying around. "I suppose I really shouldn't let it get me so bent out of shape," she admitted. "It's not like I'm overwhelmed with free time anyway. Between my work with the kids, and doing the boards and figuring out what the hell I want to do with the rooms the Kavanaghs have finished, I would've had to scramble to fit this project in. It's just…"

"It was a good plan," Ava said.

"Yes! Not perfect, I know, but a lot better than dumping three kids into the system for a first offense.

Maybe I could have made a difference in their lives." She shrugged. "Maybe not. But I sure would have liked the chance to find out. Now I'll never know."

"You still have a crack at them during the cleanup project, though, right?" Jane asked.

"Yeah, but we all know that's not going to thrill them. It was the opportunity to paint some honest-to-God community-sanctioned art that might have opened up a chink in their armor."

Ava's auburn brows pleated. "You know what? Detective Sheik may have done a lot more last fall than we first believed—but he's still a pig."

"Yeah," Jane agreed. "And from now on he's just plain Detective de Sanges. He doesn't deserve to be called the Sheik."

"No fooling." Poppy took another sip of her ale, pushed back her pint glass to make room for the steaming basket of fries the waitress set in front of her and sighed as she grabbed one and dragged it through the little dish of aioli. "How can someone who makes me so hot just looking at him have turned out to be such a cold fish?"

THE SCENT OF deep-fat-fried fish wafted up from the paper-and-twine-wrapped package Jase juggled as he rapped his knuckles against an apartment door one floor down from his own. "Murph! You in there? Hey, I brought dinner. Open up before I drop the damn thing on the carpet."

"Hold your water, kid," a gruff voice said, growing

closer as his one-time mentor and long-time friend approached the other side of the door. "I ain't as young as I useta be, y'know."

"No shit?" he muttered as locks tumbled and the doorknob turned. "Can't say as I remember you ever being young."

"Cute," Murphy said, opening the door and reaching out to relieve him of the six-pack of St. Pauli Girl he'd tucked under his elbow.

"Not trying to be cute," he said honestly. "I *don't* remember. I was, what? Fourteen when we met? I thought you were a hundred then."

"I was fifty-four!"

"Which might as well be a hundred when you're fourteen."

Murphy laughed. "I suppose you got a point." He shot a glance over his shoulder at the blue-and-white paper bundling their dinner as he led the way to the little dining table outside his almost equally small kitchen. "Spud's fish and chips," he said as he pulled a couple of longnecks out of the six-pack and set them on the table. "What's the occasion?"

"That bogus committee you talked me into joining is no more." And he refused to feel guilty about the disappointment he'd seen in the Babe's big brown eyes when the vote hadn't gone the way she'd hoped. "Figured that calls for a celebration."

Murphy slowly straightened from putting the rest of the beer in the refrigerator. Turning his head, he pinned Jase in the crosshairs of his faded but still sharp blue eyes. "I know you weren't hot to be on this thing in the first place. But how the hell'd you manage that?"

"By injecting a little reality into a harebrained scheme." He nodded at the package he'd unwrapped. "I'll tell you all about it, but right now come sit down. Let's eat before this gets cold."

They each grabbed a wad of napkins and dug into the fish, eating with their fingers. They dipped the battered fish into plastic containers of tartar sauce, scraped thick clam chowder out of tiny cardboard cups with round-bowled plastic spoons and dredged their fries through ketchup, washing it all down with beer.

Eventually there was nothing left except a couple of grease spots and a splash of garlic-infused vinegar in the bottom of their cardboard dishes. Murphy stacked them, tossed in the empty plastic condiment containers and, wadding up the wrapping paper, added it to the pile. He pushed his chair back from the table, patted his comfortable paunch and met Jase's gaze. "Good dinner. Thanks."

"You're welcome."

"So tell me about this harebrained scheme."

"Do you remember me talking about the Babe?"

"Sure. Rich girl who got you all hot and bothered a few months back."

"She didn't get me all—" He swallowed the lie. "Okay, maybe she did. But that's old news."

"So what's the new news?"

"Turns out she was on the committee, too. And she

damn near talked the rest of the people on it into rewarding the kids caught tagging."

"How's that?"

"She was all for letting them do a mural on the side
of one of the businesses."

"You're kidding me. No making them clean up after
their vandalism—just giving them something fun to do?"

"Well, no. She actually did propose making them
clean up their mess first with paint they paid for out of
their own pockets."

Murph nodded. "Okay, good. That's responsible.
But—what?—they've been in and out of the system a
hundred times already?"

"Uh, not exactly." He shifted in his seat. Tipped his
bottle up and drained the last sip of beer from it. Because he knew this was where self-righteousness got a
little shaky. "It was their first run-in with the police."

Murphy lowered his own bottle, which he'd been
raising to his lips, and sat a little straighter in his seat.
"Let me get this straight. The kids have never been in
trouble. The Babe was going to have them clean up
their mess with paint they're responsible for purchas-
ing. But she wanted to take it a step further and have
them also paint a mural on the side of a building.
So…what? She just tossed the idea out there on the
table for someone else to implement?"

Crap. "No, she offered to supervise. She wants to
'make a difference' in their lives."

The old man snorted. "Right. *That's* likely to happen," he said, deadpan. "Still, if she's willing to do the

work, why would the committee vote against the idea? It's not like it'd be any skin offa their noses."

Crapfuckhell. "I might have gotten a little carried away with my 'tagging is the first step to crime' talk. Could have maybe scared them off some."

"For God's sake, boy." Murphy scratched his thinning iron-gray hair. "Why?"

Back straightening, he looked Murph in the eye. "You know damn well why. Once you start torquing the rules it's a slippery slope. One day you're rewarding kids for trashing people's hard-earned businesses. Next thing you know you're giving in to the temptation to just take that old-lady-bashing mugger around the corner and stick your service revolver to his temple to 'help' him cough up a confession."

There was a moment's silence in which his words clanged in his head like buckshot fired into a steel chamber—and he wished he could get the past few seconds back so he could cut his tongue out.

Then Murphy said dryly, "I'm gonna take a wild stab here and speculate we're not still talking about a bunch of merchants deciding to vote down the Babe's proposal."

Burying his head in his hands, Jase groaned.

He felt Murph rub rough fingers over his hair.

"One of these days," the old man said gruffly, "I'd like to see you give yourself a break and realize you're not like your dad or grandpa or Joe."

"That's never going to happen...because I am." Dropping his hands to the tabletop, he raised his head to look at the old man. "I'm a goddamn de Sanges male, which is a lot like being a recovering alcoholic—I'm one act away from being *just* like the rest of the men in my family."

"That's bullshit, and you oughtta damn well know it by now. But, no—you're too fucking stubborn to take your head outta your butt. *You* have never knocked over convenience stores. *You* have never kited checks or destroyed bars in a drunken brawl. And I'm guessing now is probably not a good time to tell you about this, but I'm going to anyways. I got a call from your brother today, looking for you."

Everything inside him stilled. "Joe's out on parole?"

"Looks like."

"Shit." Jase laughed without humor. Then, spreading his fingers against the faux wood, he lowered his head again and thunked it once, twice, three times against the tabletop. "I guess I'd better get in touch with him quick then, hadn't I? Because God knows he won't be out for long."

CHAPTER THREE

Holy shitskis, that "Be Careful What You Wish For" thing is no joke. Just when things were starting to settle down and I was finally getting that man out of my head...this!

"SHARON, YOU want to come take a look?" Poppy twisted around on her perch near the top of the step-ladder to look for the coffee-shop owner.

The woman popped her head out of the kitchen. Brushing flour from her hands against the white apron tied around her waist, she stepped into the retail area and studied the blackboard, closely inspecting the updated menu Poppy had just completed. Then she smiled. "Lookin' good."

"Excellent." Poppy packed up her case of colored chalks and climbed down off the ladder. She slid the container into her big tote, which she'd left by the register, then folded in the ladder's legs and tipped it carefully onto its side in the narrow area behind the glass bakery case until it was parallel to the floor and she could get a grip on it with both hands. Glancing out the door at the pale glow of daybreak beginning to lighten the eastern sky, she said, "I'll just go put this back in the closet, then clean up and get out of your way."

"I took a blueberry coffee cake out of the oven about ten minutes ago," Sharon said. "You have time for a slice and a cuppa joe? My staff's going to start trickling in pretty soon and I don't know about you, but I'm ready for a break."

"That would be great." As if to demonstrate its appreciation, her stomach growled and, patting it, she laughed. "Don't tell my mother, but I skipped breakfast this morning."

She maneuvered the ladder through the kitchen to the big utility closet by the back door, where she stored it away. Then she washed the multicolored layers of chalk from her hands and joined Sharon at a table. They visited over cups of full-bodied coffee and luscious, still-warm cake.

She didn't linger long after the snack was consumed, however. She still had three other boards to do this morning at sites scattered from Madison Park to Phinney Ridge to the Ballard neighborhood where she'd grown up, and they needed to be completed before the businesses were open to the public.

When she finished the last job, a deli just off Market Street, she looked at her watch. She'd planned to drop in on her parents but schools were closed for a teachers' "professional development" day, she had a date with some kids in the Central District—or the CD, as it was called by native Seattleites—and she had to stop by the mansion first. So with a regretful glance in the general direction of her childhood home, she steered her car toward the Ballard Bridge.

She lucked into a parking space on the block below the mansion on the steeply pitched western slope of Queen Anne and, getting out of her car, she paused to look up at the house.

The sunroom that had been scabbed onto the front of the edifice was now whittled down to a size and style in keeping with the rest of the structure and the Kavanaghs had repaired the facade to match the original. Her artist's soul smiled to see the elegant bones restored to the early-twentieth-century mansion. The sound of hammers, pithy obscenities and male laughter coming from the kitchen as she approached the back door elicited yet another grin.

She let herself into a room filled with buff guys wielding power tools. Well, okay, only one of the four men in the gutted kitchen was actually operating one. As Devlin Kavanagh's drill whined into silence and he and his brothers looked over at her, she inhaled a deep breath, then blew it out with theatrical gusto. "I love the smell of testosterone in the morning!"

Raising his black eyebrows toward his Irish-setter red hair, Dev drawled, "According to Jane, babe, you wouldn't know what to *do* with testosterone in the morning."

"You are so full of it, Kavanagh. Janie would never rat me out—not even to you. And watching all this tool-belt activity does make my little heart go pitty-pat. It's. Just. So—" she batted her lashes at Dev and his brothers "—manly."

They laughed and went back to work. She headed upstairs.

Where she found herself wandering the finished rooms, thinking about the videotape Miss Agnes had left for her, Ava and Jane to view at the reading of the will almost exactly a year ago. In it the old woman had said how much the three of them had come to mean to her over the years. And she'd told them in that foghorn voice of hers that she realized they'd have to sell the mansion—but it was her wish that each would carry out one final request from her in getting it ready. Poppy sure wished, not for the first time, that she understood what it was Miss A. had had in mind when she'd requested that Poppy be in charge of the decorating part of the renovation.

The old woman had been so good to the three of them, amazingly canny when it came to knowing what each one needed, then seeing to it that they got it. For Jane and Ava that had meant a modicum of parenting to fill in the gaps left by the always dramatic self-absorption of Janie's folks and the benign indifference of Ava's. For her it had meant having her passion for color indulged. Miss A. had done what few other adults would—given a young girl a paintbrush and the paint color of her choice and trusted the kid not to make a huge mess out of her mansion. And in the matter of the dining room, she'd even allowed Poppy to choose window treatments that let in light where before heavy draperies had kept it out. But that was a far cry from decorating the entire place.

"Omigawd." She stopped dead in the upstairs hall-way. "That's it."

Grabbing her cell phone from her tote, she was punching in an auto-dial number even as she rushed from the mansion. "I finally figured it out!" she crowed to Ava as she strode back to her car. Holding the phone to her ear, she adjusted her slipping tote on her shoulder and almost tripped over a raised slab of sidewalk where an ancient Douglas fir's root had pushed it up.

"I was making Miss A.'s request way too complicated. I thought she'd completely overestimated my talents and wanted me to act as a big-time interior decorator."

"You could do that," Ava assured her.

She laughed. "You're a true and loyal friend and I love you for it. But I design menu boards and the occa-sional greeting card—"

"One of which got picked up by Shoebox!"

Yes, that was a stroke of luck she was still dancing in the streets about—that she no longer had to scramble to come up with the rent check the first of each month. "But, face it, mostly I do catch-as-catch-can low-end commercial stuff for whoever I can convince to hire me and fast-talked my way into a couple of grants to turn on underprivileged kids to art. I'm sure as hell no interior designer."

She grinned like a deranged jester. "But that's what I figured out, that Miss A. didn't intend me to be. Jane actually tried to tell me this last fall, but my thong was in a twist at the time because I thought she was about to blow the deal I'd made with the Kavanaghs, so it didn't really register. But I think all Miss Agnes wanted from me was precisely what I was always bugging her to let me do—rip down all those gawd-awful drapes that are blocking out the light, give the rooms a fresh coat of paint and new window treatments and maybe stage it the way Realtors do these days with a few of her nicer pieces of furniture and the odd collectible."

"That sounds reasonable. But, girl, don't underesti-mate yourself, because you've already done so much more. You found us the Kavanaghs and negotiated a lower bid in exchange for the publicity they'll get, and you've been the one handling ninety percent of the bills—when all you really want to do is work with your kids."

That made her flash on the three boys she wouldn't have the opportunity to work with, which made her think about de Sanges, which, frankly, she'd been doing far too often in the past week and a half since running in to him again at the merchants' meeting.

Her chin lifted even as she drew herself up to her full height. Well, she was going to quit doing that, starting this instant.

"You're thinking about them, aren't you?" Ava said.

Poppy stumbled. "What?"

"Those boys That Man robbed you of. You're think-ing about them."

"Uh, yeah." But not as much as the man himself, she admitted guiltily.

"The bastard."

Her sentiments exactly. She just wished she could shake him from her thoughts, that the image of him, all long and lean and imbued with a sexual energy that whispered to her own, would get the hell out of her head. And in truth, the more time that passed since their encounter, the better she was getting at not thinking about him.

Arriving at her car, she said goodbye to Ava, tossed her tote into the backseat and headed for the CD.

Like the rest of Seattle, the Central District was undergoing the boom of town houses or mixed retail and condominium construction that was changing the face of the city. This neighborhood was changing more than most, however, because in addition to the relentless urban-density building going up all over town, the past decade had seen the area transform from a primarily African-American neighborhood to one with a more integrated mixed-race demographic—a change not necessarily embraced with enthusiasm by the residents who'd been here the longest.

She pulled in to the community center lot on East Cherry, parked and unloaded her easels and supplies, making several trips to haul everything into the room assigned her.

She was a little early so she got started setting the easels up and putting out pencils, brushes, palettes and tubes of paint for her class. She thought of the very first time she'd done this and smiled. Miss Agnes had volunteered her when she'd heard the DAR was looking for someone to teach an art class for one of their charitable endeavors. Poppy had been less than thrilled at the time. She was twenty-seven, scrambling to make a living on her own terms, and she'd had to stretch her schedule to fit it in.

Then she'd met the kids.

Now, she sure didn't come from a family rolling in dough, and God knew there'd been times she'd had to do some pretty creative bookkeeping to make her various incomes stretch. But there was *always* enough to buy her art supplies—a fact she'd simply taken for granted.

Then she'd met the teens in her first class and realized these kids didn't have that luxury. And watching them blossom during the short time she'd had them, a new passion had taken root in her breast.

Little by little her current teens trickled in, the cardboard tubes she'd supplied to protect their drawings and paintings tucked beneath their arms or sticking out of the tops of backpacks.

It was a small group, just twelve kids in all, selected by teachers at the three high schools that her eight boys and four girls attended. The teens had been chosen both for their aptitude in art and their lack of financial—and in some cases, family—resources. This was her third group of its kind and her kids were now far enough into the course that she'd mostly gotten them over the giving-her-attitude hump and was edging them into the fun stage. At least it was a kick for her, since this was where she got to watch the myriad possibilities of art start to spark excitement in them.

She moved quietly from student to student, standing

behind them to study their paintings or drawings, praising them here and offering tips or answering questions there.

"Yo, bitch. Hand over the vermillion."

"*What*chu call me, *cabrón?*"

Poppy whipped around. "Mr. Jackson. Ms. Suarez."

Darnell Jackson, whom she knew darn well was crushin' on the girl he'd insulted, winced, but then straightened to his full six and a half feet to give Poppy a look loaded with that attitude she'd just patted herself on the back for having put in the past.

"Did you *hear* what he called me, Ms. Calloway?" Emilia Suarez stood with one hand on her hip, her head cocked and her chin thrust up in a belligerent I'm-gonna-take-you-*down* angle at a boy who—even standing three feet away—towered head and shoulders above her.

"Yes, I did. And I'm guessing whatever it was you called him in return wasn't a love ode to your BFF." Still, Emilia's slur had been a direct response to what Darnell started, and Poppy turned to the young man standing one easel over from the irate girl. Leveling her gaze on him, she kept her tone mild when she inquired, "What is my number-one rule of behavior in this class, Mr. Jackson?"

She could see his pride demanding that he hang on to his badass 'tude, especially considering how the room had quieted and all the kids had turned to see what he would do. But Darnell had been the first of the twelve to give in to the seduction that was art; he was one of her most talented students and Poppy had made it clear at the beginning of the course that she had a zero tolerance policy for troublemaking. Moreover, the teen lived with a grandmother who'd drilled manners into his head regarding respecting one's elders.

And much as it bit her butt to think of herself as part of that demographic, it was probably how this group of teenagers viewed her.

"To give each other respect," he said grudgingly.

She looked at him in silence.

He dipped his head. "Sorry, Miz Calloway."

"It's not me you owe the apology to," she said calmly.

Big shoulders curving in, he looked over at the girl next to him. "Sorry, Emilia."

"You a sorry excuse for a *man*," Emilia muttered, but color flushed her cheeks. The other girls were too busy whooping their enthusiasm over seeing one of the boys who outnumbered them being disciplined to notice.

Which was a good thing, Poppy thought, for if they had, they would have teased Emilia unmercifully about it, which would have just escalated matters. "Ladies," she said with quiet repressiveness.

They immediately settled down, but two of them bumped hips and exchanged low fives.

Poppy bit back a grin. But, damn, she loved teenagers!

She hadn't gotten as far as Darnell and Emilia in her circuit around the room and she crossed to them now. Standing back, she studied Darnell's painting. "Oh," she breathed, staring at the portrait of three women with their heads together. "This is wonderful."

"I got the idea from this picture my grandma Barb

has of her grandmother and two great-aunts," Darnell said, forgetting both his pride and his embarrassment in his enthusiasm for the project.

She scrutinized it further, admiring the way the women all but leaped off the canvas. "Do you have a name for it yet?"

"After Church."

She laughed. "Yes, I can visualize that—sprung from those hard pews and ready to dish on who was wearing what and who showed up hungover from the excesses of the night before. You captured a sense of gossip and imbued it with a definite feel of an older, bygone era. Yet the subject matter is as fresh today as it was in your great-great-grandmother's time. It's fabulous, Darnell. I love the bold use of color."

"Grandma's photo's black-and-white, but she says her people's always been lovin' color." He grinned. "And I don't doubt it, if me and her's anything to go by."

He'd painted two of the women in mostly primary-colored clothing—one in brilliant blue with a blue-and-yellow head wrap, the other in yellow sporting a large brimmed hat with green feathers and a matching sash that tied beneath her chin. He indicated the third figure, which as yet was still a pencil sketch. "That's what I wanted the vermillion for." Then he drew himself up to his considerable height and cut his eyes to the girl next to him. "But I'm sorry 'bout what I called you, Emilia. I was being a smart-ass and Grandma would scrub my mouth out with soap if she knew."

"I'll do that myself, you ever call me that again." But

Emilia handed him the tube of paint. "I'm sorry I disrespected you, too."

His teeth flashed. "Did you? I don't speak Spanish, so you coulda said anything and I wouldn't know the difference. What'd you call me?"

Her lips curved up. "It's prob'ly best you don't know." She gazed at his painting. "You're really good, Darnell. I can't do figures for sh—" shooting a glance at Poppy, she cut herself off "—um, nuthin'."

"Yeah, but you do buildings real good. I wanted to put the church steeple in the background, but I drew it and erased it so many times trying to get the proportions right I'm lucky I didn't put a hole in the canvas."

"Maybe after class sometime, I can show you how to do that. But you gotta show me how to draw them whatchamacall'ems—life studies."

"Yeah," he said, turning back to his easel. A smile curved his lips. "Yeah. That'd be good. Go to Starbucks, maybe, and grab a table where we can spread out our sh— Uh, stuff."

Poppy was feeling pretty pleased with both her kids and herself by the time she rolled back into her Fremont neighborhood late that afternoon. She'd stopped at a Home Depot on the way home to grab a fistful of paint chips for the mansion. She swung by Marketime now to pick up a few groceries—but then didn't feel like cooking when she got back to her apartment. So she tossed her paint chips on the table, took her groceries into the kitchen and put them away, then hiked over to Mad Pizza to get herself a small pie to take home.

Settling with it at the tiny table outside her kitchen a short while later, she listened to Zero 7 on her CD player and happily pored over paint color chips while washing down three slices with a bottle of beer.

She was feeling so mellow that she actually filed away the stack of paperwork that was a by-product of the grant she'd received from the Parks Department Youth Community Outreach program. It had been taking up space on the top of the bookshelf for the past six weeks. She felt a lot more righteous than the chore merited when she finished up and, noticing the pristine clear spots in the dust where the paperwork had lain, even considered digging the duster out of the closet to do a little spring cleaning.

Then she laughed and got real. "Nah." No sense in getting carried away.

She did swab down the table in order to have a clean surface on which to lay out her greeting-card supplies, then got down to work. She finished painting the design she'd been interrupted doing yesterday when something else needing her attention had gotten in the way. When that was done she started a new design and was soon in the zone where her mind drifted while her creativity soared.

It was a while before she registered the primary colors she'd been automatically applying to the new card. Realizing that Darnell's painting had inspired her color choices, it started her thinking. Maybe she should put together a proposal for a new grant—this one to teach kids how to make greeting cards with the intent to sell them. It was true she'd only sold one card to a

national company, but she did okay marketing her others
to trendy little boutiques around town. Her income from
them was pocket change compared to the one that had
gone mainstream, but it nevertheless gave her additional
credentials and demonstrated that handcrafted cards
were marketable.

Someday, when the mansion renovation was complete
and she and her friends had sold it, she'd have access to
some real money. Aside from getting a car that was more
reliable than the heap she drove now, her own needs were
few. But with Miss Agnes's money, she could reach out to
more kids—a lot more. The old lady would've loved that.

The pure, max *coolness* of that prospect made her
smile. Life was good.

The telephone rang and she jumped up to answer it,
ready to share her ideas and settle into a long, satisfy-
ing conversation with Jane or Ava or her mother.

Only it turned out to be none of them and by the time
Poppy hung up fifteen minutes later, her heart was hammering the wall of her chest like an enraged carpenter.
She didn't know whether to laugh like a loon or bang
her head against the nearest wall.

Because it turned out she was getting what she'd
asked for. And that was good, right? Her three juvie
taggers were getting a second chance, which meant so
was she—to help. So, yes. It was good.

Excellent, in fact.

All except for the part about them being monitored
for good behavior. By none other than her favorite cop:
Jason de Sanges.

CHAPTER FOUR

Did I lie through my teeth? You betcha. Do I feel
bad about it? Yeah, right.

THE FAINTEST GLIMMER of the connection between a recent
spate of burglaries that Robbery had been fielding itched
at the back of Jase's mind. He couldn't quite get a grasp
on it, but it floated close to the edge of his consciousness
then disappeared, floated nearer yet, then dove out of
reach once more. He thumbed back through his notes,
knowing that something in there must have triggered it,
but the pale flicker of whatever it was retreated. So he
emptied his mind and sat quietly in the noisy squad room
in hopes that the association he sought would swim a little
nearer to the surface of his brain. And the glimmer came
closer, closer—yes, come to Papa, baby, almost there…

"Yo, de Sanges!"

And it was gone. Swiveling his chair around, he saw
Bob Greer leaning out of the door to his closet-size
office. "Something I can help you with, Lieutenant?"

"Yeah. Come in here a minute, will ya?"

He did as he was bid and knew he wasn't going to like
whatever was coming when Greer said, "Close the door."

He did so and stuffed his hands into his pockets as he studied his superior. "What's going on?"

"Take a seat."

He took a seat.

His lieutenant perched on the edge of his desk. "I got a call from the commissioner, who got a call from the mayor."

Oh, shit, he thought in disbelief, *she wouldn't have. Not twice.* But a bad feeling crawled the nape of his neck. "And?"

"And apparently someone is seriously connected, because guess what you've just been assigned to?"

He rubbed his hand over his jaw. "Tell me this doesn't have anything to do with those merchants' tagger kids."

"Sorry, Jase. You are now the official head honcho of the—get this—Neighbors United Through Art program."

He slumped back in his chair. Breathed, "Fuuuck," stretching out the single syllable until by rights it should have snapped beneath the attenuation.

"Look at it this way," Greer said. "It puts you on the mayor's radar. Do a good job and he's gonna remember when it comes time for you to take that lieutenants' exam. A word from him could mean the difference between a decent placement and Peoria."

Right. Like the man was still apt to be in office by the time the next lieutenants' exam rolled around. But he nodded as if that were a genuine consideration and said, "Yeah, there is that. So what does a 'head honcho' on one of these committees do?"

"Make damn sure those three kids toe the line. No screwups."

He sat upright. "You're kidding me, right?" Looking at the older man, Jase could see that he wasn't. "Jesus, Lieutenant, we *all* screw up now and then— and teenagers more often than most. Are you seriously taking me off the streets to be their frigging hall monitor?"

Greer shrugged. "What can I say? The mayor wants to accommodate his friend by giving the kids a break. But he's a politician first and foremost, so he's also covering his ass by making sure they don't do anything to get the merchants or general neighborhood up in arms. And you're the lucky bastard who was nominated to ride herd on them."

"Lieutenant, we're dealing with that rash of burg—"

"Oh, you'll get to work your burglaries, trust me. You didn't think watching some baby taggers was going to be your only job, did you? Hell, no. But, hey, our Man in Office is all over sweetening the deal. While you might have to fit this in around your regular work, the mayor authorized up to—wait for it—twenty whole overtime hours."

"Oh, well, then. As long as I can die a rich man." Maintaining a neutral expression, he discussed what few particulars his lieutenant knew for a while longer. But by the time he left Greer's office, he was steaming. The second he reached his desk he flipped back to the November notes in his tattered notebook, located the Babe's phone number, then headed straight for a reverse directory.

IT WASN'T LIKE he was bending—never mind breaking—any rules here, he assured himself as he pulled up to an apartment house in the Fremont district a short while later. Miz Calloway thought she had a pet cop on a leash? Well, he was a paid public servant for the populace at large, not just her and her wealthy friends, and he was merely stopping by to let her know what she could expect from their upcoming association.

Hey, it was in her own best interest.

He frowned up at the old brick building as he climbed out of his car and locked up. This wasn't exactly where he would have pictured little Miss Ritz living. He'd pegged her more as the renowned Epi Apartment type, with its views of the ship canal and artsy stainless steel curlicues wrapping the south tower. But what the hell did he know? Maybe this was one of those…what had he once heard Hohn's wife call a piece of furniture that Jase had just thought needed a good coat of paint? Oh, yeah—shabby chic. Maybe it was one of those places.

But the joint had an elevator the size of a British telephone booth and that had an out-of-order sign on it. His brows drew together as he hiked up to the third floor, unable to visualize Calloway here. They cinched tighter yet when he saw the flimsy lock on her door. Maybe that was the reason he pounded a bit harder on it than he'd intended. But what the hell was the woman doing in a place with nonexistent security?

When his commanding knocks didn't garner an immediate response, he rapped his knuckles against the panel with even more force. At least it was made from a nice solid piece of first-growth Seattle fir.

"Hold your horses, for God's sake," he heard her say from the other side of the door. "I'm coming." A second later the door whipped open.

And he was face-to-face with her.

"Oh," she said flatly. "It's you."

He merely stood there staring at her, feeling the way he did every damn time he'd seen her—which, okay, counting this evening had only been three. It seemed like more, maybe because it was always accompanied by this hot spear of lightning ripping up his spine and electrifying neurons along the farthest reaches of every nerve path winding through his body.

He scowled down at her. "You don't even look out your peephole before you open the door?" he demanded. "And why don't you have a chain on this?" Not that chains weren't a joke in the face of a determined burglar, but since they only allowed the door to be opened so far they did offer the possibility of slowing things down for that important nanosecond the home owner could take to slam it shut again.

Her chin angling skyward, she narrowed her eyes at him. But in the next instant she flashed him a smile of such singular sweetness he knew to brace for trouble.

And he got it in spades when she chided, "Oh, *Daddy!*" and, moving faster than a cat, looped her slender arms around his neck to give him a brief, fierce hug. "You are so sweet, always worrying about me." Gazing up at him, she touched her fingertips to his jaw and for a warm, moist second they breathed the same air. "The designer stubble is new. You give up shaving, Papa?"

"Very funny," he said, even as he stood still as a statue while another of those lightning arcs flashed through him. He was ruthlessly banishing it even before she took a swift step back. Yeah, yeah, she had big brown eyes and creamy skin and a soft cloud of curly blond hair that he wouldn't mind wrapping around his fists. Hell, he'd strip her down and do her against the nearest wall in a New York minute if she'd let him.

But that wasn't going to happen, and his shoulders hitched in a barely conscious move. Oh, well, he thought mendaciously, life was just full of disappointments. You learned that young growing up in the foster system. Or—as in his case—mostly in the system, since he hadn't spent *all* his time in foster care after his mother died. Sometimes whichever male relative had been cut loose from the pen would swing by his current dwelling to spring him for a while—against Child Protective Services' rules, of course, since the state didn't consider any of the de Sanges men good parent material.

CPS rarely had to mount a hunt for him, however, because it was never long before Dad or Pops or his brother Joe broke parole—and Jase would find himself delivered back into foster care about the same time the *loco parentis* of the hour was loaded shackled into the back of a van for a fast trip back to the slammer.

So big deal; Blondie wasn't going to provide him with a handy outlet for all this electricity zinging around inside of him. It wasn't the reason he'd come here anyhow, so it was time he dragged his attention away from the subtle sheen of lavender smoothed from her lashes to the crease of her eyelids and got down to business.

He took a step forward and felt a little spurt of satisfaction when she fell back. Eradicating that as well, he watched without expression as he backed her step for step into the short hallway of her apartment and closed the door behind them.

"You've had me pulled off a crucial case to attend to what *you* decided is important for the last time," he informed her in a low, even voice. "So, here's how we're going to work this. You want me to waste my time on this Arts For Thugs project? Fine. I have my orders from the mayor and I'll follow them. But I'm doing this my way and I plan to watch those kids' every move. You better hope to hell they don't screw the pooch, Ms. Calloway, because I'm going to be breathing down their necks every minute. And if they so much as spit on the sidewalk I'll haul them in, lock them up and throw away the key." Or not. But damned if he was giving her a single reason to suspect he might not be serious.

"Oh, yeah, like *that* won't all but guarantee that they'll mess up!"

He shrugged. "Not my problem."

"Well, guess what, Detective? I'm making it your problem." She took a hot step forward. "I was feeling kind of bad about you being dragged away from your work, so I thank you. Your oh-so-sensitive approach to dealing with kids just knocked that clean out of my repertoire of regrets."

She got right in his face and he smelled clean skin, felt warm breath fan his chin. "I've got a flash for you, de Sanges, I have strings I haven't even *begun* to pull. You think the mayor is as high up the food chain as I can go? Think again. So here's how *I* say we're going to work this. You will stay ten—no, make that *fifteen*—feet away from my kids. The price for you being any closer than that is your willingness to work alongside them. I expect you to be civil. And you can bring your own damn paint-brush, too!" Cheeks flushed, breathing quick and shallow, she stepped back. "Now I'd like you to leave."

He stared down at her and the temptation to give in to the de Sanges genes sang through his veins like a sweet narcotic. He knew ways to make her back down—ways that, without issuing an actual threat, would scare the spiral right out of those long, blond curls. All he had to do was lean down and whisper a few succinct sentences in her ear.

Snapping shut the lips he had opened to do just that, however, he turned and strode to the door. He hadn't spent all these years rising above his genes just to cave in now. But he stopped with his hand on the doorknob to look back at her, raking his gaze from her chocolate eyes, to her round breasts that pushed against a surprisingly worn-at-the-seams gray hoodie, to the slice of Nordic pale skin showing between the jacket's hem and the hip-band of its matching drawstring pants, to her sock-clad feet.

Then he sent it in a reverse journey back up until he was once again looking directly into those startlingly dark eyes.

She might have won this round, but he had a little news flash of his own. "I'll stay the requisite fifteen feet from your minithugs or pack my paintbrush. But I'm putting you on notice, Ms. Calloway. This is it. I don't give a flying…flick who you know. You ever go over my head again or jeopardize my ability to do my job and there will be consequences. Count on it."

And seething in places he'd never allow to show, he let himself out the door.

HEART RACING like an Indy 500 contender, Poppy watched the door softly snick shut behind de Sanges and abruptly buckled at the knees, lowering herself without grace to sit on the hallway floor. Her kneecaps wavering in front of her face, she braced her elbows against them and lowered her head into her hands. "Holy shitskis. Holy, ho-ly shitskis!"

She couldn't believe the bluff that had come out of her mouth. As if she called in personal favors from the mayor—and people of even more influence—all the time!

A sputter of hysterical laughter escaped her. As if, indeed. No, the only one in the Sisterhood with political clout was Ava. Who, it turned out, had talked to her uncle Robert, who played golf with His Honor the Mayor most Wednesdays—and all without so much as a hint to Poppy that she planned to do so. Poppy had been as surprised as de Sanges to hear from the mayor's office that her proposed project was on after all. And although she'd been thrilled at the thought of having an opportunity to help those three kids, she hadn't been lying—she *had* felt kind of guilty about Ava going over the detective's head for a second time. But only until he'd opened his mouth and threatened to intimidate the teenagers. That had shot her empathy straight to hell.

Yet with or without the sympathy factor, she really, really wished she hadn't touched him.

Because. Lord. Have. Mercy.

She didn't know what it was about him, but she only had to lay eyes on him and she got such a visceral reaction she didn't know what to do with herself. She hadn't felt this strongly about *Andrew,* and she'd had a three-year relationship in college with him. Such an unprecedented response to a guy she didn't know and didn't much like the little she *did* know shook her up. And that pissed her off. Never a stellar combination, which she had proven by promptly getting off on the wrong foot with him the minute she'd opened the door and seen him on the other side.

She'd thought she was being so clever to treat his arrogant high-handedness over her door chain as if it were a concerned command from her father.

But it hadn't been clever at all; it had been stupid. Because she'd looped her arms around his neck and she had damn near whimpered at the heat that pumped off his long, hard frame, at the starch and soap scents she'd smelled emanating from his collar that made her want to bury her nose in his neck. His angular jaw had been bristly beneath her fingertips, making the full cut of his lips look contrastingly soft—until they'd suddenly gone hard with some unnamed determination. Whereupon she'd all but leaped out of range like a scalded cat.

She hoped he hadn't noticed, but he didn't strike her as the type who missed much.

Her subsequent embarrassment, combined with his unemotional threat against her teens, was undoubtedly what had given her the stones to look him in the eye and lie like a politician.

But, oh, she was torn about having her proposal suddenly accepted. Half of her was thrilled at this opportunity to reach the three teenagers.

The other half thought she was freaking nuts to put herself anywhere in de Sanges's vicinity.

Oh, no. The latter thought put a firm halt to the low-grade panic she'd been experiencing ever since she'd opened her mouth and started threatening him, and her spine snapped straight. *Oh, no, no, no.* She was neither weak-willed nor easily pushed around, and the idea that she should be wary of or intimidated by a little one-on-one time spent with the detective put her back up but good.

For God's sake, she wasn't some impressionable fourteen-year-old ruled by her hormones. Yes, he was dark and steely and, okay, the power of attraction she felt was formidable. But she was a big girl, one who was motivated to preserve—and hopefully enhance—the well-being of those kids. And contrary to what de Sanges might believe based on tonight and the first time they'd met, she actually did know how to act professional.

So he had better just watch his step. Because she was a woman with a mission.

But one who was going to be very careful never to get within touching range of that man again.

CHAPTER FIVE

And I'm supposed to be an artist, with an eye for detail. Some eye. Because the whole Cory-being-a-girl thing—I sure didn't see that one coming!

FOURTEEN-and-three-quarters-year-old Cory Capelli pulled her newsboy cap down low, flipped her father's battered leather jacket collar up and veered away from the group she'd been hanging with on the Ave in the U district. She liked catching up occasionally with other graffiti artists and taggers to hear the latest gossip about who was doing what and listen to everyone one-up each other's lies. But she did her best work alone.

It was a policy she should have remembered before she hooked up with Danny G. and Henry Whatshisname two weeks ago. Danny alone would have been fine. He did some of the best storytelling graffiti around, and Cory considered herself more of an artist than a tagger. She might not style elaborate wall paintings but her tag, CaP, was a work of art in its own right with its fat, two-dimensional, multicolored letters and her trademark cap hanging from the lowercase *a*. She considered it a world removed from scrawling quick and dirty chicken scratches on bus-stop signs or buildings or messing up someone else's work. She'd been working on some graphic novel–type illustrations in her sketch pad at home, but she hadn't worked up the confidence yet to give them a public try. Which was why she'd wanted to team up with Danny G.

Henry, on the other hand, was one of the chicken scratchers. So when he'd attached himself to their plan to cover a block of buildings together, in a neighborhood they weren't familiar with, she hadn't known how to say that didn't work for her.

She definitely needed to learn that, whatchamacallit…assertiveness stuff. Because just look where her silence had gotten her. Could you say *busted?* The three of them were now scheduled to meet some do-gooder tomorrow morning to paint over what they'd done. *Whoop-de-do,* Cory thought, spotting a nice wall and melting into the space between the dentist's office hosting it and the jewelry store next door. Like *that* was how she wanted to spend her Saturday morning.

Still, it beat getting a record and being sent to juvie, which would just finish the job of Mom's already broken heart. And Cory got it—she really did—that relatively speaking, she and Danny G. and Henry had lucked out with those people whose buildings they'd tagged. Well, Henry had tagged. He'd managed to scrawl his crap over every workable surface before she or Danny could so much as pull out a can of paint.

Okay, that wasn't quite true. They'd both had their cans out when the guy from the store across the street had busted them. Henry might have beaten the two of them to the neighborhood but it wasn't as if they hadn't been there to do the same thing he had done—if you discounted the talent factor, since even with their dominant hands tied behind their backs, either one of them would have done a helluva better job.

But the point was, they'd still lucked out with those store people. Because while the merchants had called in the cops, they'd refused to press charges until they had a chance to discuss among themselves what to do with her and the boys. So this cleanup gig was better than the alternative.

But not by much.

And the thought of it was putting a heavy-duty crimp in her night. She was bummed out, it was late, and foot traffic from U-Dub students had dwindled everywhere but around the area's taverns and clubs. That last part was actually a good thing, since it skewed her odds toward the not-getting-caught end of the spectrum. But it felt isolated and lonely and rain clouds were starting to blow across the moon-free sky. In the little bit of light that managed to penetrate between the buildings from the corner streetlamp, she found herself gazing listlessly at the expanse of smooth buttercream paint in front of her.

Giving herself a mental shake, she then shook her aerosol can of Patriot Blue, absorbing the comforting sound of the bead rattling around inside. By rights she oughtta be all pumped up at finding a virgin wall like this one.

Only...

She had zero vision in her head as far as putting a fresh spin on her tag went. Usually she had all kinds of ideas. But she was tired of just doing the same letters over and over again, and she couldn't drum up a lick of enthusiasm for the project, no matter how rare it was to find a clean wall.

So she might as well go home. In light of the way she'd be spending her Saturday tomorrow, it was pretty dumb to be out here pushing her luck in the first place. Plus Mom would be getting off work in about an hour and she'd freak if she knew Cory was out this late.

The knee-jerk guilt was immediate, but so was the defiance she pushed it away with. Hey, it wasn't as if she didn't stay in like a good little Girl Scout dang near every weeknight. She even studied so that she wouldn't have to see the sad look she'd put on Mom's face last spring by bringing home a truly in-the-toilet-type report card.

But the weekends were a different matter. They just seemed to stretch without end, what with Mom working two jobs and the fact that they'd only moved here from Philly a couple of months ago. Midyear changes at school sucked—she'd like to see *anyone*, except maybe one of those so-perky-you-wanted-to-smack-'em cheerleader types, make instant friends. And a girl had to have some fun.

There'd sure been precious little of that since Daddy was killed.

Grief, hard and sharp, sliced through her defenses, and she doubled over, her arms wrapped around her middle. But this wasn't the place to give in to it and she pulled herself upright. Still, she had to get out of here.

She was slipping out from between the two buildings when she heard glass breaking, so close it made her jump. There was a shout from within the store next door. Then the report of a gunshot. It was a sound that defined her nightmares and she froze in the deep shadow of the dentist's office doorway, cold sweat trickling down her sides.

A strident alarm started whooping and she made herself move, shimmying up the rough brick that formed a facade at the front of the building. It seemed like an eon but was probably only a few moments before she hooked her elbows over the edge of the one-story office's cantilevered roof and swung herself over its lip. She lay there on her back for a moment, panting and struggling to slow her heartbeat. Then she slowly rolled onto her stomach and pulled herself by her elbows to the back edge nearest the north-side jewelry store, knowing she should have simply beat feet while the beating was good, but sucked into a bad decision once again by her damn impulsiveness and never-ending curiosity.

From her vantage point she watched kids pour out of the shop's back door and realized the stories she'd thought a couple of taggers had been making up must be true: there was a youth gang robbing city jewelry stores. Given that most of the kids looked young even to her, she couldn't imagine they'd come up with the idea on their own.

The thought had no sooner flitted across her mind

than a man stepped out behind them, shoving both a gun and what looked like a black hood in the waistband of his slacks. He paused beneath the dim light that shone over the door, but with the brim of his porkpie hat throwing his face in shadow she couldn't make out his features. And that was just fine with Cory, since the most painful lesson she'd learned in her life was that the wrong kind of knowledge could kill you.

That's how it had worked with her dad.

"Move your asses," the man growled, and the kids scattered in six different directions. "Fucking amateurs," he muttered and lit a cigarette as he pushed away from the door.

And, oh, crap. The flame of his Zippo briefly illuminated his face.

She knew him. Well, she didn't *know*-him know him, but she recognized who he was. She'd overheard someone saying he was, like, the muscle for some local crime boss whose name she couldn't recall. But she knew he had a *bad* reputation. And she really, really didn't want to bring herself to the attention of the top dawg *or* his henchman. Not when it was obvious the Hench had just shot someone.

But she must have made some sort of noise or moved without realizing it, because even as Muscle Boy was stalking purposefully down the passageway between the two buildings toward the street, he looked up.

Straight at her.

Cory's heart stopped and for a moment she merely gawped. Seeing his hand go for the gun in his waistband, however, unfroze her but quick and, scuttling backward, she scrambled to her feet and raced across the rooftop, leaping up onto the roof of the south-side building with strides long and sure even as her mind screamed in panic. Her daddy had been a track star way back in his high-school years, and he'd taught her to run practically from the time she could walk. He used to say she was the son he'd never had and the daughter he'd always wanted.

But she couldn't think about that now because it made her knees weak. Shoving all thoughts of her family aside, she sprinted across the second building and up onto a third. This one had a working roof with heat or air shafts or whatever they were sticking out, and a little shedlike structure with a door that led to the building. She came to an abrupt halt. She couldn't simply keep going—at least not without trying to think it through. The Hench hadn't come up onto the dentist's roof after her, so he was no doubt headed straight for the last building to await her descent. At least she hoped that was what he would do. Because her plan was to bail midblock. She sped over to the door and reached for the knob.

It was locked. But there was a fire escape going down the back of the building. Cautiously, she approached it and peered over.

And damn near wet her pants. In the millisecond before she jerked back again she glimpsed Muscle Boy—a big, ugly boogeyman of a guy—pointing his gun at her in a two-handed grip.

A gun that he'd already proved he wasn't shy about

using. The crack of it discharging at *her* in the next second sounded louder than thunder.

Almost simultaneous with the report, the bullet hit high on the air vent thingie behind her and ricocheted off. She managed to bite back the girlish scream bulging the back of her throat, but it was a close thing. She'd learned a long time ago to dress like a boy when she went out tagging. It was just safer and even with the cops and the store owners who'd busted her two weeks ago, she'd stayed in character. She hadn't claimed to be a boy, but she was tall and she knew how to walk and talk like one when she needed to. Plus Cory was one of those names that could belong to a boy or a girl and hers even had the more boylike spelling.

If she got out of this tonight, hopefully that would stand her in good stead, since it would be way harder to track down a boy tagger than a girl.

She was already hauling ass when she heard the fire escape rattle beneath the bad guy's weight, but the adrenaline that spiked through her bloodstream at the sound acted like a turbo boost as she raced back the way she had come. She jumped down the three-foot drop to the next building, raced across that roof, then dropped another couple feet to the dentist's office roof. Reaching the edge, she plopped onto her butt, rolled, grasped the rim of the roof and dropped, bending her knees to soften the impact when she hit ground.

She still had to put a hand down to catch herself on the tiny patch of grass fronting the office and her feet scrambled in the dormant flower border before she gained some purchase and sprinted like a bat out of hell toward Forty-fifth. Reaching the main east-west arterial, she cut across a gas station lot, then slowed down and eased into a shadow as the wail of a cop siren split the night. A second later a blue-and-white flashed past, red lights swirling.

Passing only two students weaving unsteadily down the sidewalk, she left the shopping district behind, casting glances over her shoulder to make sure she wasn't being followed. She slid through the neighborhood, jumping fences and cutting through yards. It wasn't until she was blocks away that she slowed down and tried to collect herself so she could make a plan to get back home. She had to arrive before her mother, or Mom would go ballistic. And not just about her being out on her own this time of night, but over her disguise.

Which brought back the way she'd misrepresented herself to the shop-owner people, which in turn made her stomach drop. She didn't even know why she'd stayed in guy character, except that it was a form of protection. Girls were more vulnerable on the street. So if Danny G. and Henry found out, her cover was blown.

And, okay, she admitted that maybe she'd hoped the whole thing would just go away and nobody would ever have to know the difference.

But of course it hadn't, so now she had to show up tomorrow as herself. Because it was one thing to pull off acting like a guy for short periods of time in dim lighting. It was something else again to try it in broad daylight for God knew how long. The woman who had contacted her about making reparation said to plan on being at her beck and call for as long as she deemed fit.

So it presented a problem—the guys *were* going to find out she was a girl. She had a hunch that Danny G. maybe already knew, but he was a quiet, self-contained guy who mostly kept to himself, so she didn't fear him talking. Henry, on the other hand, would probably shoot his mouth off all over town. Soon everybody would know that her alter ego CaP, assumed to be a guy, wasn't. And that would blow her one ace card: the fact that the henchman wouldn't be looking for a female.

Hell, if he was even still looking for anybody at all. Maybe she was worrying over nothing. Maybe he'd come to the right conclusion—that she was too smart, not to mention scared, to tell anyone what she had seen.

But a shiver rippled down her spine and she shuddered. Because that was a lot of maybes.

And she had a bad feeling this wasn't going to go away that easily.

Up on the Ave, Bruno Arturo was pulling his cell phone from his leather jacket pocket as he strode toward Diamond Parking to retrieve his car. He punched in an auto number, then stopped on the sidewalk for a second, rubbing his free hand over his jaw as the phone rang on the other end.

It was picked up on the second ring. "Schultz."

"We got trouble, boss."

"Those aren't words I like to hear, Arturo. What kind of trouble?"

"There was an old man in the store when we got inside."

Schultz's voice grew cold. "Is he going to be able to tell the cops about the kids? Identify anyone?"

"Not now."

"Then I don't see where we have a problem."

"There was also a kid up on the roof next door. A tagger, I think." He'd seen several in the neighborhood as he'd made his way back to his car. "I think he saw my face." He pulled out a smoke and fired it up. Sucked in harsh smoke, then let it drift from his nostrils. "I know damn well he saw my gun, since I was pointing it right at him."

Schultz snorted. "How old, you think?"

"I dunno. Young. Still had that gawky all-arms-and-legs thing going. Fast little sonuvabitch, though. Ran like the wind."

"Then forget about him. He's probably scared shitless—he's not going to bring attention to himself by talking and we don't want to do it by launching some big boy-hunt. Wait a few days. If we don't hear anything about the cops looking for a kiddie gang, just let it go."

"Ya think?"

"Yes, Bruno, I do." Schultz's voice got that cold you-questioning-*me?* inflection that anyone who worked for him knew was a warning that they were treading on thin ice.

"Okay, then."

They hung up a few minutes later and Bruno continued to his Escalade. But as he unlocked it and climbed in a short while later, he was already making plans.

Because it was all fine and mofo'n dandy for the boss to say wait to make sure we're not tipping our hands. But if the kid walked into a cop shop and sat down with a sketch artist, it wasn't gonna be Schultz's ass that was hung out to dry. It'd be his.

And that didn't make him real anxious to just "let it go."

THE SEATTLE PD robbery unit augmented patrol by listening to the police scanner at all times. If they heard of a bank robbery in progress, they answered the call alongside patrol. The call that came over the scanner early Saturday morning had nothing to do with a bank. But a coworker called Jase anyhow.

"I'm off duty, slick," he growled into the receiver as he pulled into his parking slot at his apartment house.

"Yeah, sorry about that," Hohn said. "But I thought you'd wanna know. Another jewelry store heist just came over the scanner. I'm heading there now."

Jase swore. "Where?"

"U district." Hohn gave him the address and instructed him to park around back.

"Meet you in ten." Jase snapped his phone shut, backed out of his slot and was slapping the rotating LED beacon on his car roof as he hit the arterial at Greenwood.

He arrived with a couple of minutes to spare and found an EMT wagon just pulling away and a patrol car with its lights swirling and radio squawking parked in one of the two spaces behind the jewelry store. He pulled into the other and climbed out of his car at the same time Hohn pulled in behind him. Jase hung his badge from his jacket's breast pocket as he went to greet the other detective. Together they approached the back door.

"Robbery," Hohn called into the interior.

"In here, Detective." An Asian-American patrolman crossed the room to them. "I'm Greg Vuong." He indicated another patrolman just entering the work area from the showroom. "That's my partner, Mark Nelson."

Jase gave Vuong a quick once-over. Kid looked barely out of the academy but had a nice steady gaze. "What have we got, Officer?" They moved deeper into the room.

"The alarm company called us at twelve-fourteen. We arrived at twelve-twenty-six. We found the back door open and a man we assume to be the owner on the floor with a gunshot wound."

"The meat wagon was leaving as I got here. The owner gonna make it?"

"He's alive, but I don't know for how long. The paramedics said he was in bad shape."

"Any idea yet what was taken?"

"There's a loose diamond on the floor. If more were out when the robbers broke in they might have taken them," Vuong said, then looked at his partner.

"The cases in the store are empty." Nelson picked up the report. "But they're not smashed, so I'm guessing the owner probably empties them into the safe at night." He indicated a tall, industrial-strength model bolted into the corner of the workroom. "Or it's possible the robber forced him to open the cases out front before he shot him."

Jase squatted behind the workbench. He inspected the overturned stool and the bloodstains on the floor without touching either, then turned to examine the bench itself. "He had this drawer half open and there's a thirty-eight special inside. Looks to me like he was shot where he sat before he could get to it. My guess is whoever did this intended a smash-and-grab and didn't expect to find anyone still in the store at this hour. Are there any security cameras?"

Nelson nodded. "Two in the retail area. None back here."

"We'll need to check them out—see if there's anything on them."

The lab boys arrived and started searching for trace evidence and setting up to dust for prints. While Hohn organized the patrolmen to try to unearth information on the victim in order to contact the next of kin, Jase went outside to see what he could find.

In the high-powered beam cast by the Maglite he'd collected from the passenger seat of his car, he found a fairly fresh-looking Double Bubble gum wrapper that may or may not have been recently dropped where the parking area met the narrow alley. He bagged it up. The flashlight beam picked up what looked like a long drift of ash in the through-way between the store and the building next door, and when he crouched down he discovered a cigarette that looked as if it had been lit only to be tossed aside. He slid the filter into another baggie and duckwalked down the passage toward the street one step at a time, sweeping the light from his Mag over every inch before he moved a leg forward.

The front of the jewelry store was pristine and untouched as far as he could tell, the sidewalk clean and the groomed dirt that would probably be overflowing with flowers in another month or so in the narrow garden boxes on either side of the stubby walkway just beginning to sprout a few early shoots.

There wasn't much to be gleaned here and he turned to head back the way he had come to broaden his search of the alley. His Maglite, which he'd lowered when he'd hit the lighted street, flashed over the small patch of landscaping fronting the building next door, and he had taken two steps down the passageway before what he'd seen registered. Then he backpedaled and swung his flashlight at the ground in front of what turned out to be a dentist's office.

This flower bed was all chewed up and a can of spray paint lay on its side on the postage stamp–size patch of grass. He carefully picked it up, using only a thumbnail beneath its bottom rim and the very edge of a fingertip upon its blue cap. He turned it toward the streetlight.

It was a can of Krylon, a brand that could be found at any hardware store in town. But putting a slideshow of impressions together, he thought he was beginning to see a picture.

It looked like there might have been a witness to tonight's robbery. Maybe a graffiti artist or a tagger. Not exactly a huge break in the case, considering there must be dozens if not hundreds of them in the city.

Still, maybe they had their territories. And at the very least, it was a place to start.

CHAPTER SIX

Okay, I have to admit it, today was different. Usually the kids I teach *want* to be here.

SATURDAY MORNING, on the north side of Jerry Harvey's shop, Poppy faced three kids who stared back at her sullenly, their postures a study of teenage defiance. She turned to give Jason a brief glance, then concentrated her full attention on the teens. "My name is Poppy Calloway," she said genially. "You will refer to me as Ms. Calloway. This is Detective de Sanges." She looked at the lone girl in the group. "Are you Danny or Cory?"

"Cory." The red lipstick, the heavily mascaraed blue eyes beneath the long, black bangs of an otherwise short, spiky hairdo gave her attitude. But a wash of color upon her fair, fair skin hinted at nerves.

"You're a surprise." *There* was an understatement, but she buried her astonishment in a calm tone. "Lot of people thought you were a boy."

"No shit," the scrawnier of the two boys muttered.

Poppy turned to him. "And you are?"

A who-wants-to-know expression was her only answer for a long moment. But when Poppy merely looked at him and de Sanges shifted impatiently at her back, he muttered, "Henry."

She glanced at her notes, then back up to meet his gaze with a level, carefully nonconfrontational one of her own. "Well, Mr. Close," she said pleasantly, "as long as you're a part of this group, you will check your language at the door."

"Right. That's fuckin' gonna happen."

She put a hand on de Sanges's arm as he took a giant step to brush past her, aware, even through two layers of clothing, of the strength and heat beneath her fingers. He was closer to them than the fifteen feet she'd insisted upon during their last conversation. She was willing to let it go, however, as long as he let her handle matters without his less-than-sympathetic interference.

The instant he subsided, she released her grip, then moved within a foot of Henry Close herself. He was undersize even for a thirteen-year-old, but he had old eyes and she recognized a hard life when she saw one written on a child's face.

"Oh, it will happen, Mr. Close," she said amiably.

"M'name's Henry."

"If you learn nothing else while you're under my supervision," she said as if he hadn't interrupted, "you will learn this—we show each other respect. That's my number-one rule. And a large part of that is avoiding the use of inflammatory language. Another part is to address each other with courtesy. So as long as you are in my program, you are Mr. Close, who is just as valuable a member of Seattle society as Bill Gates."

"Who, technically," the third kid said, "is a member of Medina society—not Seattle's."

"Yes, who is technically a member of the snooty eastside," Poppy agreed with an easy grin, turning to the last of her trio, a tall boy with subtly expensive clothing and razor-cut brown hair. "But we like to claim him as our own when it suits our purposes to do so. And you, by process of elimination, must be Mr. Gardo."

"Most people call me Danny G."

"As I explained to Mr. Close, we're a little more formal than most people."

"What program?" Henry demanded.

Poppy raised her eyebrows at him in inquiry.

"You said as long as we're in your program. I thought this painting over the tagging gig was just for today."

"Then you weren't paying attention when I called to let you know that while you will not be going to jail for defacing the shopping district, you are mine after school and on weekends until I say otherwise."

"That sucks!"

"Funny, that's pretty much what the merchants said when they saw what the three of you had done to their buildings."

"Three of us, my booty," Cory muttered.

Poppy looked at the young girl, only to find her exchanging some heavy eye contact with Henry. "Do you have something you'd like to contribute to the conversation, Ms. Capelli?"

The girl hesitated a moment, then tore her gaze away from Henry's, glanced at Danny and shrugged shoulders burdened with a beat-up, much-too-large leather jacket worn over a black hoodie. "No, ma'am."

"Then let's discuss you for a minute."

The teen started. "Nuthin' to discuss," she mumbled.

"Now, there we'll have to disagree." Poppy smiled at Cory's unique attire. She wore a flowery black-and-tan dress over capri-length black leggings and she'd paired them with Doc Martens. Sort of Garden Party Barbie meets Urban Warrior. "Can I safely assume you dress as a boy when you go out at night for safety reasons?" she inquired gently.

Cory gave a jerky nod and Poppy allowed the girl to break eye contact.

She turned back to the two boys. "Then I suggest we all keep Ms. Capelli's identity under our hats so she may continue to be safe. Is that agreeable with you, Mr. Gardo? Mr. Close?"

"Yeah, sure," Danny said.

Henry opened his mouth to no doubt say something smart-ass, but snapped it shut again at the half defiant, half pleading look Cory shot him. "Whatever." Then, as if to make up for what he clearly interpreted as a momentary weakness, he gave Poppy a slow up-and-down. "You're hot."

"Yes, I know. It's my burden to bear. So shall we get started?" She nodded at the assortment of painting supplies on the sidewalk to her right and held out her hand, palm up. "You each owe me thirty-seven fifty."

Danny dug through his wallet and forked over the required amount, but both Cory and Henry looked stricken, although they struggled to hide the fact. Cory said sulkily, "I've only got ten-fifty."

"And I only got twenty," Henry admitted.

"Then we'll put you on the payment plan," she said easily and accepted the money they did have, making a note of it in her little notebook. "You'll contribute each time we meet until your debt is paid off. If you don't have a way to make money on your own, a couple of the merchants whose buildings you defaced agreed to give you some chores, which they'll pay you minimum wage to perform."

"Pretty damn generous of them if you ask me," Jase muttered.

She turned to face him. "The no-cursing rule extends to you and me, Detective de Sanges," she said levelly. "I will thank you to show us the same respect we're requiring of Misters Gardo and Close and Ms. Capelli."

"Yeah, Detective," Henry said. "Show us some damn respect."

De Sanges's dark brows inched toward each other for a moment, and he leveled a look on Henry until the kid shifted on his huge, laces-dangling sneakers. But he merely said to Poppy, "Yes, ma'am," and looked beyond her to the kids once more. "My apologies," he said flatly.

When it became clear none of the teens was going to reply, she turned her attention back to the two with balances left on their accounts. "Do you both understand my conditions?"

Cory gave a clipped nod.

Henry said, "Yeah, big deal. I'll wait until the old man climbs back in his bottle and see what the wallet yields."

Her heart felt bruised at the picture that comment revealed, but she knew better than to display anything that Henry could construe as pity. "Let's get started then."

Jase stood back and watched as she handed out old lab coats for the kids to use to protect their clothing and got them organized. He eyed the girl in particular as she took off her oversize leather jacket and carefully folded it before setting it out of harm's way. Calloway had the right of it: the kid was a surprise. He hadn't been involved when they'd been busted, but everything he'd heard had been about three boys. Cory was tall for her age and happily not one of those starved-looking girls that so many of today's young females strove to be. But the nape of her neck looked soft-as-a-baby's vulnerable.

My ass. He scowled. He didn't know where the hell that had come from, but he wasn't cutting her any slack just because she was a girl. *Do the crime, you do the time;* that was his motto. Her freaking nape most likely wasn't on display anyway when she was in the dark, dressed like a boy, roaming the city streets.

But a jittery feeling attacked the pit of his stomach on the heels of that visual…and just served to make him tenser still. Pulling his attention away from the girl, he focused it on the author of this charade.

And felt an edginess of a different sort. He shoved it aside, but ruminated over the fact that she was a bit of a revelation herself. He wasn't sure what he'd expected to see in her interaction with these kids, but something a little more Lady Bountiful, he supposed.

But she was good with them. Calm but strict, which surprised him. He'd assumed she'd want to be their friend too much to be anything but ineffectual. But she hadn't let a damn thing slide, whether it was about the money they owed or that respecting-each-other rule… which he had to admit was first-rate. She managed to do it, too, in a way that didn't put their backs up, and God knew that was a talent not to be sneezed at.

And that little shit Henry was right about one thing: she was hot. Amazingly so, considering she didn't try real hard. As far as he could tell she wasn't wearing a lick of makeup except for maybe some mascara and a lip balm he'd seen her smear over naturally pink lips with a pronounced bow that pulled his gaze like magnets did metal. She had all that blond hair pulled away from her face in a high ponytail, three skinny black headbands keeping the unruly curls from escaping, the first just back from her hairline, the second an inch or so behind that and the third an equal distance behind the second.

She wore well-worn jeans, a slim red fleece top and a puffy navy down vest, over which she was currently pulling on a voluminous black smock that was paint-splotched with a good dozen colors. All those layers should have made her look like the Kraft Jet-Puffed Girl, and for about one minute it did. But then she bent down to pry the lid off a can of paint and the smock rode up and her jeans stretched tight over a world-class butt.

"Dude, why you lickin' your chops?"

Jerking his attention away, wondering what had become of his trademark ability to stay on track no matter what distractions were going on around him, he glanced at Henry and said the first thing that popped to mind. "I was thinking about marshmallows and hot, gooey centers."

"I love marshmallows!" Cory looked at him over her shoulder and for a moment her screw-you armor dropped and she was just a wistful-looking little girl in too much makeup. "My daddy used to make us a fire in the fireplace and we'd toast them on a stick over it."

Henry studied him a moment, then shook his head. "You mighta been thinking of hot, gooey centers, dude, but *I'm* thinking it weren't in no marshmallows."

Jesus. Jase was disgusted with himself. *What the hell's happened to your cop face, when you can't even fool a thirteen-year-old?*

Luckily Henry didn't have time to pursue his advantage because Poppy chose that moment to hand him a roller. The boy grimaced in distaste.

Jase shot him an evil smile. "Shut up and paint, kid."

"That's Mr. Close to you, dickhead."

"Remember Ms. Calloway's rules," Cory said. "It's *Detective* Dickhead."

Danny G. laughed.

"That's enough out of all of you," Blondie said and shot him a look that said, *Aren't you supposed to be the grown-up here, Detective Dickhead?* "I want to see a little less dissing and a lot more painting."

She kept the teens on task, making them, over their vociferous protests, apply two coats of paint on the side of the shop. Not until nearly three and a half hours had passed did she step back and survey their work. "Not bad," she said.

"It's better than *not bad*," Danny G. protested. "It's damn—*dang*—good. 'Specially considering only a small portion of it was even tagged in the first place."

"Yes, I haven't heard that more than a dozen times from each of you today," she said mildly. "But that's what happens, Mr. Gardo, when you break the law— you lose a lot of the rights you've always taken for granted. Sort of like the merchants around here did when they discovered you'd vandalized the businesses they've poured their hearts, souls and bank accounts into."

Leaning down, she scooped up a bucket. "All of you put your rollers in this and take it around to the back door. Mr. Harvey agreed to let you clean them in the stationary tub in the back of his shop. I expect you to do that quickly and quietly. And there will be an inspection." She looked each teen in the eye with a steely glint in her own. "I'm hungry and feeling kind of cranky. You don't want to make me have you do it twice."

After they finished cleaning the brushes to her satisfaction, she had them hammer the lids back on the paint cans, pack everything else in the milk crates she'd provided and cart them to her car. Then she cut them loose with instructions to be back the next day at 8:00 a.m. All three kids began to protest, but she merely gave them another of those I'm-the-Woman-of-Steel-and-not-even-Kryptonite-can-weaken-me looks and they shut up and trudged away, grumbling under their breath.

The instant they disappeared from sight, she grinned and pumped a fist in the air. "Yessss!" She undulated over to him, hips swinging, arms swaying overhead and head bopping. "Am I good, or what?" she crowed, dancing in place as she beamed up at him. "Those three were a tougher room than I'm used to playing, but I think they're gonna come along just fine. And kudos to you, too, Detective D. You weren't nearly the pain in the ass I thought you'd be with them."

He raised his eyebrows at her and took an involuntary step closer. "What happened to the inflammatory language lecture?"

"Pfffft. It's just you and me now, bud—and I don't need to be a good influence on you."

Then neither did he, and he moved closer yet until he could see the specks of topaz in her dark brown irises. The color reminded him of the stones he'd tried to steal when he'd thought he might as well go into the family business alongside his brother, dad and Pops— the ones that had brought him to Murphy's attention. "I wouldn't get too full of myself just yet if I were you," he advised dryly. "It went okay today, but this is still a lousy idea. There are a thousand things that can go wrong and trust me, Blondie, they will. Probably the minute the newness wears off the so-called program for your minithugs."

"Ah, but that's where you're wrong, de Sanges." She looked up at him, all passionate eyes and glowing cheeks. "There's nothing 'so-called' about it—my programs have been forged in fire. And the longer I have these kids, the better. Or so my previous two groups and the current program I've got running in the CD have led me to believe. In my experience most teens just want someone to show a little interest in them and give them something to do that ideally engages their attention in a fun way. I admit that for this particular group, part one of my agenda isn't what most teens consider fun. But if art is their thing, and they stick with me for the work segment, part two will be. And that's when I get 'em firmly on the hook and start reeling them in."

Looking at the wild, soft curls erupting from the rubber band at her crown, he had a sudden urge to wrap them around his hands and do some reeling in of his own. He took a sharp step back, rubbing his itchy palms against his thighs. *Christ, de Sanges,* he thought in disgust. *You aren't Dad or Joe out on parole and on the hunt for the nearest willing babe.*

Those fucking family genes were going to be the death of him yet.

He shook the thought aside to tune back in on Poppy's conversation.

"We have to assume that tagging is these kids' equivalent of a creative outlet," she said. "I can supply them that in a way more socially acceptable *and* demonstrate a genuine interest in them as well. I like teenagers." The corner of her mouth quirked up. "Which I'm sure you'd say is because I still have the mentality of one."

Jase wasn't sure what the hell he would say. He looked at the conviction on her face and felt all his preconceived notions about her shift.

He tried to ignore it, because he didn't like being wrong. Hell, if you followed the rules, you usually weren't—and he'd been doing that since he was fourteen years old and Murph had caught him with his bad-seed fingers all over those topazes. But Poppy had acted a lot like Murphy with those kids today and she was telling him stuff now that made him question what he thought he knew about her. Then there was the memory of that not-exactly-high-rent-and-definitely-security-free building she lived in. Abruptly he demanded, "Who are you?"

"Well, not the rich girl you've got me pegged for, that's for sure."

He'd been so certain…but every piece of evidence except one said he'd been dead wrong.

Shit.

Still. He rubbed the back of his neck. "That mansion…"

She blew out a gusty, put-upon sigh, but said levelly, "Ava and Jane and I met Agnes Wolcott when we were twelve. She was a fascinating lady and we started hanging out with her when she attended the soirees Ava's parents threw. Then one day she invited us to the Wolcott mansion for high tea."

"What's that, something you drink on a ladder?"

"Very droll, Detective de Sanges. Ridiculous, but droll. Actually, it's laced with LSD."

His mouth dropped open.

"That woman had been all over the world and she knew where *alllll* the best drugs were." Then she gave him a jab. "And here I thought cops were supposed to be so impervious to lies and prevarications." She gave him a look similar to the ones she'd bent on the kids. "Do you actually want to hear this or just waste my time with your smart-ass remarks?"

Fascinated by her against all good sense, he gave her a by-all-means-proceed sweep of his hand.

"All right, then. At that first tea, she gave us our first diaries and talked to us like we were interesting people, not a bunch of kids too stupid to understand words of more than two syllables. And our friendship with her simply grew from there. She had no family of her own, so she left us her estate when she died."

She aimed a stern look on him. "But you've seen the mansion. It needs work and we're having it fixed up, which takes both time and a lot of money. Most of the latter is coming from the collections she also left us, but Jane is still working on getting the last of those cataloged and until we finish the renovations, actually sell the place and reconcile the debit column with the credit side, we aren't exactly rolling in dough. And even then—well, while it will certainly be more money than I've ever seen in my life, it's not exactly going to be untold wealth."

He narrowed his eyes at her, half-suspicious she was messing with him. "I've read a little about Miss Wolcott. She was quite the grande dame by all accounts. So how would girls with no money be in any position to meet her?"

"We all attended Country Day school, me on my grandmother's dime and Janie on a scholarship. Ava genuinely *is* wealthy, and the three of us were introduced to Miss A. at one of those functions at Av's parents' house I mentioned."

"Okay," he said slowly. "So what you're telling me here is that you're just the girl next door?"

"More or less." She smiled wryly. "If that next door happens to be a commune."

"You lived in a *commune?*" Jesus. This just kept getting stranger and stranger. But looking at her with her easy confidence and that I-can-make-a-difference-in-the-world attitude, he could sort of picture it.

"Until I was five. Then my great-grandpa Larsen died and left my folks a modest inheritance that included a little house in Ballard."

He narrowed his eyes at her. "So in other words, you don't really have those contacts you've been threatening me with."

"You think not?" She gave him a smoky look from beneath her lashes. "I hate to burst your bubble, Detective, but that school I told you I attended? It's quite prestigious and I rubbed elbows and had adjoining lockers with the kids of all *kinds* of Washington power brokers. Made contacts like you wouldn't believe."

He shoved his hands in his slacks pockets. "Crap."

"I know." She gave him a commiserating nod. "Life's a bitch, isn't it?" Then she leveled those cool gold-speckled chocolate-brown eyes on him. "But more for some than others, I'm afraid. And, Detective, you're still stuck playing by my rules."

CHAPTER SEVEN

Man, I so don't like feeling this way—all shook-up and shaky. But I have a feeling I'm not going to be able to blow this off as easily as I usually do.

SHE HAD BEEN feeling pretty darn invincible, but Poppy wasn't quite so insouciant when de Sanges took a hot step forward to loom over her, a storm brewing in his eyes. He had the benefit of height on his side and he used it to full advantage. Standing this close, she had to crane her head back just to look into his face.

He blocked out the mellow early spring light, all wide shoulders, dark-as-the-universe pissed-off eyes and five o'clock shadow, the latter of which suddenly struck her as probably a pretty much round-the-clock condition with him, rather than time-specific.

He was so overwhelmingly male, it was all she could do not to flinch back.

"I warned you not to mess with me," he said with a lack of heat that was belied by those narrowed eyes.

"And just how am I doing that?" she demanded, thanking the gods for the irritation that laced her voice.

It beat hell out of having it crack middeclaration like some intimidated schoolgirl, and in truth she hadn't been all that certain it wouldn't until she'd opened her mouth. "I stated a fact, Jack. You implied that because I don't hail from a wealthy family I'm without resources, and I gave you the reasons why that's not true. God, you're a buzz-kill. I was feeling so good until you had to go and wreck it." She slapped hands to his chest and pushed. "Get out of my way."

He didn't budge and she really, really wished she hadn't touched him, but she was committed now. She wasn't about to give him the satisfaction of whipping her hands back like he was some too-hot-to-handle stud and she a big-eyed, inexperienced kid too rattled to be in his presence.

Like he was the Sheik and she was the Virgin. Uh-uh, no, ma'am. That was *so* two decades ago.

It didn't help, though, that his chest was suddenly the only thing she could think about. It was warm and solid beneath his white dress shirt and narrow suspenders. Beneath her abruptly tingling palms.

To keep her thoughts off the way it made her feel, she deliberately concentrated on his retro-hip clothing. He was a sharp dresser, which was just one more thing pushing her buttons at the moment. "And another thing," she snapped, standing on her toes to get in his face, "wear painting-appropriate clothes, for God's sake! You're gonna wreck your cool threads."

She abruptly became aware of the stillness in the body beneath her hands.

But he merely said coolly, "Not if I don't paint."

So she figured it had nothing to do with her touch. "You don't know much about kids, do you? They see you standing around in your sharp clothes, they're going to end up accidentally-on-purpose flinging a little paint your way. Especially since you watch them like a hawk."

He hitched his shoulders, renewing her awareness of the play of muscles beneath her hands. "That's my job," he said.

"Is it your job to act like Boss Godfrey while you're about it?" she demanded in exasperation, giving him an even harder shove to back him up.

To no avail once again. He merely gazed down at her with his usual lack of expression. "Who's Boss Godfrey?"

"You know, in *Cool Hand Luke?*" she said, fully expecting to see a what-the-hell-are-you-talking-about expression on his face.

But he surprised her when he said, "Hey, I liked that movie." And darned if he didn't almost display pleasure for a moment. "Which one was he?" Clearly running the cast of characters through his mind, he furrowed his brow but almost immediately it cleared. "The road crew boss, right? The sharpshooter?"

"All you're missing," she said dryly, "is the rifle and a pair of mirror shades."

The slightest of smiles curved his lips and his long fingers came up to shackle her wrists. "Maybe I oughtta bring that up tomorrow—that the minithugs should refer to me from now on as Boss de Sanges." He shot her a full-fledged grin. "It's got a certain ring to it."

She sagged in his grip, her knees going weak at the flash of white teeth, the crinkling at the corners of his dark eyes. She hadn't thought the man was capable of *smiling,* never mind possessing an honest-to-goodness sense of humor that came complete with a killer grin.

The latter faded as he stared down at her and his fingers tightened around her wrists. Whispering a blasphemy beneath his breath, he slowly pulled her hands up around his neck, a movement that caused her inner arms to slide up his chest and their bodies to brush. Lowering his head, he kissed her.

And Poppy's thinking processes short-circuited. Feeling his mouth simultaneously firm and soft against her lips, her head reeling with his scent, a frisson of undiluted lust rushed to her brain, filling it with heat that immediately suffused her entire body. She rose onto her toes to get closer, *closer* to the source, tightening her arms around his neck until she darn near had him in a choke hold, reveling in the press of that long, hard body the entire length of her own. Her lips parted beneath his, her tongue slicked over the silky inner membrane of his lower lip.

Then he was gone, his hands unwinding her arms as he stepped back, dropping them as if they'd smeared his palms with slug slime. Gone, gone, gone—his lips, his scent, his body—if not that far in actual feet and inches, still an immeasurable gulf in emotional distance, judging by the remote look in his eyes.

Red tinged his high cheekbones, but his face was otherwise expressionless. "My apologies, Ms. Calloway," he said coolly.

She jerked her head back. What, kissing her was some big *mistake?* Well, it was, of course, but there wasn't a woman alive who wanted to be told she was a mistake. Nor was she overjoyed to learn that what had completely rocked her boat hadn't affected him at all.

She'd walk naked down Pike Street in a rainstorm before she'd let him know, however, so she merely nodded. But screw his apology. If he wasn't affected, *she* wasn't affected. She didn't know what that brain-function meltdown had been all about, but she would've pulled back if Detective Hot Lips hadn't beat her to the punch.

She was almost completely, utterly, one-hundred-percent certain about that. "Not a problem," she said with a carelessness she didn't quite feel, forcing a wry tilt of her lips. "As kisses go, that one was hardly worth apologizing over."

If you discount the nuclear effect. But steel entered her spine at the covert thought. Because she did. She discounted it with every atom of her being.

She got the satisfaction of seeing his eyes narrow, which for the king of the BOTOX expression she interpreted as wild displeasure. Good. Let him be unhappy. She wasn't feeling all that peppy herself.

Stepping around him, she gathered up her personal odds and ends and stuffed them in her tote as she said over her shoulder with studied casualness, "See you tomorrow." *Seeing as how I can't legitimately avoid it.*

Not that she would if she could. Hey, she could be every bit as professional as Robocop.

Really.

He didn't reply and she turned her attention back to her packing, but she could *feel* him still standing there. Then he said brusquely, "Yeah. Tomorrow." And walked away.

The instant he disappeared from sight Poppy stopped all her busywork and released a sharp exhalation. Glancing around, she was relieved to see that none of the merchants she worked for had witnessed her moment of idiocy—a possible consequence she would have been a lot wiser to consider earlier. "Stupid, stupid, stupid!" she spat, thunking the side of her fist against her forehead with each repetition. Then she rose to her feet, brushed off her clothing and headed for the car.

As soon as she'd climbed in and closed the door, she hauled her cell phone from her tote and hit speed dial.

"Hey," she said as soon as her ring was answered. "I could really use a little Sisterhood solidarity about now."

THEY ENDED UP meeting at the mansion. Jane was already in the parlor when Poppy arrived and just seeing her friend back by the fireplace, her dark hair shining under the lights as she focused on a table full of antique vases, melted some of the tension she'd been holding in her shoulders.

"Hey," she said softly as she wove through the remaining collections that still crowded the room. "I'm glad you suggested meeting here. I've been so busy lately I haven't been able to stop by."

"Tell me about it, stranger." Jane smiled at her. "I haven't seen you in, like, forever."

"I know. It's been a good week or two since we've

had any decent girl-time." Out of all the vases on the table, a tall green one grabbed her attention. She picked it up, turning it in her hands to admire the beautiful long-trunked rose tree etched and enameled on it. Something—its beauty, its lines—spoke to her. "This is gorgeous. I don't remember seeing it before."

"It's a Lamartine."

"It really is lovely. Don't you think it would look great on my sideboard?"

Jane studied it a moment and nodded. "It would—it'd look perfect there."

"Maybe I can buy it from my share of the estate. What would something like this cost?"

"Somewhere in the neighborhood of twenty-five hundred to three thousand dollars."

Poppy bobbled it, her heart pounding as she caught the vase against her stomach before it could hit the floor. Returning it to the table, she carefully placed it well back from the edge.

"Ho-ly Mary, mother of—" Blowing out a breath, she turned to discover her friend grinning at her. She pressed both hands over her still madly tripping heart. "Janie, you gotta tell me to step away from stuff that valuable. Don't let me pick it up, for God's sake—I damn near dropped the thing!"

Ava breezed into the room, a small white baker's box in her hands. "Hello, my sister hoods," she said, shedding jacket, flowing scarf and her Kate Spade handbag onto the settee. "I come bearing gifts." She opened the lid on the box to show them a golden-crusted wheel with a cranberry chutney nestled in the center of its top. "A brie was left over from a new client's party last night."

"Wow, you've got honest employees," Poppy said, pinching a small hunk of what looked like pineapple off the golden top. "I would've eaten it so fast you'd never even have known there was a leftover."

Ava grinned. "Somehow my assistant double-booked me so I couldn't be there myself, and the party was just large enough that I had to hire extra waitstaff instead of making do with my usual extras. I'm pretty sure the newbies were all set to dive into it themselves until I spoiled the fun by dropping by to check on how the party had gone."

"Where was this one?" Jane asked, then grinned. "Not that I really care. The important thing is you've got food and I'm starving. Let's take it to the dining room. The guys hooked up the appliances in there while they're working on the kitchen, and there's some pop and sparkling water in the fridge."

"Is there anything stronger?" Poppy demanded. "It's been a day—I could stand a glass of wine."

"I'll check."

Poppy hooked an arm through Ava's as they trooped down the hall. "I'm not as hungry as Janie, so I'd be interested in hearing where the new client's party was."

"In a fabulous house near Volunteer Park."

"And you were just passing by that neighborhood at what I'm assuming was a fairly late hour *why?*"

"It was the first function I put on for them and I'd told

the client I'd check in when it was over to make sure she was satisfied with how smoothly it had been handled. Besides I was on my way home from the other event. One where I was an actual guest instead of the concierge making it happen."

Jane shot Ava a glance over her shoulder. "You attended a party in a strictly social capacity? That's kinda unusual for you these days."

Ava shrugged a cashmere-clad shoulder. "They're never strictly social anymore—and it was at one of my biggest clients' house, which is why I felt compelled to go. Plus, I network whether I want to or not, since someone invariably brings up what I do. People in the set I grew up in are fascinated by my profession for some reason. A few, like my parents, find it embarrassing that I work in a service industry, while others seem to think it's pretty cool." She flashed her dimpled shark's smile. "But all of them like the idea of 'one of their own' handling their affairs...which is what keeps my business building.

"But enough about me." Ava handed off the pastry box to Jane as they entered the dining room and headed straight for the sideboard. Squatting, she stuck her head in its cupboard and emerged a moment later with a bottle of wine in her hands. Rising to her feet, she displayed it to Poppy like a four-star sommelier, then ruined the impression by wagging her eyebrows. "Eh? *Eh?*"

"Oh, bless you, my child!"

Jane lifted the wheel of brie from the box. "What do I do with this? Throw it in the micro?"

"Good God, no!" Ava regarded her with horror. "Put

it in the oven at three-fifty for about seven minutes. It's already been baked, so we're just reheating it."

"So I ask again—why not simply microwave it? It's faster and we don't really have an *oven* oven—just the toaster variety while the kitchen's out of commission."

"How did I come to be bosom buds with such a philistine? You've obviously been hanging out with construction guys too long. Microwaving turns the pastry to rubber."

"Well, eee-ow," Jane said in a bad Cockney accent, tipping her nose ceilingward with a fingertip. "I ain't a foine lydee such as yerself, Duchess." But she cranked on the toaster oven, placed the wheel on its little pan and slid it in.

Poppy smiled as she extracted the cork from the wine bottle and poured a glass each for herself and Ava. Having grown up in a household with chronic drinkers, Janie rarely touched alcohol, so Poppy fetched her a diet cola from the fridge, poured it in a glass and added ice. She transported everything to the long dining-room table. This was exactly what the doctor'd ordered—a dose of friendship, the Rx of champions.

As if reading her mind, Jane leaned against the sideboard and looked at her. "So what's up? On the phone you sounded a tad desperate. Your new kiddies giving you grief?"

"More than I expected, which is my own fault for not giving the dynamics of this group more thought. I didn't take into consideration that the kids in my other groups are in my program because they want to be. This is a first, having teens who *have* to be there. So, it is a little different. But sooner or later I'll win them over. I don't mind doing the tough-love thing until I do."

"So if it's not your new group," Ava said, propping her chin in her palm and her elbow on the gleaming tabletop, fixing Poppy with her undivided attention, "then wha— Oh. Detective Shei— Uh, Bastard Rat." Her eyes went cool and narrow. "Is he giving you a hard time?"

"Not precisely." She hesitated, not sure if she really wanted to get into this. But the wine she'd sipped had dissipated the defenses she'd slapped in place in an attempt to convince herself Jason's kiss had left her unaffected. Plus these were her two closest friends in the world and if she couldn't talk to them, she was in more trouble than she already feared. "Would you consider me a pretty confident woman when it comes to men?"

"Absolutely," Janie said.

"Hell, yeah," Ava agreed.

"I always thought I was, too," she said glumly. "But with de Sanges…" Making a face, she gave an impatient wave of her hand. "Don't get me wrong, I can hold my own with the man. But he drives me crazy. He doesn't interact with the kids at all unless it's to say something intimidating."

"Uh-oh. That's iron-clad guaranteed to put him on your bad side," Jane said.

"Damn tootin'." And if part of her insisted on drifting to the fact that he'd got it when she'd accused him of being like Boss Godfrey with the kids, she firmly brought it back on track. Because, please. Big deal.

"I've never *met* anyone so rigid and serious. I doubt he has the first clue how to have fun." Okay, so he'd displayed a hint of a sense of humor. Clearly it was an aberration and she hardly felt compelled to throw *that* into the mix. It would only confuse her friends the way it had her.

"I only met him that one time," Ava agreed, "but I remember that he never once smiled."

Oh, but when he does unbend he's got a seriously killer smile.

"That's the thing, though," Poppy said, disgusted with her thoughts. "I find myself suddenly making all kinds of excuses for him. All because I lost it when he kissed me." Boy, had she lost it!

"He *kissed* you?" both friends exclaimed in unison.

They leaned forward, all alert eyes and bristling curiosity, but Ava beat Jane to the punch when she demanded, "And you didn't lead off with that the minute the three of us were in one room? Why the hell did you let me go on and on about the stupid brie?"

"Hey, it wasn't as if it was *much* of a kiss," she said defensively. "The thing was so brief I'm not even sure it qualifies."

"If you lost it, then I'm guessing it qualified," Jane said.

Ava nodded. "Yes, tell us about that. I need a definition, because my idea of 'lost it' and yours could be two different things. Or I can just go out on a limb here and speculate it means he made you feel—"

"Like he was lightning and I was the tallest tree on the prairie? Oh, yeah."

Both her friends grinned and Ava wiggled in her chair.

"Ooh. Tell us more and don't stint on the details. It's been a long dry spell for me, so I have to live vicariously."

"It's embarrassing."

"Even better," Jane said, giving her a lopsided smile. "You're the girl who always skated when it came to those embarrassing man/woman situations that knock the rest of us on our butts. You were due."

"Oh, *nice*, Janie. I may have been dumped less often than some—but the pain when I am is still my pain. You're dreaming if you think anyone skates entirely when it comes to this kind of crap."

"Oh, kiddo, I know." Jane reached across the table to rub the back of her hand. "That didn't come out right. I didn't mean you've never been hurt, just that you never seem to be *embarrassed* by anything. You're usually so at ease with men and I used to be so awkward that I just had one of those mean it-was-bound-to-catch-up-with-you-sooner-or-later moments."

"Bitch," she said without heat, then added morosely, "I would've voted for later. But I have a feeling hanging around de Sanges for any length of time—which I can hardly avoid, given the terms of the kids' deal with the city and the merchants—is going to end up being one big kick in the head for me."

"By your own account, Poppy, it was merely a brief kiss," Ava pointed out gently.

"Yeah, but that's the thing, Av. It was so short it obviously meant nothing to him. Yet to me there was nothing *merely* about it. He barely grazed my lips and I was all over him like hot fudge on ice cream. I went from a reasonably intelligent woman to a crazed sex machine in one-point-two seconds. I've never experienced anything quite like it."

"Yowsa. And this is bad *why?*"

"Because he shoved me back like I was pumping nuclear waste all over his jazzy shoes and said—" she deepened her voice in an attempt to approximate his "'—My apologies, Ms. Calloway.'"

All amusement fled her friends' faces. Ava gaped at her. "He told you kissing you was a *mistake?*"

She nodded. See, *they* got it—it wasn't for nothing they were her BFFs.

Ava glowered. "Why, that low-down, dirty, rotten—"

"*Pig,*" Jane spat.

And suddenly Poppy felt a measure of her usual confidence return. Yes, she was still mortified and less than thrilled at the prospect of facing Studly Do-Right again. But she had the most loyal friends in the world. And that went a long way toward removing the sting from even the worst bites that life had to offer.

"Why the hell did the jerk kiss you in the first place?" Jane demanded.

Arrested, Poppy stared at her. "That's a very good question," she said slowly. And for the first time since Jason had pushed her away she thought about *his* actions: his hands guiding hers up to encircle his strong neck, the look in his dark eyes when he'd lowered his mouth to hers. Reflectively, she said, "He didn't seem to like it when I told him it was hardly worth apologizing over."

Ava and Jane snorted their amusement, but Poppy

waved it aside. "So why *did* he kiss me?" she mused softly, reaching for the wine bottle to tip another splash into her and Ava's glasses. "That brie ready yet? I think we're going to need something to soak up this second glass."

Then she leveled a look at her friends and came back to the important issue. "You know what? I just might have to ask *him* about that. Don'tcha think?"

Ava and Jane exchanged glances. Then they turned identical smiles on her.

And gave her the thumbs-up.

CHAPTER EIGHT

Man. I wouldn't be a fourteen-year-old girl again for all the world. Cory just broke my heart.

EMOTIONS BOILING, Jase headed straight to the squad room, where he started making calls on a few open cases.

Why the hell *did you kiss her?* The question kept popping up in the back of his mind whenever he was put on hold and later as he studied the surveillance videos from the series of jewelry-store robberies. Of all the stupid, lamebrain impulses! After spending half his frigging life trying to avoid the base urges fueled by de Sanges genes, he'd gone and crowded a civilian he was supposed to be working with and laid a *kiss* on her?

Terrific. Maybe he should send a postcard to the joint to let the old man know that the family talent for bad behavior was trumping his years of toeing the line.

Except he refused to believe that. He refused to be a victim of heredity. He had a choice, dammit.

So why had he kissed Poppy? Yes, as Henry had pointed out, she was hot. But he'd been tempted by hot women in the past—temptation that he'd turned away from without a qualm if the timing wasn't right or the situation was inappropriate. So what was so compelling about the Babe?

David Hohn dropped into a chair in the room where Jase was viewing the tapes. "Anything new pop?"

"No." Grateful to have his attention directed somewhere, *any*where, else, he shoved upright in his chair. "It's the same damn thing on every tape—just one guy, medium height, weight-lifter's build, wearing a dark jacket, dark slacks and a dark ninja-style hood. He keeps his head down and shoots Silly String at the camera to disable it. But the timing doesn't make sense on several of these stores. There shouldn't be enough time between the alarm going off and patrol arriving for just one person to clean everything out."

"We'll figure it out. Sooner or later we're gonna grab hold of that one piece of string that unravels the whole ball." David grinned at him. "Meanwhile, you missed the idiot-of-the-day show."

"Yeah?" He was more than happy to let the problem slide for now. "Let's hear it."

"Patrol out of south precinct sees this mope acting suspicious on the street and pulls over to talk to him. Guy's wearing a do-rag that one of the officers thought looked surprisingly smart and when she looks closer, she sees it says Versace by one of the knots. So she calls Robbery to see if we've got a blue zodiac-printed silk Versace scarf in the database and, sure enough, it kicks out from that burglary over on Sunset in West Seattle.

"She hauls him in and when they get here he struts into the room like he's got good sense, complaining to

all and sundry that Officer Manelli's doin' him wrong."
Hohn's grin grew wider. "I explained that calling the ar-
resting officer a bitch and a ho is probably not the best
way to clear his path through the system—then asked
if he understood he was under arrest for possession of
stolen goods.

"'Nah, dude,' he says, 'I *bought* this!'

"'Yeah?' I ask. 'Where'd you get it?'

"And he says—get this—'Target, man!'"

Hohn shook his head. "You gotta love how dumb
they can be. Officer Manelli tells me she went online
and discovered the scarf, which is about the size of your
average bandanna, retails for about two-seventy-five.
And you can't even buy the damn thing at Nordstrom,
let alone Tarjay." He reached for a folder on his desk,
still grinning. "I *love* this job."

Jase did, too, most of the time. But he was more than
ready to go home by the time he pushed back from his
desk a few hours later.

He stopped for a sub on the way home and decided, as
he pulled his car into a slot alongside his apartment
building a short while later, that things were a lot less grim
on a full stomach. It didn't stop him from jumping straight
into cop mode, however, when a man stepped out of the
shadows as he was climbing from his Honda CR-V. Adrenaline spiking, he crouched to make himself a smaller target
behind the open car door and reached for his gun.

"Hey, Jase, it's me," the man said softly, hands wide
of his body as he stepped under a nearby light, making
himself more visible.

Jason's hand slid away from his service revolver. "Holy shit, Joe," he said to his older brother. "That's an excellent way to get yourself shot. What the hell are you doing lurking in the laurels?"

"Waitin' for you to get home, man. I didn't wanna run into fucking Murphy." A touch of bitterness entered his voice. "Did he even bother to tell you I called before?"

"Yeah, he did. And I called the number you left with him, but I got some woman who said you were out." There was always a woman. Used to be the minute Joe or Dad or Pops were sprung, they'd come liberate him from his current foster home, then hook up with the first available warm, willing squeeze they stumbled across.

"Damn that Sherry." Joe scrubbed his hand across his face and Jase noticed a new jailhouse tattoo, a crudely inked black spider above the knuckle of his right forefinger. "Guess I shoulda known she'd forget half my messages. I didn't exactly pick her for her brains."

"Come on up," Jase said as he headed for the entrance. "You working?"

"Why? You wanna offer me the janitor position at the cop shop?"

Holding the entrance door, Jase gazed down at his brother as Joe muscled past. His big brother was shorter and stockier than he and looked a lot like their dad. Jase took more after Pops. "I was just making conversation, Joey. I haven't seen you in—what?—eight years? We gotta start somewhere."

Joe jammed his hands in his jacket pockets and shifted his beefy shoulders. "Yeah, okay, sorry. I got me a job at a garage in Lake City. You might not remember this, since I been in and out of the pen since you was fairly little, but I'm a pretty decent mechanic."

"I remember. One of the times you were out, you let me hang out while you worked on a car. You showed me how to hot-wire it."

"Yeah, well, I didn't know then you'd be working the other side of the fence someday."

"At the time I was leaning more toward joining the family tradition, so I thought it was a primo lesson."

Bypassing the elevators, he opened the door to the stairwell and they climbed in silence. But once they reached his apartment and he'd let them in, his brother said, "I'm sure you know that none of us, not me or Dad or Pops, was real thrilled with your friendship with Detective Dickwad."

"No shit? I never would have guessed that, the three of you being so diplomatic when it comes to expressing your opinions."

Joe grinned and for the first time looked completely relaxed with him. "That prob'ly explains why I got two aggravateds on my sheet—I forget to use my diplomatic skills." Then he sobered. "I'm gonna tell you something I never thought I'd say about that sumbitch, though. I'm glad he nipped your crime career in the bud."

Jase turned from where he was assembling a pot of coffee to look at his brother. Under the kitchen cam lights, Joe looked older than he had in the more forgiving shadows outside. His dark hair was shaved almost into nonexistence but Jase could see glints of gray stubble among the dark. The jaw was the same: it gleamed with a fresh shave, but still sported the ubiquitous five-o'clock shadow that de Sanges males had inherited along with all the other fun shit accompanying puberty. The rest of his face, however, appeared pasty, his eyes had dark bags under them and he looked tired. "You're glad?"

"Yeah." He rubbed his hand over his head and Jase noted a small separation in the underarm seam of his flannel shirt. "Look at you," his brother said. "You look like one a' them *GQ* models. Much as I hate that bastard's more to you than us, I gotta admit your nice clothes, this decent apartment—that's because a' him. Him takin' you under his wing when you was still young enough to influence—well, you got a chance at a real life on account of it."

It was true. He'd been well on his way to embracing his family's unsavory traditions when Murphy caught him with those topazes. By rights, the old cop could have, should have, busted his ass. But he'd cut him a break. Then, instead of doing his good deed for the day and disappearing, Murph had started dropping by Jase's various foster homes. Sometimes it was just to jaw for a while. Other times he took him out for a burger or to walk the beaches at Alki or Golden Gardens. Occasionally he sprang for tickets in the nosebleed section of the old Kingdome to catch a Mariners game.

Jase hadn't been accustomed to having a positive male influence and Murphy's continued attention had made him think about where he wanted to be in five, ten, twenty years. When the vision that popped most frequently to mind featured something more along the lines of Murphy's life than that of his blood relatives, he'd set his sights on becoming a cop.

"Those two aggravateds I mentioned?" Joe said, interrupting his stroll down memory lane. "Both were the parole breakers that sent me back to jail and I'm just a bar fight away from my three strikes. I been lucky so far—if you can call it that—to get arrested for different things and avoid the three-strikes law. But it's prob'ly only a matter of time."

Jase handed him a mug of coffee and set the sugar canister on the tiny table. Sitting down with his own black coffee, he looked across at his brother, watching as Joe shoveled three heaping spoons into his cup. "You ever consider signing up for an anger management program?"

"Took one a' them in the joint. But I'm afraid in a tight situation I'll forget what I learned." He met Jase's gaze across the table. "I'm thirty-nine years old, though, Jason. I'm not as impatient as I was as a kid for that what-ayacall it—instant gratification shit. And God knows, I'm tired of living my en-fuckin'-tire life in the pen." He took a sip of his coffee, then said morosely, "I'm just not sure I've got what it takes to live it on the outside."

"You've got a marketable skill. You're employed. That's a pretty sweet start."

"True." Joe sat straighter. "I make good money and they like me there. Sherry's got a good job, too. She works at the post office. They got good benefits and stuff. And she might not be great about passin' along my messages, but she's sweet. So maybe I oughtta just avoid bars and work on those anger management skills they taught me."

That sounded real hopeful…on paper. Jase had his doubts, however, about this playing out any differently than events in the past. He'd heard too many promises from the men in his family—assurances that this time they were going to turn things around, live clean. But it never happened. So he didn't intend to hold his breath. He wished his brother the best, but had no expectations.

But he nodded all the same. "That sounds like a real good place to start, Joe."

AT A FEW MINUTES before eight o'clock the following morning, Cory handed Ms. Calloway two fives and seven battered dollar bills. The pretty blonde accepted them with a smile, marked the amount against Cory's debt in her notebook and handed her a painting smock.

As she shed her father's leather coat and set it carefully out of reach of even the most ambitious paint splatters, she reflected that it was lucky Nina Petrocova had needed a babysitter last night. Okay, Nina was always looking for a sitter. It was Mom who wasn't wild about Cory sitting for her because their neighbor danced downtown at the Lusty Lady. Cory thought Nina was nice, though. Her little boy, Kai, was really cute, too, and it was kind of nice having something to do and someone else to talk to while Mom worked her second job—if only for a couple of hours until she put the toddler down for the night.

She wanted to please her mother, but sometimes that

just wasn't possible. So far she'd lucked out and hadn't had to 'fess up to the getting-busted-tagging business. She'd told her she was part of a community art project but had conveniently left out the illegal activity that had led up to it. Anything to avoid having to see the disappointment on her mom's face.

But she needed money to pay for her share of the paint and supplies, so she'd agreed to sit for Nina again tonight. It didn't hurt that after she paid off her last ten bucks, she'd have a couple of dollars left over for herself. Then maybe she'd talk to Mom about doing this on a more regular basis. Nina was just trying to get by like everyone else in the neighborhood, and she bet Mom didn't know that their neighbor was taking a couple classes at SCCC during the day so she wouldn't have to take her clothes off for a living for the rest of her life.

"Okay, let's get started," Ms. Calloway said and Cory realized that Danny G., Henry and the cop had arrived and everyone—even Detective de Sanges, who had worn killer clothes yesterday—was suited up in painting gear.

"Today's going to be a little different," Ms. Calloway said. "We're going to work at removing your tagging from bricks. This is a whole different ball game. On the downside, it's tougher than simply painting over something. The good news, though, is that you don't have to do the entire side the way we did on Mr. Harvey's building."

Instructing them all to grab some of the supplies, Poppy—God, that was such a dap name—led the way down the block. As the blonde walked with long-legged strides in front of them, Cory watched the filmy hem of her skirt, which peeked from beneath Ms. C.'s long paint-splotched lab coat, as it floated and flared around her legs.

The woman was seriously gamagorgeous—especially for a do-gooder. At least Cory had never run in to anyone remotely like her during her and Mom's encounters with a string of social workers after Daddy was killed. Most of them had been dowdy dressers who seemed to think makeup was the devil's toolbox.

Cory couldn't help but wonder what Ms. Calloway's story was, why someone so glamourama was riding herd over a posse of captive graffiti artists.

By the time the rest of them caught up to Ms C. in front of a brick fronted store around the corner and up the block, an older woman had joined her. "I want you to meet Mrs. Stories," Ms. Calloway told them as they walked up. "Marlene, you already know Detective de Sanges. This is Mr. Gardo, Mr. Close and Ms. Capelli." She looked at them. "I think it's important that you have a real person to put to the buildings you vandalize. Mrs. Stories pays a bundle every month to lease this place and it's my sincere hope that you'll think about the people left to clean up your messes the next time you're tempted to deface their businesses."

Rolling her eyes, Cory curled her lip to show that no one was gonna guilt her into anything. Dammit, she hadn't even done the crime!

In this neighborhood, anyway.

But she couldn't quite hold Mrs. Stories's gaze when the older woman turned soft brown eyes on her, giving her a level look. "Sorry, ma'am," she heard herself mut-

tering to the pavement in front of her—then was furious
with herself for caving. The only saving grace was that
she wasn't the only one. Danny G. and Henry apolo-
gized, too.

She scowled at Ms. Calloway when the woman
handed her a pair of rubber gloves.

Ms. C. merely smiled. "I'm not sure how harsh the
remover is. You'll probably want to wear those when
you use it."

"You're exposing kids to toxic chemicals?" Henry
demanded. "Putting us in a situation where we can
inhale them into our still-developing lungs?"

"Seems only fair to me," she said mildly, raising an
elegant eyebrow at him. "Better you than Marlene, who
suffers from asthma. And who—forgive me for beating
this to death, but you seem to be missing the basic
premise here—is not the person who decorated her
stylish business with these chicken scratches." Not until
Henry started to squirm did she release his gaze and turn
to include Danny and Cory. "Any more questions? No?
Good. One of you help me grab the buckets and we'll
review the instructions. Then we can get started."

Reacting to the authority in Ms. Calloway's voice,
Cory stepped forward before she thought it through, then
was stuck. Making a face to show the guys she wasn't
one of those teacher's-pet nerds or anything, she crossed
to where Ms. C. stooped next to a couple of plastic containers. She dropped onto her heels next to her.

They each picked up a sealed tub and had just risen
to their feet when the cop snapped, "Look out!"

Simultaneously Danny leaped across the space and shoved them hard. The bucket in Cory's hands went flying and she barely kept her footing.

"Hey!" she snarled at the same time something hit the pavement with a horrendous clamor right where they'd just been standing. She stared without comprehension at a *hugegantic* wrench sporting a wicked gouge in its silvery surface.

"Sonuva—!" A man's head appeared over the edge of Mrs. Stories's roof. "Is everyone okay down there? Sorry, dudes—I accidentally kicked it off the ledge."

Her heart still pounding out a rhythm like a rapper on speed, she watched Ms. C. grab de Sanges's arm when he took a hot step toward the building.

He looked down at her all tenselike, listened as she murmured something, then with a curt nod walked away. Ms. Calloway inhaled and exhaled a couple of times, then straightened her shoulders and shook out her hands. "Thank you, Danny. Cory, are you okay?"

"Yeah. I think. That was spooky."

"No kidding." Ms. C. bent to pick up a white plastic tub that she, too, had dropped. After reading the instructions on its side, she shot Henry a sly smile.

"Hmm. No methylene chloride, MEK or toluene. No fumes or flammable solvents. That kinda kicks the slats out from under your wrecking-your-delicate-lungs theory, doesn't it? It is caustic, though, so wear your gloves. We wouldn't want to incur any damage to your still-developing fingers."

Cory didn't want to find anything about the situation

amusing, but her lips curled up in spite of herself. Ms. C. was like no adult she'd ever met before. She was pretty as a model, but not at all snooty. She acted as if she actually liked them, talking to them in that easy way the good teachers did. And she'd just shrugged off a very near-miss accident. She was…cool.

The smile dropped from her face, however, when Detective de Sanges strode up to her.

"I'm partnering with you," he said in his nonsmiling, just-the-facts-ma'am way. "Poppy—er, that is, Ms. Calloway assigned us to this section of brick over here." He walked over to it and raised dark, slashing eyebrows at her when she didn't immediately follow. "She says after we clean it, you're to paint on the remover and I'm to apply this laminated cloth on top of it." He hefted a small plastic-wrapped bundle for her to see.

Panic scratched at the back of Cory's throat, but she raised her chin in an attempt to refute it. "Forget it. I don't want to partner with you."

Those eyebrows gathered over the strong thrust of his nose, but he merely said, "I didn't make the assignment, kid—I'm just following the general's orders."

The panic pushed harder. "Well, I'm not."

"Yeah, yeah, I got that. Except it's not your choice. Still, why don't we talk to—"

"I don't *want* to talk to you!" Taking several steps back, she crossed her arms militantly over her breasts, hoping it would divert his sharp gaze from the sudden tremble in her lips. "You're a cop. I don't like cops."

"Okay," he said calmly. "Basically we're just people

like everyone else, and if you don't break the law you've got nothing to worry about. But let me just talk to Ms. Ca—"

"That's bullshit!" Her voice came out too loud and she hugged herself against the sick tremors suddenly shaking her from head to foot. But she stood by her words: it *was* bullshit.

"Language, Ms. Capelli," Ms. C. said.

Cory wasn't listening. She glared at the detective. "That's a big, fat lie. My daddy didn't break no law! My daddy did the right thing—least that's what he *thought* he was doing by going to the police in my old neighborhood when he recognized the gunman in a drive-by shooting. And you know what your precious cops did in return? Nuthin'! They were happy enough to get the information and make an arrest, but they didn't bother to keep him safe from the shooter's gang."

Salty liquid trickled in the corner of her mouth and angrily she swiped her forearm against her cheek to wipe away tears she hadn't even realized she was crying. "Almost two years my daddy's been dead," she snapped with extra force to negate the weakness implied by her weeping. But she couldn't keep her voice steady and she ended up sobbing, "And my mom's been working two jobs just to make ends meet. So don't tell *me* how goddamn wonderful cops—"

"Shh, shh, shh, shh, shh." Warm hands closed around her upper arms and she was pulled against a softly scented female breast and wrapped in warm arms. "Shh, now," Ms. Calloway's voice crooned and one hand lifted to stroke the back of Cory's hair. "It's okay. It's okay, baby."

"No, it's not!" she wailed.

The hand stilled for a second, then resumed its stroking. "No, you're right. There's nothing okay about your father being killed for trying to do the right thing. Detective," she said in a calm voice over Cory's head, "why don't you take the boys to the coffee shop down the street and get them something to drink. Take your time. But bring us back a couple of mocha frappuccinos when you're done, will you? My wallet's in my tote over there."

"Keep your money," he said gruffly. "Come on, guys."

Stupid tears kept trickling from Cory's eyes and her nose was getting so stuffy she could barely breathe. Panting noisily through her mouth, she rested her cheek against the soft cushion of Ms. C.'s breast, feeling the paint-splotched cotton beneath it growing damp and hoping to heck she wasn't getting snot all over Poppy.

Wouldn't *that* just be the sprinkles on her cupcake.

Yet, she felt…better somehow. Still sad, but not so gut-wrenchingly lonesome.

"How long have you been keeping this in?" Ms. Calloway inquired gently, her hands still soothing the back of Cory's head and her neck.

"I dunno. Year and a half?"

"Ever since your father died? Haven't you talked to your mother about it?"

"Nuh-uh. Mom misses Daddy so much, and she's got loads on her plate, y'know? I don't wanna burden her."

"Honey, she's your mom. She'd want to know. What do you do when it hits you out of the blue, cry alone?"

She shrugged. "Mostly." And she hadn't realized how good it could feel to be held while she grieved. But the thought made her feel disloyal to her mother, so she disengaged herself and stepped back, knuckling her nose. Which only spread the snot across her cheek.

Jeezus.

Ms. C. produced a little pack of Kleenex and passed it to her. Cory mopped up her face and blew her nose.

"Here." Stepping close, Ms. C. pulled a tissue out of the pack in Cory's hand and dabbed under her eyes with it. Tipping her chin in, she inspected her for a silent moment. "You actually look prettier without all that makeup," she said with a soft smile as she balled up the mascara and eyeliner-smeared tissue.

Cory sniffed. "That's what my mom says."

"Talk to her. If your mother's anything like mine, she'd die if she knew how much you were holding in for her sake."

It was a seductive thought, but she merely said, "I'll think about it."

"She's the adult in your family, Cory. I doubt she'd like the idea of you protecting her at the cost of your own peace of mind." Then she waved her hand. "But I'm not going to nag. So let's discuss Detective de Sanges instead."

Her heart immediately began to pound. "He's mean!"

"No," Ms. C. disagreed without heat. "He's stingy with his smiles and pretty darn single-minded, but I don't believe he's mean. He's dedicated to the job to an almost ridiculous point. I imagine if he'd been on the team assigned to your father's case, he would have turned himself inside out to assure there'd be a very different outcome."

Oh, if only! But her daddy was gone and nothing was gonna bring him back. "Maybe," she said grudgingly, unwilling to give any cop the benefit of the doubt. Still, maybe he wasn't all bad. Because now that she wasn't so panicked, she kind of remembered him trying to tell her he'd get Ms. C. when she'd flipped out on him about being partnered up.

At least that wasn't bound to happen now. So, as embarrassing as crying like a baby in front of everyone was, it had *one* upside.

"I'm sorry," Ms. Calloway said. "That was hardly helpful in the face of a situation that can't be changed. But as you get to know Detective de Sanges a little better I'm confident you'll discover he's not so bad."

Uh-oh, that didn't sound good. "Huh? As I get to know—"

"Him better," Ms. C. finished. "Because you do realize, don't you, that he's still your partner? At least until this chore is complete."

CHAPTER NINE

Well, damn. Just when I'm getting comfy in my preconceptions, Jason has to go and throw a spanner in the works. I *hate* it when the facts get in the way of my prejudices!

WHEN BRUNO ARTURO spotted a teen toting spray-paint cans, he reversed his course, backtracking with long strides in the youth's direction. Sure, Schultz had said to leave the tagger situation be, but this was Kismet, man. Why else would a graffiti freak that he'd seen hanging around the streets before show up just as he was thinking how whack it was that he couldn't find *his* tagger? "Hey, kid!"

The boy glanced over his shoulder but kept shuffling along in his oversize hoodie, baggy pants that showed a good eight inches of boxer shorts where they hung off his skinny ass and huge, untied sneakers.

"You! I'm talking to you." Jesus, what the hell were these kids thinking when they pulled on rags like that in the morning? Smoothing his palm along the lapel of his own sharp gray suit, Arturo watched the kid's head turn back around and snapped, "Don't you walk away from me, punk!"

"Whaddup, dude?" The boy turned back, but his upper body angled back and his arms crossed over his chest, copping an attitude. "Whatchu want?"

"You, answering some questions about one of your species."

The teen's eyes narrowed. "What species you talkin' about, ass-can? One that be *black?*"

"No, idiot. I'm trying to locate a tagger. A white tagger," he added pointedly.

"Don't know me none a' them."

"Bullshit. I see you kids hanging out together all the time. Only color you graffiti types seem to see says Krylon on the can. So tell me where I can find this one." He described the boy who'd been on the roof in as much detail as he could recall.

But the kid merely shrugged and Bruno had a feeling he hadn't even been listening. "Like I said, dude, don't know him. I can't help you."

"Well, if you can't, I guess you can't," he said affably—then grabbed the youth by the throat and waltzed him backward into a nearby alley.

"Now," he said calmly as the kid's fingers scrabbled at his hand and his dark eyes bugged out. "Whataya say we try this one more time?"

POPPY FOUND HERSELF sneaking peeks at Jason as the group worked at painting over the black spray-paint on yet another storefront the following Tuesday afternoon.

He'd been…mellower since Cory's meltdown, not nearly as standoffish and serious.

Not that he'd suddenly turned into a smiling fool or the kids' best friend. But Poppy had noted his gentleness with Cory when he'd rejoined the girl that day, and the quiet way in which he'd allowed her to maintain her distance. So although he'd still made cracks to Poppy about her minithugs, he'd obviously done something right while he'd had the boys over at the coffee shop. She didn't know what he'd said to them, but both kids had managed to act pretty natural around Cory when they'd come back. After the girl's revelation concerning her father—and boys being boys—Poppy doubted they could have pulled that off if he hadn't said *something* to them.

So that was…good. Or at least it should be good. But, man, oh, man. Her stomach twisted as she shot Jase another glance. Because she wasn't all that certain a mellower de Sanges was a good thing.

It was bad enough she had the hots for the guy when he was being his usual I-do-not-smile-therefore-I-am gloomy Gus. This damn itchy got-you-under-my-skin attraction she felt for him made no sense, but at least his thorny personality helped her keep her distance.

Oh, yeah? How's that working for you? Blowing out a disgusted breath, she pulled a foot-long piece of an old Venetian blind out of her tote and crossed to where Henry was avoiding painting up to the corner to show him how to use the pliable length of aluminum to avoid slopping color onto the adjoining wall while he finished his section.

But her mind returned to her rat-in-a-maze musings the instant she no longer had something to distract her. Because Jason's less-than-jovial persona had been *such* a consideration, hadn't it, when he'd given her that peck on the lips and she'd wanted to swallow him whole?

Oh, yeah. *Big* turnoff. *As if it was you who pulled away.*

Damn. She so didn't get this. Because the way she felt around him? Probably *the* most libidinous of her life. She'd always had a pretty healthy sex drive, but never had she taken just one look at a guy and thought, *Want that.*

She swallowed a snort. *Giving yourself way too much credit here if you actually believe there's been any* thinking *involved.* She was all nerve endings and awareness around him. Take last fall when she'd believed he was blowing off the break-in scare they'd experienced at the mansion. She'd been furious with him, yet it hadn't stopped her from wanting to rub herself all over him like a cat in heat.

She had no idea where all these urges, past and present, were coming from. She'd always imagined the kind of guy who'd have this visceral an impact on her would be...well, worlds different from Jason de Sanges, that's for sure. She'd envisioned someone artistic and socially conscious—a guy who was maybe a little bit like her dad, in that he'd love to laugh and think that her desire to change the world one kid at a time was actually a good thing, not some giant pain in his ass.

She found her gaze drawn to that portion of his anatomy, then staying to study it in loving detail. In his usual tailored slacks his butt was round and muscular and studly enough. But in the worn jeans he had on today? Lord have mercy. Those showcased precisely what a world-class—

For God's sake, Poppy! It was all she could do not to smack her palm off her forehead. Because, for the love of Pete, what was she, a high-school girl mooning over the football captain? She hadn't done that when she was a teen!

She had a bad, bad feeling, though, that things weren't going to get better. Because it was tough enough keeping her eyes to herself and her thoughts off his ass when he was Robocop. How was she supposed to deal if he turned all Mr. New Age Sensitive Guy on her?

By taking a big step back, that's how. She blew out a quiet breath. Squared her shoulders.

Okay, she could do that. She could—and would—act professionally from now on and keep all personal inclinations under lock and key. No letting her hormones be in charge. No more checking out his butt. And except for those situations when it couldn't be helped as they worked with the kids, she was keeping lots and lots of space between them. Physically *and* emotionally.

She moved between her teenage taggers, checking their work and giving them words of encouragement. Her cell phone rang as she was praising the neat, efficient job Danny was doing and she rounded the end of the building to answer it. Turning her back to the traffic whizzing by in the street, she stuck a finger in her free ear to block out the road noises. "Hello?"

"Ms. Calloway? This is Barb Jackson—Darnell's grandmother?"

She beamed at the thought of her star student in the Central District project. "Oh, yes, Mrs. Jackson. How are you?"

Her smile faded as Mrs. Jackson's voice grew frantic and frightened the more the older woman talked. Twice Poppy had to exhort her to slow down as well as asking her more than once to repeat something in order to fully understand the situation that had the woman so distraught.

Finally, she said, "Mrs. Jackson, I'm with another group of kids at the moment, but we should be finished in about an hour. Could I come by your house? Yes? Good, hang on a moment while I grab something to write on." She raced back to her tote and pulled out her tablet and pen. "Okay, I'm ready. Let me have your address and telephone number."

Terminating the call a moment later, she tapped the tablet against her palm as she shot Jase a considering look. She really, really didn't want to take this to him. But he had resources she could only dream of.

Tossing the notebook and pen back in her tote, she strode over to where he was taping the corner where Henry worked.

He gave her a don't-mess-with-me look as she approached. "That piece of blind is fine for small areas," he said. "But I'm taping this. I want to get done here before we're all old and gray."

"Fine," she agreed. "I'm all over whatever works. But that's not why I'm here. I need—" The words stuck in her throat, because asking directly contradicted her vow to keep her distance. Still, it had to be said. *Resources,* she reminded herself. *This isn't about you, it's about Darnell, and de Sanges has the resources.* She swallowed hard.

"I need your help."

AFTER THE KIDS had taken off for the day, Jase stuffed his hands in his jeans pockets and walked beside Poppy to her car, wondering what the hell was going on. They hadn't had time to really talk and he wasn't sure why he had automatically agreed to help just because she'd asked.

It sure wasn't his usual way. He liked to have his *i*'s dotted and his *t*'s crossed before he committed to anything. But had he even once asked, *Need my help to do what?* Hell, no. The late afternoon spring sun had been casting a nimbus around Poppy's hair, weaving lacy shadows through the thick lashes fringing those deep brown eyes with their clear, clear whites, and he'd said, yeah, all right. Sure.

Almost immediately, his uncharacteristic acquiescence had brought him up short. Yet before he could retract it and demand details, Henry had climbed all over his case about finishing the tape job. Then it seemed as if one kid or another had a question or opinion they wanted Poppy to hear. Between all that, there'd been no time for conversation.

That wasn't the case now, however, and he opened his mouth to demand details of what he'd blindly signed on for. But Poppy stopped in front of her car and, taking one look at it, all other considerations momentarily fled.

Jesus, the thing must be fifteen years old and looked as if it was held together by baling wire and gum. Had he laid eyes on the ramshackle wreck at any time since that day he'd been dragged from the Lewis case to take Poppy and her friends' burglary report, it would've eliminated a world of misunderstanding regarding her financial situation. "We'll take my car."

Clearly unoffended, she shot him a lopsided smile as she stroked the car's oxidized front fender. "Why does everyone always assume Maybelline here is on the verge of a breakdown? She may not be pretty, but she runs a lot better than she looks."

"I hope to hell, since it's a rust bucket." Then he stared at her. "You *named* your car?"

"Well, sure. We've been together a long time—I could hardly just call her *it*." She gave him a droll look. "I take it you didn't name yours."

"Not in this lifetime," he muttered. But he could easily visualize her doing so. He'd discovered a…lightness to Poppy Calloway over the past several days, a sort of built-in joy that all but glowed from her.

Damned, however, if he intended to cop to that. "C'mon," he said gruffly. "I'm parked around the corner."

He ushered her to his SUV, settled her in the passenger seat, then strode around the hood. Climbing in, he slid his key into the ignition, but turned his head to look at her instead of starting it up. "All right, just what the hell do you need my help doing?"

"It's nothing illegal, I assure you," she said dryly and made a little shooing gesture with her fingertips. "Do you think you could head for the Central District while we talk?"

"No."

She sighed. "Barb Jackson, the grandmother of one of my students in the Central District program, called me. Darnell's gone missing, and she's scared sick."

He stared at her. "Contrary to what this assignment with the kids might suggest, Blondie, I'm not your personal cop. Not to mention I'm a Robbery detective, not Missing Persons."

"Which is actually a bonus at the moment, since they basically told Mrs. Jackson not to worry her pretty little head, that that was kids for you and Darnell has to be missing twenty-four hours before they'll start looking for him."

"There's a reason they wait that long. Nine times out of ten that *is* kids for you."

"He's a good kid, Jason, and what if he's that tenth out of ten? I know you have a demanding job that our cleanup project is taking you away from, and I honest to God don't expect you to drop everything else you're doing. But you've got resources Mrs. Jackson and I do not. Won't you at least talk to her?"

He should say no. He *intended* to say no. Instead, grumbling, he fired up the engine. And headed for the CD.

Twenty minutes later he pulled up in front of a neat, mid-nineteenth-century bungalow. For a brief moment after he turned off the ignition, he simply sat there staring up the walk. Then on a resigned breath, he turned to Poppy. "I don't suppose you want to change your mind about this?"

"She needs our help, Jason."

He swore under his breath and—ignoring the fact that hearing her call him by his given name did something funny to his gut—climbed from the car and strode around the hood to open Poppy's door. She beat him to it, however, and moodily eyeing the swing of her hips, he all but tromped on her heels as she strode up the short walk. Finding himself breathing down her neck as she stopped to push the doorbell, he took a healthy step backward. Jesus. The woman was making him seriously crazy.

The door opened and the author of his insanity said, "Mrs. Jackson? I'm Poppy Calloway and this is Detective de Sanges."

"Thank you so much for coming." A plump, tidily attired African-American woman who looked to be in her late fifties stepped back, opening the door wider. "Please, come in." She shot him a glance, then looked back at Poppy. "I didn't know a police officer would be accompanying you."

"I'm not with Missing Persons, Mrs. Jackson, but Ms. Calloway asked if I'd help look into your grandson's disappearance. I don't have any authority in another department's case, but—"

"It's nobody's case, Detective. When I called Darnell's school and found out he hadn't been there I went to Missing Persons. But they said he hadn't been gone long enough to create a file."

"In most instances the waiting period turns out to be valid. But I'll do what I can."

Mrs. Jackson led them into a living room that was inexpensively furnished, but clean and freshly painted in a cheerful spring green. "Please, have a seat."

He and Poppy sat on the couch, and he automatically reached for what should have been the inside pocket of his suit jacket—only to pull up short at the reminder he'd dressed casually today. "I'm sorry, Mrs. Jackson, I don't have my notebook with me. Would you have a piece of paper and something to write with?"

She fetched him a tablet and a pen.

"Thanks." Flipping back the tablet cover, he looked at the older woman and clicked the pen to extend its point. "When's the last time you saw your grandson?"

"Last night before I went to bed." She turned to Poppy. "He was still talking about your last class, and I thought at first, when he didn't come home from school, he'd maybe met up with that South American girl he likes or had gone to a friend's house. But when he still hadn't called or shown up come suppertime, I started calling his friends." For a moment her face crumpled, then she regained control. "Nobody knew anything."

"Or weren't willing to say," he said.

The older woman shifted in protest. "He's a good boy! And so are ninety-nine percent of his friends."

"I'm not implying otherwise, ma'am. But even the best of teens are still teens. They do things they don't think through very well. They all seem to believe that if there were an Eleventh Commandment it would be

Thou Shalt Cover For Thy Friends No Matter What. And sometimes they lie simply because they know you won't like the truth and they just don't want the responsibility of living up to your expectations. I don't know Darnell so I'm not saying he's done any of those things. But it is something to keep in mind. Does he have a car?"

"No, sir."

He rose to his feet. "Why don't you show me his room. Then perhaps you can get me a picture to show around and a list of his friends' addresses and phone numbers while I take a look at it."

"All right." She led them to a room off the kitchen.

When the older woman left them at the door and turned back into the kitchen, Poppy turned back to watch Jason paw through the teen's possessions.

And found herself needing to reassess.

She'd been quick to pass judgment on de Sanges last year when he'd told her things she hadn't wanted to hear, but she realized now that he simply laid out matters as he saw them, based on his professional expertise. Contrary to what she'd first assumed, he didn't do so to discourage or to hurt, but rather to impart information as truthfully as he could. And God knew his assessment of teens correlated pretty damn spot-on with her own experience working with them.

She believed what she'd told Cory—that things might have been different if there had been a cop like Jason on the Capelli case. He was just too pigheaded, too detail-oriented, to let a man's reward for courageously stepping forward to identify a killer be to forfeit his life.

"Kid's got talent," Jason said, interrupting her thoughts.

She looked up to find him studying some of Darnell's work tacked to the walls. "He does. A boatload of it."

"I don't see a computer."

"He probably uses the public ones at the library. Mrs. Jackson provides a good life for him here, but it doesn't come with much discretionary income. And things like cell phones and computers? Well, they're rarely on the have-nots' side of the equation."

He essayed a philosophical shrug that suggested he saw the divide between class privileges on a daily basis. "Sort through the wastebasket and see if there's anything in it that might point us to his whereabouts."

Mrs. Jackson rejoined them and Jason studied the wallet-size school photo she gave him. He had the older woman go through Darnell's clothing to see if anything was missing, then asked her to identify the drawings of the people in the teen's sketch pad.

"And that's me, of course," she said at one point, then sat silently for a moment as tears welled in her eyes. Sniffing, she sat straighter, but ran gentle fingertips down her likeness on the paper. Slowly she flipped the page and studied it for a moment. "I'm thinking this is that girl Darnell likes in Ms. Calloway's class."

Poppy leaned down to look. "Emilia, yes. They do seem to like each other quite a lot."

De Sanges glanced at Mrs. Jackson. "What did she have to say when you called?"

When she said she hadn't because she didn't know the number, Poppy volunteered to contact the girl.

Mrs. Jackson's face suddenly tightened.

Looking from her expression to the drawing in the book, de Sanges leaned in to study the sketch more closely. "Who's this?"

"Nobody," the older woman said flatly.

"He's someone, Mrs. Jackson, or your grandson wouldn't have sketched him."

"His name is Freddy Gordon and he and Darnell used to be friends. But then Freddy joined a gang. They don't see each other anymore."

"I'll need his address anyhow. We don't want to leave any stone unturned."

"I can tell you exactly what you're going to find under that particular rock," Mrs. Jackson muttered. But she stood and swept up the contact list she'd made, taking it back to the kitchen.

With the briefest expression-free eye contact, he passed Poppy the sketchbook. To her surprise, however, she realized she was beginning to read nuances in Detective Sobersides's poker face. And looking down at the drawing, she saw why he might have a hard time taking Mrs. Jackson's assessment at face value. It showed a youth with sad, old-soul eyes but a sweet if barely there smile.

"This kid might be trouble or a bad influence, but Darnell drew him with love," she said softly, admiring the boy's ability to bring personalities to life.

"Yeah." He rose to his feet. "That was my impression, too." Meeting the missing boy's grandmother in the doorway as she returned from the kitchen, he accepted the revised sheet she handed him and said, "Mrs.

Jackson, we're going to take Darnell's picture and this information and search for him. I'll let you know the minute I hear anything."

The older woman reached for his hand and held it between both her own as she thanked him. Then she did the same to Poppy. Five minutes later they were back in the car.

He looked over at her, something in his dark eyes telegraphing a sense that he was now as fully engaged in this quest as she.

"Let's go have a talk with Freddy Gordon," he said and started the car.

CHAPTER TEN

Oh, man, that smile. Not to mention what he *did*.

It's official. I'm toast.

FIRST THING Jase did, after turning off his car in front of a rundown house several blocks and a world of upkeep removed from Mrs. Jackson's, was unlock the glove compartment and retrieve his gun from its rig. Then he grabbed his badge and his seen-better-days notebook with its cheap pen stuck through the spirals. Climbing from the SUV, he shoved the book into one hip pocket and his badge into the other. He tucked his gun in the back of his jeans and pulled his T-shirt from his waistband to conceal it. There. Now he didn't feel so naked.

Poppy was actually still sitting in the passenger seat when he rounded the hood, instead of already halfway up the cracked walk ahead of him. He opened her door, but she didn't move, just gave him a look.

"Not thrilled with the gun, de Sanges."

"Sorry to hear it, Calloway. I'm not thrilled with the feel of this place. The gun stays."

She gazed at him a moment longer, then nodded. "I know what you mean about the feel. Why do I have the sense this kid isn't going to get the same kind of concern Mrs. Jackson displayed for Darnell?"

"Because you've worked with enough kids to get a feel for the ones in bad family situations? Or, hell, maybe just because it's still a sunny evening, but all the blinds are closed, or the fact that this place is a dump." He looked at the dirt-and-weed-choked yard littered with broken, discarded bikes and trikes as he ushered her up the uneven walkway to the front door. "Even the doesn't-require-much-money, easily fixed stuff hasn't been done."

They stopped on the sagging two-step stoop. A television inside blared *Oprah* and when Poppy once again failed to make a move—which was very unlike her—he reached around to rap his knuckles on the door.

It opened and he had to adjust his sights a good deal lower to the little girl standing on the other side. Wearing a grimy, food-stained T-shirt and corduroy pants, she planted her finger firmly in her mouth and stared up at him with solemn eyes.

And Poppy finally came to life. "Well, hello there," she murmured with a soft smile and dropped to her haunches in front of the child.

The little girl reached out to touch the blond mass of curls brushing Poppy's collarbone. Her own hair looked as if it hadn't seen a comb or brush that day. A shy smile curled her lips around the damp finger.

"Whatayou want?" demanded a harsh voice and the kid snatched her hand back, the smile dropping from her face. She gave her finger a comforting suck.

Pulling his attention from Poppy, who was trailing gentle fingertips over the crown of the little girl's head as she rose to her feet in a swirl of filmy skirts, he directed it at the irritated countenance of the reed-thin woman who'd gotten up and come to the door.

Ignoring the ash that fell from her cigarette onto the floor, she stared back at him.

"You Mrs. Gordon?"

Suspicious eyes narrowed behind the screen of smoke she blew between them. "Who wants to know?" Then she gave him a closer inspection. "Shit. A cop." Turning her attention to Poppy, she glared. "And you got that do-gooder look about ya, so you must be—what? CPS?"

"No, ma'am, I'm not with Child Protection Services. Darnell Jackson is in an art class I teach. He's missing and we're trying to find him. We heard he's friends with Freddy."

"Well, he sure ain't here," the woman scoffed, tossing her cigarette out the door. "Darnell don't come around much anymore. That was his tight-assed granny's doin', but for once I hadda agree with the old bitch. Boy's got no reason to be hangin' with my son. Darnell's got somethin'—you can see jest by lookin' at him that he's gonna be someone someday." Then the warmth bled out of her voice. "Freddy ain't never gonna amount to shit."

Jase saw the shock on Poppy's face that a woman could say such a thing about her own son. With the authority he'd been soft-pedaling until now, he barked, "Is Freddy around? I'd like to talk to him."

"I don't know where the little bastard is. Ain't seen him since Sunday night."

"You didn't get him off to school?" Poppy asked.

"He's almost eighteen, lady. He kin get hisself off to school."

Poppy's eyes started flashing fire and Jase took a lateral step to place himself between the two women. "Does Freddy have a cell phone?"

"Yeah."

When she didn't elaborate, he said in a you-don't-want-to-mess-with-me voice, "What's his number?"

Muttering under her breath, she shuffled on worn bedroom scuffs back across the living room, then returned a moment later, a fresh cigarette in one hand and a dollar-store address book in the other. She turned its pages with painful slowness until she finally hit upon the one she sought. Without looking up, she recited it aloud.

He wrote it in his notebook, then passed her his card, accompanied by a hard look. "Call me the minute you hear from him."

"Huh," she grunted and held the front door open in a clear invitation to leave.

He followed Poppy from the house and could tell by her stiff-gaited stride that she wasn't happy.

And if that hadn't been hint enough, she was less than shy about stating her opinion. "Can you *believe* that woman?" she snapped as she slid into the car.

He shut the door in her face, but she was turned toward the driver side when he climbed in seconds later.

"I wish I had been CPS—that woman was just

begging to have her children taken away. Dammit, Jason, that sweet little girl didn't look as if she'd had an ounce of care given her in I don't know how long."

He didn't like the way he kept getting all hung up on the sound of his name coming from her lips. Consequently, his voice was stiff when he said, "I agree Mrs. Gordon won't qualify for mother of the year anytime soon. But I've rarely seen the foster system add quality to a kid's life."

"At least the child wouldn't die from secondhand smoke," she muttered. But she sighed and visibly reined in her anger. "All right, I know that," she admitted softly. "I do. It's just…"

"Yeah," he agreed. "It bites." He tried calling the number he'd gotten for Freddy, but it went straight to voice mail. After leaving a brief message with his various numbers, he disconnected, then turned back to Poppy.

"Listen, work's piling up on my desk. If you can dig up Darnell's girlfriend's address we'll go by and see if she's home. But win or lose on that front, Blondie, I need to head back to the station the minute we're done."

"You're kidding me. It's already after six."

He shrugged. "Work's piling up on my desk."

Reaching across the console, she touched warm fingertips to his forearm. "Thank you, Jason. For everything. You've been great about this and I can't tell you how much I appreciate it."

Jase had a quick mental vision of her demonstrating her appreciation. With nudity. Flex-cuffs. And a headboard.

He snapped erect. Jesus. He was more, dammit, than

the sum total of his fucked-up genes. His voice developing some snap, he said, "You can thank me by hustling for that address."

"I've got it here." She'd been scrolling through her cell phone, clueless, thank God, to the direction his thoughts had taken. She rattled off an address in south Seattle. "You want me to call first to see if she's home? It'll save you some time."

"No. Calling can be a time-saver, but with kids it usually just gives them the chance to book." He fired up the engine and pulled away from the curb.

"Man, I wouldn't have your job for the world," she said. "You really do see the worst in people, don't you?"

"As opposed to through your Pollyanna-rosy glasses, you mean?"

"Yeah." She grinned at him and launched into a story about her art-class kids. One thing you could say about the Babe, he mused during the crosstown drive, you never had to worry about digging for things to talk about. After regaling him with an anecdote of one of the boys in her project, she segued into the logistics of the selection process of the three Seattle high schools that had contributed kids to her program. Emilia, for instance, the girl they were traveling to see, had been culled from Chief Sealth on the recommendation of a teacher. Jase was cresting Highland Park Way—more commonly known as Boeing Hill—and headed toward White Center by the time Poppy finished praising the girl's apparent aptitude for drawing landscapes and buildings and shit.

He turned off the arterial before they reached Rox-bury, the main east-west street cutting through the area shopping district, then turned again and cruised down Tenth until he spotted the house he was looking for. It was a small but beautifully maintained wood-frame single-family residence with a landscaped yard. After he parked in front of it, they got out of the car and for the third time that evening walked up to a front door. He stood one step behind Poppy while she rang the bell.

A pretty teenaged girl around Poppy's mid-five-feet height opened the door, and he took a wild stab and guessed it was the much-touted Ms. Suarez—a conjec-ture he figured was right on the money when the girl's big brown eyes went wide and she said in patent sur-prise, "Ms. Calloway!"

The look she gave Poppy was at once thrilled and horrified…and Jase's professional radar went on red alert over the latter.

"Hi, Emilia," Poppy said. "I'm sorry to bother you at home but—"

"The hell with that," he interrupted gruffly and the girl jerked, as if just now noticing him. He stepped forward, towering over her. "Where's Darnell?"

Emilia blinked rapidly as Poppy whipped around to stare at him through narrowed lashes. The Babe slapped a warm-fingered hand against his chest to hold him away from the girl and snapped, "Back off, Detective!"

He gave her a level look and dipped his head to mouth, *Good cop, bad cop.* She immediately whirled back to the teenager and he didn't have a clue whether or not she'd play along.

"Ms. Suarez, this charming gentleman is Detective de Sanges," she said dryly. "Darnell's missing, his grandmother is worried sick and Detective de Sanges has some questions he needs to ask."

With a quick look over her shoulder, Emilia stepped out onto the porch and closed the door behind her. "I don't know why he'd wanna ask me, Ms. Calloway," she said, but couldn't hold Poppy's clear gaze and wouldn't look at Jase at all. "I don't know nuth—"

"I suggest you put some thought into playing the I-know-nothing card," he interrupted in a hard tone and shot the girl a feral smile when her gaze snapped to his. He jerked his chin at Poppy. "The teach here might buy that, but I don't. And you don't want to know what I can charge you with for hampering my investigation—" not a damn thing "—should I discover you're lying. Which you are, Ms. Suarez." Then he added more gently, "But I'm going to give you a chance to rectify the situation. Where's Darnell?"

Grabbing Poppy's hand, the teen hauled the blonde along with her as she leaped off the porch and headed around the house. She shot Jase a sullen look over her shoulder. "Let's take this to the backyard."

He fell into step behind the two females and they rounded the south end of the house, then edged single file down a narrow side yard that was mostly dormant garden. A moment later they stepped out into a deep backyard with a lush lawn and even lusher grasses and plants surrounding it. In the corner of the property stood a little shake-covered shed built to look like a microscopic house. Trees and shrubberies offered strategically planted privacy from the neighboring houses that encroached on either side.

"Emilia, this is gorgeous!" Poppy exclaimed with the uninhibited enthusiasm Jase was learning characterized her.

The girl smiled with pride. "My papi did it," she said. "He works for a landscape and yard service guy who says he's got a real green thumb."

Jase allowed the teen to show Poppy around and point out specific features for a few minutes. Then he said, "Where's Darnell?"

Reluctantly, she turned to face him. "I told you—"

He crossed the distance separating them in two long strides. "And I told you what the consequences would be if you lied to me again. Don't mess with me."

"I'm *not* messing with you! Just because me and Darnell go out sometimes don't mean I know where he is." But she looked at him and gave a significant thrust of her chin toward the corner of the yard.

Following the trajectory, Jase found himself looking straight at the little shed. He looked down at her and raised an eyebrow.

Looking miserable, the girl sketched a barely there nod.

"You better not be lying to me," he said for Darnell's benefit—if indeed the boy was in there—and started in that direction. "I'm sure you don't mind if I look around to make sure for myself." Slowly approaching the structure, he reached under his T-shirt and drew out his gun.

"Jason!" Poppy exclaimed at the same time that Emilia screeched, "No!" and raced to his side, where she grabbed for his gun hand.

With an easy twist, he slid his wrist out of her grasp and pinned her in place with his coldest cop expression. "Interfering with a police officer in the performance of his duty is a serious offense, Ms. Suarez."

"You don't need a *gun*," she cried fiercely, giving the weapon in his hand a look of loathing.

"Probably not," he agreed. "Everything I've heard about Darnell paints the picture of a good kid. But he's disappeared for no good reason. I'm guessing he's holed up in your shed and for all I know he has a weapon of his own. I do not go into that sort of situation unarmed."

"Wait, wait, wait," came a muffled voice from within the shed. "I'm opening the door."

Jase drew on it in a two-handed grip. "Do it slowly, Mr. Jackson. You don't want to make any sudden moves."

"For heaven's sake, de Sanges," Poppy said as he watched the door down his gun's sight. "Is that really necessary?"

"I hope not. But too many good cops have been killed in situations where they trusted in the goodness of man, and I don't plan on joining their ranks. I do this by the book."

"Don't shoot, man!" The door slowly creaked open. "We're coming out!"

We? "Put your hands out the door first, then slowly step out one at a time," he instructed.

A young medium-skinned black man did as he said, bending to clear the door opening before straightening to a height that had to be a good six and a half feet. In his wake came a shorter and darker-skinned teen, who upon closer inspection looked like he'd recently had the crap kicked out of him.

"Misters Jackson and Gordon, I presume," he said dryly. "Step to the side, both of you, then turn and face the shed and put your hands against the wall."

They complied and he quickly frisked both youths. Finding them clean, he shoved his piece back into the waistband of his jeans and stepped back. "Okay, you can turn around."

They did, looking both scared and sullen, and he swallowed a sigh. Damn, teenagers were work. "Let's hear it."

Neither boy spoke and Jase said dryly, "Don't everyone talk at once."

Silence reigned and he turned to Darnell's friend. "Okay, let's start with you, Mr. Gordon. Who beat you?"

No answer.

He looked at Darnell. "You care to field this one?"

He, too, remained mute. And Poppy, whom he knew to be firmly in the boys' corner, lost patience.

But, surprisingly, not with him.

"Darnell Jackson," she snapped. "You've worried your grandmother sick and tied up the better part of Detective de Sanges's evening, when he's here as a favor to me. *I* am here as a favor to your grandmother and because I, too, was worried. So you had better start talking, mister." When the teen failed to immediately respond, her voice snapped like a whip. *"Now!"*

The boy remained stubbornly silent. Then Freddy said, "It's my fault."

Darnell shifted. "Freddy—"

"No. You think I don't know who she is?" He jerked his head at Poppy. "That's your teacher from that class you got such a big love-on for. And you ain't gettin' bounced outta it on account a' me." He peered at Poppy through swollen, slitted eyelids. "Don't be mad at him. He was just trying to help me."

"Why don't we sit over here?" Jase said and led the boys to a set of wooden benches under an old lilac tree. He looked over at Emilia, whose gaze kept jumping from Darnell to Freddy to him and back again. "Do you think you could get your friends a glass of water or something?"

Looking relieved to have something to do, she raced to the back door. He turned back to the boys.

"Okay, let's start with something simple. Why were you in the shed?"

The boys admitted that Freddy had needed a place to hide so Emilia had let them in the house while her folks were at work, and then again when they left after dinner to visit their married daughter.

"So you were there when Ms. Calloway and I arrived?"

Darnell straightened from his slump on the bench. He looked toward the kitchen where Emilia had disappeared then met Jase's gaze squarely. "She's not gonna get jammed up over this, is she?"

"No. So far I don't see that anyone's done anything illegal."

He nodded. "Then, yeah. We were in the kitchen but slipped out the back when the doorbell rang."

Jase turned his attention back to Freddy. "Who beat you?"

"I had a difference of opinion with my homies."

"And that difference was?"

He essayed a shrug, but dark shadows haunted his eyes. "I want out. They don't believe in quitters."

Shit. That wasn't good. Remembering some of the stories he'd heard from gang-unit detectives, he thought fast. The kid's home life hadn't struck him as wonderful and he doubted the mother was likely to smother him in TLC anytime soon. He studied the boy's contusions, trying to assess the damage. "How badly are you hurt?"

Another shrug. "I'll live."

He established the boy didn't have any broken bones, double vision and wasn't peeing blood, then took a deep breath. "You have any family outside Seattle?"

For just a second hope flickered across Freddy's face, but it was immediately subdued, making Jase think the boy probably hadn't had many of his hopes realized. "Got an uncle in Alabama."

"What's his name?"

"Conrad Gordon."

"Your father's brother, huh?" When Freddy nodded, he inquired gently, "Have you considered calling him?"

"Yeah. But I ain't got no money for long distance and my cell phone's got a dead battery."

Man, when it rained it poured for this kid, didn't it? "I've got a phone. Why don't you give me his number and let me see what I can do?"

That hope flickered a little stronger before Freddy once again stuffed it down. But he had clearly memorized his relative's number because he rattled it off without consulting anything.

Jase entered it in his notebook, then looked at his watch and figured it was late enough in Alabama to improve their chances of finding someone home. "Poppy, why don't you give Darnell your phone so he can let his grandma know he's okay," he suggested. He shot her an assessing glance, surprised at her reticence since they'd arrived. He would have expected her to jump in and take over with the teens, but except for that once, she'd pretty much stayed out of his way. Then, shrugging the matter aside, he crossed the yard to make the call.

Living a cop's life meant he usually saw the worst in people, and he wanted to be out of Freddy's hearing if the uncle didn't come through. The boy would need to know one way or the other, of course, but if it was bad news, at least Jase would have a minute to find a way to break it to him.

Hell, he shouldn't even be doing this. The kid was a minor and regardless of the fact that he thought the mother was just this side of abusive, his job was to return Freddy to her.

But for once he didn't care. His cynical side doubted the teen would get his fairy-tale ending, but he could at least see if anyone else was willing to be responsible for him.

Freddy's uncle Conrad surprised him. After hearing Jase out, the man admitted he'd suspected things weren't great and knew he should have done something sooner, but he'd been tied up in his own life and had let it slide. He offered now to assume guardianship of the boy, stating that he couldn't do a worse job of it than that bitch Arlene, whom Jase had no trouble identifying as Mrs. Gordon. He also mentioned some cousins for Freddy to hang out with and said the small Alabama town where he lived was a good place for a boy to grow up.

"We have some gang problems here, too, unfortunately," Gordon said. "But there's plenty of good kids in this town and you can be damn sure I'll steer Freddy their way and monitor things to see he stays on the right path." He blew out a breath. "I doubt Arlene will kick up a fuss, but she might just because she can."

"If that happens, tell her I'll be over to talk to her personally. And this time I will bring CPS." If she knew the law, Freddy was sunk, but he was betting on her indifference.

"In that case I'll get back to you as soon as I get him a ticket. I might not be able to score one today."

"I know a good man I'm pretty sure will take Freddy in if you can't." Making a mental note to give Murphy a call, he found himself wondering if this was what Murph had felt like when he'd yanked him off the path to destruction.

He called Freddy over to talk to his uncle and handed him the phone.

Then watched with a rare smile as a battered boy's face lit up with joy.

CHAPTER ELEVEN

I am so over that frickin' sheik fantasy. Swear to
heaven I am!

DEFINITELY NOT ONE of my brighter ideas, Poppy thought
as she stood outside Jason's Phinney Ridge apartment
at half past seven the next evening. She set down her
cloth Trader Joe's shopping bag on the corridor carpet,
smoothed the fine gauge of her aqua sweater over her
hips, fussed with her curls for a moment, then—giving
up on them as hopeless—shifted her purse strap more
securely over her shoulder. Finally, practicing a yoga re-
laxation breathing technique, she stooped to pick the
red-and-white Hawaiian print bag back up. After
straightening, she knocked on the door before she could
lose her nerve and talk herself out of it. Hey, she was
here; no sense in turning into a big chicken, thus making
the carbon footprint she'd burned on the way over here
even more of a waste than it already was.

She knocked once more for good measure, then
didn't know whether to be relieved or disappointed
when no one answered. Considering the way she'd been
trying to talk herself out of this ever since it had occurred

to her to bring Jason a homemade meal as a thank-you for his marvelous handling of not only the Darnell situation, but Freddy's as well, she should be downright giddy at the reprieve, right?

And part of her was happy about it. She felt lighter, the way she had that time back in the fifth grade when she'd escaped having to take a test she'd studied insufficiently for because of a rare snow-day school closure, which had given her a second chance to prepare. Now, as then, she'd been saved from her own less-than-brilliant impulses.

Yet at the same time…

An excitement she couldn't deny had percolated inside of her as she'd assembled the Stroganoff, taken a quick shower, shaved her legs and donned the new undies she'd bought from a sale bin at Victoria's Secret last week. Facing her intentions squarely, she admitted that feeding de Sanges probably hadn't been the primary motivation driving her.

That leg-shaving thing was the big clue.

Grinning to herself—because, really, she had a feeling the man was waaaay out of her league, sexually speaking—she put the bag back on the floor in front of his door, hunted up a pen and notepad in her purse and scribbled a quick thank-you note. Ripping it out of the pad, she placed it atop the casserole dish in the cloth bag, which she left behind as she headed back down the corridor to the elevator.

Only to have the door to the stairwell open and Jason step out before she reached it.

They both stopped short, and while Poppy guessed his heart probably wasn't doing a sudden tap dance, hers sure was. "Um, hi."

"What are you doing here?" He jerked his tie loose, directing Poppy's attention to his snappy suit. Then his eyes narrowed. "How the hell did you get my address?"

"Jeez, not paranoidly suspicious or anything, are you?" Still, she couldn't help but smile. "I don't suppose you'd buy me looking you up online?"

"I'm a cop, Blondie. You could search the Net until your pretty tight skin sagged around your ankles and still find damn few of us with a published address or listed phone. So which politician did you buy off this time?"

"Same guy as the past two times—the mayor. He looooves me. And get over yourself. I'm not stalking you and I'm not here to bomb your apartment house. I brought you a pan of the famous Calloway beef Stroganoff to thank you for all you did yesterday."

He went still. "You cooked for me?"

"Sure. And not just anything, pal. Chefs all over the greater Seattle area weep when my mother refuses them this recipe. It's to die for." Then she shot him a wry smile and admitted, "Not that I could always make that claim. You'll just have to trust me when I say it's come a long way since Mom's tofu period."

His face registered the proper horror and a visible shudder rippled his strong shoulders.

"Tell me about it," she agreed. "And you never even had to eat it. I lived on that crap for two, maybe three, years. I can't remember the exact number, but it felt like ten."

"That's just plain cruel and unusual punishment."

"Amen to that, brother. There oughtta be a law. If I ever have a kid, I will never serve her tofu. You can take that to the bank."

He hesitated for two long heartbeats, then craned his head forward, his bony nose raised like a cartoon character following a beckoning finger of scent. "I think I smell it. You better come in and show me how to cook the thing. I've never had much homemade food, and I'd hate to screw it up."

"Not sure that you can." He'd never had homemade— Catching herself, she fell into step beside him. "It's merely a matter of heating it through, which you can do in the micro. But I can toss the salad while you do that."

He turned his head to stare at her over his shoulder. "You brought me salad, too?"

"Uh-huh. And a baguette and a bottle of white." She raised her eyebrows at him. "You're not an alcoholic, are you?"

The corner of his mouth ticked up, which Poppy interpreted as riotous amusement. His teeth were very white against his swarthy skin and five-o'clock shadow. "Nah."

"Glad to hear it. 'Cuz this baby's got a cork and everything. I probably wouldn't go so far as to give it a minute to breathe, but if you're particular we can do that."

"I'm still stunned at the cork part. That's a big step up from the last bottle I bought." Arriving at his door, he swept up the Trader Joe's bag, unlocked the door and stood back for her to precede him into his apartment. "Although I gotta admit that once I fished the glass out of the neck I'd opened against the counter it was a very fine three-buck-chuck."

Oh, God, oh, God. A sense of humor. She'd thought the hardly-even-a-hint she'd caught of it a while back had been a one-off thing, but that was a joke he'd just made. An honest-to-God joke!

She wanted to have his baby.

She'd settle, however, for checking out his apartment. Absorbing as many impressions as possible, she followed him down the short hallway, taking the opportunity to look around when he ducked into his bedroom to hang up his jacket.

The place turned out to be another surprise. Not the fact that it was neat as a pin—that was hardly astonishing, considering. But she'd pegged him as the minimalist type and if she'd put any thought into it she would have predicted his style as Early Military Barracks, a sort of no-frills bare-essentials look.

Instead, it put her in mind of his sharp suits: clean lines, understated and nothing bargain basement about it. She could see a few good pieces of furniture where the end of the hallway opened up into a living area. And a couple of interesting art reproductions that he'd probably spent more money on matting and framing than he had the prints.

But what amazed her most was the personal stuff. She really had to quit trying to pigeonhole him, she realized. Because the truth was she'd half expected all the surfaces to be bare and clean. And while they were the latter, they were far from the former.

Books were crammed into the gorgeous mission-style bookcase and atop it were a couple of candles, one of those Japanese-style trays with white sand, another candle and some interesting rocks. He even had a fairly healthy plant, for God's sake. Plus a couple of framed snapshots.

Her fingers nearly itched, so badly did she want to get her hands on those photos. But Jason came out of his bedroom, minus his jacket and gun, and crossed to the small kitchen as she was edging down the hall. With a sigh, she followed. She supposed it would be rude to just blow past him in order to paw through his stuff.

First opportunity, though, she intended to check it out.

Then Jason grinned as he began pulling the groceries out of her shopping bag and her intentions evaporated like so many tears in the desert. "Wow," she said, her heart skipping as she made herself at home, opening cupboards until she located his quartet of wineglasses. She grabbed two. "You oughtta do that more often."

"Huh?" He looked up from the container of Stroganoff that he'd opened and brought up to inhale deeply. And…good God. He looked like a guy who'd just got his. All he lacked was the cigarette.

Oh. Not a smart comparison. She was way too aware of him as it was and certainly didn't need that kind of image scorching through her thoughts. Forcing lightness into her voice, she said, "Smile. You should smile more often. You have a very nice one, but you hardly ever use it. I guess it's true what they say, though. The way to a man's heart really *is* through his stomach."

His smile grew wider, making her notice the long

creases bracketing his mouth. "You have no idea how true," he agreed. "Except for grilling the odd chunk of meat, I'm not much in the cooking department. Restaurants and takeout is more my speed, but it gets old. And, man, even cold this stuff smells good."

"Go ahead and put it in the micro and set it for—" eyeing his clunky counter model, she saw it was pretty ancient "—maybe two minutes to start, then give it a half turn and zap it for another two. After you start that, grab me a salad-size bowl and you can cut the baguette."

"Bossy little thing, aren't you?"

"I don't know about little, but bossy? You betcha. You can save yourself a heap of aggravation by simply letting me have my way from the get-go."

"Right." He snorted. "You keep clinging to that raft, sister."

She sighed and poured the greens she'd cut up earlier from her Ziploc bag into the bowl he handed her. "Fine, do it the hard way. You'll learn. They all do." She reached for the bottle of Asian Caesar dressing and unscrewed its top.

"All who? Men?"

She looked at him, saw the sudden intense glitter in his eyes and the walls seemed to take a giant step inward. The air suddenly grew warmer, thicker, moister. At the same time her mouth went dry. She cleared her throat. Attempted a careless shrug. "Men. Women. Children, dogs. The world in general, pal."

"O-kay. Nothing wrong with your ego." He handed her a glass of wine.

"What can I say? I was born to rule the universe. Just ask my folks. Dad claims he knew commune living wasn't going to work for me practically the minute I emerged from the womb." She took a sip of the crisp pinot grigio, resisting the urge to knock back half the goblet in one gulp.

"Good wine," he said.

"Yes, and you should take a moment to feel the pride of using a corkscrew to open it rather than breaking the top off against the nearest hard surface."

The corner of his mouth tugged up, that long crease forming once again in his stubble-darkened cheek. He turned back to slicing the bread.

When he finished, he removed two plates from a cupboard and handed them to her. "Want to set the table? Just toss the stuff on—I don't have any place mats or those napkin ring things. Or napkins, come to that."

"How will I get by?" Then she laughed and gave him a friendly hip bump. Another ill-conceived move as it turned out, given her instant awareness of the warmth and hardness of his body, but she forged ahead as if she hadn't registered that in her bones. "You don't think I eat like this every day, do you? Like you, I rely on a lot of takeout or slap together a sandwich or a salad. Occasionally I cook, but when I do, I make it count and cook up enough to last me the week. Either that or invite my friends or family over. I've got a container of Stroganoff in my fridge that matches the one I brought you."

"Hell, I'm not sharing mine then. Go home."

"Wanna make me? I don't have any of that pinot grigio back at the homestead, so I'm ready to rumble."

He took a long-legged step forward, his dark eyes locked on hers, and the air surrounding her threatened to catch fire. Her heart was trying to pound its way out of her chest when he suddenly went still. Looked down at the glass in his hand.

And tossed back the remainder of the wine in it. "Okay, fine," he said, running a knuckle over a drop clinging to his lower lip, his eyes still on her. "But I'm only sharing a little. So don't go eating like a trucker."

She couldn't unglue her tongue from the roof of her mouth to save her soul, but gave him what she really, really hoped was a careless look that said, *You don't affect me, big boy.*

She feared, however, what it probably looked like was closer to, *So, Sheik. Looking for a sex slave?*

Somehow, however, she survived the meal, finding her voice and dredging up innocuous subjects until the image of him clearing the table with one sweep of his arm and slamming her down for some set-the-world-afire sex finally loosened its grip on her imagination. She almost felt back to normal by the time they set their forks across their plates.

"Damn, that was good," he sighed, wadding up his paper towel and tossing it atop his cutlery. "I could eat that for the rest of my life."

Tickled, she flashed him a genuine smile. "I'm pretty sure it would wear thin if that was your sole diet."

"I suppose. But not for a long time." He pushed

back from the table and climbed to his feet. "You want some coffee?"

"No, thanks. Much to the disgust of my Norwegian grandpa I have to cut myself off by five or I toss and turn all night." Rising as well, she gathered their dishes and followed him into the small kitchen. Taking them to the sink, she turned on the hot water.

He looked up from the gold filter he'd balanced atop a coffee mug. "Hey, you don't have to do that. You cooked. I can do the dishes."

"I'll wash. You dry." She found the plug and squirted soap under the stream of hot water.

"Is this one of those 'just let you have your way from the get-go' moments you were blathering about?"

"I don't blather, bud. But feel free to categorize it as a control thing if you want. Me, I'd be more practical."

He actually laughed. "You've got a point, considering you're offering free labor. So, okay." He hitched a shoulder. "I can live with that." After hefting the stainless teakettle from the back burner as if to test for sufficient water, he replaced it and turned on the burner.

He rolled up his shirtsleeves and dried as she washed, then, when the kettle whistled, flipped the towel over his shoulder to make himself a single cup of coffee. Sipping it, he tackled the few dishes left in the drainer. Poppy turned away to wipe down the counters, resolutely ignoring his strong forearms with their feathering of black hair. Trying not to notice how long, how strong-looking his brown-skinned, white-nailed fingers were.

She wanted those hands on her.

Involuntarily she squeezed the sponge in her own hand and water dripped onto the stove top. *She wanted his hands on her. Had* wanted them on her from the first instant she'd clapped eyes on him. And what was she doing about it?

Nothing, that was what.

Okay, so the man had shot her down once already when he'd offered that lowering apology following the one and only kiss they'd shared.

Nevahtheless, declared a voice in her head that sounded suspiciously like Katharine Hepburn in *The African Queen,* and Poppy infused some steel into her backbone.

Was she not the woman who'd just told the good detective he should always let her have her way? She had never been shy about going after what she wanted, but for some reason she acted unnaturally missish around de Sanges. Maybe because he had the ability to command such strong reactions from her—stronger than she'd known with anyone else. And she could admit it: that shook her a little.

Okay, more than a little.

Still, she had a reputation to uphold. So it stopped right here, right now.

She wiped up the pool of water she'd created and set the sponge back in its dish. Drew a slow, calming breath to steady an unsteady heartbeat. And sauntered over to Jason, putting a little swivel action into her hips. She watched his dark eyes grow darker. And cop-wary.

He was smart to be wary. She might not be a burglar, armed and dangerous. But she'd made up her mind, she was loaded for bear and that made her dangerous in her own way.

Stopping in front of him, she stood just a touch closer than was polite but not so close that she risked having him back her up a step, since she didn't doubt for a second that he was just mean enough to do precisely that. She reached out to lay her fingertips on his chest in the most meager of touches. "Thank you," she said quietly.

Brows furrowing over the prominent thrust of his nose, he stepped back, causing her hand to drop to her side. "For what?"

"The way you went out of your way to help last night. I think you're probably a very good cop, Jason. I know we've had our differences when it comes to my kids and my programs, but you're better with them than you let on when we first got into this. You totally rocked with Darnell and Freddy. So this is for them. And for whatever it was you said to Danny G. and Henry the day Cory had her meltdown." And rising onto her toes, she pressed a soft kiss on his lips.

She almost jerked back, so electric was the sensation from what should have been a simple buss. And in execution it was simple: gentle, no tongue, no full-on press of bodies straining to get closer. But there was nothing simple about the way it made her feel.

Nothing simple at all.

But maybe that was merely her. Reluctantly—so much so that it hurt in places she hadn't even known she possessed—she withdrew her lips from his in glacially slow increments, lowering her heels back onto the floor.

And looked up at him with a level gaze, her eyebrows raised in question.

He stared back at her. Then muttered, *"Damn."* And quicker than a striking snake, he whipped out those long-fingered hands to wrap warmth around her nape and haul her back onto her toes. He rocked his mouth over hers.

This was not gentle. This was all fierce lips and teeth and tongue, with a heat that turned her mind to smoke. But one thing remained constant. He kissed her and she lost all reason.

Plunging her fingers into his hair, she plastered herself against him. He waltzed her backward until her back hit the fridge and something atop it made an off-center spinning sound. Pressing her against the appliance, he bracketed her in with his inflexible torso, long, strong arms and longer, stronger legs. The contrast of cool metal against her back and the heat that pumped through Jason's clothing to steam-press her front elicited a tiny moan from some atavistic stranger living inside her. Sucking at his tongue, she yanked his shirttails from the waistband of his slacks.

Making a feral sound, he ripped his mouth free, fisted the material of her delicate aqua sweater in his hands, growled, "Raise your arms," and pulled it off over her head when she complied. He leaned back from the waist and gave her a comprehensive inspection from her mussed hair to her well-kissed lips to her bare collarbone to her unlined, ivory lace bra. When his gaze reached that it stopped dead.

"Jesus." He traced the patterns of the lace and his

forefinger contrasted darkly against the bra's ivory and her own ivory flesh glowing through it. He circled her nipples, which Poppy could feel poking eagerly against the lace, in ever closer, tighter figure eights. Then he swept his thumb in to trap one and gave it a tug.

Sensation streaked south from the point of compression and Poppy sucked in a sharp breath. Her head fell back. "Gaaaawd," she moaned at the ceiling as she thrust her breasts in the direction of his fingers as they retreated, her breath hitching as they went back to circling both nipples. "The opposable thumb's a marvelous thing, isn't it?"

He caught the one he'd neglected before and gave it another hit-and-run pinch. Rising onto her toes, she hooked a leg around his hip and yanked, slapping their pelvises together.

He swore and abandoned finessing her breast in favor of sliding both hands up the backs of her thighs beneath her skirt until they reached the bare cheeks exposed by her new Rio thong panties. Filling his hands, he hiked her up and Poppy wrapped her other leg around him as well. His erection sparked a new uproar inside her as it slid against the soft furrow between her legs.

Breath gusting out, he shifted his grip and his fingertips brushed the small triangle that dwindled into a narrow band riding the division of her buttocks.

"You *are* wearing something under here," he said, tightening his fingers around her bottom, and Poppy almost aspirated her tongue as she felt her cheeks separate and his fingertips curl into the crease. Lowering his head, he kissed her again as his thumbs slid under the twin strings that connected the back triangle to its slightly larger counterpart in front.

Poppy wrapped her arms around his neck and kissed him back hungrily.

She nearly jumped a foot when someone suddenly pounded on the door and a man's voice called, "Jase! You home, boy? Saw your car out in the lot."

Jason dropped her back on her feet and stepped away so fast she staggered and had to slap her hands against the refrigerator at her back to keep from wheeling into the counter. He stared at her with dawning horror and, plowing a hand through his hair, opened his mouth.

She narrowed her eyes at him. "If you apologize again after kissing me like a starving man at the all-you-can-eat buffet, I will personally see to it you never father children."

"No, okay." Holding his hair off his forehead, he stared at her. "I'm not sorry," he said. "But I still shouldn't have started this."

"Which—hello—you didn't. I did."

"But I fell right in with the program, didn't I? And mixing it up with someone in one of my cases is against both my and the SPD's professional code of ethics."

Pushing away from the fridge, she glared up at him, her back erect and chin raised. "I'm not *in* a case of yours, pal."

"Okay, someone that I work with then, which is the same difference— *Shit!*" The man out in the hall knocked again. "I gotta get that." Looking unaccustomedly frazzled, he bent and grabbed her sweater off the floor. "Here. Get dressed," he said, tossing it to her. "We'll talk as soon as I get rid of—" His sentence faded away as he strode from the room.

"No, I don't think we will," she said to herself, pulling the garment on over her head, then smoothing her hair as best she could. She pulled in deep and even breaths and exhaled them slowly in an attempt to calm herself. This was the second time he'd gotten her all worked up only to slap her down.

Looking around, she located her purse and the empty Trader Joe's bag and snatched them up. She marched down the hallway and pushed past Jason and an older man, who stared at her openmouthed.

"Poppy, wait."

Dodging Jason's outstretched hand, she blew past the two men. Because she agreed with that old maxim. Fool me once, shame on you. Fool me twice, shame on me.

And damned if she intended to be a fool a third time.

CHAPTER TWELVE

I hate that this hurts so bad. It shouldn't. I don't know him well enough. But it does. It hurts like crazy.

"Damn, Jase, I'm sorry."

Yeah, you and me both. Jase reached out and gently closed the door Poppy had just barreled through, resisting the urge to bang his head against the jamb. Man, she hadn't even looked at him.

But he shrugged and led the way into his living room. "No need to be sorry," he said. "Ms. Calloway was just leaving anyway."

"O-kay." Murphy gave him a who-do-you-think-you're-kidding? look as he lowered himself onto the couch. "You might wanna let your woody go down and tuck your shirt back in your pants before you try floating that horseshit," he said dryly. "Not to mention that grab you made for your lady friend to keep her from hoofing it out the door."

"Yeah, whatever," he said curtly. "In any case, it's not a problem."

"Hell, yeah, it's a problem," Murphy said indignantly. "I screwed up your evening."

"No, you interrupted it. I did the screwing-up part all on my own." Then he straightened. "No, dammit, it *wasn't* a screwup. I just told her the truth. I shouldn't have let things get started with her that I have no intention of continuing."

"That you have no intention…?" Murph gave him an incredulous look. "Why the hell not? Are you blind, boy? Even with whisker rash all over her face, that was one seriously pretty young lady."

Oh, man, you don't know the half of it. A vision of Poppy's eyes all heavy-lidded with arousal and of her lips, so pink and moist and swollen from his kisses, exploded like a hand grenade in his mind. He thought of her breasts, round and ripe and pale beneath her sec-through lace bra, of their spiky little nipples and the wetness between her—

Sternly, he put the skids to those thoughts. Because it was pointless, wasn't it? "She's off-limits," he said flatly. "I'm working with her."

"Oh." Murphy deflated. "Well, shit. That's a cryin' shame. So which case is she a part of?"

"It's not exactly a case…"

Murph shot him the same level-eyed what-the-*hell*-are-you-talking-about stare he'd used to such good effect when Jase was a teen and the old man was on the job. "What exactly is it, then?"

Feeling defensive, as if he were somehow in the wrong, Jase said, "Look, she's the one who used her influence with the mayor to pull me into this bullshit cleanup project with the taggers." Only it turned out the project really wasn't all that bullshit after all.

Murphy sat upright. "The Babe? That was *the Babe?*"

He shrugged his agreement.

"Whataya know."

"It gets worse," he said morosely, ignoring the speculative look on his friend's face. "Turns out, she's a frickin' good girl." Which he figured pretty much said it all.

Apparently, however, he seriously overestimated Murphy's intelligence, because his longtime friend and mentor snapped, "So what?"

"So, get real, Murph. I'm freakin'-ass wrong for her."

"Because she's a *good girl?* What the hell does that even mean?"

"It means her tough-girl attitude is all for show. She's a goddamn marshmallow who undoubtedly plans to go the white-wedding-and-kids route one day. Not exactly the let's-screw-our-brains-out-then-walk-away-with-no-regrets-or-recriminations sort that I go for. Poppy's… shiny. She's all about the kids. And thanking people with home-cooked meals." But mentioning that made something inside him hurt, so he repudiated it by pretending he hadn't brought up the subject in the first place and that the event itself had never happened. "She does good works, for cri'sake."

"I thought you said she was a rich-girl user."

"I did." An unamused laugh escaped him. "Yet another instance where I was wrong, which should probably give you a clue. She grew up in a fricking hippie *commune* and from the looks of things lives paycheck to paycheck. Her entire place is about the size of my living room, has shit for security and she drives a rattletrap that shouldn't be allowed on the road."

"I'm not gonna ask how you know all this. But you like her," Murphy said shrewdly. "I'm guessing, too, that she must like you right back or I wouldn't have interrupted the two of you about to get busy. So why not just relax and see where it takes you?"

"Because she's a good girl!"

"And you're a good boy!" Murphy roared.

"I'm a fucking de Sanges. I quit being a good boy around the time I turned eight."

"That's just horseshit. You were heading down the wrong track when I met you, but you were still a good kid then and you're a good man now." Murph scrubbed his hands over his cheeks and jaw, then lowered them to grip his knees. "Jesus," he sighed irritably. "I have never met anyone who works as hard as you do to undercut his own happiness."

"I'm happy!"

"No, you're at best content—and only then if you've got a lot of work to keep you occupied."

"Don't tell me what I am, old man—I'm fuckin' ecstatic!"

Murph snorted. "My ass. But, okay, we're not going to fight about this, too. I'll concede you're happy, okay?"

"Damn straight," he muttered, his stomach in knots.

"Trust me, kid, you'd be a whole lot happier with a woman in your life. Take it from someone who knows— being alone ain't all that great. Maybe the Babe could

put some balance in that all-work-and-no-play ethic
you pass off as a lifestyle. And it seems to me a so-called
good girl might actually be a positive thing to have in
your corner, not the reverse. Didn't I hear you say something about homemade food? That alone would be
worth whatever it is you seem to see as the downside."

Jase brooded about the conversation long after the
old man had gone back to his apartment. Murphy simply
didn't understand. People who grew up with normal
childhoods rarely did.

Until he'd met Murph, he'd run wild with no one to
set him down and tell him in no uncertain terms that this,
that or the other action would not be tolerated. He'd
known deep down when he was doing wrong, of
course—he wasn't stupid—but no one had ever en-
forced a zero tolerance policy to reinforce that knowledge. And by the time Murph had come along and done
so, it had been too late. By then nothing could completely eradicate the first fourteen and a half years of bad
influence and worse genes.

Maybe if Murph had gotten his hands on him when
he was younger, things would have been different. What
was it the Jesuits said? Give me a child in his first seven
years and he'll be mine for life?

Well, Murphy hadn't appeared until Jase was going
on fifteen—so that made him the de Sanges' for life.
Nothing could eradicate his genetic makeup; *that*
required constant vigilance to keep it from wrecking his
world. He'd totally gotten it when his brother Joe had
claimed to be a single bar fight away from his third

strike—the one that would send him back to the pen for the rest of his natural-born days.

Because knowing the difference between right and wrong sure as hell didn't deliver Jase from temptation. He was tempted to cut corners every damn day, to do whatever was necessary and not worry if it was *right*. He was always one false step away from blowing everything he'd worked so hard to build. Enticement was a constant siren singing its addictive song in his ear. It would be so easy to give in to the shortcuts that would get him his convictions, to take the occasional diamond bauble from a store that was already burgled instead of supporting his lifestyle by careful saving and controlled spending. He heard his dad's and Pops's voices in his head sometimes saying, "Go ahead, boy—take it. Who's it gonna hurt?"

But that way lay disaster. So he'd long ago constructed a life built around rules. He'd erected a box for himself, and as long as he stayed within it, his life would stay on track. He had rules for work, rules for play—such as it was—and rules for the people he associated with.

Including women.

Hell, maybe especially women. Because one of the first rules he'd ever made for himself—and the one he still stuck to most rigidly—was his strict policy not to mess with the shiny girls.

He used to watch them back in middle and high school. They were the girls who came from families that he envisioned sitting around the dinner table every night, sharing a meal and discussing their expectations—the girls you just knew would go on to college and marry some decent schmoe and raise kids whom they could inoculate with the same values they'd learned from the cradle.

And for a short while he'd wanted that for himself. It had been a burning in his gut, a secret wish—a *futile* wish, and no one had to tell him so. He'd known it intuitively, which still hadn't stopped him from going after one or two of the good girls.

Okay, who was he kidding—it had been exactly two. It wasn't as if he'd forgotten either Hilary or Megan.

Because for a short while both relationships had actually worked out. He'd felt different when he was with those girls. Better about himself. He'd felt *great*.

But he'd learned the hard way that it didn't pay to get in too deep, to grow too dependent. Because the minute he had, he'd done something, said something to bring the relationship to a screeching halt. The genes had won out every time. With Hilary it had been beating the crap out of an ape of a boy he'd caught bullying some runty kids for their lunch money; with Megan it was boosting a car to take her for a ride. But the grand theft auto, which luckily no one had caught him doing, was probably just extra nails—he was pretty sure his frank talk about having relatives in the pen had already slammed the lid on the coffin of that relationship.

In any case, in both instances his getting comfortable and acting like the de Sanges he was had signaled the end with the objects of his affection. Much to their families' relief, he was sure. He'd finally wised up to the fact that good girls weren't looking for a guy like him to chuck a spanner into their organized worlds…and their parents sure as hell weren't looking for him to tarnish their sterling-silver daughters.

So, hey, big deal. If there was one thing he'd understood, even from a very young age, it was that disappointment happened. But life had ways of doling out compensations as well.

A big one, for him, had been the fact that he'd shot up and filled out when most boys were still standing eyeball-to-chin with their female counterparts. That's probably how he'd attracted Hilary and Megan in the first place. But the real bennie of his taller, fitter body had been the loose girls who'd come sniffing around, ready and willing to take his mind off what he couldn't have. All *they'd* wanted in return was to be shown a good time.

And he'd done his best to accommodate them. They'd taught him things beneath the bleachers and on musty gym mats stacked in the corners of school equipment rooms. He'd paid attention and he'd learned. Then he'd returned the favor in the backseat of his eleven-year-old Chevy Cavalier, which had been a piece of shit but his pride and joy all the same.

And thinking about it now, he realized it had been a while since he'd hooked up with the adult equivalent of those girls. Maybe it was time to go find himself a loose woman. Because Poppy's kisses, her touch, had made him feel wild and reckless and dangerous. That session up against his fridge had built to blow-the-top-of-his-head-off proportions and he'd wanted nothing more

than to step fast and furiously outside the box he'd constructed for himself with no concern for what the rules
were, let alone adhering to them.

But he was damned if he intended to revert to that ir-
responsible kid. No one had been hurt by tonight's
episode, but that could change in a red-hot hurry if he
continued to let Poppy cloud his brain. So his mind was
made up: it wouldn't happen again.

And as soon as he could free up a couple of hours
he planned to head for the nearest cop bar and pick
up a groupie.

No time like the present, boy.

"Jesus!" It wasn't bad enough he heard Pops's
voice encouraging him into illegal activities, now he
was hearing it in his fucking love life? That was just
what he needed.

Well, he wasn't about to be hustled into conforming
to anyone's schedule but his own. Hey, he *would* do it
tonight...except he'd be lousy company. And if he had
nothing else to offer, a woman at least deserved a guy
who would pay attention and show her a good time for
the short while she was with him.

So soon, for sure. God knew he needed to blow off
some of this steam.

Poppy's flushed, willing expression again flashed
through his consciousness, but he sternly pushed it
away. Not, however, before he felt a fierce tug of desire.

He set his jaw. Hell, yes; he'd say it again. He had to
blow off some steam.

Before he did something stupid.

"WHAT THE HECK are you doing?"

Poppy jerked, slopping a bit of the paint she'd been loading onto her roller brush over the edge of the pan. She scowled over at Jane, who stood in the doorway of the Wolcott mansion's upstairs bedroom. "What does it look like?" she snapped, turning back to wipe the edge of the pan with the wet cloth in her hand before shoving it in her lab coat pocket and rolling another swath of April Mist onto the wall. "Painting."

"Feeling a bit peckish, are we." It wasn't a question and, giving Poppy's lousy mood the zero attention only a close friend dared, Jane strolled into the room, her dark hair gleaming beneath the overhead lights. "You gonna snap my head off if I ask why? It's almost ten o'clock at night."

"I know what time it is!" Then, sighing, she set the roller back in the paint pan and turned back to her friend.

"I've let my obligations here slide, and this is the time I had available," she said with hard-won composure, firmly quashing her conscience when it urged her to expand her answer.

But that wasn't necessary. It wasn't as if she'd told a lie. Perhaps she hadn't told the entire truth, but she *was* behind in her obligations to the mansion's restoration project and she *had* been meaning to get over here to start painting. She had simply allowed herself to be sidetracked.

But she felt no burning urge to admit to a foible that she was *so* over.

"You know what Ava would say, don't you?" Jane

demanded, closing the distance separating them with long-legged strides.

"You'll have to narrow that down a little for me," she said dryly. "Ava would—and does—say a great many things."

"I'm talking about if she saw you painting this room all by yourself. She'd say that when Miss Agnes requested you be in charge of decorating the mansion she never intended for you to manually do every room yourself. And that we should hire someone."

The last of Poppy's ire collapsed, and she felt as if she were about to follow in its footsteps, suddenly so fatigued she could barely hold her head up. "That would be nice. Great, actually. I don't mind doing a portion of it myself, but I get worn to a nub just thinking about doing the entire thing." She perked up a little. "Hey, maybe I can hire my taggers. They've proven to be halfway decent house painters and surprisingly responsible. Plus, they could probably use the money." Well, Cory and Henry could, at least. She didn't know what Danny's story was, but she doubted a lack of money factored anywhere into it.

"Uh, I hate to pull a de Sanges, but I have to ask if it's safe to have those kids in the house."

"They're not thieves, Janie. But, okay, I understand your concerns—you don't know them and you've been burned by one thief already. Most of your collections are in the parlor, though, right? We could close the pocket door and keep that area locked." She sighed, weary to the bone.

"So now that we've got that settled, what's really

bothering you?" Jane asked out of the blue, and only fast reflexes kept Poppy from bobbling her roller.

Mind spinning, she bought herself a second by carefully placing the roller in its paint tray once again, aligning it just so. Ordinarily she wouldn't have a problem dumping news of tonight's events all over one of her best friends. And if what she felt was merely anger, she probably would have started doing precisely that the minute Jane cleared the door. Because anger was empowering. She never felt girlie or weak when she was pissed.

And God knew she was furious that Jason had kissed her— *more* than kissed her—twice now, only to reject her. But there was a healthy dose of hurt mixed into her fury and that wasn't something she longed to share. She knew Janie wouldn't think any less of her for it, but right or wrong, she felt diminished by her own weakness.

Diminished by *him*.

She knew better than to lie about it, however. The three of them had been friends forever and had a sixth sense about each other's emotional vulnerabilities. "I can't discuss it, Janie," she admitted quietly. "Not tonight, anyhow." When her friend gave an understanding nod, she said, "What are *you* doing here, anyway? It's just as late for you to be dropping by as it was for me."

"Dev and his brothers are having a poker party at our place tonight and I couldn't take all the scratching and spitting."

"Ew. Literally?"

"No, but trust me, it's almost as icky in the figurative sense. None of them is a smoker, yet they all insist on lighting up these nasty, skinny little cigars. And I swear every other word out of their mouths is *fuck*. They don't talk like that when they're smashing their thumbs with a hammer."

Poppy gave her a skeptical look and Jane smiled wryly. "Okay, we've all heard them when that happens. But their general speech isn't fifty-percent obscenities. Put a deck of cards in front of them, though, and…" She shrugged. "So I got out before I landed on Mama K.'s bad side by knocking together her baby boys' heads and went over to Ava's. We called you to join us, but you weren't home."

"No, I haven't been there since late this afternoon. It's been a busy day. Hell, it's been a busy week." She considered telling Jane about Darnell going missing yesterday and all that had happened during the attempt to find him. But Jason was too intertwined in the story and she was simply too exhausted to pick through the land mine it'd become if she attempted relating it without including him. "I'll tell you about it tomorrow." Hopefully she'd have figured out what to incorporate by then.

And what to leave out. She wondered what it would be like to have what Jane had—a sheer happiness that radiated from her even when she was bitching about the man responsible for it.

"So you went to Ava's. That still doesn't address what you're doing here."

"When I left her place I knew it was still too early for the Kavanagh boys to have wrapped up their game. So I thought I'd take the opportunity to finish cataloging one of the collections I didn't have time to complete the other day. So here I am. And speaking of Av, she's got a sudden wild hair to go dancing. You up for it one of these nights if we can find a time that works with all our schedules?"

"Right now it sounds too tiring to even think about. But I imagine I'll feel differently after I've had a good night's sleep. So, sure. Count me in."

"Meanwhile," Jane said, stripping off her little black cashmere sweater, "you have an extra paint smock? Find me one and I'll give you a hand."

"Aw, man." Poppy slung an arm around her friend's shoulders and gave her a hug. "I love you to pieces for offering. But the extra lab coats I've been supplying the kids are out in my car and you've got your own job to do. So go ahead and get to it. I think I'll finish this one wall, then call it a night and head for home." Turning her head, she pressed a kiss to Jane's temple. "But thank you. I'm still worn to the bone, but you've made me feel much, much better. And I love ya for it."

Jane hugged her back. "Then I guess my work here is done."

CHAPTER THIRTEEN

*He didn't show up today. I wonder if he's through.
With me. The kids. The whole damn project.*

USUALLY IT WAS a treat for Cory to have her mother come home during the day. Today, not so much.

Not when Mom had caught her making arrangements to babysit for Nina tomorrow night and had promptly dragged her into their apartment as if she were a six-year-old she'd discovered decorating the walls with crayons.

Sandy Capelli slammed the door behind them and tossed her Kmart purse on the secondhand couch. "You are not babysitting for that woman."

"I know," Cory said, deliberately misunderstanding. "Nina doesn't work tonight."

"I'm not talking about just tonight, Cory Kay, and you damn well know it. You are *never* to sit for her again. Nina Petrocova is not the kind of person I want influencing you."

Cory was used to bowing to her mother's wishes, but for once she didn't fret about adding to Sandy's burden. Because Mom was just plain wrong about this. "You don't know the first thing about Nina except that she dances at a strip club."

"And that's all I need to know!"

"No, it's not! You can't just blow off the fact she's going to school so she can make a better life for herself and Kai. Or that she's a really good mother."

"I've said my piece and the subject is closed. Tell Ms. I-take-my-clothes-off-for-a-living she'll need to find someone else."

"No!"

Her mother froze. Then, crossing her arms over her chest, she fixed an eagle eye on Cory, the exhaustion generally cloaking her like a worn coat nowhere in evidence. "Ex*cuse* me, young lady?"

Cory's heart pounded, but she said in a hard, flat voice, "I'm babysitting for Nina. I can use the money and it's nice having someone to actually *talk* to at night."

"No, you aren't. I forbid it."

"Screw that! How are you gonna stop me, Mom? It's not like you're ever home." Grabbing Daddy's jacket from one of the hooks by the entrance, she whipped it on and slammed out the front door, ignoring her mother's strident command to come back here this instant.

Her stomach churned as she raced down the stairs and pushed through the heavy metal door that led out onto the street. It wasn't fair, she fumed as she stomped down the sidewalk to the bus stop. Mom *wasn't* hardly ever around and Cory was tired of always being in the apartment alone. It was creepy at night, with its random creaks and groans and all the people who came and went. Mom would be smarter to worry about the guy in 308 who was dealing drugs instead of focusing on Nina, who was just trying to get along!

Besides, when did *she* get credit for being good? Ever since Daddy was killed she'd been bending over backward to spare Mom from her problems. Cory hadn't given her a single, solitary reason to doubt her judgment. Since moving here a few months ago she'd kept up at school, even though she was a big zit on the student body's ass. It wasn't only her who thought so, either—hardly anyone ever talked to her. Yet had she taken her worries to the streets to try to work them out with the one thing that usually made her feel better, her art? No, sir. Not since the night she'd had the run-in with the henchman whose name, she'd learned by asking a few cautious questions, was Bruno Arturo.

Bruno. She shivered. The name reminded her of that bully Bluto from the old Popeye cartoons, so it seemed fitting. He was definitely someone big and mean and— even without the gun—not a man she ever wanted to come across again.

All the same, being a goody two-shoes had, like, zero rewards. So maybe she oughtta chance going out to paint a wall with one of the graphic 'toons she'd been experimenting with in her sketch pad. If she was careful, kept her eyes peeled and just went the once, returning to the streets somewhere other than the U district might be okay. And it would probably be a good idea to hang around with someone instead of going it alone. Couldn't hurt, anyhow.

She wondered what Danny G. was doing tonight.

And if she'd have the nerve to invite him to go along with her.

It turned out he was just crossing the Ace parking lot to Mr. Harvey's shop next door when she arrived. In fact, everyone had beat her to the corner lot except Detective de Sanges.

"I thought we were all done with this crap," Henry was grousing as she walked up, his attention glued on Ms. C. "We painted over everything I...er, that is, the stuff that was tagged, didn't we? So how come we hadda come back here today?"

Cory would never admit this to a soul, but she was going to miss these sessions.

Kinda.

Sorta.

Well, it wasn't like they were *important* to her or anything. She just enjoyed spending time with Danny G., who, aside from being studalicious cute, was something of a mystery—so therefore intriguing beyond belief. Ms. Calloway...well, Ms. C. was over-the-top dap, and Henry wasn't nearly the pain in the butt she'd thought he was at first. Well, he could be, for sure. But she'd come to understand from little things he'd let drop that his father was a serious drunk. She'd lost Daddy way too soon, and she was still angry and mystified and in a world of hurt over it. But at least she'd been lucky enough to have the father she'd had for almost thirteen years.

Even Detective de Sanges wasn't a complete jerkaholic.

"I *said*," Henry said louder, "I thought we were—"

Rising to her feet from where she'd been stooped to pull stuff out of the big tote she never seemed to leave home without, Ms. C. turned and leveled a gaze on him. Henry shut up, as they'd all learned to do when she gave them that look.

"Were you speaking to me, Mr. Close?" she inquired mildly. "I assumed you were not when I failed to hear you address me by name." She closed the distance to where the three of them stood clustered together. Stopping first in front of Danny, then Henry, then Cory, Ms. Calloway handed each of them an Aquabee Co-Mo sketch pad—the big size!—along with a tin of a dozen Faber-Castell color pencils.

Cory stared down at the latter in awe. She'd never owned actual artist's pencils before. She'd always made do with the drugstore variety of colored pencils. And their leads were generally too soft for any kind of precision work.

"I was intending to wait for Detective de Sanges to arrive before we had our little ceremony, but he appears to be held up somewhere," Ms. Calloway said and a flush of pink inexplicably washed across her cheeks. It apparently had nothing to do with the detective, however, because she promptly waved her statement aside with an airy sweep of her hand and added, "But you know what they say—you snooze, you lose. So his loss."

Then she went all solemn, as if this were some big momentous moment. "I'm very proud of you three. You've been marvelous. You showed up where and when you were asked to show up and did an exemplary job of cleaning up the tagging." A wry smile tugged up one corner of her mouth. "With darn near the bare minimum of complaints."

She studied each of them individually, taking her time with Danny G. before she moved on to Cory, and with her before moving on to Henry. Cory didn't know about the guys, but during the moment that Ms. C.'s warm, probing regard was directed solely at her, she felt it light up places inside of her she hadn't even known were in shadow. In that instant, she felt cocooned—soothed and relieved in some unfathomable way of the ragged feeling that had been lodged in her stomach since her fight with her mother.

She felt…special.

Then Ms. C. grinned, and things went back to normal. "So phase one of your ordeal is over."

"Say what?" Henry bristled with indignation. "Whatchu mean, phase one? We're *done* here, right?"

"Not quite. You've completed the work part. Now it's time to move on to the fun part."

"Which is where you cut us loose?"

"No, Mr. Close. Which is where I give you the opportunity to produce a piece of art the entire neighborhood can enjoy. Art that will be around for years to come." She gave a little shrug. "Well, if some tagger doesn't come along and scribble over it, that is."

She gave a nod to the sketch pads and pencils she'd given them. "That's where your supplies come in. I'd like you to think about what you'd like to paint on the side of Mr. Harvey's building." She tipped her head toward the still-pristine wall they had painted a couple of weeks ago. "Put some thought into it. Work up some proposals. It can be anything."

"Yeah, right," Henry scoffed. "S'long as it's boring old-people art, you mean."

"No, I truly mean anything. Well, anything legal at any rate. No porn and no severed, gore-and-blood dripping body parts. But it doesn't have to be representative art. It can be, if you want. But it could also be graphic, mural, storyboard or graffiti-based. Or something else that I haven't touched on. The possibilities are only as limited as your imaginations, so show me some examples of what floats your boat. If you're blocked, check out some of the public art in the various neighborhoods."

"Like what?"

Henry's tone was sulky but Ms. Calloway gave him a gentle smile. "Well, I could send you to West Seattle, to either the Alaska or Morgan Street junctions. They've got several murals in their business districts. But I bet you'd like Piece of Mind in Fremont better. It has totems and monsters and dudes with dreads and leans toward graffiti in its execution and bright colors."

"When were you planning on us doing this?" Danny asked coolly, and Cory noticed that although he asked as if he didn't give a big fat rip, the same spark of excitement she felt catching fire in herself burned deep in his eyes.

Ms. C. dug through the tote she'd dragged over with her and consulted her day planner. "How about next Saturday? That'll give you almost a week to research ideas and work something up." When they didn't respond, she looked up at them. "That actually wasn't a rhetorical question—I'm giving you a choice this time. So how about it? Does that sound agreeable?"

Henry hitched his shoulder and scowled, but both she and Danny G. nodded. Not with so much enthusiasm that they'd look like a couple of geeks, of course. They merely tipped their chins in cool agreement.

And Ms. Calloway laughed. "Excellent. Let's meet at the Fremont Coffee Shop at eight."

"In the *morning?*" Henry looked aghast.

"Yes. That way if we find a direction we'd like to take, we can dive right in. C'mon, Henry." It was the first time since beginning this project that she'd addressed any of them by their given names. "Let's produce some art. I'll even spring for muffins and the drink of your choice."

Once everyone agreed, Ms. C. excused herself, telling them she had to run because of a date with a black or white board or something—Cory didn't quite get it. Henry barely waited for Poppy to stride away before he, too, took off. Cory gazed at Danny.

And swallowed dryly, then tried to take a calming breath.

Tried to think of a way to ask him if maybe…

Possibly…

Perhaps…

"Whataya say we go over to Fremont and see that Piece of Mind place Ms. C. was talking about?" Danny asked while she was still running all the pros and cons through her mind.

"Hey, I was just thinking the same thing!" she said—

then could have smacked herself. She probably sounded like a dorkana, all wriggly with puppy eagerness and practically piddling on his shoes. "Uh, I wonder what bus we should take?"

"Number none." He shot her a lopsided smile. "C'mon. I've got a ride."

She walked by his side, thinking if this went okay, maybe she'd broach the idea of hitting the streets later on to practice a little graffiti. Then she wondered what kind of car he drove. If he was like most kids their age, it was probably some secondhand beater. Not that she'd sneer at that if it was.

Like people in glass shoes could afford to kick rocks! She probably couldn't even aspire to owning the oldest wreck on the road—something even worse than Ms. C.'s heap of glued-together scrap metal—until she was really old. Like twenty-five or thirty or thereabouts.

When Danny G. stopped in front of a brand-new-looking, shiny pearlescent tobacco-colored SUV, however, her jaw sagged. "Holy crapoli, *that's* your ride?"

He grinned at her.

"It's not stolen, is it? 'Cuz I'm not getting in any stolen car."

He twirled a set of keys beneath her nose. "It's not stolen. It's mine." He beeped the doors open and leaned in the driver's side.

His dad's, more like. Or maybe his mother's. But, man, she couldn't even imagine her mom driving something this nice, let alone letting Cory borrow it. She stared at the long stretch of Danny's back as he rummaged through one of those thingamajigs you Velcroed to the sun visor.

He backed out of his car and handed her a small, flat, black folder. She shot him a puzzled glance before turning her attention to it. Flipping it open, she saw a pale green Department of Licensing certificate and, noting that it was a car registration, focused in to read the entire thing.

Jeeeeez. It was made out to Daniel Gardo and she studied the pertinent parts in awe yet again before slapping the folder closed and handing it back to him.

"This is, like, brand-new. How did you get a brand-new car?" An awful thought occurred to her and she narrowed her eyes at him. "You don't deal drugs, do you?"

"For crap's sake, Cory," he snapped. "First you accuse me of stealing the car and now I'm a *dealer?*"

Her crushin'-on-Danny self demanded she scramble to take back the question, or at least to laugh it off—*anything* so he wouldn't be mad at her and retract the invitation. But she stiffened her spine. She would not *talk* to—let alone get involved with—a gang member or a drug dealer, and she tipped her chin up at him. "You didn't answer the question, Gardo."

"Yeah, because it was stupid. I'm not a goddamn drug dealer." He scowled at her.

Good enough, good enough, good enough, her inner Danny groupie moaned. He'd answered the freakin' question. At least the second part of it. But something inside of her that no longer accepted anything at face value made her cross her arms over her chest and tap her foot.

He rammed his fingers through his hair and stared at

her. Then he said in a low, sullen voice, "My mom's husband is loaded, okay?"

"Okay." She went around to the passenger side and climbed in, looking over at him when he got in the driver's side. "You say that like it's a bad thing. I wish my mom was loaded."

But that reminded her of their fight and equal parts anger and guilt, which she'd forgotten for a while, immediately started duking it out in her stomach.

No. Determinedly she pushed them away. She refused to feel guilty today. *She* wasn't the one in the wrong this time. Mom was.

"There are worse things than not having money," Danny G. said, and his tone was quiet, fervent.

But Cory snorted. "Spoken like someone who's probably always had plenty."

"Yeah, well, you know what they say," he muttered darkly. "Money doesn't always buy happiness."

She swiveled as much as her seat belt would allow to look at him. And saw something she couldn't quite define in his expression. But he looked sad, even if he was projecting an I-don't-give-a-damn nonchalance. "Well, neither does being poor," she said quietly. "My mom and I had a fight today."

"Yeah?" A little of the tension eased from his shoulders. "Over what?"

She told him about it as they drove to the Fremont district, growing passionate about her mom's blatant unfairness all over again.

"She was wrong," he said when she concluded and Cory felt a rush of warmth that he understood.

"Still," he added.

"There's a *still?*" She bristled. "Still what?"

"Nothing." But he immediately pulled himself higher in the driver's seat and shot her a look that held an edge of hostility. "No, dammit, it's not nothing. At least *your* mother sounds like she cares. Like she wants to protect you."

Well…sure. But that wasn't the point. The point was—

She blinked, realizing what he was inferring. "Doesn't yours?"

A bark of humorless laughter escaped him. "Mom cares about keeping her cushy berth with her rich new husband. I come in a poor second. Or maybe third, after her Tuesday, Thursday and Saturday afternoon masseuse. She really likes those massages."

"She has a masseuse?" Cory slapped her own cheek, knowing that was hardly the important issue. "I'm sorry," she said. "I've just never known anyone with one of those." She studied Danny's profile. "How long's she been married to your stepfather?"

"Don't call him that," he snapped. "Richie the Rich is no kind of father, step or otherwise. They've been married about six months."

"They're probably still in the—whatchamacallit— the honeymoon stage. But I'm sure she loves you," she added, because she truly couldn't envision a mother who wouldn't love her kid.

"Are you?" He glanced over at her, then turned his

attention back to the road, a small, bitter smile twisting the corner of his mouth. "Yes, I'm sure you're right."

But she felt him withdraw and reached out to touch his arm as he pulled up in front of the spectacularly painted building they'd come to see. "I'm sorry," she said again, rubbing the knotted muscle beneath her fingers. "I'm obviously talking out my butt, since I've never even met your mom."

For a moment he merely gazed at her as if she bewildered him. Then the curtains came down in his eyes. "Forget about it, okay?" Averting his gaze, he looked past her to stare out the side window. "Look at this place! We gotta check this out."

The narrow lot alongside the building was full, so he took his foot off the brake and drove on. Finding a parking spot a block and a half away a few moments later, he wheeled into it.

Feeling as if she'd somehow failed him, she climbed out of the truck and followed him back to the store or whatever it was. In silence they looked at the graffiti-like mural that covered two sides of its building.

The more Cory studied it, the more enthusiastic she felt. "This. Is. *So.* Dap! Could we do something like this, you think?"

"I don't know. Fremont is a lot more laid-back than the neighborhood we're doing. I don't think they'd go for a straight graffiti mural, no matter what Ms. C. says."

"Maybe not like the front part," she agreed. "But this side, with the mountains and totem and things—I bet we could get away with adding in some graffiti elements if we keep most of it Pacific Northwest–themed. We could do waves and fish and—"

"Incorporate subliminal stuff," he added, his eyes lighting up. "Subversive stuff within the bigger landscapes, you know?"

"Tiny fairies," she breathed.

He gave her a wry look. "I was thinking more like little demons and shit."

"Well, you do your little demons—I'll do my fairies."

They looked at each other. Laughed out loud. And exchanged high fives.

"Let's both draw up something to show Ms. C. with the general PNW theme," Danny said. "This could maybe work."

"Yeah." Excitement coursed through her. "It really could."

She glanced over at a black SUV that was cruising at a snail's pace down the other side of Fremont Avenue. Even as she noticed it, the dark tinted driver's-side window slowly lowered. "Hey, kids!" the man inside leaned out to say.

Oh, shit, oh, shit. Her heart thundered and her legs momentarily froze. She knew that face; it had inhabited her nightmares since that night in the U district. She gripped Danny G.'s arm. "We gotta go," she said quietly.

"Huh?" He gave her a puzzled look.

"Yo, you two!" Bruno Arturo called impatiently. "I'm talking to you. C'mere!"

Adrenaline hit like an electric prod and Cory transferred her grip to Danny's hand. "Move!" she snapped.

"You don't want to have a run-in with that guy." She gave his hand a hard jerk. "Danny, come on!"

She could only imagine what her expression reflected. Whatever was on her face, Danny took one good hard look and without exchanging another word, they both took off at top speed in the opposite direction from that in which Arturo's car was pointed.

Weaving their way through the streets in a circuitous route, they made their way back to Danny's car. When he'd driven them out of the district via the Fremont bridge, he glanced over at her. "Man, you can run. Wanna tell me what the hell that was all about?"

Oh, she did. She really wanted to unload her fear, to just dump it all at his feet.

And yet...

It wasn't safe. Not for her, not for him. "I'm sorry," she said. "So sorry I got you involved. Sorry I can't talk about it."

He pulled his attention away from the rearview mirror to look at her again. Then he shrugged.

"When you change your mind, you know where I am."

CHAPTER FOURTEEN

Twist-your-guts teen pathos and Jason. It was a freaking four-star day. Okay, so it actually turned out pretty good. But why does everything have to be so complicated?

SONOFABITCH! Bruno drove the streets of Fremont for another twenty minutes. But the two kids had vanished.

He kept shaking his head as if he'd taken a sucker punch to the temple. The boy he'd been hunting was a *she?* Who the hell would have guessed the kid was a mofo'n *girl?*

Hell, he'd only rolled down the window to talk to her and the other kid in the first place because they'd been gawking at that bullshit graffiti building like it was the holy-fuckin'-grail or something. So he'd thought, *Hey, good, maybe they know some of the local taggers and graffiti freaks.* The fact that he'd been addressing the very person he'd been rousting every artsy-fartsy street kid he could find over, breaking a finger or two on the ones he'd thought were withholding information on the boy—girl!—never once occurred to him.

There was no mistaking the way that kid ran, though.

She had a way of picking up her knees and streaking from zero to sixty like some hopped-up horse out of the gate at Emerald Downs. The boy with her'd had longer legs, a longer reach and more muscle mass. Yet he'd barely kept up when she'd taken off, never mind come anywhere near passing her to take the lead.

Giving up the search, Bruno wheeled out of the neighborhood and headed back to his own part of town. He didn't know what the hell to do now. It shouldn't matter that she was a girl—she was still the witness who could sink him with a single misplaced sentence.

Yet…

It did. He would rip the johnson offa anyone with the stones to actually say so to his face, but it mattered. He had a niece about that girl's age, and now that he knew his witness's gender, he could hardly believe he hadn't cottoned to the fact sooner. Yes, the all-arms-and-legs gawkiness that he'd ascribed to youth was a characteristic that could be attributed strictly to a tender age— no doubt about it. But now that he knew what the hell he was looking at, recognition of the coltish stage little girls went through as they changed into young women nearly blinded him.

Shit.

Well, he'd hunt the kid down. Dig up as much information as he could.

Then he'd figure out what the hell to do about her.

THE FOLLOWING WEEK, Jase left the Harborview trauma center, where he'd been checking on the man who'd been shot in the jewelry-store robbery in the U district. The victim was still in a coma, and the doctors weren't seeing imminent signs of recovery. Not exactly the news with which Jase had hoped to start his Saturday morning.

Arriving at his SUV, he climbed in and consulted his notes for a second before putting the vehicle in gear and pulling out into the street. He was cruising down Yesler moments later when he saw an informant he'd been trying to track down for the past several days. He swerved his CR-V over to the curb half a block from where the mope was shuffling down the street.

He had no sooner shoved the car into Park and was opening the door to go grab his snitch for a talk, however, when his cell phone rang.

What was this, some cosmic conspiracy trying to prevent him from hooking up with this guy? Because this was the third time this week that something had come along to interfere.

He glanced down at the phone's screen. Seeing Poppy's name, he scowled at the way his pulse immediately went ape shit.

But he hadn't spent a lifetime staying on top of his emotions for nothing. Wresting back control, lowering his heart rate by sheer willpower, he hit the talk button. Barked, "What?"

"Jason?" she said, her voice a stroke that went straight to his—

Uh-uh. No, sir. Straightening in his seat, he grasped the fabric near the crotch of his slacks and adjusted it with a yank. What was he—seventeen? Dammit, he had to get out, go to a bar, one of these nights. He didn't know why he kept putting it off. It had been way too long since he'd been with a woman.

Other than her, that is. And since *that* hadn't had a real satisfactory conclusion— "What do you want?"

"A civil greeting would be a start," she murmured. "Or, barring that, you keeping your word. But I guess avoiding me these days takes up all your time."

She had that right. Not the keeping-his-word part— he'd more than honored his part of a bargain he'd been coerced into making in the first place. But avoiding her? Oh, yeah. "This is probably gonna come as a shock to you, sweetheart, but I've got this job that the taxpayers actually expect me to perform to justify the paycheck the city cuts me every other Friday."

"You've got a commitment to these kids, too," she snapped. Then her tone softened. "Sorry. I'm sorry." She sighed. "Believe it or not, I didn't call to bust your chops. If you really don't want to be part of the project any longer, I'm through fighting you over it. But Henry didn't show up this morning and I'm worried."

"He probably got a better offer than slapping paint on buildings for you." But Jase shifted uneasily. Because all three of those kids had stuck with their obligation a helluva lot better than he had ever expected. And Henry's old man sounded like a piece of work. He blew out a breath. "All right. Give me his address. I'll swing by his place."

"*Thank* you. This was the day we were going to start doing the fun part. I can't imagine him missing it, even if he did pretend it was a great big pain in his behind."

"Yeah, yeah." But he shook his head at her unrelenting faith in the teens she taught. "The address?"

She rattled it off, and he wrote it in his notebook, along with the name and location of the coffee shop where she was waiting with Danny and Cory. "When I know something, you'll know something," he said curtly and snapped his phone shut.

His informant was no longer in sight and it turned out Henry didn't live that far away, so within ten minutes Jase was knocking on the youth's tenement door. He didn't really expect an answer and was surprised when Henry himself pulled open the door.

The kid looked equally surprised to see him. "Shit," he muttered in disgust. "It's you."

"You were expecting the blonde herself? Ms. C. tells me you stood her up."

"So she sent out the big dog to haul me in? I thought you didn't like us anymore—we ain't seen you around much. Whatza matter, Ms. C. wouldn't let you into her undies?"

"Don't make me hurt you, kid." He wished the words back the minute he saw Henry wince and gentled his tone. "Everything okay with you?"

The boy's chin shot up. "Macadoodledandy."

"Then let's go. They're waiting for you at the Fremont Coffee Shop."

Henry's narrow shoulders hunched in. "I ain't going."

"Why not?" He studied the boy for bruises but didn't see any. Not that that meant a helluva lot—Henry was covered from neck to ankle in baggy black clothing.

"I don't wanna, all right?"

"Ms. Calloway says this is the fun part."

He scowled. "I did what I was supposed to do. I painted all those fucking walls to cover the tagging. I'm done."

"There's just one problem with that," Jase said softly, because he could see that the boy was genuinely upset. "Ms. C. said to fetch you. So fetch you I gotta do."

"I can't draw, okay?" Henry yelled.

He blinked. "What?"

"She says this is s'pose to be the fun part and let's do some art, but I'm not like Danny G. and Cory. I can't draw." He snatched up a brand-new-looking sketch pad that had been under a tin of colored pencils and thrust it out at Jase. "She gave us each one of these and said to work up some ideas for the wall. But I can't." He whipped the cover back, showing Jason the ragged edges where page after page had been ripped out. "I got ideas, but I can't draw 'em!"

And it was eating him up, Jase saw. He rubbed his temples. "Okay, let me think about this." Doing so, he came to the only possible conclusion. "I have to call her."

"No!"

"It's better to tell her straight up what's going on, Henry. She'll handle that a helluva lot better than you just blowing her off. You agree that she's a pretty nice woman, right?"

"*Yeah,*" he said fervently.

"Then you gotta trust her. It'll break her heart if you up and disappear on her. She was really worried about you, you know. That's why she called me. Plus, you think she'll just give up on you? The woman is a pit bull—once she gets something in her head she doesn't let loose until she has what she wants. So let her help us figure this out. Because, trust me, she won't just say 'oh, well' and walk away. She'll hound you till your ears bleed. And you might as well save yourself that, because in the end, kid, you *will* rejoin the fold."

"Fine," Henry muttered, hitching a shoulder as if it didn't matter to him one way or the other. But he turned aside to swipe the heel of his hand over his cheeks.

Pretending he didn't see the tears the boy was mopping up, Jase walked to the far side of the small living room and called Poppy.

She exclaimed in distress after he explained the situation to her and said in a low, fierce voice, "You tell that child we can fix that. I can't turn him into Rembrandt — or even Gary Larson—overnight. But I can walk him through some basics and there are other options for this project besides the actual drawing. I'll prep Cory and Danny. You just get him down here."

Pocketing his phone, he turned back to Henry. "She said everything's going to be all right. Grab your stuff. Apparently Ms. C.'s got a muffin with your name all over it."

Prepping or no prepping, he was impressed with the other two teenagers when he and Henry arrived at the café a short while later. They didn't jump all over the kid for holding things up the way teens could do, but instead simply moved over to make room for him at the table.

Then he recalled the boys' horror the day Cory had her meltdown. They'd asked him, of all people, how they should act around her and had actually followed his suggestion that they refrain from commenting on it unless she brought it up first.

Apparently these kids had each other's backs.

"Check this out," Cory said and flipped open her sketchbook with one hand as she reached for Danny's with the other. The two started pitching their Northwest-themed graffiti idea so fast and furiously, half the time they both talked at once.

"So?" Cory demanded when they finally stopped to draw a breath. "Brilliant, right?"

Henry stuffed an oversize bite of muffin into his mouth, then buried his nose in the glass of orange juice Poppy had placed in front of him. But if he hoped to avoid the conversation, he didn't know teenaged girls.

Or any woman, for that matter, Jase thought wryly.

"So?" she insisted, giving him a poke. "This is where you're supposed to say, 'Brilliant, Cory.'"

"What do you care what I think?" he muttered. "Looks to me like you and Danny got it all figured out and it's not like I got sumthin' to contribute. I don't even know how to draw." His thin shoulders hunched up under his ears.

"You know how to color, though, right?" Danny said easily.

Henry nodded slowly, losing a fraction of the tightness gripping his narrow frame.

"This is going to be the biggest project any of us have ever done," the older teen said.

"No kidding," Cory agreed.

"And it's going to take all of us. So how about Cory

and me and Ms. C. do the drawing and you and Detective de S. help with coloring it in?"

Wait a minute. Jase mentally jerked upright. How did *he* get to be part of this equation?

Danny stole a pinch off Henry's muffin and popped it in his mouth. "And were you paying attention to the part where we're gonna hide trolls and stuff inside the bigger picture?"

"I'm gonna do fairies," Cory interjected.

Danny gave Henry a look. "You see what I'm dealing with here, bro? We need more man-stuff to counterbalance her girlie influence."

"Hey!" she protested.

Henry sat a little taller in his chair. "Lizards," he said emphatically and turned the sketchbooks around to study the drawings more closely. "Lizards are cool and come in all shapes and sizes, from those little rock ones to Komodo dragons."

"Reptiles." Cory sighed. "Wonderful. You're such a guy." But her lips curved up.

He ducked his head again, but this time Jase watched him hide a little smile of his own. "Lizards are cool," the boy said to the preliminary drawings in front of him. "They're like the last of the prehistorics. And we could slip them into all kinds of places. Like here," he said, pointing. "Or maybe here or here."

Poppy shoved her dishes away and said, "Open up your sketchbook, Henry. I want to show you something. Cory, if you can spare a page or two, I'd like to use yours for a minute."

The kids did as she asked and she hitched her chair closer to Henry's. She dug two pencils from out of her massive tote and handed one to Henry. "Do what I do," she instructed and drew a long oval in the middle of the page.

He drew a similar one on his pad. She added another, smaller oval toward the top of the first one, then attached a long, skinny triangle to the larger oval's bottom curve.

He followed suit and after several more minutes of adding a line here, refining or erasing an existing section there, a lizard began taking shape on both pages. Henry gawked. Then he looked up at Poppy, his face alight. "I drew that!"

"Yes, you did," she agreed. "I can walk you through a couple of other types of lizard as well, and maybe a snake or two. The trick when you're beginning is to do them a layer at a time."

He tore his glance away from the reptile he'd drawn to look at her.

As if answering a verbalized question she said in her easy way, "Look, if we start over from the beginning and use two different colors of lead, you can see both how we begin with the core shapes and how we refine the design from there. It won't turn you into an artist overnight, and you'll have to practice at home from the sketches we work on today. But it's a start, huh?"

"Yeah." He stared down at the lizard he'd drawn. Cleared his throat. "Yeah."

Jase leaned over to study the sketches with a critical eye, surprised to see that while Henry's lacked some of the realism of Poppy's, it was pretty damn proficient for a kid who couldn't draw.

And he heard the mental snap of a trap springing closed.

He had been avoiding looking at her as much as possible ever since he and the kid had arrived at the busy coffee shop, but he glanced at her now.

And swore under his breath.

She was so freaking…extraordinary. Pretty, sure. Nice—he'd already established that. One hell of a teacher, without a doubt.

And he was in the mother of all fixes.

Because he found himself saddled with a stupid-ass investment in this project, an investment he'd neither sought nor wanted. Found himself caring more than was smart about what became of these kids. He wanted to know why, while she seemed totally pumped about this project, Cory kept shooting nervous glances at the café door. How Henry would do with a few basic art lessons under his belt. What the exceedingly well-spoken Danny's story was.

So, sure, he could cut back on how often he participated in the upcoming art-on-the-side-of-the-wall venture. He could try to keep things to a minimum.

But there was no way in hell he was going to be able to just walk away from it entirely.

It was all Poppy's fault. She was like a damn Venus flytrap, and he was the poor sucker who'd made the mistake of leaning too close to check it out.

Only to have her—all big, soft eyes and satin skin—suck him in and take him prisoner so fast he barely knew what had hit him.

CHAPTER FIFTEEN

Man, when it rains, it fricking pours, doesn't it?

JASE PUSHED through the padded fake-leather door of Sessions, currently the hottest blues bar and dance club in Seattle's Columbia City neighborhood. The hot riffs of a guitar, combined with a wailing harmonica and sax, hit him like a one-two punch to the solar plexus. He felt surrounded in a sound so visceral it tugged at his senses. He wasn't much for dancing, but the music had a driving rhythm that made it hard *not* to move.

The joint looked like a dive, housed as it was in a squat no-frills building with a décor that ran to scarred wooden tables and neon signs advertising alcoholic beverages. He imagined that the owners probably had no burning need to make the place attractive in order to haul in the crowds since it consistently got the best bands in the city. But the bar had one big, fat negative in his book, and that was its location. Columbia City was no place for an unescorted woman to be running around after dark.

And Henry had told him late this afternoon that Poppy was coming here tonight with her girlfriends.

He couldn't freaking believe it. He'd thought she was smarter than that. Dammit, it was Friday night and he had plans of his own—he was supposed to meet Hohn and a couple other detectives at a cop bar up north at eleven, which was just a little over an hour away. But here he was, compelled to make a ten-mile trip so he could impart a few security tips to the Babe and her friends. The minute he made sure there was a plan in the works for getting them safely home when they decided to hit the road, however, he was out of here. So the quicker he found them, the better.

The only problem was, he didn't see them. He circled the room until he ended up back near the bar without catching so much as a glimpse.

Of course half the bar appeared to be on the dance floor—it was a writhing mass of people dancing with various degrees of talent. As usual, more women than men crowded the area, since females these days no longer sat around waiting for men to ask them to dance, but rather hit the floor on their own schedule. He could hardly say that he blamed them—women who liked to dance must outnumber the men who did four to one.

He saw Poppy's friend Ava first. She was hard to miss. It wasn't only the sleek red hair or her spectacular retro body. And just when the hell *had* it become more rule than exception for so many of today's females to be built like concentration camp survivors, anyway? Not that her attributes didn't contribute to her noticeability, of course. But mostly, the woman could *dance*. Her arms flowed and her curvaceous hips swiveled and she simply moved as if she were an integral part of the music.

Then the couple dancing next to her moved together in some sort of dirty dance move and he saw Poppy.

Jesus. He backed up until his butt bumped against a stool at the bar. Wrenching his attention away from her, he saw that the seat was unoccupied, which was lucky since he sure as hell hadn't been paying attention. Hitching a hip onto it, he braced one foot on the floor and hooked the other over the stool's lower rung. His gaze went straight back to Poppy.

He was accustomed to seeing her in one of her midcalf, flowing skirts or the occasional pair of jeans or sweats. But she'd dressed to kill tonight, wearing a short, tight bronze-colored dress and skyscraper fuck-me shoes, with stiletto thin heels, open toes and skinny little straps that circled her ankles. Her hair looked somehow even curlier than usual and she was wearing more makeup than he'd ever seen on her, her eyes lined in smoky black and her lips painted a gleaming near-red. Guys all over the bar were checking her out.

He didn't like it.

Not that it was any of his goddamn business, but ask him if he cared. She had no business looking like that in a joint like this without someone packing a 9 mm, minimum, to stand guard. You asked him—hell, asked *any* cop—she should be wearing something more sensible, say one of those granny dresses. Or, hey, maybe a nice, loose burka.

"Get you something to drink?"

Tearing his gaze away once more, he glanced over his shoulder at the bartender. "Give me a glass of whatever you got on draft."

"You got it."

He turned his attention back to the dance floor. Poppy had disappeared from view, but now that he knew her general location on the floor, it was easy enough to find her again. And once he had, he settled back to sip the beer the bartender brought him and wait for the dance to end. As soon as she came off the floor, he'd have a short, succinct talk with her, then get the hell out of here so he could start his own evening.

Great plan—except it never occurred to him that she might not come off the floor. When the first song ended she simply talked to some of the other people milling around, then started dancing again when the band launched into the next number.

Well…shit. He took another slug of beer. Okay, the end of this song should bring her to wherever it was the women were sitting. He looked around for an empty table holding at least three purses, but that was about every other one.

He rolled his shoulders. Okay, what the hell. He'd just enjoy this number, which really was good.

Four songs later, he had finished his beer and she was still on the freaking dance floor. He'd swear her dress was getting tighter, too, as perspiration from her exertions shrink-wrapped the damn thing to her body. That same humidity seemed to make her hair grow fuller and fuller.

Two men suddenly sandwiched her between them,

moving in concert with her rhythm. The dark-browed redhead looked familiar but Jase couldn't place him off the top of his head. The dark-haired man with him looked like some damn nun-debauching priest or something, and Jase slammed his empty glass on the bar and surged to his feet when the guy wrapped long hands around Poppy's hips and rocked them side to side while he all but dry-humped her round butt.

Stalking over to the floor, Jase wove between dancers without much regard and the minimum of apologies to those whose space he invaded. He didn't have the entire goddamn night to wait on Poppy and her friends—he had a social life of his own.

By the time he reached her where she'd moved deeper into the crush of dancers, the men had moved on and she was once again dancing on her own. He stepped in front of her and leaned down to yell over the music, "We gotta talk."

He wasn't prepared for her to act as if he wasn't even there, but she looked through him as if he were a pane of glass before boogying in a half turn that left him staring at her right profile. He maneuvered to face her again. "Did you hear me? I said we need to talk."

"Is one of my kids in trouble?" she asked, without looking at him.

"No."

"Somebody burn down one of the buildings they worked on?"

He scowled. "No."

"Then we've got nothing to talk about." And she

swiveled around in a complicated undulation of hips and arms that this time left her back to him.

"What the hell?" He moved around her until they were nearly chest-to-chest again. "What's your problem?"

"Got no problems, copper. It's Friday night and I'm copasetic. A little buzzed, perhaps, but, hey, that's all right. I'm not driving." She shooed him away with a languid sweep of her hand. "Move along."

"Not until I know you've made arrangements for a safe ride home." He stared at her, puzzled and frustrated by her attitude. When a dancer behind him knocked him into her, he gritted his teeth at the warm, plush press of her body.

"Didn't I just say I wasn't driving?" Stepping back out of touching range, she stopped dancing for just a second, then picked up the rhythm again. "What the hell do you care how I get home? Isn't involving yourself in my transportation arrangements against your precious *professional code of ethics?*"

Shitfuckhell. It's what he had said to her the day Murph interrupted them making out against the fridge: that getting involved with her was against his and the city's code of ethics. And wasn't he just one hell of a detective, though? Every time he'd freed up a half hour to drop by the project to check on the kids this past week, he'd been so busy trying to avoid spending one minute more in Poppy's company than was absolutely necessary that it had entirely skipped his attention she hadn't exactly been tripping all over herself to catch his interest.

On the contrary, given the way she'd just thrown his

words back in his face, he'd take a wild stab here and guess she had been avoiding him with a diligence that rivaled his own. A fact that shouldn't be catching him by surprise now, given the way she had slammed out of his apartment without a word that day.

She opened her mouth—no doubt to lambast him— just as the music segued into something slow and bluesy. A man strode toward her with clear intentions, but before he could ask her to dance, Jase grasped her wrists and pulled her into his arms, giving the other guy his best *back-off!* cop eyes.

"What the hell do you think you're doing?" she demanded, staring up at him.

"We're going to finish this conversation."

She stood rigid in his arms, but he pulled her hands around his neck and started to sway in time to the music, expecting her to shove him away at any second. After a moment, however, she loosened up enough to follow his less than *Dancing With the Stars*–worthy lead. But she angled her chin up as if to say, *You're here, so I'll dance with you—same as I would do with any guy.* His hands tightened around her wrists for a second.

Then, exhaling a quiet breath, he loosened his grip and wrapped his arms around her, splaying his hands against her back. Resting his cheek against her hair, he inhaled the scent of her shampoo.

And for a moment he felt almost…peaceful.

In tacit détente, they slow-danced without speaking. Then, just as the song was winding to a close, he felt her lips move against his collarbone as she said something he couldn't hear over the music. He tucked his chin to gaze down at her and a strand of blond hair clung like spider silk to his stubble for a second before pulling free to drift back to her temple. "What?"

"You should go home, Jason."

His jaw tightened, the peaceful feeling slip-sliding away as if it had never been. "Yeah. And I will. As soon as you assure me you've got a plan in place for getting home safely when this place closes down."

Her brows snapped together over stormy eyes. "What are you, my daddy?"

"No, dammit, I'm a cop who knows too much about what can happen after dark in this neighborhood!"

There was a scramble at a nearby table, and he glanced over to see a young woman retract a fistful of bills while the man sitting opposite her slid what looked like a quarter gram of weed out of sight. On an ordinary night he'd have had a little talk with them, but he was a bit preoccupied here and his attention immediately snapped back to Poppy when she poked him in the chest.

"Fine," she said. "Then you can trot off contented in knowing I have a plan in place for exactly that."

Which should have been sufficient, considering the way he was still smarting over the daddy crack. Yet he heard himself demanding, "What is it?"

"I've enlisted the help of a couple of fine strapping Irish lads to see us to Jane's car." The band announced a break and she disengaged herself from his arms and stepped back. "In fact, here comes one now."

She was looking past him and he turned to see the guy who'd had his hands all over her hips.

The jerk had the stones to look at him in return as if *he* was the lowlife, then transferred his attention to Poppy. "This joker giving you trouble?" he demanded. Then he studied Jase more closely. "Do I know you?"

"This is Detective de Sanges, Finn. He was just leaving." She turned to him. "I'm not stupid, you know. We realized this wasn't the best neighborhood to be out and about in at night. Ava, of course, was all for renting us a door-to-door limo. But Jane and I opted to go the cheaper route and enlist Jane's husband, Dev, and Finn here. They're twice as effective as any chauffeur and they work for beer."

"And close contact with hot babes," Finn put in, slinging an arm around Poppy's shoulder and staring at Jase, daring him to say something.

He felt his blood pressure rising.

Poppy nodded. "And the occasional dance," she agreed. "They're also Kavanaghs—as in the construction company remodeling the Wolcott mansion? I think you met them when you came out last fall."

Kavanagh didn't offer to shake and neither did he. "I talked to Devlin, I think it was," he said stiffly. Who, of course, was the redhead he'd thought had looked familiar. "I didn't meet Finn."

"Yeah, I remember now." Finn's expression didn't grow any friendlier. "I saw you arriving as I was leaving the day Jane was attacked."

"So, good," Jase said, turning back to Poppy, who

had stepped out from under the drape of Kavanagh's arm. "That's all I wanted—to make sure you got home safely. I've got plans of my own, so I'll let you get back to your evening and I'll get on with mine."

"Have a good one," she said as if she couldn't care less whether he did or not, then turned away without another glance to start weaving through the tightly packed tables toward one back in the corner where her girlfriends sat with the redheaded construction worker. The guy named Finn raised a dark brow at him, then ambled off in her wake.

Leaving Jase, stringing obscenities together beneath his breath, to head for the door.

POPPY COULDN'T catch her breath. For several long moments after arriving back at the table, she simply sat as her friends' conversation swirled around her. She didn't absorb more than one word in ten.

Damn him.

Damn him, damn him, *damn* him!

What *was* it about Jason de Sanges, anyway? She reacted to him in ways that never in a gajillion years could anyone else make her do. She couldn't think of one circumstance in which she'd ever have allowed another man to pull that macho bullshit on her—she would have chopped him off at the knees so fast, he'd be four foot two before he ever felt the blade.

But had she done anything even remotely like that with Jason?

Oh, no.

Instead, like little Miss Wishy-washy, she'd let him pull her into his arms after she had sworn—*sworn!*—to herself that he would never get another opportunity to mess with her head, her ego, her libido that way. She should have pushed him away, had fully *intended* to push him away, when he so high-handedly drafted her into that dance.

Then she'd smelled the clean scent of his skin, felt the warmth and firmness of his body through his soft navy cashmere sweater and charcoal slacks, and had simply…yielded.

Which was so, so, *so* not her usual M.O.

Dammit, she'd been in love before, had had her heart broken before—what thirty-year-old woman hadn't? She'd wanted men, had experienced wanting them with what she'd always assumed was every fiber of her being.

Except, it hadn't been. Every fiber of her being was what she'd felt the two times Jason had kissed her—crazy with wanting him, so out of control she'd barely recognized herself.

And she'd liked it. Right up until the moment he'd shoved her away and to all intents and purposes told her she was a mistake.

Twice.

"I should've pushed him away," she muttered.

Jane leaned over the table, her slippery brown hair sweeping her collarbone as it slid forward over her shoulder. "What's that?"

"I said I should have, um, grabbed the waitress." She

nodded at the young woman working the tables a short distance away. "I could really use another drink."

"Sure, that's what you said." Finn gave her a remember-me-I-saw-you-clinging-to-that-clown look. "But I'll get her for you." And, tipping his chair back on two legs, he waited until the waitress moved closer, then reached out to run a single callused fingertip down her arm as she leaned in to take an order at the table behind him.

The young woman immediately straightened and turned to him.

"My." Poppy's lips curved up in a sardonic smile. "Very impressive."

"Damn straight, buttercup. You're not hanging with the bush league players tonight." He indicated her empty martini glass. "Cosmo, right?" He made a swift assessment of everyone else's drinks, placed an order, then—as soon as the waitress finished using her pen to jot down their requests—borrowed it to write her telephone number on the back of his hand.

Poppy shook her head. "You're a scary guy, Kavanagh." But all joking came to an abrupt end as she caught sight of an unwelcome face over Finn's shoulder. "Shit!"

"What?" He craned around to look behind him. "Is your detective back?"

"He's not my detective! But, no, this is worse than de Sanges. Crap, crap, crap—ten times worse." She leaned across the table to warn Ava, but she wasn't quick enough.

"Hello, Ava," Cade Calderwood Gallari said in his

damn smooth, deep voice and Poppy could only sit there and watch her friend lose all animation and go very, very still. For a moment Ava looked so vulnerable Poppy wanted to leap from her chair and scratch Cade's Newman-blue eyes out.

Then Ava rallied. Lounging back in her chair, she hooked her right elbow over its top, a move that thrust her lush breasts against her black chiffon halter.

Cade's gaze dropped to the shift of white skin against midnight-dark fabric, then rose to meet hers.

"What do you want, Gallari?" she asked coolly.

"Five minutes of your time."

"No," Ava said with cool, quiet finality, while Jane and Poppy, exclaiming the word in unison with her, displayed an overt anger much hotter.

"Why would you think she'd have *any*thing to say to you?" Jane demanded. "You kissed that right goodbye with that bullshit bet back in high school."

"I don't know, maybe I thought that this time she'd grant me five lousy minutes to try to explain," he snapped back, thrusting both hands into his expensively cut blond- and bronze-streaked rich brown hair.

"What bet?" Finn asked.

Poppy watched her friend lose what little color she'd had as she clearly braced to hear her humiliation publicly discussed yet one more time. It might have happened a long time ago, but gifting her virginity to Cade, whom Ava had thought cared for her—only to discover that his friends had bet him he couldn't bag the "fat" girl—wasn't exactly the sort of thing a woman just laughed and walked away from. "None of your business," she informed Finn quietly. "It's not something that needs rehashing here."

Ava met Gallari's gaze with a look so frigid, he should have flash-frozen on the spot. "Go away, Cade. There was nothing you could say then, and there's nothing you can say now. Just leave it, leave *me,* alone. I know this is a tough concept for you to grasp, but not everyone in the world is gonna love you. Deal with it."

A bitter laugh escaped him. "Oh, trust me, I was *born* dealing with it. Look, could you please just give me five fucking minutes?"

"No. I gave you that and so much more once upon a time. And just look how swell that worked for me."

Finn and Dev pushed their chairs back and rose to their feet, but Cade didn't even glance at them. He obviously knew they were there, however, since rubbing the furrow between his brows, he told Ava, "All right, fine. I'm leaving. But one of these days you are going to deal with me."

"Been there. Done that. Not planning on doing it again."

He whispered an obscenity, then turned on his heel and strolled away. Poppy watched him go, thinking there was an almost defeated look to the slump in his broad shoulders.

Then she snorted. This was Cade Calderwood Gallari she was talking about—with his looks, money and connections, he'd probably never spent a defeated moment in his life. And she'd invested all the thought into him she intended, especially since Ava seemed to be holding it together just fine. If the jerk had problems, she didn't need to know about them.

She had her own to worry about. Like how she was going to quash this inconvenient heat she felt every time she thought of a certain infuriating cop.

CHAPTER SIXTEEN

I could happily go the rest of my life without another day like this one. At least the near-death-experience part.

"GOOD JOB WRAPPING up that Pinehurst mini-mart case, de Sanges."

Pausing with one hand primed to scoop his gun up off the desk and the other with his badge worked half-way into his hip pocket, Jase looked over at his lieutenant. "Thanks. We caught a break or two on that one."

"It was good, solid police work that did the trick in the end, though. You heading out to catch up with your kids project?"

Surprised by the question, Jase slowly straightened. "Don't tell me Calloway called the mayor again." And was that a flicker of *hope* he was feeling that she had?

Hell, no. He'd been making himself scarce for the past week and a half because it was the smart thing to do. For her, for him. Probably even for the kids. He gave his badge a shove to seat it in his back pocket and slid his weapon into its holster.

Lieutenant Greer laughed. "Nah—haven't heard

of any calls from that quarter in quite a while." Then he sobered. "But it's good PR and the suits upstairs love it—especially since that quickie spot about the project on the news the other day. It didn't even matter that you weren't actually there. The youngest kid—Harry, is it?"

"Henry."

"Yeah, he obliged us by mentioning your connection. How did he put it—'Dude's not half bad for a Robbery cop'?" Greer laughed, then gave Jase a significant look. "It doesn't hurt to have your name being bruited about by the people who'll be filling positions after the next lieutenants' exam, either. So take the rest of the shift off." The lieutenant waved him away. "Get on over to the project site and accrue more of those brownie points."

"Uh…"

"Go on." Greer's gaze cooled at Jase's hesitation. "That mighta sounded like a request, but it wasn't. It's an order."

"I don't have Calloway's itinerary on me. I'm not even sure we're supposed to meet today. She works with a couple other groups like this one and has a mess of odd jobs around town on top of it, so the schedule is convoluted."

"Luckily, I happen to have a copy in my office and, unlike you, I even check it now and then. Like every day since that sound bite with Calloway and her kids hit the airwaves and the kudos from upstairs started trickling down. You're meeting today. They started about ten minutes ago, so I'm sure there's still plenty of time to get your butt over there."

Shit. But Jase gave his lieutenant a clipped nod. "Right," he said without inflection. "I'll head over."

As he drove across town he brooded over the attitude Poppy had given him at the bar the last time he'd seen her. Or rebrooded, since he'd *been* brooding about it for the past week and a half. It bugged him that she'd been so pissy. All because he'd—what?—stepped away from violating an unspoken departmental edict against sleeping with someone on his case? Yeah, yeah, so maybe technically she wasn't an official part of any of his cases—but that was only because their involvement on this project had kept the kids from being arrested.

Shit. He followed the rules and she acted like that was a bad thing.

Still, an attempt to imagine *her* adhering to them made him snort. That'd be the goddamn day. Poppy was the artsy type. She was a rule-breaker, not a follower.

And, hey, he got that—people were what they were, and trying to change their basic nature generally only earned the changer a massive headache. What he had a tougher time getting was the way Poppy had totally busted the mood with which he'd started out that evening. He'd been all geared up for a quick talk with her that night, after which he'd planned to kill two birds in one cop bar by having a couple beers with Hohn and the guys while scoping out a hook-up with some nice easygoing woman who could douse these damn fires that flared to life every time he got close to the Babe.

A plan that had been blown to hell when Poppy had first ignored him, then melted in his arms for about three and a half minutes before publicly commanding him to take a hike. Face it, a cranky woman tended to color a guy's desire to even *talk* to another of her species.

So once again he'd gone home alone. Which was why he was feeling more than a little cranky himself these days.

Wheeling into Harvey's parking lot a few minutes later, he was more than ready to shelve the entire subject. He'd barely killed the engine, however, when Danny G. came striding up.

"Detective," the teen said the instant Jase opened the door. "You gotta talk to her, man."

Jase sighed. There could only be one "her." Resigned, he looked across the lot to see Poppy packing a huge-ass aluminum stepladder. Ignoring the little kick in his belly at the sight of her, he shoved down his first inclination, which was to go take the damn thing away from her and carry it wherever she intended to set it up. Instead, he tore his gaze away and gave Danny a level look. "About?"

"The ladder, dude! She says she doesn't have insurance that'll cover me or Cory if we get hurt on it. Like we're fuc— That is, we're damn—" He pulled his hair in frustration. "Like we're babies, man! Look at that!" He waved at the nearly done detailed combination of scenery and graphic urban comic they'd drawn across the entire south wall of Harvey's building—a blueprint for their as-yet unpainted masterpiece. "The drawing stage is almost done, but now that we've finally got a ladder to finish the top part she won't let us climb it! She's gonna do it. This is *our* project!"

"It's her project, too. In fact, without her, the three of you would have just done the cleanup work then gone home—not to mention been arrested and charged. There would be no cool mural."

"I know, but—"

"She had to fight like hell to get permission for you all to even do that part of it."

"Even so—"

"Does she strike you as rich, Danny?"

"No, but—"

"She ever lied to you or shined you on about anything?"

"No."

"Then you have to trust her when she says she can't afford to have anyone injured on her watch. Because if that happens, kid, even if nobody sues her ass I imagine every one of her teen projects will be pulled so fast she'll be left with nothing but a bad case of road rash."

Danny exhaled gustily. "I guess. But it still sucks."

"I hear that." Eyeing the round press of Poppy's butt against the seat of her worn jeans as she set up the ladder and bent forward to wrestle its legs apart, his mind drifted for a second to those brief moments he'd held her on the dance floor. Then the image of being kicked to the curb immediately afterward pulled him back to the present. He gave the teen a nod of understanding. "Sometimes stuff just sucks big-time."

FEELING DANNY'S eyes burning a hole in her back, Poppy glanced back over her shoulder, wondering if it would be a waste of breath to try explaining things to him one last time. But it wasn't his gaze that hers clashed headlong with. It was Jason's.

Great. Turning back to the heavy-duty ladder that her father had left for her last night between this building and the business next door, she took out her irritation over the sudden racing of her heart by kicking its legs the rest of the way apart and slamming the locking crosspieces in place. *Just* what she needed to round out her day.

Things were sure out of whack this afternoon. Danny was all bent out of shape and Cory was skulking around in the shadows, looking upset and blue. De Sanges hadn't bothered showing up the past two times they'd gotten together and despite the fact that Henry at least had seemed a bit disappointed that he wasn't there, Poppy had been perfectly fine with the situation. So why did he have to pick today to put in an appearance?

Then she shrugged the question aside. She had things to do; more important matters to worry about. The kids' wall plan in hand, she climbed the ladder, whipped out her pencil and started rapidly sketching the missing top section of the mural. She wasn't wasting any more emotion or brainpower on this. *Screw him.*

A cough of involuntary laughter erupted in the back of her throat. Okay, regrettable choice of words, considering that was exactly what she wanted to do to him every time they got within touching distance. Still, she stood by the sentiment. She was through allowing him to mess with her head.

Finishing what she could reach, she climbed down,

stood back to make sure the proportions were correct, then scooted the stepladder a few feet down the line.

"You're fast," Danny muttered behind her. "And good."

If his voice was grudging, at least he was talking to her again. She'd been surprised by how upset he'd gotten, since he was the most even-keeled of the three. But she thought she understood his reasons and smiled at him as she headed back up the ladder. She'd given them a project they could sink their teeth into and he thought she was taking it away again. "I'm not trying to usurp your baby, Mr. Gardo. You guys will still be doing ninety-five percent of the work."

"Yeah." He shuffled his feet. "We're cool. Detective de S. said to chill because if any of us got hurt on the ladder—" he made a derisive like-*that's*-gonna-happen noise "—all your other projects would be yanked."

"He did?" Twisting around, Poppy stared at Jason where he was talking to Henry across the lot. Damn the man—just when she had him pegged as a total ass, he had to go and smooth things over for her. Could he just once be consistent?

As if he felt her stare, his head started to come up and she spun back, not wanting to make eye contact again. The ladder seemed to take a spongy dip beneath her weight and she grabbed the top. Yet her precautions to protect the kids aside, she knew darn well her father kept his stuff in tip-top shape. So this sudden unstable feeling likely had more to do with a case of the whirlies from her quick turn than a problem with the stepladder. Pulling her pencil out from behind her ear, she consulted the master drawing again and set back to work.

A short while later she leaned out to finish a mountain peak that, after all her big talk about safety, she knew she shouldn't attempt before moving the ladder. Just as she stretched to her fullest extension, she felt a slight jolt beneath her. Immediately the stepladder's front right footing torqued in a direction it was never intended to move. Then both sets of legs started sliding beyond what should have been their securely locked position. The front set hit the wall and abruptly stopped, throwing her off balance.

Her hands shot out to prevent her head from coming into contact with the wall, then scrabbled for a grip on its ungrippable flat surface while the section she stood on kept going in the opposite direction. The space between her hands and feet grew wider and wider as the ladder angled away from the wall toward the ground.

She heard Danny yelp and jump away from the heavy-duty aluminum legs skittering toward him across the concrete as the ground rushed up at her at warp speed. As her hands slid down the wall while her body became less and less upright, she had just enough time to realize that when she pancaked on the concrete it wasn't going to be pretty.

Then a hard arm hooked her around the waist and jerked her against a harder body before she could plummet that final few feet. Having her descent halted in such an abrupt manner folded her in half, which cut off her breath. Jerking back to a less hinged position, she cracked her right elbow against the wall.

"Sssssshit!" Pain zinged up to her shoulder and down to her fingertips. But when Jason set her gently on her feet and supported her back against his strong torso, it dawned on her she could probably stand on her own.

She didn't bother to try, but it was good to know that she could. Drawing a few unsteady, deep breaths, she took stock.

And discovered that thanks to a much less nasty landing than she'd anticipated in those few eternal freefall seconds, she was in damn good shape.

She felt Jason's heart pounding against her back as his hands slid up to her shoulders then down to her wrists before slipping beneath her underarms and running down her sides, his fingertips brushing impersonally across the sides of her breasts on their way to her ribs, which he palpated lightly as if seeking fractures.

"Are you okay?" his voice rumbled in her ear.

She sucked in a breath. Blew it out. "Yes."

Stepping back, he turned her to face him. "What is it with you?" he demanded, sounding surly and on edge. "First you're nearly clocked by that wrench and now your ladder fails?" He squatted to examine the cross-struts that should have held it upright.

"You're asking the wrong person, because I don't get it, either," she said, stooping down next to him. The kids swarmed over to join them around the fallen ladder. Cutting across their exclamations, she informed Jason, "This is my father's and he takes excellent care of his equipment." Watching him run his fingers over the twisted holes—all that was left where the rivets anchoring the struts to the legs of the stepladder should have been—filled her with sick confusion and she said again, "I just don't get it."

WATCHING THE activity down the block from his car, Bruno Arturo admitted that dicking with the rivets had been a lame impulse. Well, tough. When he'd come across the ladder while scoping out the site late last night he'd still been pissed off from that short news feature he'd seen on KING-5. Here he'd tried to cut the kid a break. He should have known better than to go soft over some little girl.

Information on the Capelli kid had been surprisingly hard to come by. He'd made the mistake of assuming that the street kids knew what he had not—that she was a girl not a boy, so it took him longer than usual to even discover she went by the name of CaP on the street. Then when he finally did have a name for his inquiries, nobody seemed to know her well. It wasn't until one kid said that CaP had let slip once that he was from Philly that Bruno's luck began to change. That's when he'd contacted a numbers runner he knew there and got the story on the girl's father.

But he still didn't know where she lived, which astounded the shit outta him, because that was usually the easy part of running someone to ground. But the girl was wily, taking circuitous routes home, cutting through yards and racing down one-way streets the wrong way until she seemed to disappear into thin air. His record for sticking with her before she vanished was four and a half blocks. She also wasn't among the Capellis listed in the phone books, which, given what had happened to her old man, he figured was her mother's handiwork. Losing someone to murder had a way of making a person cautious.

He'd come to the conclusion his boss was right: the girl wasn't a threat. Seeing exactly what stepping up had gotten her old man had no doubt taught her to keep her yap shut. So for the first time in what seemed like weeks he'd taken a deep breath and relaxed.

Only to turn around and catch that news clip on the tube.

He'd blown sky-high to discover that while he'd been preparing to cut the kid a break and just walk away from this the way Schultz wanted, *she* was working with a cop. A fucking Robbery cop.

Still, sabotaging that ladder had been a dumb-shit response. Hell, there was no predicting who'd climb the thing. Not to mention that, at most, the strut failures would maybe crack the skull of whomever did—but more likely merely inflict a couple of bruises.

At least he'd thought far enough ahead to wrap a chamois around the tungsten blade he'd used to loosen the rivets and avoid leaving shiny silver scratch marks all over the ladder. He didn't aim to have a cop crawling up his ass.

Which brought him full circle to messing with the fucking ladder in the first place. He still didn't know how he was going to handle the kid when he did catch her. But he knew he didn't want any previous "accidents" scratching at the back of the cop's mind.

On the other hand, this might have shaken the kid up. And an off-balance mark was easier prey.

Of course, until he could separate her from the detective that meant bugger all. So he might as well remove himself from the neighborhood before someone noticed him.

He fired up the engine.

Then he blinked, realizing he'd been staring at the action down the street without actually paying attention for a few moments now. Capelli and the blonde were no longer in the group around the busted ladder. Looking around, he saw the girl crossing the street right in front of him, if down a ways. As he watched, she stopped in the middle lane and turned to say something over her shoulder.

And. Holy. Shit. He sat forward in his seat.

No one was out on the street at the moment.

The cop's back was turned.

And the opportunity he'd been presented was just too fucking good to pass up.

He floored the gas.

JASE WAS SQUATTING next to Danny G., going over the busted cross braces one last time, when he heard a car suddenly accelerate out on the street. He was twisting around to see who the hell was driving so fast when Henry shoved to his feet and sprinted away, exclaiming, "Jesus, are you guys okay? Cory, Ms. C.? You okay?"

Heart pounding in his chest not only at the words but at the shaken tremble in the boy's voice, Jase surged to his feet, his gaze sweeping the area. Poppy was sprawled facedown on the sidewalk with Cory draped half on top of her, and even as he spotted them Henry came to a halt so abrupt that it jerked the boy up onto his toes before he caught his balance and dropped to a squat alongside them.

Neither of the downed women so much as twitched a finger and Jase's heart seemed to come to a crashing halt. For one second. Two.

Then he jerked back into cop mode.

"What was that guy, *drunk?*" Henry demanded, shooting a glance at him over his bony shoulder. "Did you *see* that, dude? It was almost like he was aimin' for Ms. C. If Cory hadn't shoved her outta the way, they'da both been creamed."

Jase was already striding over to assess the damage for himself when Danny pushed past him. Although it took two seconds max to catch up, the teen had all but muscled Henry aside and was helping Cory to her feet.

"Easy," Jase cautioned. "You want to make sure nothing's broken before you go hauling her around."

"Not," Cory wheezed. "Harda…breathe…though."

"Just draw it in slow and easy," he advised. "I know it feels like it won't come back, but if you can let that fear go, you'll find it easier to inhale." He squatted down next to Poppy. "How about you?"

"Gimme a minute."

He did until she flapped a limp hand in his direction,

then he and Henry helped her to her feet. He brushed her off, gave her his second hands-on inspection of the day, then felt a knot in his gut unclench when he found her sporting nothing more than mild abrasions. He looked back at Cory. "You sure you're all right?"

She nodded shakily and he returned his attention to Poppy. "Can you tell me what happened?"

She stared at him with wide brown eyes showing too much white around the irises. "A dark car," she said shakily. "A big—no, God, *huge* car." She swallowed audibly, staring up at him. "Holy shitskis, Jason, the thing was barreling right at me! And I froze."

She shook her head. "One of my kids was in the street about to get run down and I froze." She turned to Cory. "God, I am so sorry. If you hadn't tackled me, we both would have been run down."

"No, it wasn't your fault!" Cory hugged herself as she stared at Poppy with anguished eyes.

Jase didn't give a shit whose fault it was. He knew it wasn't rational, but anger was starting to take over his usual professional detachment. "What were the two of you doing in the street to begin with?" he snapped.

"I saw Cory leaving and I wanted to talk to her for a minute. She seemed so down today, I wanted to make sure she was all right."

Cory made a choked sound.

"So you thought you'd have a heart-to-heart in the middle of a damn arterial?" He was taken aback by his combative tone. *Jesus, man. Take a deep breath here. Where the hell is your objectivity?*

Poppy's eyes narrowed and for the first time since he'd scooped her up off the ground, she looked like her usual take-no-crap-off-anyone self. "No, Detective. As I'm sure you'd be the first to point out, I wasn't thinking, period. I caught up with her and before we could get out of the street that big honkin' car was barreling right at us."

"About that." He pulled his ever-present notebook out of his hip pocket. "What kind of car was it?"

"I told you—a freaking huge dark one!"

That was helpful. "Dark as in black? Charcoal? Navy maybe?"

"Yes."

He gave her a look and she snapped, "I don't *know,* okay? It was big and it was dark, that's all I saw. *You* experience a ton of screaming metal bearing down at you at fifty miles an hour and then we'll talk about powers of observation."

He sighed and turned to Cory. "Can you do a little better?"

She shook her head.

"It was black," Henry said. "I don't know squat about models, but it was a new-looking SUV. I think maybe one a them high-end ones."

"Like an Escalade?" Danny demanded.

Henry shrugged. "Beats the hell outta me."

"Don't swear," Poppy said, but it was clearly automatic.

"How come?" Henry asked. "You did."

She blinked at him. "I did?"

Jase snapped his fingers to redirect her attention to

what was important. "Have you made yourself an enemy that you haven't bothered to mention?"

"Not so far as I know."

"Then what the hell is going on here? Because you've had three close calls in as many weeks. Now, maybe you're just having a real bad run of luck. But me, I don't believe in luck, good or bad. And I'm not big on coincidence. So if you think I'm going to stop digging before I get to the bottom of this, you can think again." He braced himself for her argument.

Instead, shoving her hair off her forehead, she gave him a weary nod. Her teeth started chattering as if the temperature had suddenly dropped thirty degrees.

"Works for me."

CHAPTER SEVENTEEN

To paraphrase ol' Charlie D: It was the best of days, it was the worst of days. ☺

"YOU'RE BLEEDING."

Cory gave Henry a blank look.

He pointed to her elbow. "Bleeding."

Lifting her arm, she cocked her elbow in. Sure enough, a viscous line of blood crept down her arm from an oozing scrape. And, seeing it, what had been blissfully numb began to sting. "Crap," she breathed.

Would this day never end?

"Let me see." Poppy came over at once, concern etched on her drawn features.

Cory stepped back. God, she couldn't stand this. Ms. C. had been nothing but nice to her, and it was all her fault that her teacher/mentor/whatever had almost been run down.

Queasiness roiled in a great greasy wave in her stomach. She was probably responsible for those other "accidents," too. And Jesus, Jesus, she didn't know what to do. "It's nothing," she said. "I'll slap a Band-Aid on it when I get home."

"Let's at least get it cleaned up. I'm sure Mr. Harvey would let us use his restroom. He probably has a first-aid kit, too."

"I'll take her," Danny G. said, stepping between them. He smiled at Ms. C. without the ever-present if slight distance he usually used like an invisible force field between himself and the rest of the world. "You look ready to drop. Why don't you go on home and I'll help Cory clean up and then drive her home, too."

"Oh, I don't know—"

"I do," Detective de Sanges said, taking her arm as carefully as if she were constructed of that special-effects glass that shattered beneath the slightest pressure. "Danny's right, you do look ready to drop. I'll take you home."

"But what about my car?" Then Poppy sagged, looking worn to the bone. "Never mind. I'll have my dad pick it up." She nodded at the cop. "Thank you, Jason, I'd really appreciate a lift. It's been…a day." But she rallied to look at Cory, Danny and Henry. "I can't seem to get my brain to track, so I don't remember offhand when we meet again. But check your schedules and I'll see you then. And thanks for being so great today."

With her drawn skin and tired posture, she looked very un-Ms. Calloway-like as the cop led her away.

Danny said, "C'mon," in a brusque voice and Cory's attention shifted to him as he guided her to the back entry of Mr. Harvey's store without actually touching her.

She was pretty sure he was pissed—and she knew at whom.

Henry trailed them, verbally reliving the afternoon's events, wringing every drop of drama from them as if the other two hadn't been right there. Rather than be irritated by it, however, Cory actually felt grateful for his nonstop chatter. If it kept her from having to deal with Danny, she was all over it.

Arriving at the storeroom door, she watched Danny rap on it with his knuckles, then test the lock when there was no answer. The knob turned under his hand and he stuck his head in. "Mr. Harvey?"

Voices murmured out in the store, but no one answered and he called the man's name louder.

"Who's there?" The shop owner's voice preceded him into the back room. "Ah, the Three Amigos. How's the project going? What can I do you for?"

Danny explained what had happened and, in the wake of the man's exclamations, asked if they could use the employee restroom to clean Cory up.

"You bet." Mr. Harvey gazed at her elbow. "There's some triple antibiotic ointment and a box of Band-Aids in the medicine cabinet over the sink. Should be a bottle of aspirin or ibuprofen in there, too, if you need it."

"Thanks, Mr. H.," she said. "I'll try not to get blood on any of your stuff."

"Don't worry about it, sweetheart. We have plenty of paper towels."

It didn't take long to disinfect her scrape and slap a Band-Aid on it. Cory knew Danny was still pissed at her, but despite that, despite her painful scrape, she couldn't ignore the little thrill she felt at the warmth of his hand cupping her arm, at the gentleness he displayed tending her wound.

They used a couple of the paper towels to clean the sink when they'd finished up, then Danny offered Henry a ride home. But Mr. H. said if Henry was interested in making some money he had about an hour and a half's worth of chores that needed to be done around the store. Since Henry was always strapped for coin, he jumped at the opportunity.

She and Danny left without him.

Danny didn't say much when they first got in his car. He concentrated on his driving, looking in the rearview mirror often and taking sudden unannounced turns, doubling and tripling back on his route. Ten or so minutes later, he pulled to the curb in a neighborhood Cory had never been in before, parking beneath the shade of an ornamental cherry tree that was shedding its flowers in drifts of pink. Shutting down the engine, he turned to look at her.

"Let's have it."

She thought about playing dumb—for about two seconds. The hard glint in Danny's eyes warned her against the idea.

She thought about saying she didn't want to talk about it, but the truth was, she did. She was tired of keeping all this crap to herself. It was like drinking a slow-acting poison: it was tasteless and odorless and for a while she'd convinced herself it was nontoxic. But it was eating her alive.

She *really* thought about crying, but bucked up.

That's what her daddy used to say: "Buck up, baby. Things probably aren't as bad as you think."

In this case he'da been wrong, but she sniffed air deep into her lungs, blinked back her tears and sat a little straighter.

She told Danny everything.

"Holy shit," he said when she finally paused for breath. "Holy, *mo*fo'n sh—" He swallowed. "Damn."

"Yeah. I don't know what to do."

"You can tell de Sanges, for starters."

Except that. She knew better than to do that. "No!"

"Cory—"

"No! How can you even suggest that?"

"Because it's the right thing to do."

She just looked at him, feeling as if he were speaking Swahili. "I've *told* you what those gangbangers did to my father. He was doing 'the right thing' and they killed him for it!"

"So how's keeping your mouth shut working for you, Cor? Because from where I sit, it's not looking so great. You never so much as *whispered* what you saw the guy do—yet he just tried to run you down! And apparently he doesn't give a shit who he takes out with you."

"I know!" she screamed at him. "You think I haven't been *thinking* about that every fricking minute since it happened? You think I haven't been torn in a bazillion little pieces knowing because of me Ms. C. nearly got taken out?"

"Then do something about it! Tell de Sanges and let him take care of it."

All the fight went out of her. But the fear of talking to the cops, indoctrinated by hard experience, remained. "I can't," she whispered. "I just…can't. The cops can't protect me or my mom. Nobody can."

"You're wrong about that. Detective de S. isn't exactly Officer Friendly, but that's what I like about him. Because he doesn't try to bullshit you. He doesn't say trust me, I'm your friend—then turn around and saunter off into the sunset without giving a good goddamn the one time you might actually need his help. I get the impression he takes that protect-and-serve shit real serious. You know what he said the day you went apeshit on him?"

Heat surged under her skin at the reminder of her public anger and—worse—crying that day. She shook her head.

"He said you had a right to your grudge against the police—that they'd fucked up their obligation to protect your father."

"He actually said fu—"

"Nah, but that's what he meant. And when Henry wouldn't let go of the fact you'd cried, de S. told us that he didn't know much about girls, but that he did know they handled things differently than guys. And he looked right at Henry when he said he'd skin us alive if we gave you a bad time about it." Danny looked her in the eyes. "Tell him what's going on, Cory. The guy's in the Robbery division. He's the ideal person to get to the bottom of this."

She knew he was probably right. Knew it deep down on a cellular level.

And yet…

"Give me a couple of days, okay? Please, Danny, just let me wrap my head around this, then I'll find a way to tell him, I swear. I need a little time to come to terms with going against everything I've believed in since Daddy was killed."

He studied her with a hard stare for a moment. Then he sighed. "Okay, but only a couple. You can't afford to put this off. You ask me, that Arturo guy is seriously whacked."

BRUNO WAS SEVERAL miles away, on the downtown side of the neighborhood he'd just left, when the fact that he'd screwed the pooch hit him like a bullet from a sniper's rifle. He didn't need to debate it; he wasn't misinterpreting the facts. And there were no do-overs.

He'd fucked up, big-time.

He should have thought things through more thoroughly before giving in to the impulse to run the girl down. Either that, or done a better job of actually *running* her down. Because it occurred to him now that if Capelli hadn't already told the cop what she'd seen that night in the U district, he'd just removed any incentive for her to keep her mouth shut.

Shit. He should have stuck to his first impression when he'd learned about the kid's old man: that she'd had a goddamn compelling example of what happened to people who talked out of turn. But hearing the boy on that damn television spot mention a Robbery cop on the art project Capelli was part of had thrown him off his stride. Made him feel she'd betrayed his generosity.

And he'd maybe overreacted.

Shitfuckshit. He turned around at the next light and headed back, knowing he was a good six or seven miles away and likely too late to track her this afternoon.

On the other hand, she probably wasn't moving as swift as usual. She sure as shit wouldn't be moving at the speed she'd sprinted to get that blond woman, who would have been unfortunate collateral damage, out of his way. Swear to God the kid could be a contender if she ever decided to try out for an Olympic track and field event.

He shook his head impatiently. This was no time to go off on a tangent. His point was, there was a chance Capelli was still where he'd left her.

And this time he'd keep up with her. He would finally discover where the hell she lived.

And if that somehow didn't happen today? Then he'd goddamn see to it that it happened tomorrow or the next day.

Because he'd set the clock ticking this afternoon. Had wedged himself solidly between a rock and a hard place. Either the cops were going to be looking for him. Or Schultz would hear that he'd disregarded his order to leave the kid be.

And of the two?

He'd just as soon take his chances with the cops.

JASON ASKED Poppy more than once, on the drive to her apartment, if she was all right. She wouldn't have minded that so much, since it was always nice knowing someone worried about your welfare. But he generally followed his solicitousness up with "Who do you know who could have done this?" And when she said, "No one," he urged, "Think, Poppy. It's important."

She knew that, dammit. But she *didn't* know anyone who had a reason to hurt her. So finally she rested her head against the passenger-side window and pretended to doze so she wouldn't have to keep addressing his questions.

Because how do you answer the unanswerable when the response you have given isn't even a hundred-percent true? Well, it was in the sense she *was* fine, physically—she'd seen worse scrapes on a playground full of kindergartners. But on the emotional front?

She was a wreck.

She knew she should probably call her parents. Let them know what had happened, both to her and to her dad's ladder.

But she wasn't quite up to the task. Not when she knew Mom would immediately get on the horn and spread the news. And that she and Dad would then descend on her with homemade chicken soup and a lot of TLC.

Not that the last part wouldn't be just what the doctor ordered.

But Aunt Sara—who was actually no relation but still family—would also show up with her crystals and her tarot cards. In the ordinary run of things Poppy would enjoy that, but she simply wasn't up to it today. Not to mention Uncle Bill, who was Aunt Sara's partner of thirty years and one of Poppy's all-time favorite people in the world. She knew he would accompany

Auntie Sara—no doubt bearing one of his personal pan-size brownies that he'd have thrown together, complete with a healthy dose of marijuana, at the last minute.

To be baked in Poppy's own kitchen, no doubt, as he wouldn't want to waste time if he felt she was in need of his support. She sighed against the cool glass.

Because she could just imagine Mr. Law and Order's reaction to that. Uncle Bill would probably be in the slammer before you could say, "Call the bondsman."

That was her last thought before drifting to sleep for real. She didn't awaken until Jason parked on the street in front of her apartment building. He'd shut down the engine and climbed from the car before she even lifted her head off the glass. As he rounded the hood she surreptitiously swiped her thumb and index finger down the corners of her lips, thinking, *Please, God, don't let there be drool.*

He opened her door and squatted down in front of her. "You want me to carry you?"

Yessss. "No, of course not," she murmured, angling her knees toward the door in preparation to swing her legs out. Still, she half expected him to ignore her demurral. His rules of behavior seemed to be governed by such rigid values.

He merely shrugged, however, and rose to his feet in an easy, economical motion. He extended a long-fingered hand to her. Sliding her own across his palm, she tried to ignore the wash of skin-against-skin heat that wrapped her in awareness as he gently hoisted her from the seat.

Because that's all she needed to round out her day, a case of the do-mes with a guy determined not to. God knew he'd told her every way there *was* to tell a woman that he didn't mix business and pleasure. Never, ever, ever.

She got it already.

So she wasn't going there. It would be faster and less humiliating to just borrow his gun and shoot her little toe off than to embarrass herself in that arena again.

"Here, why don't you lean on me?" He reached out as if to pull her to his side, but she stepped away.

"Thanks, I'm good."

He gently cupped her elbow, instead. Giving the ancient elevator a doubtful look, he nevertheless led her over to it. It opened right away, since it was almost always on the first floor as hardly anyone in the building trusted its inconsistent "in order" record.

She should have avoided it now, as well. But it was too late, so she stepped aboard, then stood as far away from him as she could. Which, considering the car was the size of a broom closet, wasn't nearly as far as she would have preferred.

It was as if her near brushes with mortality had made her supersensitive. Well, okay, she knew mortality was probably a stretch for what had been a quick ride down the ladder and kissing the sidewalk beneath the weight of a hundred-and-twenty-pound girl as a ton of screaming metal flashed by.

Then again: *a ton of screaming metal.*

So maybe not.

They had to be accidents, though. Jason's I'm-not-big-on-coincidence to the contrary, she *didn't* know anyone who bore her that sort of enmity.

The elevator slid to a bumpy halt and the doors opened. Jason walked her the few steps to her apartment, then took her keys from her and let them in.

"You want something to drink or some aspirin or anything?"

"I can get it. You don't have to stay, Jason. I'm going to take a shower then probably take a nap. I'll call my folks a little later."

"You go ahead and start your shower," he said. "I'll just make sure your place is secure."

"Okay." She headed for the bathroom, but then paused to look back at him. "Thank you. For bringing me home and...well, everything."

Their eyes locked for a long moment. But true to form, she felt her libido start to spark, while he only said, "Not a problem."

She went into the bathroom, locked the door, then shook a couple of aspirin from the bottle in the medicine chest. She washed them down with so many Dixie cups of water the little paper receptacle started falling apart at the seams. Tossing it in the wastebasket, she climbed in the tub. She pulled the curtain, turned on the shower, then adjusted the water temperature until clouds of steam began to billow.

Ten minutes later, she climbed out, feeling cleansed in ways that went deeper than simply having removed the parking lot and sidewalk grime. She wrapped her freshly shampooed hair in a towel, patted herself dry and dabbed ointment on her scrapes. Then she moisturized from head to foot and finally began to feel halfway human. Maybe she'd complete the transformation by pouring herself a glass of wine, then call her mom.

The air out in the hall felt cool after the steamy bathroom when she stepped out a few minutes later, and she zipped her favorite threadbare gray hoodie over a white tank top that she'd paired with equally raggedy gray sweats. She considered detouring to the bedroom to grab a pair of socks.

Wine first, she decided. Then socks. She strode into the living room.

Then stopped short at the sight of Jason sprawled out on her couch. He'd kicked off his shoes and his head rested on one of her throw pillows against the arm of the couch. One long leg stretched the length of the cushions, its stocking-clad foot propped on the far arm. His other leg spilled over the edge, the angle of that foot against the floor cocking his leg in such a way that she could see he dressed to the left.

She hastily redirected her attention upward. His arm was thrown over his eyes and she approached him cautiously. Had he fallen asleep?

Apparently not, for when she was a mere foot away he lowered his arm and looked up at her. His gaze traveled from her terry turban to her bare toes, then back up again in a quick, comprehensive assessment. "You look like you're feeling better."

"What are you doing here?" Dammit, the shower

had helped wash away that confusing, unwelcome mixture of lust and frustration she felt every time she was around this man. But she looked at him lying there, with his rolled-up sleeves, loosened tie, dangerous—if holstered—gun and even more dangerous eyes, and it came roaring back, stronger than ever. She shoved her fists into her hoodie's shallow pockets.

"You didn't really think I was going to just walk away and leave you here defenseless, did you?"

She blinked at him, dragging her attention back from an unbidden fantasy of ripping his shirt open hard enough to make buttons fly. *Stop it, stop it, stop it!* Furious with herself, she took it out on him. "I have told you and *told* you, I don't need defending!"

"No, you've told me you don't know of anyone who would want to hurt you," he corrected, sitting up in a lithe movement that looked effortless but had to take abs of steel to pull off. His knee brushed hers as he swung around to put both feet on the floor, and electricity zinged up her thighs.

She stepped back. "Same thing."

"Not even close." He rose to his feet and she backed even farther away. "Maybe I should call the station— get a policewoman to stay with you until we can figure this thing out."

She knew it was contrary to be angry about him not wanting to be here himself when all she wanted was to see his backside going out her door. But, oh, man, he couldn't *wait* to be shed of her, could he? She stopped retreating and took a hot step forward. "Read my lips, de Sanges. I. Do. Not. Need. Police. Protection. I can take care of myself!"

His eyebrows lowered. "Oh, yeah. I can see you're all kinds of tough."

"I'm plenty tough!"

A temper where she was accustomed to seeing a carefully controlled expression snapped in his eyes. "Well, let's test that theory, whataya say? Let's pretend I've just broken in and I've got it in my mind to kill you because—" He shook his head. "Well, we don't really know why, do we? Maybe simply because you're so goddamn stubborn." He narrowed his eyes at her. "But first, I'm going to have a little fun. You might not think it's a whole lot of fun, but, hey, what do I care? I'm a fuckin' psychopath."

The way he stared at her with flat, dark angry eyes, he looked like a psychopath. Goose bumps ran down her spine and the backs of her thighs. "You're scaring me, Jason," she whispered.

"Why? You're plenty tough, remember? So what are you gonna do?" He feinted at her, and with a burst of fury that he was deliberately trying to frighten her she ran for her tote, with its little canister of pepper spray. He wanted to act like this was real? She'd show him real!

Except, she wasn't tough at all. Hell, she wasn't even fast. She didn't get a full yard away before he swept her feet out from under her. She tumbled to the floor and in a flash, he'd dropped down, rolled her over and had her pinned, her wrists stapled by his long hands to the aged fir on either side of her head.

He was hot and heavy and smelled of worked-up man. Fear disappeared and lust took its place. God, she wanted, wanted, wanted him.

"So what are you gonna do now, hotshot?" he demanded. But his eyes were suddenly wary.

She closed her own eyes and gave her lips a nervous lick, praying she wouldn't embarrass herself. She had done that too many times with him already.

Then feeling him grow still atop her, she snuck a peek upward. He was staring at her lips, but he slowly raised his gaze to meet hers.

"Damn you," he growled in a low, hoarse voice. Then slammed his mouth over hers.

CHAPTER EIGHTEEN

I always thought I was pretty hip when it came to sex. Thought I *knew.* Man. I didn't know squat.

THE TASTE Jase'd had of Poppy that evening she'd brought him dinner had been way too meager. He might have fooled himself otherwise, but it only took a hint of her flavor now for every remnant of good sense to collapse beneath the white-hot fingers of lust spearing like sheet lightning through his veins.

Propping himself over her just enough to keep his weight from crushing her into the wooden floor, he burrowed his hands under the towel wrapped around her hair. Its turban-tuck promptly unraveled and the cloth spilled in a ruby-colored waterfall, pooling on the floor beneath her head. Poppy's damp curls tumbled free from their confinement. Plunging his hands into them, he was only vaguely aware of the clinging strands that wrapped around his fingers.

Because in that same instant her lips opened under his. His focus shifted, honing in like a high-tech missile on the heat, the taste, the textures of her mouth as his tongue plunged in to stake its territory.

With a sigh of pleasure that flowed sweet and soft from her mouth to his, she countered the thrust with a silky stroke of her tongue, its slow, sinuous twine laying claim to some territory of its own.

"Ah!" Breath exploding, he tunneled his fingers deeper into her curls, gripping her head and tipping it back so he could kiss her with even fiercer intent.

He wanted deeper, closer, wanted to climb inside of her and never come out. He wanted…

Christ. He had settled all his weight on her and was crushing her breasts beneath the inflexible press of his chest. His thighs, wedged between her own, had widened, spreading hers open while he rocked and swiveled his hips, thrusting and rubbing against the warm damp furrow between her legs.

For God's sake, man, she had a ladder collapse out from under her today. Not to mention she'd damn near been run down by a speeding car, which—according to Henry, at any rate—had been deliberately driven right at her. And here he was, grinding her into a hard floor while dry-humping her like a teenager with his first shot at getting lucky.

Was he a prince or what?

Ripping his mouth free, he pushed up on his palms, his head hanging low and his breath sawing like he'd run a four-minute mile.

A dissatisfied little hum purled out of Poppy's throat and her lashes slowly raised. Licking her lips, she blinked up at him with a hazy lack of comprehension.

But her dark, liquid eyes cleared as they focused on him. And her brow furrowed.

She raised one hand and touched it to his jaw, then trailed her fingertips down his throat to his collar.

Where she abruptly wrapped her fist around his tie and yanked, dragging his face so close to her own they were all but nose-to-nose. Her eyes flashed a dire warning. "You better not be thinking of leaving me high and dry again," she whispered.

"No," he answered honestly, even though he knew it would be best all around if he did precisely that. "I should, but I just don't have the chops. My willpower's toast." And how the *hell* this five-foot-five package of curls and attitude had managed to drain him of it he couldn't say.

Neither, however, could he prevent himself from brushing the backs of his fingers down her soft, soft skin from temple to jaw. "You've had a rough day, though, and I thought you might appreciate moving this show to a soft bed." Then he raised his eyebrows at her. "Still, if you'd prefer sex on a hard floor..."

She grimaced. "No. Now that you mention it, I'm kind of feeling my various bumps and bruises. A bed sounds like a real good plan."

He pushed up off her, then leaned back down to extend a hand, pulling her to her feet when she slid her fingers into the cup of his palm. Their eyes met and held, and he lowered his head to kiss her again.

Mistake. He realized it the minute he found himself waltzing her over to the small dining table and bending her backward as he prepared to sweep everything atop it onto the floor so he could get her horizontal. He pulled her back upright. Straightened the gray hoodie his arm had gripped into creases along the small of her back.

Man, what *was* it about her? He got anywhere near those lips and all his circuits fried, reducing him to nothing more than impulses and nerve endings. "Sorry," he muttered.

She grinned at him. "Yeah, women just hate it when a guy loses all control over them." She cocked her head at his feet. "Lose the gun."

"I'm happy to take it off, but I don't leave it behind. It goes where I go."

"That would be down there." She led him to her bedroom.

Stopping moments later next to her bed, which was piled high with those incomprehensible little girlie pillows women seemed to get off on, she pointed to the end table, then looped her arms around his neck as soon as he set his gun on it. "Whataya say we try this again?"

"Oh, yeah," he agreed with a fervency he feared was too damn revealing. Yet, looking at her lips so soft and full, her skin so smooth and flushed and her eyes so heavy-lidded and carnal, the fact that he'd exposed himself just didn't seem worth worrying about. At least not right this minute. Grasping her ass, he hauled her up.

She laughed and wrapped her legs around his waist. And he kissed her.

Heat, barely banked, roared back to life and his fingers dug into the firm cheeks they cupped. He wanted her.

God, worse, he *needed* her. The thought sent a cold lick of unease trickling through the hot quagmire of his mind.

But before it could give him second thoughts, it struck him he wasn't in this alone. Poppy's laughter turned to breathy moans that constricted his gut. She strained against him, her legs tightened around his hips and her arms around his neck as if she, too, felt driven to get closer, closer.

Sweeping what seemed like fifty pillows onto the floor, he settled her on the space he'd cleared and peeled her arms from his neck so he could access the zipper on her hoodie. A satisfied grunt sounded in his throat when its sides fell apart and he saw the high, round shape of her breasts pressing against her white tank top. They jiggled enticingly when he peeled her out of the sweatshirt and her nipples formed pale spikes that tented the thin, stretchy cotton.

"God," he whispered and dropped down over her. Catching himself on his palms, he lowered his head to kiss her again.

Now that he finally had her prone on a comfortable surface, some of that fierce gotta-do-her-*now* urgency faded. Not that he still wouldn't die to eat her whole. But he had her where he wanted her and felt like he could take a breath. Take his *time*. She'd gotten a little beat up today. The last thing she needed was him going at her like a starved dog on a juicy bone.

His mouth softening, he sipped from her lips, leisurely savoring their supple give in their still-closed state, their slick heat when they parted on a tiny moan.

He spent long, fervent moments simply kissing her, reveling in her sweet essence. But when he felt his hips start that age-old rhythm against her, first easily, then with serious intent, he lifted his mouth and slid down her body. Cupping her breast in his hand, he pushed it up and kissed the pale curve that spilled above the tank's low neckline.

Sinking his face into her cleavage, he pressed both breasts together and inhaled. Then, drunk on her scent and the warm, plush rub on either side of his scratchy jaw, he pulled back to gently bite her nipple through the fabric.

"Jason!" she breathed and arched her back, offering herself up for more.

He was happy to oblige, but first he needed to see what he had touched. Snaking a hand beneath the hem of her tank top, he worked it up her midriff, shoved the stretchy fabric above her breasts.

He left it there, bunched from armpit to armpit. Because the sight that greeted him, soft curves ivory-fair and round, stiff little nipples the palest pink he'd ever seen, derailed his thoughts entirely, never mind whatever intention he may have started out with.

"Sweet," he said hoarsely, touching the tip of his finger to one straining nipple, arrested by the sight of his brown-skinned finger, so dark against her porcelain flesh. "God, these are sweet."

She hissed in a breath, raising her hands to spread her fingers against his chest. Heat seeped through the cloth of his shirt, but almost in the same heartbeat that she'd touched him, she tore her hands away to begin fumbling at his buttons.

"You'll help me if you want to keep your shirt intact," she muttered. "'S not fair you get to look at me and I haven't even seen a glimpse of you."

He pushed away to kneel astride her thighs and started working the button placket from the top down, while she unfastened from the bottom up.

"I fantasized ripping this off you," she said, her eyebrows furrowing as an especially recalcitrant button refused her attempts to work it through its hole. "And if the damn thing doesn't get in gear, I still may."

"You had a fantasy about me?" He stilled for a second, his heart unaccountably racing at the idea.

She flapped an impatient hand at the button he'd quit manipulating with the job only half-complete, and he unbuttoned it, then yanked down the knot of his tie.

"Yes," she answered, as she worked on the final fastener. "And you may have featured in one or two of my Sheik daydreams as well."

"Chic?" he said, confused. "What, you like the way I dress?"

"No." Shaking her head, she gave him a wry little half smile. "Well, actually I do. But I'm talking white-hot sex in the oasis—you know, like Valentino? The *Sheik*." She glanced up at him, her irises bitter chocolate–dark against the startling whiteness surrounding them. "I wouldn't get a fat head about it, though, because the fantasy didn't originate with you. It's been my running favorite since Ava and Janie and I made up increasingly raunchy stories about the guy when we were twelve, thirteen years old."

"So this sheik," he inquired. "He—what? Abducts you to his tent in the desert or something?"

"Yeah." She gave him a crooked smile and shrugged. "That race across the desert on his midnight-black Arabian is usually the starting line."

He slipped his tie through its loop and shrugged out of his shirt. "I could get into that." To his surprise he thought he could actually get into it big-time. Who knew? Sexual role-playing wasn't something he'd ever included in his bag of tricks.

The moisture in Poppy's mouth dried up as Jason's shirt slid from his shoulders. He was svelte in his clothing, but *sans* the shirt he looked much less civilized, more in keeping with that always blue-black jaw of his. His shoulders were wide and bony, his arms long and leanly muscled, feathered with black hair and traced with soft, standing veins that snaked down the inside bend of his elbow and along his forearms. And his chest—

She swallowed hard. God, his chest and abs were corded with muscle and covered with more fine black fur, this spreading fairly densely across his pectorals before descending in an ever-narrowing stripe down his abdomen. He *was* the Sheik of her fantasies and she wanted to sink into him, to feel that dark hair abrade her nipples, marvel at the differences in their coloring when they were skin-to-skin.

What had he said? That he could get into the fantasy? She wiggled out from between his legs, then rolled up to knee-walk back to him, stripping her tank top as she went. Looping her arms around his neck, she pressed herself close, savoring the hardness of his chest flattening her breasts, the cloud of hair both crisp and soft that her nipples sank into.

"Me, too," she agreed. "But for now I'm happy just to get into this." Gently, she bit the stubble-roughened thrust of his chin.

His hands splaying across her bare back, he lifted her against him, raising her until her knees cleared the beloved tea-stained quilt a former commune member had made her when she was a teen. Laughing, she parted her legs to wrap herself around him once again.

Hanging her weight from his front while he was leaning into her wasn't her brightest move, however, and they overbalanced. She tumbled onto her back, Jason atop her, pressing her into the mattress.

It was the first time she'd borne his entire weight and she moaned with pleasure.

"Sorry." Breathing hard, he started to push off.

"No. Stay." She tightened her arms around his neck. "You feel *gooood*."

He froze for an instant, hot, dark eyes blazing. Then his weight came back down atop her and his long fingers grasped her head. He slammed his mouth over hers.

Gone was the slow, erotic gentleness he'd treated her to moments ago. He was all muscular heat now. All rough-skinned hands and male aggression.

And it made her so hot she thought she'd explode.

She couldn't catch her breath. Couldn't think. God, she'd believed she was sexually excited before, but that paled compared to the arousal roaring through her veins in this moment.

Shooting fire through every nerve ending.

Turning her nipples so hard it was nearly painful.

Saturating swollen tissues deep between her legs.

Barely recognizing those breathless moans rising in the air as her own, she writhed beneath Jason's weight, digging her nails into his nape, trying to widen her legs between the hard thighs holding them captive.

He raised his head and stared down at her. Then he slid down her torso. Palming her left breast, he pushed it up at the same time he lowered his head. Holding her gaze, he wrapped his lips around the projectile point of her nipple. And sucked.

Head punching back into one of the remaining pillows, she chanted his name in rhythm to the suction pulling at her breast. Lust was a dozen flaming arrows shot straight to that pulsing target between her thighs.

As if he knew it, Jason slid onto his side without relinquishing her nipple. Easing his hand from the breast he'd been plumping up, however, he brushed his fingers down her diaphragm, leaving a trail of heat all the way to her waist, and from there down her stomach. Insinuating his hand beneath the hip bands of her sweatpants and panties, he eased his forefinger between the lips of her sex.

Poppy sucked air...then held her breath as his fingertip continued downward, following the intimate curve until his long finger disappeared into her hot, wet depths with one deep, devastating plunge.

An atavistic sound exploded from her chest.

Her nipple popped free as his head jerked up. Licking his lips, he looked from her expression to where his hand disappeared beneath the waistband of her sweats. Then he raised his eyes to hers once more. That middle finger pushed deeper as his palm flattened over her mound. "Shove down your pants," he commanded. "I do my best work when I can see what I'm doing."

His words exploded a sharp, hard little contraction inside her. Her sheath clamped tightly around his finger and she watched as the fires already burning in the backs of his eyes flared.

"Shove 'em down," he growled.

Raising her hips, she did as he ordered.

"Oh, God, look at you," he said hoarsely. His gaze roamed from her breasts thrusting ceilingward to her sweats tangled around her knees—then honed in on the blond curls between her thighs. "You are so pretty."

His thumb slid up and down her furrow and he hissed when it set off another small orgasm. Leaning down, he bestowed a quick, sharp nip to the tip of her nipple, then withdrew his finger from her as he slithered down the quilt toward the foot of the bed. After stripping her of her sweatpants, he applied his hands to the insides of her knees and pushed them wide.

Before she had time to feel the slightest bit awkward, he lowered his head and gave her a slow lick up the soft split between her legs, ending with a flick of his tongue against her clitoris.

"Oh, God!" Jackknifing halfway to a seated position,

she fisted her hand in his hair, not quite sure even as she did it what action she intended to take.

Then, his dark eyes watching her every reaction, he lapped at her again and, panting, she realized it wasn't to pull him away.

She flopped back down onto her pillow.

He grinned up at her, all flashing white teeth and long, strong tongue flattened against her most intimate tissues. Looking at him, feeling what he was doing to her, she came for real this time. Her orgasm rolled through her, a hard, clenching interior earthquake that had her thrusting her hips high while her attenuated moan kept time with the sensations that just kept coming and coming and coming.

"Jesus." Looking up the length of her body, Jase watched as she went wild. Spreading his hand just above her mound, he held her down while he lapped her through another set of spasms. God, he wanted to be inside her, wanted to feel her wrap all around him like a rubber band when she went off. This time was for her though.

But, holy shit, she was so damn beautiful getting off it was hard not to climb all over her like a kid on a new set of monkey bars.

He was so hard he was hurtin' by the time she went limp, and he fished his wallet from his hip pocket to extract the condom he'd been carrying since the night he'd planned to score at the cop bar.

Looking at Poppy sprawled, naked and satiated upon her bedspread, he had the oddest moment of gratitude that he hadn't.

Not quite sure what that was all about, he shoved it aside and shucked out of his slacks and socks. Then he rolled the protection on. Coming back to lie alongside her on the bed, he tenderly brushed her hair, which was growing to almost scary proportions as it dried, off her face, and leaned to press a gentle kiss on her lips. "You okay?"

Her lids slowly lifting, she hummed a little nonanswer that nevertheless sounded pretty damn happy, and breathed in deeply through her nose. Then, gentle as a zephyr, her exhale drifted through softly parted lips. "Better than," she breathed, the corners of her lips curling up. "Way better. *Hugely* better."

"Good." He leaned down to give the curve of her neck a nuzzle.

Then a nip. "Because there's more where that came from." And going back to the basics, he kissed her for the umpteenth time. Then he set about arousing her interest in Round Two.

To his gratification, it didn't take long. Mere minutes into his ministrations, she rolled them over so she was on top.

"Aw, Jeez-us!" He gasped when she plopped herself directly atop his dick.

Grinning down at him, she wiggled around, and it didn't matter that she knew *exactly* what she was doing to him—he was pretty sure his eyes were crossed. Then she shifted back onto his upper thighs and all that wondrous wet heat she'd been teasing him with disappeared. His cock sprang upright so fast it nearly slapped her in the stomach.

Her hand wrapped around it. "Lookie, he's all suited up." She shot him an ironic smile. "You're such a Boy Scout."

"Yes, ma'am," he groaned even as his hips shot up when she squeezed him through her fist from tip to root. "Be prepared," he wheezed. "Those are words to live by."

She laughed and climbed onto her feet to crouch over him, holding him in place while she centered herself over his blindly seeking dick. Lowering herself a fraction, she rubbed its head along her slick, swollen furrow.

And her laughter died. "I wanted to tease you into insanity," she whispered, gazing down at him. "And I really thought, since you took such good care of me, that I could hold out long enough to do it." She made an adjustment and lowered another inch and Jase gritted his teeth as he felt the head of his cock start to push into her. "But I can't," she said. "I wanna know what you feel like inside me too much."

Another inch and the head popped past the ring of muscle at her entrance. Then she just kept on going until her sweet round butt settled against his balls. And *fuck, oh, fuck,* she was so hot and slick and tight inside.

His hips shot up again. Bracing her feet, she rode him like a Saturday-night cowgirl on the mechanical bull. The resulting sensation had him nearly blind with need. But it was time he took charge.

So, clasping her hips in his hands he raised her up. Almost,

nearly,

just about off him.

Then he slammed her back down. Raised her up and pulled her back down.

Her eyes closed and her white teeth clamped over her rosy lower lip and she crossed her arms in the air over her head as a soft moan escaped her.

He crunched up and took a fast hard pull on her nipple. She hissed, her eyes flying open.

"I want to be on top," he growled around the tight little morsel between his teeth. He gave it another tug, then turned it loose and looked her in the eye. "I want to hold you down and fuck you—*love* you—till you scream."

A helpless little mew sounded in her throat and, taking it as assent, he flipped them over. Lacing their fingers together, he pressed the backs of her hands into the quilt on either side of her head, spread his thighs until hers were wide-open and braced his toes in the mattress. And he sank into her, a long, slow push that ended with an emphatic up-tilted thrust at its apex.

He knew he was hitting her sweet spot when her eyes lost focus, and he pulled out so slowly he felt the drag of every single millimeter of those slippery tissues trying to retain their clasp on him.

Then he pushed back in.

Pulled back out.

Pushed—

"Omigawd, omigawd, omigawd," she started to chant, her voice climbing with each imprecation. "Omiga— Jason? Oh, *God,* Jason!" Her legs wrapping tightly around his hips, her head rocked back into the pillow, she started coming all around him.

The look of her, wild hair, flushed cheeks and inward-looking dazed eyes, the *feel* of all those tight, sharp contractions squeezing and releasing, *squee*zing and releasing his cock broke his grip on the slow, controlled strokes he'd been employing. *Mine,* he thought savagely and thrust into her harder, faster, disengaging their fingers and pushing up onto his planted hands to gain more leverage. *Mine, mine, mine, mine, mine.*

She kept coming all around him and his world went red. God, he was so close, so clo— *Oh. Fuuuuuuck!*

He shoved deep one last time and held, throwing back his head and growling long and low as the spasms milked him dry. When it was over, when she had wrung every last drop of sensation to be had out of him, his head flopped forward, too heavy to hold up.

Then he slid bonelessly atop her.

For the longest time he merely lay there feeling his heartbeat slowly descend out of the red zone. Eventually, however, his brain reengaged.

Okay. He didn't know what the hell all that *mine* crap was about. Hell, he didn't even have a clue what it was he felt when it came to her. It sure as shit wasn't love, though. He was a de Sanges; what did *he* know from love?

So this…whatever it was between them wasn't the stuff of happily-ever-afters. But neither did he like what was going down around her all of a sudden. It would kill him if something happened to her. Serve and protect— that was what he knew, what he did. Who he was.

And what he intended to do—whether Poppy liked it or not.

Raising his head far enough to look down at her, he said in a voice that would have been a lot more impressive if it didn't sound as if it had been run through a shredder, "Clear out some room in a drawer for me, Blondie. I'm moving in."

CHAPTER NINETEEN

Okay. On behalf of independent women everywhere, I should have protested Jason's big tell-
don't-ask policy much more strenuously. Or,
okay—here's a thought—at all.

IT WAS ONE WEEK today since Jason had moved in with
her, lock, stock and barrel. Well, barrel anyhow. He'd
brought several armloads of clothing over, but not much
else—except for his ever-present gun. *That,* Poppy
admitted as she stood in the parking lot beneath the
kids' mural, was taking a bit of getting used to.

"Hey, watch it!"

Glancing up from the paper plate where she was
mixing yellow into Henry's lizard-green paint for him
to dot along his much-adored reptile's legs and belly to
give it texture and depth, she saw that Danny had
dribbled some paint from his own piece of Chinet, just
missing Henry by inches.

"Sorry, dude. I got sort of involved here and didn't
realize I was tipping my plate."

"Palette," Henry corrected him, taking a hit-and-miss
swipe at the spill with one of the wet rags she'd given

the kids. "Jeez, and you call yourself an artist? Show a little pride in your tools, man."

No harm, no foul, obviously. After checking Cory to be sure she, too, was doing all right on her part of the wall, Poppy went back to her mindless mixing and her thoughts.

Because the truth was, the whole situation took some getting used to. She not only hadn't talked to her best friends this week, but she'd also actively dodged two calls from Ava. She sure as hell hadn't mentioned to her folks yet that Jason was living with her. With luck he'd be gone before she had to.

Ignoring the funny pang she got at the thought of him moving out when he had barely moved in, she concentrated on her parents' probable reaction if…when…*if* they discovered it. Not that they'd have a problem with her living with a member of the XY species. They had raised her, after all, in an atmosphere of free love.

But free love with *the Man,* as she'd grown up hearing cops called? Not so sure they'd be happy about that. And she *knew* they wouldn't love the fact that the guy whose suits were taking up more of her closet space than any man's clothes ought to went around with a weapon snugged under his arm. Pretty much 24/7. No, as roommates went, he wouldn't be her folks' first choice.

She snorted softly as a blast of heat suffused her veins, her loins, her face. Because the way the two of them had been going at it, one, two and once *three* times in one night, the word *roommate* just seemed sort of a…weak, pallid—oh, my—definite misnomer.

Unable to help herself, she looked up again. Her

brow furrowed when she didn't spot Jason in the lot or working with the kids. Although come to think of it, she vaguely remembered him mentioning something about going to Marlene's shop to talk about…well, she didn't know what exactly, since she was pretty sure he hadn't actually said.

Like a tongue to a loose tooth, her mind went back to the possibility—no, *probability*—of him moving out every bit as precipitously as he had moved in. This whole mysterious-madman-wanting-to-harm-her scenario was ludicrous and sooner or later Jason would realize it. And she already knew—the dilemma of explaining a gun-toting lover to her pacifist folks aside—that she'd miss him when he admitted she didn't need protecting, threw his classy suits in his car and hit the road back to his own place. She'd miss him big-time.

She had come to enjoy not only the four-star, toe-curling sex he brought to the table, but all the day-to-day stuff they did together as well. It was mostly just little things like brushing their teeth together or making the bed. Left up to her, she would have just tossed the blankets up. But Jason was much neater than she was and she found she didn't mind taking the time so much when he was across from her chipping in.

He made her feel…complete. Which was funny, considering she'd never judged her life lacking. But when they were together there was…hell, she didn't know— a sort of airiness to her soul. At the same time she felt grounded, connected. Plugged in.

She shook her head, because could she *be* any less

coherent? This was the main reason she'd avoided her friends this week. If she sounded this stupid to herself— who at least appreciated these never before felt emotions, even if she couldn't intelligently define them—how was she supposed to describe the suckers to Ava and Jane? To her mother or her father?

Jason had made her laugh several times this week. She should no longer be caught by surprise by what a great sense of humor he had—and she wasn't, really. Still, she did find herself tickled every time it manifested itself. As she realized she was grinning like an idiot but not caring, her mind drifted back a few days....

POPPY HEARD the front door close and poked her head out the bathroom door to see Jason stripping off his suit coat in the living room. As she gathered her hair at the top of her head, she watched him sling the jacket over his shoulder. His free hand lifted to rub the furrow between his brows.

She went out to meet him, whipping a rubber band around the ponytail she'd gathered as she walked.

"Rough day?" she asked and saw some of the rigidity in his shoulders lessen.

"More frustrating than anything," he replied. "I feel like I'm spinning my wheels on some cases I've got going."

Wrapping both hands around his wrist, she backed toward the kitchen, tugging him along with her. "Come on," she said. "You can fill me in while we get dinner ready. There's a bottle of wine on the counter." She pointed to it as they squeezed into the small space.

"Why don't you pour us a glass. Or there might still be a beer in the fridge, if you'd prefer that. I'm just going to throw together some eggs and Canadian bacon."

She gathered her supplies from the fridge, then bumped it closed with a hip and looked over at him as she began cracking eggs over a bowl. "Tell me about the pain-in-the-patootie cases."

His shoulders shifted. "There's nothing concrete to tell. That's the problem. Hohn and I have been working a series of burglaries. I know they've gotta have a common denominator—but aside from the fact that they're jewelry stores, we haven't discovered what that is."

"Yet." She stopped whisking eggs to look at him. "You haven't found the common denominator *yet*."

"Right." The corner of his mouth ticked up. "I haven't discovered it yet. Part of it's because I haven't got my rhythm yet living here, so I'm a little off my game. Usually I'd go home to an empty apartment and obsess all night."

"And how's that usually work out for you?" She poured the egg mixture into a hot pan and gestured toward the fridge. "Grab a couple slices of that sourdough bread from the loaf in the freezer and throw them in the toaster."

He did as requested, pressed down the toaster button, then turned back to lean against the counter. And answered her question. "Most of the time? I don't accomplish a lot. Occasionally, though, something shakes loose. Or sometimes I go up and talk it over with Murph." As if he could read the question forming in her mind, he smiled wryly. "With, okay, pretty much the same results. So maybe I oughtta try setting it aside for the night. God knows it'll still be there in the morning."

Her spatula poised midturn beneath a Canadian bacon round, she beamed at him. Because, really, if she'd learned nothing else the past several days he'd been living here, she'd come to understand that the man would work himself into the ground left to his own devices. That made his willingness to set aside his concern over his cases a sacrifice on his part.

A sacrifice made to accommodate their living arrangement. "Maybe giving it a rest will enable you to look at it with fresh eyes."

"Maybe it will." He crossed the tiny kitchen in a single long step and hauled her in for a kiss. Then he set her back on her feet and brushed back a curl he had disarranged. "You're one smart tomatah, aren'tcha."

"Yes, I am." She scrambled the eggs in the pan, sprinkled a pinch of kosher salt over them, then sent him a sidelong glance. "You're one good kisser."

"I am, aren't I?" Leaning back against the counter again, he grinned at her and—bam!—her knees went weak.

The toast popped and she pulled herself together. "Butter that and we'll eat." She dished the eggs onto two hand-tossed pottery plates and added the Canadian bacon. "You want milk?"

He declined it in favor of the wine they were still working on and they carried their dinner to the couch. Poppy grimaced as they sat down. "I really do need to clear enough space off the table so we aren't constantly having to balance plates on our knees."

"I wouldn't know how to act," he commented and dug into his eggs. They ate in silence for a few moments, then he shot her a crooked smile. "These are great."

He was consistently appreciative of her cooking—far beyond what it merited—and it never failed to grab at something way down deep inside of her. To counteract the sappy feeling, she assumed a motherly smile as she reached over and patted his knee.

"Yes, well, I do live for the challenge of preparing these gourmet meals."

"Smart mouth." His gaze on her lips, he wolfed down the last few bites, then set his plate on the floor. "I've got a much better use for that mouth than listening to it make fun of me."

She dabbed her fingertip at a drip of melted butter on her plate and slid the digit into her mouth. Looking him in the eye, she gave her finger a little suck. *"Ooh,"* she murmured around it.

Then laughed as he dove for her, divested her of her plate and glass and drove her flat against the couch cushions with the weight of his hard body.

POPPY JERKED, coming back to her surroundings with the bump and burn of a space shuttle reentering earth's atmosphere. Blinking, licking her lips, she looked down at her hands, which still held the plate of yellow-green paint, although the Popsicle stick she'd been using to stir it with was frozen midwhisk. Holy sh—

She blew out a gusty exhale. Had she gotten sucked into the waltz-down-memory-lane time/space continuum, or what? Shaking the last of the lingering memories that trailed like cobwebs from her mind, she rose to her feet and took the paint over to Henry.

She was soon absorbed in showing the teen how to dot the color along the lizard's underbelly and around its protuberant eye. Yet her head inexplicably lifted several moments later. Looking toward the corner, she saw Jason rounding Harvey's building.

He moved with his habitual loose-limbed grace, a long, lean man in white shirtsleeves, loosened tie, slacks and suspenders. He had his hands in his pockets and his suit jacket looped over one arm. He must have locked his gun in the car, because he didn't appear to be wearing it. That was a direct contradiction of the man she'd come to know this past week. Still, the day had turned sunny and warm, so perhaps he hadn't wanted to publicly reveal the weapon when he'd removed his jacket.

As she watched, his step developed an almost imperceptible hitch and he extracted a hand from his slacks to dig through his jacket's inside breast pocket. His rummaging around made the jacket shift over his arm, and Poppy nodded.

Aha. Mystery solved. The butt of his gun stuck out from his waistband, disguised up until then by the way he'd been carrying his suit coat.

Retrieving a cell phone, he flipped it open, glanced at its screen and brought it up to his ear. He continued toward them as he listened to the person on the other end, but then stopped. Looking across the distance that separated them, he met her gaze and held up a lean finger in the universal gonna-be-a-minute signal.

And why that simple gesture should trigger the abrupt rush of emotion that boiled through her like steam through a clam cooker she could not say. Yet all of a sudden she was suffused with dead-certain knowledge. She stared at him in wonderment.

Ho-ly—

Ohmigaw—

She sucked in a breath. Blew it out again.

And faced her reality head on. Dear. Freakin'. Lord.

She'd gone and fallen in love with the man.

JASE SNAPPED his phone closed a longer while later than he'd anticipated and noticed that the kids, directed by Poppy, were packing up their supplies in the trunk of her POS car. Watching her laugh as she supervised the positioning of the paint cans and various other materials and supplies, he was visited again by a suspicion that had been nipping at him for a few days now.

Hell, more than a few. Truth was, except for the day they'd first made love and he'd announced his intention to move in, the feeling that he was chasing the wrong lead had nagged at him this entire past week. He'd been going 'round and around the track with no more apparent purpose than a greyhound blindly pursuing its mechanical rabbit. The more time he spent with Poppy, the less likely it seemed that she was the one who'd attracted the ladder-sabotaging, car-as-a-weapon-wielding enemy they appeared to be dealing with.

God knew the woman wasn't shy about giving attitude. For the most part, however, that was reserved for him.

And even then, usually only when it came to her kids. She was the height of professionalism or easy friendliness with everyone else he'd ever watched her deal with. Hell, Poppy was an open book, period. What you saw was what you got. People always knew exactly where they stood with her; she simply wasn't the type to hide her feelings. Which made her keeping a deep dark secret that would attract someone bent on taking her out of the picture very unlikely.

There had been problems at the mansion last fall, but as far as he could see it had been centered strictly around her friend Jane. The Kavanaghs had come up clean when he'd run them in conjunction with the break-in there, and he wasn't sure just where he could take an investigation beyond that.

He'd been trying to deconstruct the situations that had gone down around here. So his first order of the day today had been to talk to Marlene Stories to find out whether she'd hired someone to work on her roof the day the wrench had damn near bounced off Poppy's head.

It turned out that, yeah, she had had a guy up there patching a leak around her skylight. A guy who matched the description of the man who had poked his head over the edge to apologize after the tool plummeted from the roof. So that appeared to have been a legitimate accident.

Which was good. It cut down on the fricking psycho factor.

But damned if Jase intended to write off the other two incidents as accidents as well. Like he'd told Poppy last week, he didn't believe in coincidence. And while two back-to-back accidents were statistically possible, they sure as hell weren't probable. Neither could he discount Poppy's adamant conviction regarding her father's dedication to keeping his equipment in tip-top shape. Or Henry's oath that the car that had almost hit her and Cory had barreled without hesitation straight at them.

At *them*. Her and Cory. Once you took the wrench out of the equation and figured that there was no eff'n way of knowing in advance which of them would have used the ladder that day, Poppy was no longer odds-on-favorite as the intended victim.

Much as he wracked his brain, however, he couldn't come up with a scenario that made any more sense for someone wanting to harm Cory. Still, something had been up with the kid lately. And his instincts told him she was the common denominator in this scenario. The connection he'd been looking for.

Unfortunately, he knew demanding answers of a teenage girl before he had a glimmer of what the hell he was even looking for would be one huge exercise in futility. Might as well grab a ball-peen hammer and smack himself in the head with it a few times—he'd probably have the same degree of success.

Not to mention the headache waiting to happen if he gave the girl the third degree in front of Poppy.

Oh, yeah. He could just visualize *that* going down. Like the Babe would ever, in a million years, sit still for it. Hell, without probable cause, she'd be right not to.

But that had been his snitch on the phone. And the guy promised some very interesting information about tagger kids disappearing and how it might connect with Jase's jewelry-store robberies.

"Yo, copper!"

He looked over to Henry, who yelled, "See ya!" and headed for the back door to Harvey's, where he'd been working off and on.

The other kids took off as well and Poppy was closing the trunk as he strode up to her. "Gotta go," he said. "I've got an informant with a possible lead that might be connected to the shit going down around here."

She raised her eyebrows at him. "And he couldn't just tell you over the phone?"

"Snitches aren't big on giving away intel without seeing the green." He started to lean in to kiss her goodbye, then caught himself and snapped upright. "Where are you headed next?"

"I'm free for the rest of the day. I'm gonna go to the mansion and get a little painting done on Miss A.'s bedroom suite."

"Anyone else going to be around?"

"The Kavanagh bros are still working on the kitchen, so I imagine some of them."

"Okay, good. I'll see you later."

She grabbed him by the tie, rose up on her toes and pulled his head down for a kiss. Immediately fired up, he was sinking into it, bracing himself against her car and pulling her close, his hands diving into her hair to grip her head, when she broke the connection and settled back on her heels.

"Yes, you will," she agreed, stroking his jaw. Then she stepped away and climbed in the driver's seat. "See you at home."

Thrusting his hand through his hair, Jase pushed away from the car, then stood gripping the back of his neck as he watched her drive away. When she turned the corner and disappeared from sight, he crossed the lot to his own car.

Jesus. Ever since he'd made love to her, he barely recognized himself. They'd had sex one time and he'd moved in?

He could still see Murph's face when he'd gone back to his place that day to grab some stuff and stopped by to tell his friend where he could be found for the next whatever. The old man hadn't said, *Are you out of your mind!* He hadn't tried to talk him out of it. He'd followed Jase up to his apartment then sat around grinning while Jase gathered his toothbrush, shaving kit and an armload of clothing. Grinning, for Christ sake. As though it were *natural* for a guy with Jase's dicked-up history to move in with Poppy.

What the hell was that all about? Sure, Jase had been determined on his course. That hadn't stopped him from questioning himself. Yet Murph thought it was all just swell?

And *that* had been when Jase had genuinely feared Poppy was in danger.

Now he was ninety-some-percent certain she wasn't. She didn't need his protection. Yet all the same…

See you at home, she'd said. *Home.*

Where she hummed as she worked over her greeting cards while he pored through case notes across the table from her.

Where she fed him homemade meal after homemade meal.

Where he felt…good.

She hadn't called it her house. She'd said home. As if it were his, too.

And in that moment he lost what feeble intention he'd ever had of moving out.

CHAPTER TWENTY

The Big L? Am I really contemplating the Big L?

POPPY HADN'T BEEN in the mansion half an hour before Jane and Ava showed up. "Hey," she said, looking up from the trim she was painting. "You two have radar or something?"

"Nah, something better. A husband who's been warned he better give me a jingle the minute he lays eyes on you." Jane pinned her with a look. "You've been avoiding us, Missy."

Ah, hell. She carefully placed her brush across the corner of her paint tray and rose to her feet.

And tried to prevaricate. "What are you talking about?"

Okay, she obviously stunk at it now every bit as much as she had as a kid, because Ava said, "Oh, *please,*" and Jane tapped her Michael Kors patent leather demi-wedge shoe on Miss A.'s gleaming wooden floor.

"Give it up, Calloway," she said. "You never could lie worth a damn. What the hell have you got to hide anyway? It's not like you've been holed up with a hot stud all week and are holding out on us instead of sharing all the steamy details as per the BFF bylaws."

"Ooh, that's a good one," Ava said. "Funny, though, how you never mentioned any bylaws when you were making time with Dev." She waved her hand. "But that's just nitpicking, since you've got the bottom line right. Poppy hasn't had a hot date in, well, almost as long as me—never mind being shacked up with a hottie." She flashed Poppy a comrade-in-arms grin.

Come on, face, don't fail me now. C'mon, c'mon, you can do this—shit!

Both friends' jaws went slack and Ava said, "You *have*, haven't you? You've been shacked up with a hottie this past week! Who on earth—? Oh, my God. Detective *Sheik?*"

"Tell me he's not the one," Jane begged. But that, too, was apparently written on her face, because her friend heaved a big sigh. "Hell. It is." She sank down to sit cross-legged on the floor with no regard for the panties she was flashing beneath her rucked-up skirt.

Ava joined her, but demurely curved her legs to one side, even though she was wearing slacks and could have sprawled out any which way. Her dimples nowhere in evidence, she bent a stern look on Poppy. "You will dish if you know what's good for you, sister."

And she did; grabbing her own spot on the floor, she told her friends everything. Well, almost everything; she didn't mention the so-called threat that had driven Jason to move in with her in the first place, because she knew she wasn't in danger, and she didn't want her friends to worry. And she kept the sexual details to herself.

But she spilled all the rest in minute detail.

When she finally wound down, Jane studied her quietly for a moment. Then her lips curled up in a faint smile. "So I'm guessing that maybe de Sanges is not the rigid Nazi you first painted him to be."

"Oh, man." She drew in a deep breath. Shook her head. "He still has his Nazi moments. But he also has sweet moments, funny moments. And he's been downright amazing with the kids."

"Oh, boy. That's it. She's a goner," Ava breathed.

Poppy raised her brows as if she hadn't the foggiest notion what her friend was talking about.

"C'mon! He's good-looking, he's built, he's good with your precious kids? All we're missing is testimony that the man is a demon in the sack and— Uh-huh! Uh-huh!" She jabbed an elegantly manicured finger at Poppy. "He is! I can see it on your face. You are *so* gone on this guy!"

"Can't deny that."

"And him?" Jane asked. "Is he equally gone on you?"

"That I don't know," she admitted. "We haven't really talked about any of this stuff."

"Okay, I suppose it's only been a week," her friend conceded. "So we're going to be generous here and allow him two, three, maybe four more before we expect him to man-up and declare himself. Then Detective de Sanges had better come through for you, if he knows what's good for him."

"That's right," Ava agreed. "Or we'll see to it he pays in ways that'll make him scream like a girl."

"I THINK CORY might have seen something illegal go down," Jase said the moment he cleared Poppy's door several hours later. "And I think I know when."

Poppy was working on one of her greeting cards. Or so he assumed, since she was hunched over her little dining table. They'd been sharing workspace at that table nightly, but it was a piece of furniture he'd never actually eaten a meal on, since it was constantly covered by a bunch of her projects in progress.

And she always had a mess of those in the works.

She set her colored pencil down now, however, and rose from her workspace. Crossing the room to him, she reached out to rub his arm. Gave him a soft smile that made his gut clench.

Then knotted her fist in his tie and yanked his head down on a level with her own. And said, "*Tell* me."

He almost smiled because it was just so…Poppy. She cared so damn much about everything pertaining to her kids. Add to that the fact she wanted him to open up to her more about his work—and she got twice the bang for her buck with this peremptory demand.

Every damn night she asked him about his day—his cases. What was he supposed to say? He could discuss the former in generalities, but divulging details of the latter to a civilian? He couldn't seem to make her understand that he wasn't like her—that he didn't chat about every damn thing he knew.

Still, just knowing she cared eased some of the tension he'd been carrying. It didn't make sense, because it wasn't as if her interest changed anything when it came to the new concerns set in motion by the intel he'd collected today. He could be damn sure nothing would be improved by talking to her about it. And even if it was, wasn't that just exchanging one set of problems for another?

As abruptly as she'd grabbed it, she untangled her fist from his tie. Carefully she smoothed its silver-blue and gray and white stripes against his blue button-down. Then, lacing her fingers through his, she tugged him deeper into the room.

"Please," she said quietly, reaching out to snag her mug of tea from the table as they passed it. Swinging him around, she looked at him with concerned eyes as she backed him toward the couch, steering him around the low table in front of it. "Tell me about Cory. I need to know."

And for the first time in his career he found himself willing to discuss a case with someone who wasn't a cop. "Some weeks ago I was called out on a robbery that was just another in a series of jewelry-store heists we've been dealing with around town."

"The ones you mentioned the other night that have been giving you fits?"

He nodded as the backs of his calves hit the couch. She gave his chest a nudge and he sat. Their knees brushed as she took her own seat on the coffee table facing him and he reached for one of her hands. Fiddling with her fingers, he said, "This call differed only in that the owner had the bad luck to be in the shop when it was broken into, and he got shot. He's still at Harborview."

"I think I heard about that on the news." She sat a

little straighter on her wooden perch. "The guy who's in the coma?"

"Yeah. What you didn't hear was that I found a can of spray paint and some chewed-up garden in front of the dentist's office next door. I think a graffiti artist witnessed at least part of what went down."

"Oh, God." She surged to her feet, paced a few feet away, then stopped to stare at him. "And you think that someone was Cory?"

"Yes, I think it was. According to my informant, there's been a big attrition in the ranks of taggers who considered the U district their territory. Kids have been disappearing from the streets lately."

Poppy drained her tea, then hugged the empty mug to her breast. "Disappearing how?" she whispered. *"Killed?"*

"No." He jumped up and, closing the space between them, reeled her in for a quick hug. "Sorry, I didn't mean to scare you. But they have been getting hurt." He led her back to the couch and sat her down, then dropped down beside her and shifted to face her. "One kid abruptly moved—he was sent to stay with an aunt and the family doesn't trust cops worth a damn, so they won't say what happened to him. Another had a broken arm and yet another had bruises on his neck that he couldn't or wouldn't explain to his family."

She looked at him with troubled eyes. "Doesn't that sound an awful lot like what happened to Freddy Gordon?"

"Yeah, I thought of that myself. It would be a pretty

big coincidence, though, and you know how I feel about those. On the other hand, Freddy was beat to shit around the same time and a teen not telling the truth to avoid incriminating himself? That wouldn't exactly shock my socks off. I tried calling him but got his uncle's message machine. I haven't heard back from anyone yet."

"How on earth do you stand the wait? I would go *nuts* with your job." Her slender eyebrows meeting over her nose, she gave him an accusatory glare. "Did you learn anything from anyone?"

A slight smile pulling up the corners of his mouth, he reached out to run his finger down the delicate slope of her nose. "I talked to the boy with the bruised neck. He's scared and I don't think I would've gotten squat out of him, except his mother sat with him on their couch and held his hand at the same time she informed him that no one was budging from that room until he talked to me—and to her, too, since she was through allowing him to keep her in the dark. As soon as it became clear she meant business—that he'd have a cop camped in his living room until he talked—he caved."

"And?" she demanded impatiently.

"And apparently some thug was looking for a boy known only by his street tag." He hesitated, then admitted, "Of CaP."

She went very still as she stared up at him in alarm. "As in Capelli."

"That's what I'm thinking. *And* that the thug clearly now knows that Cory's a girl, not the boy he was asking about earlier. How he made that leap I can't say, but the fact he tried to run her down indicates he discovered it somehow. I need to talk to her, Poppy." He braced himself, marshaling his arguments for when she jumped down his throat.

"I agree."

Relaxing his muscles one by one, he leaned back to study her face. "You do?"

"Of course I do. I'll fight you to the death if you mess with my kids when I think it's to their detriment. But when you're doing your job by trying to keep them safe? Jason, I'm all over that."

He hauled her across his lap for a kiss. Then he set her back on the couch next to him and gently smoothed the clothing his abrupt handling had tweaked out of place. "I've said it before, but I'll say it again—you are one smart tomatah."

"And once again I'm forced to agree." She gave him a wry smile. "Just don't expect me to keep telling you that you're an excellent kisser."

"No need to tell me what I already know, Blondie." He grinned at her, feeling pretty darn good. "You got a contact number for Cory?"

"Yeah. It's in my work address book—the red one in that stack under the phone. Here, I'll get it for you." She climbed to her feet, then crossed the room to unearth the address book. After flipping through a few pages, she read him the phone number.

Thinking it'd be smarter to call the station and have someone look it up in the reverse directory so he could simply show up on Cory's doorstep, Jase nevertheless did something he never did when it came to a case—gave in to the expectation on Poppy's face. He punched in the numbers on his cell.

A minute later, he snapped the phone shut again.

"What?" Poppy demanded. "Nobody home?"

"Worse," he said flatly. "It was an operator intercept. She gave you a bullshit number."

Poppy's jaw dropped. "She gave me a false… Why that little—" She drew a deep breath, slowly eased it out and turned to him. "Okay. I think we'll be finishing up the art project tomorrow and I had planned on taking the kids out for pizza to celebrate. Let's let them have that…then we'll talk to Cory."

"I'll talk to Cory," he corrected. "But you can be present to look after her interests until we can contact her mother if you want."

She scooted closer. "You know something, de Sanges?" she said, laying her head on his shoulder. "You are so much better with the kids than I ever would have dreamed when I first initiated this thing."

"Yeah, about that—about you roping me into this deal with them—" Suspicion had been growing in him for a while now and he turned his head to stare down at her. "Do you even know the mayor?"

Her lips curled up. "Nah."

He had to admire her brass, because she'd sure as hell had him going. But he bent a stern look on her…which apparently didn't faze her one bit, since she merely batted those brown eyes at him. "So, who sicced him on me, then? No, wait, lemme guess." He didn't even have to give it five seconds' consideration. "My money's on Ava."

"She's got connections like you wouldn't believe," Poppy agreed, then gave an impatient wave of her hand. "But we were talking about you. About how good you are with the kids. Man. Who woulda ever figured that?"

"Not me," he answered truthfully, since his experience with teens up until now had been fairly minimal—and that usually with some kid he'd been in the process of busting for knocking over a mini-mart. "Sure as hell not me."

SEATTLE DAWNED warm and sunny the following morning—one of those rare preview-of-summer days that hinted at a possible hot spell. Cory pulled a sundress from the back of her closet, one that her mother had bought her and she'd never worn because she'd considered it just too freaking cheery. Too so not her.

But it was really kinda pretty with its spaghetti straps and empire waist, and she supposed the fuchsia fabric with its orange color-block stripes around the bust part and forming the dress's short hem wasn't *too* sucky. A little too pep-rally-girl for comfort, but she could live with it for one day.

Especially after she pulled it on and saw that she actually looked kinda hot in it.

She fixed her hair and put on makeup. Looking at herself in the mirror, she paused for a moment with the liquid eyeliner in one fist and the mascara wand poised over her lashes, thinking about what both her mom and Poppy had said about her looking prettier without all the makeup. Maybe...?

Nah. She shook her head. She looked like a damn not-quite-fifteen-year-old—and a *young* not-quite-fifteen-year-old at that—without her eyes made up. Maybe when she was sixteen or seventeen, she'd revisit the idea of cutting back.

Or not. In either case, it wasn't something she had to worry about today. Which was good, because she already had a boatload of crap to consider.

Ms. C. seemed to think they'd probably be finishing the art project today. Cory had mixed emotions about it.

On the one hand, they'd put in a ton of hours on the project and she was beyond excited to see the total result of all their hard work.

On the other, though, she was gonna miss seeing everyone involved in the project. Even Henry and Detective de S. And, oh, man. Ms. Calloway, for sure.

But she was especially going to miss seeing Danny G. on a regular basis. She sure wished they went to the same school.

She wondered if he would just disappear from her life. She'd pretty much decided to give up her nighttime graffiti outings, since it wasn't safe for her to be out on the streets these days. Besides, she'd gotten a taste for bigger projects, working on this one. Still, the streets had been her only contact with Danny. So what would she do if he just disappeared? God knew he was close-mouthed about where he lived and stuff. She'd already tried to look him up in the phone book and online, but that had been one big no-go.

She'd thought they had become friends. But she also knew he was a little p.o.'d at her for not telling de Sanges about Goonzilla and all the jewelry-store robbery stuff. She actually thought she might do that after they finished this afternoon. Because she really, really didn't want this to follow her home someday. She'd die if she put her mom at risk. And while she may have outrun Arturo so far, there was no guaranteeing her luck would hold out.

Besides, she didn't want to spend her entire life squirreled away inside her apartment. She'd go five kinds of crazy.

Then she shook her head. What was she doing—she didn't need all this crap wrecking her day. She had to deal with it later but until then she was going to try not to worry about it. Because for now, she looked kinda pretty, she was going to see a boy she really liked and work on a project she loved with a woman she admired.

So, please, God. Just let that be enough for the next few hours.

CHAPTER TWENTY-ONE

I wonder what kind of mother I'd be. Man, talk about killer responsibility! There are just so many ways to screw up.

THE PIZZA PARLOR where Poppy took the kids to celebrate the completion of their project was crowded and noisy. They found a table in the back, however, and the two extra-large everything-on-'em pizzas they'd ordered—along with all except maybe a pint's worth of their second pitcher of Pepsi—were nearly gone by the time Jason arrived.

She watched him wind through the tables and smiled when Henry, seated beside her, spotted him as well and hollered, "'Bout time you got here, copper!"

"That's Detective Copper to you, short stuff," Jason said mildly as he pulled out the chair they'd saved for him and sat.

"Yeah, and that's *Mister* Short Stuff to you," Henry shot back around a mouthful of pizza.

Jason flashed one of his rare grins. "Fair enough. I did a drive-by of the wall on my way here and it looks good. Really good. So, congratulations on a job well done." He included all three teens in his look, then added to Poppy, "Sorry I'm late. I caught a new case today and it kept me pretty tied up."

A curvy, five-foot-nothing waitress blew past two parties trying to get her attention and made a beeline straight for their table. She rocked to a halt at Jason's side. "Can I get you a plate?" she asked, leaning down with a megawatt smile. "Or perhaps you'd like a beer?"

Poppy bristled at the way the woman was, well, maybe not hanging all over him, precisely—but definitely sending out vibes. *Do-me* vibes.

Still, she could hardly claim not to understand why, since Jase had drawn her own undivided attention from the first moment she'd lain eyes on him. He might be composed of way too many harsh lines and angles to be considered Mister Hollywood material, but he had chemistry to spare. He was just so…male.

It must be that old hunter-gatherer thing. One look at him and a woman simply knew when it came to the three Ps—protect, provide and procreate—that he had the goods. And then some.

A dawning awareness that Henry had stiffened next to her yanked her from the mental path she was wandering down. She turned to see what was wrong and found him staring at the table talker, which advertised beers from the bar, that Jason had picked up.

Oh, crap. She'd forgotten about his father. And once reminded, she wasn't sure for a second which would be less damaging to a child who lived with what she feared was a sometimes abusive alcoholic: to see that an adult male could drink a beer and not turn all scary on him, or for him to see that there were men who could have a perfectly good time without adding alcohol to the mix.

Before she could decide, Jason simply set the tri-angular menu down and asked the waitress if she had any club soda.

"Oh, I'm sorry, we don't." She looked at him with more regret than a failure to provide the beverage warranted.

"I'll just have a glass of water then. A tall one, okay? And that plate would be appreciated." He turned to the kids and indicated the last quarter of the pizza. "Do we need another one?"

"Heck, yeah," Henry said.

"Okay, and another of these," he told the waitress. "I've seen you pack it away," he said to Henry, "so I'm no longer amazed at the amounts you can eat." He shifted his attention to Danny and Cory. "The question is how much more you two can eat. Should we order a large or an extra-large?"

"I'm pretty much done," Cory said.

"Not me," Danny said. "I could eat another piece or two."

"Then make it extra-large and bring another pitcher of pop," Jason said to the waitress and pulled the pan with the two pizza slices still on it toward him and ripped off one. Looping the strings of cheese back onto the triangle with his fingers, he gave the boys that level cop look he did so well. "But one of you is going to have to wait for the new pie to get here, because this piece is mine. I'm starved."

Poppy almost asked if he'd managed to eat anything since breakfast, but bit down on the impulse in time. That would be brilliant. Might as well make a big sign that read *Ms. C. is Shacked Up with Detective de S.* and be done with it. Good grief.

She watched his strong teeth carve off another bite and the muscles in his jaws bunch and lengthen as he chewed. And realized they'd probably have to talk about her feelings for him sooner rather than later.

Because she had a feeling she wasn't any better at this keeping-her-emotions-to-herself business than she was at lying to her friends.

JASE ENJOYED the pizza and watching Poppy interact with the kids. He even did a little interacting of his own. Very little, it was true, but hey.

A beer would have tasted good, but he'd seen that flash of fear on Henry's face and no tall, cold brew was worth that. Damn all fathers who put their addictions above their kids' welfare. There oughtta be a special spot in lockup reserved just for them.

But brooding about things he had no control over was no way to preserve his mellow mood, so he shut down the bitterness that clawed for attention every time he thought of Henry's old man making the kid's life so insecure when his job description was supposed to be protecting his son. He knew he had his own issues with the whole dad-copping-out-of-responsibility subject, even if his father's problem hadn't been substance abuse but rather the fact that he couldn't keep his butt out of the state pen long enough to do his job.

Either way, Jase wasn't going there today. This was supposed to be a celebration.

The closer it came to winding down, however, the quicker his unaccustomedly laid-back mood started swirling down the drain. Because as soon as the party was over, he had to deal with Cory. And he doubted they'd get through that without the whole nine yards of teen-girl tear-soaked drama.

Which, frankly, he couldn't believe was making him edgy. When it came to his cases, his usual reaction to histrionics was simply to wall himself off and power through it. He sure as hell didn't get sucked into that crap. But there was just something about these three kids that got to him.

Dammit, he'd *known* all this one-on-one shit would turn around and bite him on the butt. And what the hell had he been thinking to tell Poppy she could represent Cory's interests until the girl's mother could be contacted?

This was what happened when you got involved. Let down your professional guard just once and pretty soon it was slip-sliding to hell and gone.

His teeth were clenched in impatience by the time they all stood on the sidewalk outside the pizza joint. Hoping the goodbyes would be short and sweet so he could cut Cory out of the herd, he eased out an exasperated breath when Poppy said with her trademark easiness, "Oh, man, I can't believe I almost forgot. I've been meaning to offer you guys a business proposition."

Now what, for cri'sake? She hadn't mentioned any business prop for the kids to him.

"Okay, it's nothing real exciting," she qualified when everyone looked at her with varying degrees of anticipation. "I have a lot of painting I need to get done—décor painting, nothing particularly artistic. But if any of you would like to earn some spending money on Saturday, I'd love the help. You did such a good job not only of the wall, but also of all the grunt work that came before it. I'd be honored to work with you again. I pay twelve-fifty an hour and it's at the Wolcott mansion, which I thought you'd get a kick out of seeing."

"What's the Wolcott mansion?" Danny asked.

She gawked at him a moment, then sighed. "Okay, now you're just making me feel old. I thought everyone was familiar with the mansion and its old unsolved murder mystery."

"I can't," Henry said with palpable regret. "Shit!" He grimaced. "Sorry, Ms. C. I meant shoot. No—that's weak. Uh, I meant…hell. That I just can't, I guess. I told Mr. Harvey I'd help out in the storeroom Saturday."

The mention of Jerry Harvey broke Jase's brood-on. Because the guy seemed to be adopting Henry. Several times now he'd had the kid do chores and odd jobs around the store for him. Plus Henry had mentioned Harvey buying him a piece of pie and a glass of milk at Slice of Heaven.

Jase's suspicious reaction to hearing the latter had been to run Harvey through the system to make sure he didn't have a record. Henry had trouble enough with his old man. And just to be on the safe side he'd run a discreet check through a detective he knew in Special Assaults. Nothing had popped, and in truth Harvey wasn't doing a damn thing that Poppy wasn't. God knew Jase had never suspected *her* of anything kinked.

That was the downside of being a cop. You saw too damn much of the ugly not to have it color the way you looked at everything.

"Maybe another time," Poppy was saying to Henry when he tuned back in on her conversation with the kids. "I'm doing the entire mansion and have barely made a dent in what I need to get done. So maybe you can give me some time when school goes to summer break. Here. Let me give you…" Voice trailing, she dug through her big tote and came up with a small leather folder. She pulled out business cards and offered one to each of the kids. "Both my phone numbers are on that. You can call me when you've got time and we'll compare schedules," she said to Henry, then turned to Cory and Danny. "You two don't need to decide right this minute, either. Give me a call if you think you can make it and I'll give you directions."

"I'd like to," Danny said. "I'm not sure about this weekend, though. I think Gloria wants to play her annual mother gig this Saturday. But I'd like to another time." He turned to Cory. "So you want a ride?"

Jase braced himself to intercede, but to his surprise the girl shook her head.

"Thanks," she said. "But I need to talk to Detective de S."

Danny inspected her a moment, then nodded. "Good

idea." He turned to Poppy. "Thanks for everything, Ms. C. You turned this into something a lot different from what I expected. You're really…awesome." Color climbed his lean cheeks and as if to counteract it, he turned briskly to Jase. "You aren't half-bad, either," he said and stuck out his hand.

Jase shook it, then watched as the kid whirled on his heel.

"I'll see you two around," Danny said to Cory and Henry. "Good project." He started to stride off without a backward glance, then turned back to Henry "You need a ride?"

"You mean it?" At Danny's nod, Henry grinned. "Coolicious, dude. Maybe you could take me back to Harvey's?"

"Sure."

And a second later, they were gone.

Jase immediately turned to Cory. Before he could launch the interrogation he'd been itching to get to, however, she cleared her throat and said, "I have something I have to tell you."

He blinked, momentarily thrown off balance. Then he nodded. "Shoot."

She looked around at the people coming and going on the sidewalk outside the pizza parlor. "Could we, um, maybe go to your car or something?"

"Sure. Do you want Poppy—Ms. Calloway—to come, too?"

She nodded jerkily and sent Poppy a nervous, uncertain smile. "If you wouldn't mind?"

"Of course not." Reaching for the girl's hand, Poppy gave it a squeeze.

The three of them walked the half block to where he'd parked and he held the door for Cory to get in the front passenger seat and then the back door for Poppy.

The teen sat without speaking for a moment after all of them were settled inside. Then she blinked her overmascaraed eyes. Wiped her palms down the pretty skirt of her dress where it draped over her thighs. Cleared her throat.

Then swiveled to face him. "The night before we first started this project," she began, "I went to the U district to see if I could find a good wall for a little graffiti…"

CRAP.

Crap, crap, crap! Cory scowled at the back of Detective Hardass's head as he wove his car through the freeway traffic toward her apartment. Not about to ride shotgun next to him when he refused to listen to reason, she had insisted Ms. C. trade seats with her.

They were going to her real address. He'd demanded it in such a you-don't-*even*-wanna-mess-with-me tone after she'd finished telling him about Arturo and the jewelry shop that she'd recited it without thinking twice. Pissed about that, about *everything,* she visualized a burn hole beginning as a small smoking speck in the amber-brown skin where his dark hair met his neck, then rapidly widening to a huge, black-edged hole.

And said for the umpteenth time, "We do *not* have to involve my mom in this."

His wide shoulders didn't shift. His attention remained firmly on the road. "Yeah," he growled with finality. "We do."

"Ms. *Ceeeee,*" she said, looking for backup from the blonde she'd come to admire so much.

Poppy twisted to look at her over the seat. "Cory, I'm one hundred percent on Detective de Sanges's side on this one. Not only does your mother have a right to know, she *needs* to know."

"Oh, big surprise you'd side with him," Cory snarled bitterly. "We all know he's doing you."

The moment the words left her mouth, she went hot, then cold, then hot again, feeling kinda sick to her stomach. She held her breath, hardly believing she'd just said that.

Detective de S.'s gaze snapped to the rearview mirror and locked on hers as if he couldn't believe it, either. His dark eyes burned hot beneath aggressively lowered brows, and he didn't have to open his stern mouth for her to know he was not happy with her.

Ms. Calloway's expression, on the other hand, went very cool, which was so unlike her that it made Cory's stomach pitch even further.

"Setting aside for a moment that my love life is my business and none of yours," the blonde said in a calm voice that held not one speck of the warmth Cory was used to hearing in it, "you clearly didn't learn the first thing about me these past several weeks if you think sex—or anything else for that matter—could ever turn me into a yes woman."

Jason snorted and turned his attention back to the road. "That's the goddamn truth," he said under his breath.

Ms. C. didn't reprimand him for his language and she didn't turn back to face front. She simply pinned Cory in place with a level gaze.

Which made her squirm and duck her head, wishing her bangs were longer so she could hide behind them. Because she was ashamed she'd said that. She and the guys had kind of speculated their teacher and the cop might be doing the deed, but even if they were, Ms. Calloway wasn't one of those females whose every thought originated with her boyfriend of the moment. She had never once acted like anyone but her own woman.

But Cory was desperate. At practically any other time, her mother would have been working, so it wouldn't have been as big a deal to be dragged home by the cops. This *would* have to be the day her mom had one of her rare half-days off. There was no way she could keep her from discovering the real reason Cory had been part of the project she'd talked about so enthusiastically.

But all the same…

"I'm sorry," she muttered to her lap. And she was. But twisting her fingers together, she whispered to them what was really foremost in her mind. "I never wanted Mom to know I was on the art project as a punishment for tagging."

"Is that what it felt like to you, Cory? A punishment?"

"At first it did." Sneaking a peek at the pretty blonde, she was relieved to see that her teacher's brown eyes weren't as distant as they had been. "Not so much after I'd been there a couple of days, though." She slid Ms. C. another sidelong peek. "It turned out to be fun."

"Good. Because I've enjoyed working with you. And I'd like you to trust me about something. You need to let your mother be your mother. Give her the opportunity to do what moms do best."

She heaved a big sigh. "Whatever," she muttered. Because she didn't think Ms. C. did know best in this instance.

They reached her building way too soon. Reluctantly, she led her jailers up to her apartment.

Her mother looked up from the laundry she was folding when Cory trooped through the door with Detective de S. and Ms. C. in tow a few minutes later. "Cory?" she said, alarm chasing across her face as her gaze darted between the two adults. Setting the T-shirt she was folding on a stack of them perched on the arm of the couch, she rose to her feet.

Detective de S. stepped forward. "Mrs. Capelli, I'm Detective de Sanges and this is Poppy Calloway."

The fear that having a cop show up on her doorstep had flashed in her mother's eyes turned to arrested interest at Ms. C.'s name. She turned to Poppy. "Cory's teacher in that art project?"

"Yes, ma'am," Ms. C. agreed.

"Oh, how nice to meet you! She's *loved* being a part of that."

"And I've loved having her in it. Cory is very talented. We just finished our wall today. You'll have to have her take you over to see it."

Cory let out the breath she'd been holding as her mother agreed that was a great idea. Apparently Ms. C.

didn't feel compelled to mention the manner in which Cory had been drafted into the project.

Then Detective de Sanges shifted and she shot him a nervous glance. Because there was no guarantee he wouldn't blow it for her. The guy wasn't big on torquing the rules.

But ratting her out must not have been all that high on his list of important stuff, because he stepped forward and said in a gentle voice, "You might want to sit down again, Mrs. Capelli. Because Cory's got some trouble and we need to talk to you about it."

Her face losing all color, Cory's mom reached for her hand. "Honey?"

They sat side by side on the couch and her mother's face grew whiter with every word Detective de S. spoke. But she slipped an arm around Cory's shoulders, and hugged her to her side. When he finished, she turned and gathered her even closer, holding her tight. Pulling back a few moments later, she smoothed Cory's bangs back from her face. Gave her a look filled with fierce love.

"Why didn't you *tell* me this was happening?"

"I didn't want to worry you."

"Didn't want to—" She gave her a little shake. "Who's the mother here, Cory Kay?"

"You," she admitted in a little voice.

"That's right. I am. You do not protect me. *I* protect you. And I can't do that if you're keeping the fact you're in danger from me." She turned to the detective, resolve written all over her even though Cory knew it must have felt like nightmare déjà vu to have her last remaining family member be a witness relying on the cops to keep her safe. 'Cuz just look at how good that had turned out last time. "What do we do?" she asked.

And even though Cory knew she wasn't out of the woods yet, even though she understood that she was still in very real danger from Arturo and that her mother was bound to have something to say about the fact she'd been out to paint graffiti on other people's walls the night all this had begun, she went limp with relief against her mother's side. Because for the first time in almost two years, she realized something.

She didn't have to be the strong one in the family. She didn't have to save her mother's sensibilities. All she had to be was a kid.

And that was one heck of a—what had Henry called the ride Danny G. offered him? Oh, yeah.

That was one heck of a coolicious load off.

CHAPTER TWENTY-TWO

How can everything turn upside down so damn fast?

POPPY HAD BEEN home almost four hours and was talking to Jane on the bedroom phone when the doorbell rang.

"Gotta go," she said, interrupting her friend in mid-sentence. "Jason's home and I need to find out what happened at Cory's after I left." She'd been anxiously anticipating news practically since the moment he'd tossed her his car keys at the Capelli apartment and told her she might as well go home.

He had been on the phone at the time, waiting to talk to someone about getting protective custody for Cory. After informing her it could be a long process that was bound to take a while, he'd assured her he could catch a ride back to the apartment when he was done.

Dying to find out how everything had transpired after she'd left, she raced to the front door.

"I didn't realize until I got home that you forgot to take the house key off your chain," she said with a smile as she yanked it open.

It wasn't Jase. Instead, a strange man stood there.

A rough-looking, stocky stranger, sporting a couple

of thick, black, badly rendered tattoos on his knuckles. She swallowed hard and started easing the door closed again, knowing she didn't have a prayer of shutting it if his intention was to muscle his way in.

He merely slid his fingers into his jeans pockets, however, and gave her an easy smile. "Hey," he said. "Jase around?"

He knew Jason? "Um, no." Oh, crap, considering all the stuff that had been happening lately, should she have told him that? Let him know she was here all alone?

Then she blew out a breath. Dammit, she wasn't used to regarding people with distrust. "No, I'm sorry," she said. "He's out on a case."

"Oh." Disappointment flashed across his face, then disappeared behind a neutral expression. "Detective Dickwa—um, that is, Murphy, gave me your address." He thrust out his hand. "I'm Joe. Jase's brother."

Shock was a punch to the lungs. Jason had a *brother?*

Her expression must have been as poleaxed as she felt because Joe grimaced.

"Shit. He didn't tell you, did he? Well, I s'pose me and the old man and Pops—that's Jase and me's grampa—we ain't exactly the relatives to write home about. We spent more time in Walla Walla or Monroe than we was ever around to take care of Jase when he was growin' up."

Holy, holy shitskis. And the surprises just kept piling up. She stepped back, opening the door wider. "I'm hoping he'll be home soon." Belatedly, she offered her hand. "I'm Poppy. Would you like to come in?"

"Thanks. That'd be real nice." But once inside, he refused her offer of a beverage and perched uneasily on her couch.

She studied him. "You and Jason don't look much alike, do you?" Then, looking at his chin, she smiled. "Well, except for that five-o'clock shadow."

That made him smile as well and he rubbed a hand over his jaw. "Yeah. All the de Sanges men got this damn beard." Then he lapsed back into an uncomfortable silence.

She searched for something to say that would put him at ease, then finally had to acknowledge, "I'm not sure what's acceptable to ask a man who admits to spending more time in jail than out."

To her delight, it seemed to restore the uncomplicated manner with which he'd started out. "Yeah," he said with a wry grin. "I'm guessin' an uptown girl like you ain't seen many the likes of me."

Poppy snorted. "Uptown, my butt. I have a friend who's one of those, but I grew up in a commune."

"No shit?"

"Well, okay, 'grew up' might be stretching it a bit. But I did spend my first five years in one." It occurred to her that this was a golden opportunity to learn a little something about Jason. Sure, pumping his brother for information wasn't exactly a heroic pursuit, but she could at least safely ask what Jase had been like as a kid without stepping over that line between curiosity and prying. "So tell me, what was—"

The front door slammed shut and Poppy realized she

must not have closed it behind them all the way when she let Joe in. "This time it probably really is Jason," she told Joe with a grin and leaned back to check, prepared to tell Jase they had company.

Only to have her stomach sink with unspecified dread when she caught sight of his expression. His scowl was a black thundercloud darkening his face as he ripped his tie from under his collar and hurled it across the narrow hallway.

The neckpiece was too lightweight to go very far. The jacket he tossed in its wake did a much more impressive job. It hit the wall and slid to the floor as he turned away to stalk into the living room.

He stopped dead in the archway, staring at his brother. "What the hell are you doing here?"

"Jason!" She surged to her feet, but Joe put a hand on her arm as he, too, stood.

"It's okay," he said, then turned his attention to his brother. "I was in the neighborhood and stopped by to see you at your place. Murphy told me you was staying here for a while, so I thought I'd try ta catch ya. Poppy and me's been getting to know one another." When Jason's expression didn't change, Joe shrugged. "But I can see you got things on your mind, so I'll get outta your hair. Maybe we can get together another time."

"Yeah, sure. Maybe."

Poppy patted Joe's arm as she walked him to the door. "I am so sorry. I don't know what's gotten into him."

"Don't worry about it. Like I said, I wasn't there for him much when he was comin' up. I can hardly kick if he ain't dying to get to know me now. Saying that this time I really mean it that I'll stay outta jail isn't *stayin'* outta jail—and Jase's heard the lies before. Anyhow, it was real nice meeting you. You take care, now." And squaring his shoulders, he let himself out.

Poppy stormed back into the living room. "What is the *matter* with you?" she demanded. "That's no way to treat a family memb—" Then the reason she'd been so anxiously awaiting his return, temporarily forgotten by the discovery he had a brother—and a father and grandfather as well, apparently—suddenly came roaring back.

"Oh, my God," she whispered, dread settling in the pit of her stomach. "What happened at Cory's?"

He turned furious dark eyes on her. "What happened? I'll tell you what happened. Fucking budget cuts!"

Her hand went to her heart. "They aren't going to protect her?"

"According to the powers that be, there's no need to put Cory in a safe house, because there's no real evidence that anyone is trying to hurt her."

"That's crazy! What about the ladder—"

"Unfortunate accident."

"The hell it is! But forget that for a moment—how did they explain away someone trying to run her down in a car?"

"Oh, those crazy-ass drivers these days," he said with an insouciance that was belied by the tension in his shoulders, his big hands balled into fists at his sides. "Pedestrians just aren't safe in the streets anymore. Oh, and guess what? Freddy got back to me right in the middle of all this. Turns out he wasn't telling the truth, the whole truth and nothing but the truth after all."

"Arturo beat him up, too?"

"Yeah."

"Then *he* can press charges, right? That will give you something to hold that bastard on—" A bleakness in Jason's eyes stopped her. "What?" she whispered.

"Freddy doesn't want to get involved."

"*What?* You bent over backward to help him!"

"Proving once again that no good deed goes unpunished." He ground the heel of his hand into his forehead. "Except...you know what I really think?" He dropped his hand to his side. "I think Freddy might have been involved a lot deeper than as a tagger Arturo was questioning. I think he may have been one of the kids Cory told us came out of the jewelry store after the owner was shot. He was beaten more severely than the other kids. I think he may have made the mistake of telling someone he hadn't signed up for shooting anybody. But we'll never know for sure because he won't admit to anything beyond being beaten for information."

He jabbed long fingers through his hair and stared down at her, frustration snapping like lightning in his dark eyes. "I know in my *gut* Arturo's trying to eliminate the only witness to his crime. But without a license plate number, an eyewitness ID, *something,* I can't prove it. And without probable cause, no one will give me the manpower I need to watch Cory around the clock."

"So that's it?" she demanded bitterly. "Just...too bad, so sad for Cory?"

"As far as the department is concerned it is. But I put out an APB on Arturo. I have enough to at least bring him in for questioning." His stubble rasped as he scrubbed the backs of his fingers over his chin and lower lip. "I also called in a couple of favors. I've got two patrolmen who will keep the kid's apartment under surveillance for the next few days. I'm not sure what we'll do after that, but I am *not* failing her the way those Philly cops failed her father. Even if that means I have to hog-tie Cory myself."

"Cory? Why wouldn't she do everything possible to help you help her?"

"Because I told her and her mother that she has to stay inside, to keep a low profile, until I can get Arturo off the streets. Apparently the guy doesn't know where they live at this point, and we need to keep it that way. But little Miss Capelli says that she'll have to repeat the ninth grade if she misses too much school and that she'll go crazy, be bored stiff, stuck inside. *Bored!*" He gave her an exasperated look, but he was clearly baffled as well.

Reaching out, Poppy rubbed comforting circles on his forearm. "She's not quite fifteen, Jason. Kids that age can't see past Friday night—a week seems like an eternity."

"Yeah, I get that. Which is why I invited her to see herself in a coffin and her mother left all alone to cry over it. Mrs. Capelli comprehends the concept just fine. She said she'd see to it that Cory stays out of sight, but the woman is holding down two jobs just to make ends meet, so I'm not sure how she intends to do that. But if she can't, I damn well will. Me and my crew."

Oh, Lord. Looking at the fire of conviction burning in his eyes, at the steely resolve, she couldn't believe she'd ever thought this guy was an iceberg. Slapping her hands to his chest, she gave him a shove.

He landed in the chair behind him. "What the—"

Climbing onto his lap, she straddled his thighs, clutched two fistfuls of his shirt on either side of its partially unfastened button placket and pulled him to her as she rocked her mouth over his.

Jason detonated faster than gas fumes meeting a lit Bic. His hands plunging into her hair, he gripped her skull and took immediate *I'm*-in-charge-here command of the kiss.

She conceded control with a shiver, his dominance arousing her almost beyond bearing. He was all hot lips and hotter tongue as he kissed her, as he told her in blunt language that fueled her fire even further what he was going to do to her. His strong fingers combed through her hair, explored her neck, her back, the curve of her hips, the division of her buttocks. They deftly stripped her of her clothing from the waist down, then touched her, stroked her, gripped her, rubbed.

"Now, now, *now*," she chanted as a single talented finger commenced a slow slide up and down the soft, wet slit between her legs, and she rose onto her knees on the chair cushion to fumble between them for his zipper.

A second later his penis sprang free. Wrapping her hand around its base, she positioned herself over it.

Then paused. "If you've got a condom, you'd better give it to me quick."

"Wallet," he panted, rolling up on one hip to push his pants farther down so he could fish it out. "I've been making sure there's one in it all the time because I can't seem to keep my hands off—" He sucked in a breath as she rapidly suited him up, then slowly sank down upon him.

His hands slapped down on her butt and splayed wide, gripping her cheeks to hold her tightly against him as his hips hammered upward in short, deep, powerful thrusts.

Poppy tried to hold out, to make it last, but her body wasn't in an asking-for-permission mode. Not when Jason was hitting all the right spots. Not when she could look into his face and see the fierce concentration as he drew nearer his own climax, as he gritted his teeth and tightened his grasp on her bottom.

Not when he raised her onto her knees with the vigorousness of each new thrust. The sensations, the visuals, brought her—oh, God—so close. And closer yet.

Then he tilted his head back and gazed up at her like carnality incarnate with his slitted, glittering eyes and his lips parted, a hint of upper teeth showing and his tongue pressing his bottom lip.

Her building orgasm ignited with enough pyrotechnics to make the Fourth of July displays at Lake Union and Ivar's look like pikers in comparison.

Flushed, satiated, boneless with radiating pleasure, it was pretty hard to wish you'd held out.

But that didn't keep her from being fiercely pleased when Jason immediately growled deep in his throat, his control in smithereens as he shot his hips high one last time and held her to him, groaning long and loud as he ground against her in release.

Seconds later, he sank back into the seat and she collapsed in a mellow heap atop him, her boobs flattening against the hard plane of his chest, her cheek snuggled in the crook of his neck. She was a jellyfish, floating in a warm sea of contentment. "Whoa," she murmured against his smooth, hot skin.

"No shit." A laugh rumbled in his chest and his hands caressed the backs of her thighs from the crease where they met her butt, down past the backs of her knees to her calves, then all the way to her ankles. He slowly stroked his way back up again. Down once more, then up; down, then up, in a hypnotic rhythm. "Your legs always feel so amazing," he murmured, rubbing his cheek against the top of her head. "Smoother 'n butter."

She sighed, happy in every fiber of her being. She pressed a soft kiss into the bend where his neck flowed into his shoulder, then rearranged herself to press her ear against his chest to listen to the reassuring beat of his heart. "God, I love you."

Jase jerked as if the words were an electric prod, then forced himself to go still. As though a brilliant white light had exploded warmth inside his chest, his first knee-jerk reaction was *Want that.*

But he shoved it away. Locked it in an airtight box. Because he was a de Sanges and, face it, de Sangeses didn't know shit about love.

He'd like to continue blaming that lack on his family, but he couldn't. He'd had options over the years; he could have chosen to learn how to develop relationships. And he had, with Murphy and Hohn. But he'd steered clear of anything deeper than a weekend relationship with women…and old habits died hard.

Hell, if they even died at all. Because, face it. It was damn late to reverse his entire lifetime's point of view.

He almost told Poppy she was wrong, that she didn't love him. But he shut his mouth because he could just see how that would play out. She'd hand him his balls on a plate. She was a woman whose feelings went strong and deep and he wouldn't insult her by insisting he knew better than she did what those feelings were. It would be better for them both if she didn't love him. Hell, if he was a better man, he'd wish that was truly the case.

But he wasn't. He wasn't a better man at all. Which was pretty damn dicked up, because where did that leave either of them?

Feeling hollowed out, he reached for her hips to move her off him, but she beat him to the punch. She climbed to her feet and stared down at him as she gathered her panties off the floor and stepped into them.

"It's not a death sentence, Jason."

She was flushed and tousled, clad only in her satin thong and a baffled smile, and his heart clenched like a fist. "No, it's not." His mind went blank for a moment, then he cleared his throat. "And I don't want you to think that I don't know it's an honor and a gift—"

"Oh, please," she interrupted. "Let's not do the whole 'It's not you, it's me' routine, okay?"

"It is me, though, Poppy. I don't *know* how to love."

Climbing to his feet, he straightened his clothes. "You think I wouldn't glom onto you if I did? I'd do that so fast your head would spin." In a blast of clarity he realized he'd been happy here with her.

But that was getting into sloppy-emotions territory, and *that* was a place he wasn't prepared to go—never mind talk about. So he said instead, "You're great. I really like living with you. I dig the meals we've shared and, Jesus, the sex is off-the-scale hot."

Stiffening, she gave him an incredulous look. "*That's* what the two of us mean to you—eating together and rolling around under the sheets?"

"No, of course not. Or at least not only that." When she shot him a look that made him feel cornered, he demanded, "What the hell is it you want me to say?"

"Not a damn thing, if you need to ask."

"Are you kidding me?" He was almost grateful for the indignation that sliced through his burgeoning regret. "I *hate* it when women do that kind of shit!"

She crossed her arms over her bare breasts. "Wonderful. Now you're lumping me with other women."

"No. *God*." He rubbed the small ache that was beginning to thump between his brows. But he dropped his hand and took an unprecedented plunge, exposing the soft underbelly he liked to pretend he didn't have. "Okay, you want me to bare my soul like some damn new-age metrosexual?" Taking a breath, he admitted something he'd always known but had managed to shove down deep inside of himself so he wouldn't have to deal with it. "Look, you met my brother. I'm guessing he told you about how he and Dad and Pops spent most of my childhood—hell, of my life—in the slammer?"

"Yeah, about that—just what does it take to earn your trust, anyway? You didn't think that was something I might've wanted to hear from you?" She narrowed her eyes at him. "So tell me. Would you have ever told me if Joe hadn't come by?"

Shit. Not voluntarily. Well, maybe. Eventually, probably.

Oh, hell. "I don't know." He shrugged helplessly. "That's a problem, I take it."

"Your unwillingness to share the first thing about yourself?" She smacked him on the chest. "Dammit, Jason, you're living with me—*sleeping* with me, but you haven't told me about the important stuff that makes you *you?* Yeah, I'd say it's a problem."

"Nobody taught me all these rules!" he roared. His gut rolled but he quieted his voice and admitted something he'd always known but had managed to shove down deep inside so he wouldn't have to deal with it. "But here's the thing, Poppy. I don't know if it's my family situation or if it's just me, but the bottom line is, I'm...damaged."

"*What?* That's ludicrous!" Her opinion prompt and her surprise evident, she dropped her arms to her sides. "You're stuck in the past, maybe, but there's not a damn thing wrong with you. I'm guessing it weighs on you that the men in your family are in jail more than they're out. But, Jason, their mistakes are theirs, not yours. You're clearly nothing like them."

"How the hell do you know?" It had taken something for him to confess that he knew he was fucked up, and she'd just blown it off? Ignoring the fact that she saw him in a much more positive light than he saw himself, he zeroed in instead on the fact that while he'd allowed her her feelings, she wasn't doing the same for him. "You spent—what?—fifteen minutes with my brother and now you're an authority?"

"I know *you,* and I've never encountered a guy so by-the-book. You chose an entirely different path from the one your relatives took, so why would you think you're anything like them? The only thing you have in common as far as I can see is that your father and grandfather are locked behind steel bars and you're locked down in a prison of your own making."

It was a hit out of the blue, and his stomach roiled even as his mouth tightened. "That's funny," he snapped. "I don't remember seeing your psychology degree."

Hurt flashed in her eyes, but she didn't snarl back at him as he expected. Instead she tilted her face up to his and said steadily, "You know what I just don't get? I don't understand why you won't see what I see in you. You've got such a huge capacity for love in you, Jason. I've heard it in the way you talk about your friend Murphy. Felt it in the way you treat me. Seen it in how good you are with the kids. But from where I'm standing, you're just flat-out choosing to deny it."

Pushing her hair back from her face, she looked him squarely in the eye. "It just burns a hole in my heart that I can't make you see it. But I can't. Only you can make the choice, and I can see by the look on your face that you're not willing to. So under the circumstances…" She hesitated, then glanced at the door as if measuring the distance.

Jase went cold, then red-hot. "What?" he demanded furiously, towering over her. "You're throwing me the hell out?"

Again, she hesitated. Then she nodded. "I think it might be best if you went back to your place."

No! Every atom of his being protested the idea. "Best for who?"

"For me." For the first time, her voice wobbled. "I don't think I can take this, Jase—loving you but knowing you don't care enough in return to even try. You and I could have something really special, but it takes two. I can't do it by myself."

She stepped back. Squared her shoulders. "So, yes. Under the circumstances I do think it would be best if you packed your suits and left. It hurts knowing you won't fight for me—for *us*. Hurts so bad I feel broken in so many pieces you could make a mosaic out of me. But if you can't see our relationship as something that's worth working toward, then I need you to stay away from me so I can put myself back together."

Heart thundering, he stared at her, torn by so many emotions he hardly knew what to address first. The stuff she'd said before the hit-the-road-Jack part resonated on a level deep inside of him. Yet he'd lived his entire life with one mind-set and it was a mountain that he couldn't see his way around.

He didn't want to leave her.

He didn't know how to change.

So in the end he did what she asked. He packed his clothes and left.

CHAPTER TWENTY-THREE

If only I had handled everything better, smarter…

"JESUS, BOY, would you sit your ass in the chair and quit wearing a path in my carpet?"

Jase looked over at Murph and saw the old man scowling at him from the kitchen. "Sorry." He threw himself down on a chair. Crossed his ankle over his opposite knee and jiggled his foot. Picked up the TV remote and turned on a game. Turned it off again twenty seconds later.

He thumped his foot back down to the floor, then climbed to his feet and resumed pacing once again.

"For gawd's sake," Murphy muttered.

The next time he stalked past the kitchen, Murph was exiting it and the old man snagged his wrist in a grip of steel. He stabbed the forefinger of his free hand at the chair Jase had abandoned. "Sit!" he snapped. "Stay."

Jase yanked free. "What am I, a fucking dog?"

"Hey, if it snaps like a hound and barks like a hound. Christ Almighty, son, I once saw a cage full of half-starved pit bulls who were better humored than you. Working with you's gotta be one helluva joy—what's your unit had to say about your piss-poor attitude?"

"How the hell would I know?" *Since no one's talking to me.* Everyone was, in fact, giving him a very wide berth. He rolled his shoulders. "I've maybe been a little grouchy."

"Son, you passed 'a little' last Sunday. Why don't you do us all a favor and just make up with the girl?"

Pain splintered through Jase. God, he wanted that. Wanted it so bad he was bleeding inside.

But he couldn't have it—why the fuck couldn't anyone *understand* that? "I've told you why, but you obviously haven't listened to a thing I've said over and goddamn *over* again. I am through having this conversation."

And emotions beat to shit, feeling carved hollow, he slammed out of Murphy's apartment.

Poppy walked out of the field house where the Merchants' Association had just met to discuss the completed art project. They had been pretty enthusiastic about it. Apparently everyone had already received a lot of feedback from their customers and it was overwhelmingly positive. Poppy was pleased to hear it.

It was, in fact, the first bit of enjoyment she'd felt in six long days.

Quietly escaping the post-meeting socializing, she headed back to the parking lot behind Harvey's store. Once she reached her car, however, she simply stood gazing blankly at the completed wall, eyes narrowed against the late-morning light.

Because for a rare time in her life, she didn't have the first idea what to do next.

It was Saturday, the day she'd invited the kids to join her at the Wolcott mansion. But Henry and Danny had plans, and Cory was under quarantine, for lack of a better word, so Poppy didn't have a time frame she had to race over there to meet them in. Nor did she have an art class to teach, and weekends meant no menu boards to design.

She always had greeting cards in the works but she couldn't stomach the idea of going home. She had stripped the bed and washed the sheets—along with every towel she owned. She had vacuumed, dusted and scrubbed surfaces until they shone. But still she swore she could smell Jason's scent. Or maybe it was his ghost or spirit that had embedded itself in her apartment. She might not be able to define it exactly, but she knew it was too painful to be there when he wasn't. She'd been spending as little time home alone as she could.

The problem was, she didn't want to visit with anyone. Not her friends. Not her folks. She simply wasn't fit company.

Maybe she should go sit in a theater somewhere and pretend to watch a movie. Except…

She heaved a sigh. She didn't want to do that, either.

She climbed in the car and started the engine. The day stretched out in front of her like its own Paleolithic period, and she simply didn't know how she was going to fill up all those unwanted hours. She supposed the mansion was her best bet. It had the fewest associations with Jason and the Kavanaghs didn't work on Saturdays so she wouldn't have to pretend to anyone that she was doing just fine. She'd have the entire place to herself and heaven knew there was plenty for her to do.

Putting the car in gear, she maneuvered through the lot to the street and pulled into the flow of traffic, pointing her car toward Queen Anne. She might as well get some work done.

RUMP-SPRUNG from spending so damn much time in the car, Bruno Arturo snapped to attention when an old wreck of a station wagon chugged past him and he recognized the blonde behind the wheel. It was the babe who'd been directing the punks as they'd slopped their crap on the wall. Putting the Escalade in gear, he pulled out into traffic a few cars behind her. It might not be much—in fact it was pretty damn weak —but spotting her was the closest thing he'd come to a break all week.

Word on the street was that there was an all-points out on him, which had forced him to go underground before the cops came knocking on his door. So he was avoiding them for now, but if he didn't get his hands on the Capelli kid but *soon,* he was fucked, no two ways about it. Because once the cops brought him in for questioning, you could be damn sure they'd have the girl there within the hour to pick him out of a lineup. And that would be the start of one hurkin' fast track to a charge of robbery and attempted murder.

And as if that wasn't grief enough, there was Schultz, who had told him to lay off the kid in the first place. The prospect of jail was a wet dream compared to what the boss could—and probably would—do to him for ignoring instructions. Rumor had it Schultz was looking for him—and that he was not happy.

Bruno didn't know how many times he'd heard Schultz say he didn't like loose ends. According to the boss, loose ends had a habit of turning state's evidence in order to save their own skin.

Bruno couldn't disagree. He was considering the option himself if he didn't get his hands on the kid today. What other choice did he have? He was ass-deep in alligators—gators with bone-breaking teeth longer than his arm—and that wasn't a position with great future potential. He had the law to the left of him, a crime lord to the right—and he was smack in the middle about to be eaten alive.

Which brought him here, trailing a curly-headed bimbo in a sorry excuse of a car and telling himself he wasn't on a fucking chump's errand.

He lit a cigarette and forced himself to look on the bright side. Because, hey, who knew, spotting this chick could be a sign. Maybe things were finally turning around for him.

When the blonde drove her low-rent ride into a high-class driveway a short while later, he nearly missed it. Forced to hang way back to keep her from spotting him once she'd exited the main arterial and begun wending through a high-dollar neighborhood, he'd lost sight of her for a second. It was pure blind luck that brought him around the corner in time to catch a flash of her brake lights—the only part of her old heap that hadn't been blocked from view by a low wall and an ancient tree in full leaf as the car disappeared into a drive that led to the back of a huge mansion.

Tempted to swing his Escalade—complete with false plates—in bchind her, block her in and do what he did best—extract information from a mark who didn't want to give it—he had to force himself to cruise past thc drive instead. Hc was losing patience and that's when things generally turned to shit on him. He *knew* better than to jump the gun. It usually just led to dumb-shit decisions that ended in an impulsive action he came to regret.

IIe didn't get it, though. The blonde didn't look like she belonged in a place like that one. Her car sure didn't fit with the mansion *or* the surrounding neighborhood with its multimillion-dollar views. But she'd driven right up to the back door like she belonged, so she obviously had some sort of in—even if she was just the hired help.

Which led him to another fact he needed to consider: he didn't know who else might be in there with her. He had to think smart, because these were the kind of cribs that were bound to have monitored systems…and security guards cruising through the 'hood like clockwork.

So until he knew what he was dealing with, he would play it cool. He'd come too far, had managed to evade lockup when odds in his favor had been for shit. He wasn't about to blow it now because he was too impatient to do things right.

He found a spot to park and settled in to keep an eye on the place.

AT A LITTLE AFTER one that afternoon, Cory made her way slowly down the street the Wolcott mansion was on, checking her MapQuest directions one last time. She knew she shouldn't be here, and if Mom came home before she got back, she'd be in so much trouble.

But she couldn't take being cooped up any longer. She just wanted to paint with Ms. C. for an hour or so, then she'd head back home again. Was that so much to ask?

And it wasn't like she wasn't being maximum cautious. Before she'd even stepped outside the door, she'd made sure she had good directions and had looked up the shortest routes by bus. Now that she was out, she was watching everything around her as if she was freaking Fruit Fly Girl with, like, eight hundred eyes in her head.

It was nice just to be breathing fresh air. But she had to admit that while she felt free for the first time in practically an entire week, she also felt awfully exposed.

Take that black Escalade over there. Man, that brought her up on her toes for a minute, because that was exactly like the one Arturo had driven that day in Fremont, the one she'd last seen bearing down on her and Ms. C., going, like, a hundred miles an hour. She froze in the shade of a huge old tree while she checked it out. Maybe leaving the apartment hadn't been such a hot idea after all.

But then she realized no one was lurking in the SUV or anywhere else, and the tension in her shoulders eased. *Jeez, girl. Get a grip. Rich people don't have to be gangsters to drive a Caddy.*

And this was definitely a rich people's neighborhood. She'd never seen so many big houses in her life. And the view! This was where half the Seattle pictures she'd ever seen must have been taken from, because with her back to the tree trunk she could see the Space Needle with downtown rising behind it and Mount Rainier behind that. How dap was that?

But which was the Wolcott place? She peered at each of the rooftops until she picked the one she was pretty sure had been pictured in the article she'd read on the Internet. With a final glance at the Escalade to make sure it truly was empty, she raced down the block and up the drive of the mansion.

Breathing a sigh of relief to be off the street, the secluded yard making her feel more secure, she climbed a couple shallow stairs to what had to be the kitchen and rapped on the door.

When no one answered she swallowed hard. Because she hadn't considered this possibility—that Ms. C. might have decided not to come here at all today. Or that she had made plans to come later or had been here and already left.

Suddenly desperate and feeling as exposed as if she were naked, she pounded on the door. Oh, God, she shouldn't have left home. Her mom and Detective de S. were right. She wasn't safe out of the house.

Then suddenly the door opened and Ms. C. stood framed in it, her lips parted in disbelief.

"What the—?" She reached out and grabbed Cory's arm with a paint-splotched hand and hauled her into the room. Leaning out the door, she looked around the yard

before straightening back inside. She slammed it shut
and bolted it. In two long strides she crossed to a keypad
mounted on the wall and punched in some numbers,
making its red light quit blinking.

Then she turned back to Cory. "What are you doing
here?"

"I came to help you paint." She flashed her best big-
eyed innocent look.

Ms. C. clearly wasn't buying it, for she narrowed her
own eyes and looked far from charmed. "What part of
'you've got to stay in your house, out of sight, in order
to keep safe' don't you understand?"

"I was going *crazy!* You don't know what it's like—
I can't go to school, which, okay, maybe I don't love,
but I sure don't wanna have to take the grade *over* again.
And Mom stayed home for a couple of days, but she has
to work so we have a roof over our heads, which means
I'm left by myself all day and half the night. It can get
scary-noisy sometimes and most of the neighbors aren't
the kind you associate with, you know? Except for Nina.
I like her but my mom doesn't want me hanging with
her and besides, she's taking classes and leaves Kai in
the day care at the CC while she's in school, so I don't
even have him to babysit."

"So you put yourself at risk because you're bored?"

"I'm lonely!"

"I'm sorry, Cory, I'm sure that's not easy. But Detective de Sanges is putting his career on the line for you
and you can't just—"

"Of course you'd find *his* issues more important than

my little problems. Hey, we don't want to make things tough for Detective de S.!" She could feel herself losing it, but she was *so* damn lonely and she just couldn't take it anymore. She'd thought Ms. C. would understand, because she was always so warm and smiley and had a way of making you feel so welcome.

But Poppy wasn't smiling now and Cory didn't feel welcome. Ms. C.'s expression, in fact, had gone downright frigid and shuttered, and that shook Cory more than it probably should have. It was just too much on top of everything else, though, and hating the tears she felt rising to the surface, she embraced the injustice that surged in her chest—or at least the anger that was its end result. "I thought you'd understand, but you probably have all sorts of friends and stuff, and now that the project is done I guess I'm just a big pain in the butt to you."

"Honey, of course you aren't."

"But you don't want to be responsible for me—I get it, all right. Well, guess what?" Angrily she dashed the welling tears from her eyes. "I don't want to be a rock around your neck, either, so why don't we just forget I was even here." She whirled around and reached for the lock on the door.

"Cory, wait!"

Ms. C.'s fingers brushed her arm, but she shook them off and got the lock undone. She couldn't bear to see the pity or impatience or whatever on her teacher's face. Wrenching open the door, she dashed out into the yard.

"Sonova— Cory Capelli, get your butt back here!"

Not freaking likely. Cory put on the extra burst of speed that carried her down the drive and out into the street.

BRUNO'S HEAD came up when he heard someone call the Capelli kid's name. Holy fuck. He couldn't be that lucky, could he? But a second later the kid herself burst out of the drive and started sprinting in his direction. He ducked down behind the rear bumper of the Escalade nearest the sidewalk, unable to believe his good timing. He'd just returned from a quick recon of the mansion and the properties adjoining it.

He heard the footsteps pounding up the street and when they reached the front of the vehicle he hit his keyless remote to disengage the alarm and open the SUV. He'd counted on the chirp startling her and knew he was right when her footsteps faltered. Springing out from the back of the car, he whipped his arm around her waist, lifted her off her feet and clipped her hard on the chin. She went limp in his arms and he stuffed her in the car.

"Hello, sweetheart," he murmured as he buckled her in. "You've been causing me all kinds of problems, haven't you?" He slammed the door shut and rounded the car to the driver's side. "But that's okay. Because I'm about to fix all that."

FOR THE SECOND TIME in as many minutes Poppy punched the code in the alarm. Then she bolted through the back door in pursuit of Cory, but the girl was incredibly fast and was already out of sight.

Dammit, why hadn't she handled that better? A bitter

laugh escaped her. Because Cory had brought her personal relationship with Jason into it, that's why. She'd heard the teen's reference to a bond she no longer had with him and quit thinking like a rational adult faced with an emotional kid in desperate need of kid-glove treatment.

And look what wonderful results that had brought.

She was still beating herself up with all the possible ways that she could have, *should* have, controlled the situation when she reached the end of the drive. She looked frantically in both directions.

And was just in time to see a man shutting the passenger door of a black SUV. The sun hitting the car's tinted windshield showed a shadowy spiky-headed form within—a form that hung from the seat belt with a frightening lack of animation.

"Shit!" Whirling on her heel, Poppy ran like she'd never run before back to the house. That had to be Arturo and she could not let him get away. Cory's life was in the balance and it was her fault.

Barreling through the door she'd left wide-open, she snatched up her tote, which she had dropped behind the counter in the newly renovated kitchen when she'd gotten here earlier, then ran back out, slamming the door behind her. She climbed in her car and started it up, hoping to hell the man hadn't disappeared.

The only thing in her favor was that he'd been parked facing this direction, so she craned forward to look to the right as she nosed the car up to the street. Then swore. He was nowhere in sight.

She took a right anyway and raced up to the next

corner. Slamming on the brakes, she looked in both directions and spotted him to the west, turning at the end of the block. "Thank you, *thank* you, God!"

Creeping cautiously up to the corner where he'd turned, she rummaged with one hand through her tote. Where was her phone? Dammit, why the hell did she always have to carry such a freaking big bag?

Her hand sweeping frantically among all the crap she'd accumulated in her tote, she paused at the corner. She watched the SUV take a right up the hill, then turned her own vehicle onto the block he had just vacated. She was scared to death the guy would see her and even more scared that she'd hang back so far she'd lose him.

Her fingers brushed her cell phone just as she, too, turned onto the arterial and she yanked it from the tote. Flipping it open, she pressed in a speed-dial code she'd only used once before. "C'mon, c'mon," she urged as the phone on the other end rang for what seemed like forever.

Then it was picked up. "De Sanges," came Jason's cool, level voice.

"Jase? Oh, thank God! He's got her!"

"Poppy? Who's got who—" He cut himself off and his voice was sharp as a scalpel when he spoke again. "Arturo?"

"Yes! He's got Cory!"

"How the hell did that happ— No, never mind, that's not important right now. Where are you?"

"I'm following him in my car. But, Jason, she's not moving. I'm hanging back hoping to hell he won't see me, and in truth I couldn't see through the tinted windows on his car all that well when I *was* close enough, but I could see that she was slumped over and not moving!" She could hear the hysteria creeping into her voice and sucked in a deep breath. This was no time to fall apart.

"Hohn! With me," she heard Jason snap, then he spoke into the phone again. "I need you to stay calm."

"I know." She inhaled another deep breath and let it out. "I'm okay, I'm good. It's just… It's my fault. He must have followed me to the mansion, then Cory showed up and I let the situation get away from me when she—" She cleared her throat. "Well, that doesn't really matter. What's important is that she ran out of here before I could stop her and—"

"Tell me where you are," he interrupted.

"On Queen Anne Avenue." She took a deep breath. "I'm not positive, but it looks like we're headed for the underpass to the Aurora Bridge."

"Okay, hang in there with me. Hohn and I are heading in that direction. You just do your best to stay off his radar and keep me up-to-date on your whereabouts."

She did that. For ten minutes that dragged out into dog years, she followed the black Escalade and kept sane because she knew that Jason was not only on the other end of the line, but on his way to save Cory.

Then Arturo, whom she'd let pull quite a way ahead of her when he'd turned onto a rutted street bordering a mixed-use portion of Lake Union, suddenly pulled into a lot next to a square building. Without traffic between them, she feared he'd spot her and she whipped into another business's parking lot. "Oh," she whispered into her phone as if the thug could somehow hear her. "He's stopped."

"Are you still on East Northlake Way?"

"Yes. West of the freeway. He's in front of what looks like a warehouse or one of those marine-type businesses that are all along here—I'm not close enough to tell which." She sat tensely as Arturo climbed out of the car and came around to the passenger side. He stood looking out over the roof of the SUV for a moment, then opened the door and hauled Cory into his arms.

She blew out a ragged breath. "He's taking her out of the front seat, and she's limp as a noodle, Jase. Oh, there, she moved her head! Thank God, she's alive!" She'd been so frightened that maybe Cory wasn't—that her efforts were too little, too late.

Arturo disappeared with the teen down the side of the building. "I think he took her inside. I'm going to drive by and get the address."

"Good idea. Just don't get too close."

"He's got her in a windowless building out of sight, Jason. Her chances of staying alive just went down."

"And so will yours if he gets his hands on you."

She tapped the brakes in front of the building. It was a concrete warehouse and she read the address stenciled over the garage-type door into the phone.

"Good," Jason said. "We're not far away." Then he swore.

"What?" she demanded anxiously.

"Nothing. Just a little traffic snarl. We'll get it straightened out and be there in five minutes, tops."

"Cory might not *have* five minutes!"

"Look, Poppy, you've got to calm down and trust me, okay?"

"Right. The way you trust me, Jason?" She regretted the words the instant they left her mouth.

He went silent for a heartbeat, then said in his no-emotions cop voice, "Just stay away from the building until we get there."

"Uh-huh." She parked her car one lot over from the warehouse. Shutting down the engine, she rummaged through her tote until she came up with the little canister of pepper spray her father had given her. She tucked it into her waistband, climbed from the car and closed the door. "We've got to stop him."

"Not *we*, Poppy," he said and his voice wasn't nearly as emotionless as it had been a moment ago. "Me. *I'll* stop him. You just sit tight and do not—I repeat, do *not*—do anything impulsive."

"I'll try my best."

"Shit," he said. "I know that tone. Listen to me. Sit tight. I know how fierce you are about your kids, but this is a matter for professionals. Do not interfere—you'll just end up making things worse."

She approached a regular metal door on the side of the building. Listening for noises from within, she reached for its doorknob. "Get here soon, Jason."

"Dammit, Poppy, do you hear me? Sit tight! Stay on

the line with me, you hear? Don't hang up. *Do not hang up!*"

Snapping the phone shut, she tried the knob.

And took a deep breath when it turned silently beneath her hand.

CHAPTER TWENTY-FOUR

After what happened I sort of thought I'd be all cranked up and revving about a hundred miles an hour. Instead, I just feel numb.

SWEARING WITH vicious inventiveness, Jase snapped his phone closed. "We've gotta get the hell out of here and over to that warehouse *now,*" he snarled. "I know she's going in."

"No, she wouldn't," Hohn disagreed. "She couldn't possibly be that stu—" Jase's expression must have warned him not to go there, because he shut up midword. Instead, he hitched a shoulder. "You look like you could tear the head off a chicken with your bare hands," he commented, scowling at the traffic stopped ahead of them. He flipped a switch to make the siren give a small whoop to direct people's attention to the fact there were cops present. "Makes you the perfect candidate to clear me a path to drive through."

"Oh, trust me, it will be my pleasure," Jase said savagely, climbing from the car. "But get Patrol out here to take care of the rest of it." Hanging his badge from the breast pocket of his suit jacket, he started snapping orders at drivers, directing them to inch up a little here, pull a foot to the side there.

Some idiot texting on his iPhone had rear-ended the car in front of him, causing a chain reaction that had culminated in a truck with its wheels already cranked to turn left getting bumped into oncoming traffic. The driver who found the truck suddenly face-on in his lane had performed some damn good defensive driving and avoided a collision. But the recreational trailer he'd been towing had jackknifed, snarling traffic in both directions.

It took Jase seven minutes that felt like seven hours to clear a space large enough for Hohn to drive up onto the sidewalk. He loped back to the car, gave the roof a slap and dove in. "Sonovabitchin' morons."

Hohn turned on the siren and hit the gas, rocking up over the curb.

Jase leaned forward in his seat, his shoulders tense and his hands clenched between his spread knees as they left the congestion behind. It wasn't until they were out of the district that he sucked in several deep breaths to get a handle on himself, then shot a glance at his friend. "You've been married a long time," he said.

"Seven years of wedded bliss, bro," Hohn agreed.

"How do you do it?"

"Same way recovering addicts do, my friend—by taking it one day at a time."

Jase turned his head to stare at him. "Wow. A ringing endorsement like that almost makes a guy wanna go get hitched himself."

"Hey, it's like the all-knowing one says, man—"

"Do *not* quote Nietzsche at me," he interrupted impatiently. Hohn had an unnatural attachment to everything the guy had ever written and usually Jase just shook his head. But he was in no mood for it today.

"No, listen, I'm telling ya. This one is dead-on." He took a deep, theatrical breath, took one hand off the steering wheel to place over his heart and said, "'Ah women. They make the highs higher and the lows more frequent.'"

"Shit." Thinking that this was what he got for broaching the subject of marriage—or hell, not even that, just relationships in general—from a smart-ass, Jase went back to staring out the windshield, silently willing his friend to get them to their destination.

Now.

POPPY CREPT on cautious feet a little deeper into the dim, cavernous warehouse. The place was still and silent and she was at a loss about what to do next. Pausing, she looked around her, trying to get a feel for the layout.

That was more difficult than it should have been considering the space was basically a vast concrete cube. But while it might lack room-type walls, it was piled high with row after row of boxes that stacked nearly to the exposed steel girders overhead.

But as she stood trying to figure out where to look first for Cory, she suddenly became aware of a murmur of sound. She realized it was either a man talking or a radio playing. It seemed to be coming from the lake end of the warehouse. Nervously palming her little canister

of pepper spray, she slipped down a narrow passageway
between two rows of boxes, trying to get closer to the
murmuring voice without making any noise herself.

Her heart was already pounding like a kettledrum and
she didn't know what she'd do if Arturo suddenly
popped up at the end of her cardboard canyon. Nothing
that ended well, she was sure. If heart failure didn't get
her, a hail of bullets was sure to do the trick.

She froze for an instant before forcing herself to start
moving again. But she could have done without that last
thought. Of course Arturo would have a gun—he was a
gangster, for cri'sake. She'd be a lot happier, however,
without the *Godfather*-style imagery suddenly burrow-
ing into her consciousness.

Not that it mattered. It wasn't as if she had the luxury
of turning tail and leaving Cory to fend for herself. She
was probably too stupid to live for coming in here
instead of waiting for Jason, but living with *herself* if
the girl was injured—or worse—and she hadn't tried to
help wasn't exactly a workable option, either.

And, hey, the good news was she'd reached the end
of the row without incident. It was always nice to have
one thing go right.

Even if she was promptly faced with a new problem.

Breathing a little too fast, she stared in frustration at
yet another towering wall of cardboard, this one at a
right angle to the chute she'd just left. What was this
place, a goddamn fun-house maze?

Taking deep, calming breaths, she constructed a mental strongbox for her stress—fueled anger the way Aunt

Sara had taught her a long, long time ago, back in their commune days.

Apparently good tips never died, because the exercise was still effective. If she got out of this mess alive she'd have to be sure to thank the older woman. Barring that, she felt calmer, more in control, and tuning in on what had to be Arturo's voice she allowed the sound to guide her as she inched forward.

"...probably won't believe this," she heard him say clearly as she neared the end of yet another row, "but I'm not really thrilled with the idea of hurting a little girl."

Warily, Poppy craned her neck to take a peek around the end boxes. Heart pounding, she immediately whipped back behind the protection of her wall, images from the strobe light—quick glimpse seared with surprising detail on her retinas.

Of a small cleared space in the surrounding forest of boxes.

Of a stocky, well-dressed man standing with his back to her, casually scratching behind his ear with the barrel of a gun.

Of Cory, all scared eyes, trembling lips and that damn stubborn chin raised just slightly despite the bruise starting to darken it, looking pale and frightened as she huddled on a sagging couch.

Thank God she's all right.

"Uh-huh," the teen said with a transparent show of bravado. "That must be why you've got that gun."

"What, this?"

Poppy peered around again in time to see he'd

lowered the weapon and had it aimed at the girl. Saw, too, that Cory had seen her. Poppy put a cautionary finger to her lips, then pulled back out of sight. And wondered what the hell to do next. *God, I have got to get her out of here.* Somehow, some way. She glanced around her for inspiration, but all she saw was boxes.

"I really don't wanna use it," Arturo said. "But I will, of course. Because if it comes down to a choice between you or me, kid, I choose me every time."

"I'm sure the gangbanger who killed my daddy had the same attitude," Cory retorted bitterly. "But what do you care that I learned my lesson about talking to the cops from what happened to him—you had to try to run me and my teacher down anyway."

"That wasn't one of my better ideas," the thug agreed. "I saw the cop there and thought you'd given me up."

"Sh-yeah right," she muttered. "Haven't you listened to a word I said? Talking to cops leads to nothing but trouble. No way would I squeal you out to them. And if you kill me, they'll never quit hunting you. So why don't you just let me go? I'll go home to my mom and you can go back to whatever it is you do."

Poppy marveled at the girl's coolheaded negotiation skills when Arturo didn't immediately shoot the idea down. This just might work.

Then, hearing a sound from the direction in which she'd made her way through the warehouse, she whirled to face the possible new danger, hoping it was help for her but fearing it might be backup for Arturo instead.

Swinging around too fast, she cracked her elbow

against one of the boxes. A soft cry escaped her as pain zinged from her funny bone to her hand. The pepper spray canister fell from fingers gone lax and skittered across the concrete floor.

She froze, hoping, praying, that the thug hadn't heard—then lunged for the pepper spray when she heard footsteps crossing the cleared area. There was no place to hide and she shook the little container to activate the ingredients before tucking it into her palm.

Although why she thought it might help her against a *bullet*—

Arturo stepped around the wall, his gun pointed straight at her. "Well, well," he murmured. "If it isn't the blonde."

You think maybe this is why Jason wanted you to wait outside for him, genius? Poppy took a step forward, then stopped. Brushing a curl out of her eyes, she watched him slowly approach. When he stopped and gave her an impatient get-over-here gesture with the gun she saw that the wall of boxes was solidly between the teenager and his weapon. "Cory, run!"

"Fuck!" Lunging forward, he snatched her wrist in his fist then all but yanked her off her feet as he sprinted back down the wall of boxes, dragging her behind him. Rounding the end, he came to a dead halt, causing Poppy to stumble against his back. "Sonuvafuckingbitch!"

She peered around him, relief nearly dropping her to her knees when she saw that Cory was nowhere in sight.

Unfortunately that left her the sole focus of Arturo's attention. And he was not happy when he swiveled to face her.

Her confidence that she'd someday die in her own bed surrounded by her great-grandchildren wasn't enhanced by the knowledge that her tiny canister of pepper spray was in the hand going numb beneath the punishing grip on her wrist. Slowly, trying to keep the movement off his radar, she inched her free hand toward it.

He raised his gun and pressed its cool steel against the damp skin between her eyebrows. "Give me one good reason why I shouldn't blow your head off."

"Um…you might need a hostage when the cops get here?" Terror clogged her throat, but she was grateful at the moment simply to still be among the living.

And crazily enough, that she hadn't wet her pants. Talk about sweating the small stuff. Still, it had been touch-and-go there for a second when she'd realized she probably wouldn't even hear the shot that killed her—and she'd just as soon Jason not find her in that condition.

"Don't try to con a con man, lady. No cop in his right mind would let you just waltz in here by yourself the way you did."

"You've had her for, what, five minutes?" Jason's voice demanded coolly. "Try dealing with her for months."

With the speed of light, Arturo whirled her around and pulled her back against his chest, releasing her wrist and clamping his arm across her upper body so fast she had vertigo. All she understood for a second was that she was suddenly pinned against him with his gun now pressed against her temple instead of between her eyes.

It wasn't a huge improvement.

Neither did it help that she was looking into Jason's gun, which was braced by his opposite hand and pointed at her as well. Dragging her horrified gaze from the muzzle, which appeared to be the size of a cannon's, she raised her eyes to look into his steely gaze. *Try dealing with her for months?*

"I didn't give the bitch permission," he continued flatly. "But as you're no doubt finding out, she does exactly what she damn well pleases."

Okay, he wasn't happy with her—she got that. But Jason didn't call women *bitches.* And to sympathize with the man who had tried to run her and Cory down, who had *kidnapped* the teen? That was so not the man she knew. The man she loved.

Slowly, her fog of fear began to lift.

"It doesn't have to be this way, though," he said companionably to Arturo. "She may be a pain in the ass, but my job is to serve and protect—even her. And so far, Mr. Arturo, no one has died. There's no murder charge pending against you, no Man One. And you've got something I'm willing to bargain for."

The arm around her loosened a fraction, the pistol against her temple pulled back so that it was no longer digging into her skull. "Schultz?"

"Schultz."

Arturo seemed to be considering it. Then he stiffened behind her and she knew on a visceral level he wasn't going to take the offer. "I've thought about that—I won't pretend I haven't," he said slowly. "But Schultz's got long arms. And I ain't spending the next however many years you get my sentence reduced to looking over my shoulder waiting for some Bubba with tats on his knuckles to take his homemade shiv to me."

"So we talk to the feds. Get you into Witness Protection."

She felt the rude noise Arturo made rumbling in the chest against her back. "Living in a cinder-block motor court in Butt Fuck, Idaho? Might as *well* be dead."

She unclenched her fingers from around the canister, flashing it at Jason.

Who didn't so much as blink. "I'm an excellent shot, Arturo, and she's not big enough to hide behind. You might want to rethink that as your final answer."

"What for? I'm pretty much screwed no matter how you look at it." The arm around her torso started cinching up and she could feel the hand with the gun moving back toward her temple.

"You've got the wrong idea about Witness Protection," Jason said as if he had all day to discuss its merits. "It amazes me, frankly, how high on the hog some of you mopes live on the taxpayers' dollar." His eyes shifted briefly to her. "Now," he said without changing tone.

She shot the gas over her shoulder, scrunching her eyes shut against stray fumes and wrenching to the left at the same time that a shot rang out.

The grip on her slackened, then fell away entirely, and she felt Arturo's body slide away from hers, heard it as it hit the cement floor. She stumbled toward Jason on uncoordinated feet.

Reaching out, he grabbed her, swinging her behind him in one smooth move. "Get behind the boxes."

"Jason…"

"Get behind the boxes." His voice was surgical steel, slicing with cold precision to the bone.

She got behind the boxes. But peeked around them to watch him.

"Hohn," he roared and moved cautiously across the open space toward Arturo, his gun still firmly trained on the fallen man. "Should have taken the deal, chief," Poppy heard him murmur. Kicking Arturo's gun away, he knelt at the thug's side and reached out two fingers to feel for a pulse in the man's throat. Swearing, he yelled his partner's name again.

Hohn's voice replied from a distance.

"Call 911. We need an ambulance. Stat!" He turned his attention back to Arturo. "Come on, you sonofabitch. Don't you die on me. I don't appreciate being executioner." He glanced in her direction. "Where's Cory?"

"Somewhere in the stacks. She got away."

Poppy could hear the man she assumed was Hohn barking directions into his phone, his voice growing clearer by the moment. He rounded the corner a second later. Looked her over with the same assessing cop eyes she was accustomed to seeing from Jason, then looked at the man on the floor. "He alive?"

"Yes. But I think I nicked something major—he's bleeding pretty bad. I need something to compress the wound to slow it down."

"There's a towel under the newspaper on the couch,"

Cory's voice said from behind yet another wall of boxes. "Though I wouldn't cry too much if the bastard croaked. He was ready enough to kill Ms. C. and me."

The next hour was a blur. Poppy and Cory huddled together while Jason and Hohn worked to keep Arturo from bleeding out. Then paramedics showed up and took over and soon the warehouse was swarming with cops. Hugging the teen to her side, Poppy found them a corner where they'd be out of the way.

They watched the medics trundle Arturo off on a gurney. Cory, who had been quiet, suddenly rolled her head into Poppy's collarbone. "I'm sorry, Ms. C."

"Yeah, I know." She stroked the girl's hair with her free hand. "You made some lousy choices today, but you know, everyone makes those at times. I would like to think, though, that this experience will make you stop and think before you follow your next impulse." *A lesson you might want to consider as well.*

"Oh, I will. Trust me." Pale and wan, the teen looked up at her with swimming eyes and a trembling bottom lip. "I was so s-scared. And not just for me. I'm so, so s-sorry. I never would have forgiven myself if you'd been killed because of me."

"Cory!"

They both started at the sound of Sandy Capelli's frantic voice calling from the other side of the cardboard barricade. Then Cory screeched, "Mom!" pulled free from Poppy's embrace and tore across the opening to fling herself into her mother's arms as the older woman was escorted around the wall by a patrolman.

Hohn came over to Poppy. "Jase asked me to take your statement and then see you safely home. Okay?"

"Yes." Suddenly she was more than ready to go. She needed to step back from the day's violence; it had left a miasma of grime on her soul and she wanted nothing more than to wash it away with a hot bath and a cool glass of wine. And once she felt clean once again, she was going to break her self-imposed isolation and call her mother. Or Jane or Ava. Or all three.

But first there was the statement to get through. Quietly, she answered Hohn's questions until he was satisfied, then let him take her arm to escort her away.

There was no way, however, she could leave without looking back one last time. Jason was talking to a man across the room, but as if he felt her stare, he suddenly glanced straight at her. Without thinking, she gave him a tiny wiggle of her fingers.

He didn't acknowledge the impulsive gesture with so much as a blink. She couldn't read, in fact, emotion of any kind in his expression. He turned back to his conversation.

Poppy's heart clenched. Forcing herself to turn and walk away, it occurred to her that this might be the last time she'd ever see him.

That he truly didn't love her the way she did him.

And never would.

CHAPTER TWENTY-FIVE

Talk about the highest of highs and lowest of lows.
And all in the space of a day.

JASE ASSURED HIMSELF during the drive over to Poppy's apartment that he was just stopping by to check on her. It was the right thing to do. She'd been through a nightmare ordeal—even if it *was* the result of her own fricking recklessness—and someone needed to pay her an official visit to make sure she was all right. Double-check her statement.

Yeah. Climbing out of his SUV, he stared up at her apartment building, then straightened purposefully. This was business. He was doing his job, that's all.

He only intended to stay a few minutes before he hit the road again. Hell, maybe he'd stop on the way home and pick up some KFC for Murphy—the old guy loved the extra-crispy kind in particular. The two of them could sit down and discuss Jase's freakin' huge backlog of cases. Murph might be retired, but Jase didn't respect anyone more for his intelligent insight when it came to police work.

So, okay, he thought, as he paused outside Poppy's

door, the operative word here was *professional*. That bore repeating, he decided when he knocked on the solid fir panels perhaps just the slightest bit more forcefully than he needed to.

Then she whipped open the door and her entire face lit up at the sight of him, as if just by showing up he'd made her entire fucking day or something. It was like that little finger wave thing she'd given him at the warehouse and it hit him like a fist to the solar plexus exactly as it had then.

And his professionalism went down the tubes.

"What the *hell* were you thinking?" he demanded in a growl maybe a bit too loud and definitely enraged. Grasping her upper arms, he backed her across the short hallway until her shoulders were pressed against the wall. A bright piece of framed Poppy art shifted on its hanger near her head. "Your grandma Ingles laid down the big bucks for that fricking expensive education of yours, but did you bother to exercise your brain at all? I *told* you to wait for me! Didn't I tell you not go into that warehouse?" His gut iced over with the same dread he'd felt when he'd been caught in that traffic snarl, unable to stop her.

When he'd been too far away to protect her and left with nothing but the shakiest of goddamn hopes that he'd get there in time to stop her from being hurt.

From being killed.

"But did you *listen?*" he yelled, his nose a scant inch from her own. "Hell, no—not little Miss Leads-with-Her-Heart! You go barreling into an unknown situation armed with nothing but a quarter ounce of Mace against a thug with a fucking *gun!*"

"Not Mace," she whispered, staring up at him and trembling in his grip like a cat catching a whiff of the vet's office. "Pepper spray."

"Well, hell, yeah. Because God forbid you peace-and-love types should actually *harm* a guy bent on killing you!" She trembled harder and his brows snapped together. "Don't you shake! Don't you goddamn shake on me now! That's what you should have been doing in that parking lot instead of charging into the warehouse!"

"I was so scared, Jason."

"You don't *know* what scared is! You weren't stuck miles away knowing you couldn't stop the woman you love from walking into danger. That the job you thought was the be-all and end-all of your existence didn't mean shit if you couldn't protect her. *You* didn't come around those boxes and see a man holding a gun to your head!" And yanking her off her feet, he lifted her to meet his furious kiss.

Her soft lips immediately yielded beneath the press of his own and he tasted wine on her tongue. She wrapped her legs around his waist and her arms around his neck and without raising his head, he gripped her butt and stumbled into the living room, careening off the archway lintel when his eyes refused to open beneath the pleasure, the sheer killing relief of having her alive and warm in his arms again.

He'd truly believed he'd never get to hold her again for as long as he lived—which, without her, he realized with absolute if sudden clarity, would stretch into an eternal empty wasteland.

"Dear God," a woman murmured in hushed horror from only feet away. "Is that a *gun* strapped under his arm?"

"Beth, you can't seriously care about a little thing like a gun," Ava Spencer's voice replied dryly, "when a man who can kiss like that declares his love for your daughter. Man, where's the popcorn and Jujubes when you need 'em?"

His head jerked up and he stared openmouthed at Poppy's two best friends and a woman who could only be Mrs. Poppy, if the chocolate-brown eyes and curls escaping a long, graying braid were anything to go by.

Jesus. He never walked into a business, house or apartment without noting everything around him. But he'd taken one look at Poppy and his never-before-failed-him second nature had taken a vacation. So there sat three women on her little couch and overstuffed chair, staring back at him with emotions ranging from fascination to doubt.

But Mama or no Mama witnessing his hands on her daughter's ass, he wasn't putting Poppy down. Fingers tightening around sweet firmness, he rearranged her to a more comfortable grasp. Their gazes met and he got caught up in the topaz flecks within the darkness of her eyes. "So I guess you have company."

She licked her lips. "They were just leaving." She looked over at her mother and friends. "Weren't you, Mom? My sisters?"

"Oh, yeah," Ava said at the same time Jane murmured, "Is that a desert breeze I feel?"

The redhead laughed and gently pulled Poppy's mother to her feet. "Come on, Beth," she said goodnaturedly. "I'll buy you a drink and tell you a story about a little girl who wanted to grow up to marry a sheik."

"And here I thought I knew everything there was to know about my baby girl," Beth murmured. She gave Jase and her daughter a severe look. "You two at least practice safe sex. And I'm not talking condoms. You put that damn gun up on a shelf or in a lockbox."

"Yes, ma'am," he heard himself agree, then watched in relief as the three women left the apartment with a minimum of fuss.

Poppy leaned back the moment the door clicked closed behind them, her fingers locked behind his neck. "Out in the hallway you said 'the woman you love.'"

He nodded. Cleared his throat. "Yeah. Yeah, I did."

"And that would be me?"

His brows slammed together and his hands tightened on her butt. "Of course it's you!"

"Hey, you can't blame a girl for being confused. That's quite a turnaround from the last time we talked. You told me you didn't know how to love." But Poppy felt a lightness growing in her heart and expanding throughout her. "Let's sit down," she suggested softly. "You want a glass of wine or anything?"

"No." He didn't release her. Instead he dropped into the nearest chair and carefully arranged her legs on either side of him until she knelt over his lap, her lower legs wedged between his thighs and the soft overstuffed arms of the chair. "You got enough room there?"

She nodded. Then she patted her fingers over his face and stroked his eyebrows with her thumbs when he raised them at her. "I had quite a bit of wine when I got home," she confessed. "I want to make sure I'm not having a drunken dream here."

Wrapping his fingers around her wrists, he brought her hands down to press against his chest and his heart beat hard and fast beneath her palms. "Feel that? This is no dream. And you're not drunk. Or if you are, you disguise it pretty damn well."

Then he hesitated. Took a deep breath. And eased it out.

"You're right, though, my attitude is a turnaround. One I didn't even know I was going to make when I came over here. No, don't pull away." He flattened his palm over her hands, still stacked over his heart. "It's not like I've had some sudden big change of heart. It's more that I finally quit lying to myself."

He laughed suddenly, a huge, uninhibited head-thrown-back guffaw that bounced off the walls of her cramped little living room. "God, I feel—I don't know—a hundred pounds lighter! I thought I came here to make sure you were okay so I could go back to my ordered world. But when I saw you, with your joy and your generous heart, something inside of me just cracked wide-open.

"And I knew you were right, Blondie. I built a box an eon ago to keep my de Sanges impulses under lock and key. And knowing I had those walls around me helped—it kept me on the straight and narrow. But what you tried to tell me—what Murphy's been telling me for years—is even truer. That cage is every bit as ironclad as the state pen that my dad and grandpa and—well, not Joe, I guess, since he's out right now—but the entire de Sanges line except me has been locked in."

Bringing her fingers to his lips, he kissed the tips that stuck out beyond the loose fist he'd wrapped around them.

Poppy's butt hit his thighs with a soft plop, and she realized she'd been half up on her knees, which were suddenly weak, weak, weak with happiness.

His dark eyes locked with hers. "You're the key to getting me out, Poppy. I was so fucking scared when you went in that building—so terrified when I saw you in Arturo's clutches."

"You didn't look scared." He'd looked cool and competent and detached.

"Because I shoved my emotions in that box in order to do my job and get you the hell out of there in one piece."

"Is Arturo dead, Jason?"

"I don't know. They took him to Harborview and I haven't heard yet if he made it. I hope to hell he did. I don't want his death on my head."

"It's on his head, not yours!"

"I know, sweetheart. But it's never easy knowing you took a life."

Poppy's heart felt so full she thought it might explode. "I love you, Jason. God, I love you so much."

"Oh, man. I love *you.*"

She grinned at him. "So, you gonna move your suits back in?"

"Yeah. We might have to find a bigger place eventually, but for now, yeah."

"Your place is bigger. I could always move in there."

He went very still. "You'd do that?"

"Well, sure. We'd have to rearrange some of your stuff so I can put my stamp on the place, too. But Murphy is there and your apartment has quite a bit more room than I've got here. Maybe I could carve out a place to work on my greeting cards in a section of your second bedroom or office or whatever that extra space is so we could actually eat from a table for a change."

"You can have the whole damn room if you want."

"Nah, I just need a worktable and maybe a cupboard or some shelves or something. It'd be very cool to have a place to organize my stuff."

He carefully pushed back a curl that had flopped over her eye. "Maybe we oughtta get married."

Heart hammering, she stared at him. But she forced herself to be practical. "We're barely even back together. Maybe we should wait a bit to see how we do with the living-together part first."

He seemed fascinated with the finger he was running down her thigh. Then suddenly his sooty lashes raised and he gave her an intense look. "But you're not totally against the idea?"

"Are you kidding me? My first inclination was *want that!* But I'm impulsive—you know I'm impulsive. And this is too important to rush into without giving it the thought it deserves."

She squealed in surprise when he abruptly surged to his feet. He whipped her around in his arms, then carried her with long-legged strides to her bedroom.

"You're right," he said as he tossed her onto the bed. "Let's be responsible. Hell, that's my middle name—I ever tell you that?"

Staring down at her, he pulled his tie through his collar, put his gun on the highest surface he could find and reached for the buttons on his shirt. "So we'll talk about it again next week."

EPILOGUE

I feel like the sun is shining out all my pores!

Memorial Day

POPPY CAME TO an abrupt stop at the top of the stairs that connected Ava's Alki beach penthouse condo to its lushly planted rooftop terrace, suddenly unable to concentrate on her friends' chatter behind her. Her gaze was locked on Jason doing the guy thing at the grill with Murphy and Dev and Finn. Jase's head was tossed back as he roared one of his rare, full-throated laughs and her heart swelled so fast and furiously she thought it might burst.

"Ooh, someone's got it bad," Jane murmured, stopping beside her. She removed the tray from Poppy's hands. Then she abruptly set the load down on the beautifully appointed table with an uncharacteristic disregard for Ava's careful staging. Fruit bobbed, sangria sloshed and crystal glasses chimed like soprano bells as their delicate edges rattled together.

"What's this?" she demanded, her shiny dark hair swinging forward as she bent her head to stare down at the antique white- and yellow-gold diamond ring on Poppy's finger. "Ava! Have you seen this?"

"Well, it's about time," Poppy said. She'd been filled with suppressed excitement ever since waltzing through Ava's door, just waiting for her best friends to notice.

"Damn right," Ava muttered. "I've been waiting since Friday to see this ring."

Jaw dropping, Poppy whipped around to stare at her friend.

So did Jane, only she added the Kaplinski—no, *Kavanagh* now—evil eye. "You *knew* she was getting an engagement ring?"

"Detective Sheik asked me to hook him up with a couple of estate dealers. He didn't want to get her some big, new-age rock that she'd have to spin around to keep from feeling like she was rubbing it in the face of her low-income kids." Ava strode over to join them. "But once past the introductions, he wouldn't let me have any input. In fact, the bum made me stand across the room while he made his selection so I wouldn't know which one he'd bought until Poppy saw it first." She grabbed Poppy's hand. "So let's see it."

She inspected the ring's octagonal setting and flush-set round diamond, then breathed, "Oh, God, it's you." She looked up at Poppy. "I guess he's good enough to marry you, after all."

Jane bent over it as well. "It's beautiful, Poppy. It looks very old."

"It's Edwardian—from around nineteen-ten or so,"

Poppy told them. "Mom says it has an aura of being well-loved."

"She'd know." Jane slowly straightened. "So let me get this straight. *Everybody* knew about this before I did?"

"My first impulse after I got my breath back was to call you both," Poppy admitted. "But then I decided to see how long it would take you to notice. So I dragged Jason over to my folks' instead."

"I would have exploded if I'd tried to keep my engagement a secret for even an hour," Jane said.

Poppy laughed. "I thought I might. And you," she said, pointing an accusatory finger at Ava, "you could have put me out of my misery a half-hour ago."

"I was too busy trying to sneak peeks without you seeing. And I must say, wondering why the hell you didn't come in screaming and flashing your hand."

"And here I thought I *was* flashing it and you two were just too slow to pay attention." Her gaze drifted to the built-in barbecue area where the men were grilling salmon. She felt a fatuous smile crooking the corners of her lips as she cocked her chin in their direction. "What do you say we join them?"

Jane gave a little wiggle. "Works for me."

"Of course it does," Poppy heard Ava mutter as they crossed the terrace. "What's *not* to work when mad-for-you hunks are waiting for you?"

A few yards away, Jase tipped back his beer bottle, took a swig and decided he was having a pretty damn good time. The Kavanaghs were turning out to be decent guys and they'd included him and Murph seamlessly in today's barbecue. He had a lot to celebrate. Arturo had survived not only his gunshot wound but an attempt on his life in the hospital, which had convinced him to testify against Schultz after all. Considering a good portion of Jase's caseload had been invested in the rash of Arturo-led jewelry heists, it had lightened significantly. Several new cases had already taken up the slack and they'd probably never round up the kids who'd been involved—but it had been nice seeing so many cleared at once.

The icing on the cake—at least for Poppy and, okay, maybe for him as well—was that Cory and Danny G. had been to the Wolcott mansion several times in the past month to help Poppy paint. It had given them the chance to see that the girl was recovering well from her ordeal.

Things weren't generally wrapped up so tidily in his experience. But he could get used to it.

Dev pointed out a sailboat on the Sound but when Jase turned to look, he saw Poppy skimming toward them ahead of her friends and he gave her his immediate undivided attention. Catching himself about to simply walk away from the men without a word, he excused himself and skirted one of the many huge urns full of spiky greens and lush flowers to meet her.

She looked so pretty in her red dress, little white sweater and radiant smile. She must have kicked off her sandals in Ava's condo because her feet were bare even though the sun kept going in and out of the clouds and it was only warm up here part of the time.

"Hey," he murmured, bending his head to give her a kiss. Then he twirled her around and pulled her back against his chest. Wrapping his arms around her waist, he rested his chin atop her warm cloud of hair and looked out at the view of salt water and soaring mountains, cupping his fist around her left hand so he could rub his thumb over the diamond he'd put on her finger last night.

He felt happy, peaceful and possessive and grinned with no-bones-about-it exhilaration first at Jane as she whizzed past, headed for her husband, then at Ava as she brought up the rear. This little diamond said Poppy was *his*.

Ava stopped in front of them. "Okay, I admit it. That ring shows you pay attention and that you know who Poppy is." She glanced at Poppy's face and Jase assumed she was seeing the same luminous smile he'd been seeing all day, for the redhead's eyes went soft and remained that way when she turned her attention back to him. "You did good."

"I'm going to take good care of her, you know."

She studied him for a minute, then nodded. "Yeah, I think you probably will. Good thing, too. Because you hurt her, and Jane and I will see to it that you talk in a high, squeaky voice for the rest of your natural life."

"Av!" Poppy remonstrated, but Jase merely tightened his arms around her and nodded at Ava.

"Fair enough," he said.

"Hey, congratulations, de Sanges," Dev called from the barbecue. "I hear Poppy's put a ring through your nose."

"Yeah, she saw Jane leading you around by yours and thought it looked like something she'd like to try herself," he agreed, smoothly shifting Poppy beneath the drape of his arm as he turned them to face the group around the barbecue.

A grin splitting his face, Murphy came over to shake Jase's hand and thump him on the back. Then he pulled Poppy in for a hug. "Congratulations, kid," he said over her head. "You gonna tell Joe?"

"Already did. Ava said to invite him today, but he had plans with his girl's family, so I told him over the phone." He'd had mixed feelings when he'd issued the invitation, but it turned out he wouldn't have minded having his brother here now to share in his happiness. "He seems to be doing well, Murph. Maybe he really is serious about staying out of jail this time." He sure hoped so.

The salmon came off the grill and the women brought out salads, bread and veggies. They dished up from a buffet that looked more uptown restaurant than your average, basic picnic, but Jase figured that probably had to do with Ava's occupation. Once they were all gathered around a boomerang-shaped table that allowed everyone to sit Last Supper-style facing the spectacular view, Ava poured anyone who didn't have a beer a glass of sangria. Toasts that were sometimes sentimental but mostly rude were made to his and Poppy's engagement.

Sitting with her shoulder pressed against his arm, Jase listened to the conversations going on around him and felt so content he barely recognized himself. As if she knew what he was feeling, Poppy gave his knee a squeeze under the table.

He leaned in to her. "I knew I wanted you the minute

I clapped eyes on you," he murmured in her ear. "But I sure never knew I could love somebody like this. I thought that—and being happy, really happy—was for other people. Real people."

"You *are* real people," she said with a fierceness that caused the conversations around them to stumble. Then Murph said something to Dev that made the Kavanaghs laugh and the volume picked up again.

"I know," he said in a low voice. "That didn't come out right. I guess what I meant was that I thought it was for people from families like yours. Not for guys with my kind of messed-up background."

She tilted her head back to look at him. "I don't care what your background is. I don't love your antecedents, Jason. I love you."

"Aw, Poppy." He rested his forehead on hers for a minute. Then he gave her a soft kiss and his lips curved up in a smile against hers. "That day I walked into the merchants' meeting to settle Cory, Danny and Henry's future?" he said tenderly. He snapped his fingers. "Luckiest day of my life, doll."

Poppy's lips curved to match his. "Mine, too," she said softly. "Mine, too."

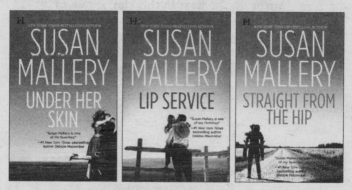

REQUEST YOUR FREE BOOKS!

2 FREE NOVELS
FROM THE ROMANCE/SUSPENSE
COLLECTION PLUS 2 FREE GIFTS!

YES! Please send me 2 FREE novels from the Romance/Suspense Collection and my 2 FREE gifts (gifts are worth about $10). After receiving them, if I don't wish to receive any more books, I can return the shipping statement marked "cancel." If I don't cancel, I will receive 4 brand-new novels every month and be billed just $5.74 per book in the U.S. or $6.24 per book in Canada. That's a savings of at least 28% off the cover price. It's quite a bargain! Shipping and handling is just 50¢ per book.* I understand that accepting the 2 free books and gifts places me under no obligation to buy anything. I can always return a shipment and cancel at any time. Even if I never buy another book from the Reader Service, the two free books and gifts are mine to keep forever.

185 MDN EYNQ   385 MDN EYN2

Name _____ (PLEASE PRINT) _____

Address _____ Apt. # _____

City _____ State/Prov. _____ Zip/Postal Code _____

Signature (if under 18, a parent or guardian must sign)

Mail to **The Reader Service:**
IN U.S.A.: P.O. Box 1867, Buffalo, NY 14240-1867
IN CANADA: P.O. Box 609, Fort Erie, Ontario L2A 5X3

Not valid to current subscribers of the Romance Collection,
the Suspense Collection or the Romance/Suspense Collection.

Want to try two free books from another line?
Call 1-800-873-8635 or visit www.morefreebooks.com.

* Terms and prices subject to change without notice. Prices do not include applicable taxes. Sales tax applicable in N.Y. Canadian residents will be charged applicable provincial taxes and GST. Offer not valid in Quebec. This offer is limited to one order per household. All orders subject to approval. Credit or debit balances in a customer's account(s) may be offset by any other outstanding balance owed by or to the customer. Please allow 4 to 6 weeks for delivery. Offer available while quantities last.

Your Privacy: Harlequin is committed to protecting your privacy. Our Privacy Policy is available online at www.eHarlequin.com or upon request from the Reader Service. From time to time we make our lists of customers available to reputable third parties who may have a product or service of interest to you. If you would prefer we not share your name and address, please check here. ☐

BOB09

Susan Andersen

77419	HOT & BOTHERED	___ $7.99 U.S.	___ $8.99 CAN.
77304	CUTTING LOOSE	___ $7.99 U.S.	___ $7.99 CAN.
77213	COMING UNDONE	___ $7.99 U.S.	___ $9.50 CAN.

(limited quantities available)

TOTAL AMOUNT	$ _____
POSTAGE & HANDLING	$ _____
($1.00 FOR 1 BOOK, 50¢ for each additional)	
APPLICABLE TAXES*	$ _____
TOTAL PAYABLE	$ _____

(check or money order—please do not send cash)

To order, complete this form and send it, along with a check or money order for the total above, payable to HQN Books, to: **In the U.S.:** 3010 Walden Avenue, P.O. Box 9077, Buffalo, NY 14269-9077; **In Canada:** P.O. Box 636, Fort Erie, Ontario, L2A 5X3.

Name: _____

Address: _____ City: _____

State/Prov.: _____ Zip/Postal Code: _____

Account Number (if applicable): _____

075 CSAS

*New York residents remit applicable sales taxes.
*Canadian residents remit applicable GST and provincial taxes.

HQN™

We *are* romance™

www.HQNBooks.com

PHSA0709BL